PERFECT ACCORD

MYSTERIOUS ARTS
BOOK THREE

CELIA LAKE

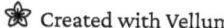

PERFECT ACCORD

Nothing too horrible can happen in a fortnight. Right?

Charlotte is worried. Her friend Victor - the man everyone expects she'll marry - has fallen in with a new circle. Growing up in the family she has, Charlotte knows there's something odd going on. The new friends are older, united in a passion for ancient legends, and there's something just a bit too intense about all of them. When Charlotte and Victor are invited for a fortnight at a remote country house with the rest of the group, she goes along to keep him out of trouble.

It's hard to get by as a working alchemist.

Lewis hopes his arrangement with Morgen will let Lewis keep his brother in a much-needed potion and begin to build up his own business as an alchemical perfumer. He doesn't mind being stuck in an isolated cottage on a rural estate while he does it.

But when Charlotte appears in his kitchen - an impossible idea - they have to figure out what's going on at the main house and how to stop it without causing more problems. All they have to work with are the skills they already have and whatever is stocked in the alchemy lab.

Perfect Accord takes place in the magical community of Great Britain in 1923, as Charlotte is preparing for her older brother Gabe's wedding. Third in the Mysterious Arts series, it can be read in any order. Join Charlotte and Lewis for a short tour through mangled Arthuriana, a long stint of forced proximity, and a sensual romance full of perfume, cooking, and time in bed.

CHAPTER I
MARCH 18TH AT VICTOR'S FAMILY ESTATE

"I'm bored." There was an unappealing slight whine to Victor's voice, even if it were understandable in the circumstances. It was possibly not intentional, in which case his characterisation was slipping. Charlotte vastly preferred Victor as himself, not putting on a show at all. But she'd learned long ago - the first month she'd known him - that the smallest tension would send him flying into a persona.

Now, Charlotte looked up from her reading. She'd been stretched out on one of the long lounge chairs in the solarium while Victor had been doing something. She wasn't entirely sure what. Some kind of charmwork, but he hadn't wanted to talk about it and it hadn't looked like much.

"Bored?" She pushed up on one elbow. "We could do something." She held up a hand. "Not at home. I came here to escape the planning, remember?"

"Mother was very pleased you did. You know she enjoys having you around. You keep me on the straight and narrow." Victor sounded pleased by that, more than usual. Today's character of the moment might be the rake redeemed, or at least Victor seemed to be trying it on for size.

"Your mother," Charlotte pointed out, "likes having the visible reminder that someday you will get married and give her grandchildren. I am simply the most reliable source of that."

"Well, you did promise. And you're going to. Eventually. When we're ready to do that sort of thing." Another time, even in Victor's mouth, it might have been melodrama, but at the moment it was rather more like relief. Charlotte had solved a significant problem for him, ages ago, and Victor did not take it for granted, even now.

Victor twisted over toward her. He was, actually, rather attractive by general standards. There were three problems with that, from Charlotte's point of view. First, that he knew he was handsome, and he had no qualms about using it. Second, that it meant a lot of other people flung themselves at him. And third, the only people he was interested in bedding or flirting with were male.

Right now, he'd be rather appealing to a lot of people. His dark hair was artfully tousled in waves that made him look like a Romantic poet. That was entirely his goal and probably took him at least an hour in the morning. Several locks, the ones tossed away from his face, were charm dyed in brilliant jewel tone purples and teals, a perfect match to the lavender of his shirt and blues and purples of his vest. He looked ravishing, and he knew it. It was not at all good for him, on the whole, and Charlotte did not praise him for it. He got enough of that from other sources.

They'd been friends since tutoring school, the two there

who were the artistic ones. They were both much more interested in drawing class, literature, music, and dramatic readings than being outside in the fresh air. To be fair, Charlotte liked the outside just fine, as long as it either involved a horse or the more leisurely sort of nature walk. The others in their years at tutoring school had been gungho for active sports, dashing everywhere in outdoor kit. They went about climbing small mountains for pleasure on a Saturday and practising every bohort skill under the sun and moon. Charlotte left the mountains to her brother Gabe, who had an ongoing inexplicable fondness for the things. Someone should, she supposed.

Charlotte and Victor had made an agreement then that they'd make a thing of seeing each other unless and until someone better came along for their particular desires. No one had, not all through their years at Schola, not in the two years since. In a year or two, maybe three, given how Victor's apprenticeship wasn't going, they'd get married. Mama would get to plan another wedding, with an entirely different set of expectations behind it than Gabe and Rathna's.

It wasn't all bad. Victor was clever and funny and creative. He didn't have nearly as many foul moods or depressive fits as a number of other artists of their acquaintance. He loved small kindnesses, he delighted in figuring out what would work. In some, that would have been an act of the benevolent Heir-presumptive, strewing largesse on the masses. Victor might dither a great deal about what would be best in those cases - Charlotte had talked him through plenty of those - but then he'd glow with pleasure when it came off the way he'd hoped.

His father was heir to the land title, though whether he

named Victor as his heir in due course or Victor's younger brother probably depended on whether there were any extant grandchildren when it became relevant. Charlotte wasn't upset by any of those obligations. She'd been born and bred to them, like Mama had been, like Papa had been.

Most importantly, Victor was going to let her do what she wanted with her time, once they married. Other than having children, of course, but that would be true whoever she married. Some things were expected, and that particular expectation got codified in the marriage agreements among their sort of people. Two children, then she could do what she liked. Or in her case, she could do as she liked from the start, so long as there weren't any children resulting. She and Victor would figure out the mechanics when needed. The Healers had solutions for that sort of thing ranging from the potion-aided to the utterly impersonal and clinical.

Not that she'd had overmuch interest in the more personal forms of intimacy, it turned out, at least so far. She knew she was expected to marry - some of the family inheritances would be easier if she did. She'd never had any hints of desire for a grand romance, which was for the best, since getting one seemed rather far-fetched. It was certainly not a priority in the Great Families.

Her family didn't have any particular obsession with virginity or protecting such virtue as might be held in it, and Victor's family didn't care much about it either. She'd had a couple of rounds of sex with people, two at school, two since. It was enough to make it clear she rather enjoyed the actual sensuality of the sex, but she hadn't much wanted to do the dance of flattery and romantic protestations with anyone who'd been open to the sex itself. Being married might well make it easier to get the physical without the emotional, at least if the gossip Mama shared about the Great Families after social events was anything to go by.

Marrying Victor was the best choice, for all sorts of reasons. She knew him, she understood him, they got along well. Most importantly, they got along particularly well in close quarters, navigating the day or the week. They rarely quarrelled about splitting up tasks or what was most important. She knew how to live in a landed family, with all the magical and pragmatic obligations that brought. There were many worse matches to be had, and Charlotte had seen enough of how things went in the Great Families to know it.

The rest of her own obligations weren't exactly simple, but she felt competent enough with them. Charlotte knew how to run a big estate, or at least she'd be ready to do it by the time she actually got married. She'd been helping Mama for the last two years, learning from the steward at Veritas about all the moving pieces. She rather liked that part, especially how to think well ahead about each thing, a year or more in advance.

Planting a particular crop not only meant planting it and harvesting it, but figuring out where to get the seed from, turning the soil over so it could rest. And of course it meant knowing what enchantments would make sense to renew the ground, all the things about crop and livestock rotation. It was also a lot of knowing how to find people who were experts in all those pieces, and treating them well, so there was institutional knowledge of this field and that cow. Charlotte enjoyed that particular kind of ever-changing puzzle.

Now, even better, she was doing a bit of an apprenticeship herself, though nothing as all-encompassing as Victor's was supposed to be. Certainly nothing like Gabe's had been. But he'd come back from Scotland after meeting Rathna bubbling over with plans, as well as everything else. In between arranging a trip to India, he'd cajoled Charlotte into asking their parents about doing something more involved than the weekly lessons she'd been taking.

Now she spent four afternoons a week, learning all she could. Mistress Lucasta was an illusionist and illustrator, skilled at using the art form to create images that near lived and breathed on the page. Charlotte wasn't sure she'd ever get skilled enough to show other people, outside some amusements for her family, but she enjoyed the learning a great deal. She also had some sketch work to do before tomorrow, though at least these didn't need daylight to do.

Victor's apprenticeship both played to his strengths and ignored them completely. Victor, through some combination of chance and birth, had particularly strong magic. The trick was getting him to apply it. It was what gave his inherent charm and charisma a boost in performance, and if he'd come from another sort of family, he could have been a star of the stage. That wasn't seemly for someone who might well inherit the land magic, however, so he'd been apprenticed to a master of enchantments, in the hopes he'd learn how to take his gifts and use them to some benefit of others. Or, if he didn't do that, at least he'd gone through the expected steps of the necessary dance to prove his magical skill sufficiently that his less respectable theatrical desires might be politely ignored.

He didn't talk a lot about the details, apparently most of them were tedious by his standards, but he was supposed to be learning the sort of enchantments set as part of building or renovating spaces, or the designs for grand social occasions. Set design, as he put it, that allowed the actual actors on stage to flourish. That he would rather have been one of them was of no account to anyone who mattered.

She and Victor had worked that out as well. It would take time and some understanding connections on his side. For her part in it, Charlotte had to get better at her illusion work. For one thing, she was formally training for illustration. Anything involving movement was a wholly different sort of challenge, especially faces. However, when those three things converged, Victor could set himself up as a theatrical patron who took minor roles. Illusions could provide cover for more major ones, if he could carry off the role itself. She liked the challenge of it. Victor was dramatically and passionately enthused by the idea, though she hadn't heard him talk much about it for a few months.

Victor sighed and flopped dramatically on his back on his own chair. "Mother won't even let me go anywhere. I mean. Not after ten. Am I still at Schola? I am not." He hit the perfect pitch on it to get across his sense of pique, without crossing the line into obnoxiousness. Professor Hallerton and Professor Ahmadi at Schola would both have given him high marks for the performance, whatever play or show it had been in.

"Last time you went out, you turned up drunk at three in the morning, after your parents had an exceedingly delicate political supper," Charlotte pointed out. "When the last of the guests were leaving." It had involved unfortunate messes on the ground and an entirely unguarded comment or three. Not something Mama and Papa had to deal with from either child in their household, admittedly.

Whatever Gabe's other impulses - and he had many -

his overindulgences tended to be reading, learning, and duelling. Also exploding things in the workroom, but those were largely self-contained. Gabe did have reasonable manners. Mama had made sure of that. It struck her now that Gabe had also been brought up to be himself, not an ever-changing rotation of stock characters, some more noble or virtuous than others, starting with 'respectable Fox scion of a family with responsibilities to the land magic'.

"I said I wouldn't do it again. Besides, I'm a changed man. Reformed. Inspired." Victor waved a hand in the air, though in this case it had more of an effect of the mast of a slowly sinking ship. She was fairly sure that wasn't what he'd intended. His poses tended towards the vague and overdramatic when he was not receiving competent theatrical feedback.

"Mmhmm." Charlotte had heard it before. About three months ago, actually, Victor was remarkably regular about that sort of thing for someone who otherwise scorned calendars, clocks, and the regular progression of time. He claimed it got in the way of inspiration. It would have worked better if he'd actually made progress with the results of whatever inspiration he was granted. "And the apprenticeship?" He did better with some grand and shining goal to aspire to. Those had not been coming from his apprenticeship itself for some time.

"Bugger." Victor rolled over on his side again, peering at her. The switch in mode made her raise an eyebrow. Not that she was unfamiliar with that particular kind of swear, certainly not from Victor. "Did Mother tell you to ask? Father?"

"Your mother beamed at me and told me to go see what you were up to and perhaps encourage you a titch. Your father was in the library when I came in. He just sort of grunted at me. You know how he does." Charlotte pursued the question. "The apprenticeship?" He hadn't actually answered her question, and her role in this play was to get answers. He knew that, or at least he ought to by now.

It did get her a response. "Not going that well, honestly. He's thinking about giving me a leave for a month or two to get myself together. Mother's fuming about it, I'm sure that's why she wants me at home. But I met such wonderful people, and they're older, and it's such a deadly bore to have to say 'I've got to be in by ten'. They're just getting started at ten. You can't do any proper ritual at ten. What kind of hour is ten? Midnight, give me midnight!" Victor had lifted up on his arm, declaiming to the ceiling of the solarium more than to Charlotte. Then he turned his head and grinned. The grin got her every time, impish and honest and knowing he was full of himself.

She threw a small pillow at him, hitting him smartly in the face. He should have known it was coming. She did it most times he got like that, if there was anything safe to throw handy. "Who are the new ones?" He'd gone out with people last week, but she'd been busy, what with dress fittings and Mama and Rathna wanting another set of eyes on flower arrangement choices.

"Oh, they're wonderful. Ever so evocative. The clothing, you'd like the clothing a lot. And one of them, Gareth, he's an illusionist, really quite good. Do come along with me, sometime, say you will."

"Depends on if I can get free?" Charlotte didn't often let him drag her out. He favoured faster crowds, the ones like them who were just too young to have fought in the Great War. Or, alternately, the ones who were running as fast as they could from what they'd seen and done there. It was harder on the men, the ones who'd lived on the knife edge of maybe needing to go fight, and then not. She felt that Gabe was sensible about his feelings about all that, and most people weren't.

More to the point, most people were messy about it, in ways that got them and others around them hurt, and Charlotte was not in favour of that. Papa had to go clean up that sort of mess, as one of the Guard, and sometimes Gabe did too, if the Penelopes got called in to deal with unexpected magic. She'd rather have them both at home, or at least doing things they loved at work without so much urgency mixed in.

"Come on, the planning can't be that bad, can it?" Victor said. "Mother's had ideas for, oh, at least a decade now, what she'd like whenever we..."

"Mama's not only arranging all the mother of the groom bits, but all the mother of the bride bits, well, the more active ones. Even if Mistress Levy is more properly Rathna's mother, or the closest thing to. But her family traditions are very different. So it's figuring out how to include the things Rathna actually wants, be respectful of the other bits, and weave that into our family traditions. Which fortunately aren't as difficult as they might be? Golden yellow veil's easy enough, and the flowers apparently aren't a problem, or the actual ritual work. But figuring out the food is a thing, there's lots of things Mistress Levy and her family don't eat, and some additional things Rathna doesn't. And mostly Mama wants them to have a solid send off, making it really clear Mama and Papa both approve."

"Whatever." Victor shrugged. "You know it's terribly boring." This was why she didn't talk about it with Victor, he would brush it off. He would usually do it charmingly, of course, and generally with something she enjoyed and found distracting. Now, however, it jarred a tad. Certainly, he hadn't found a way to keep up the bit and keep the conversation theatrical.

"You were the one who brought it up," Charlotte pointed out. "But I do need to be around for a fair bit, for at least a fortnight. Dress fittings and things. once that's done, it's more the last minute parts, and there's a gap between this bit and then."

"Mother said there's five other couples terribly annoyed they picked the sixth. It's so terribly hard to get a good date in June, between the Solstice and the Midsummer Faire." Wednesdays were exceedingly lucky, and so was June, and of course Mama had aimed straight at both. There were some advantages to the sort of social status the Edgartons held. A Council wedding would have topped it, or one of their children, but that wasn't an issue this year.

Charlotte shrugged. "Mama was very determined. And we're doing it at Veritas, so it's not like we were competing for a hall or anything. Who are these people you want me to meet?"

"Oh, most of all, Morgen - with an e, the old spelling, the mythical one. And Gareth. And they've got a number of friends. I've met, let's see, Iseult."

"Iseult is hardly a distinguishing name." There'd been a huge fad for them, she knew a dozen women named Iseult within a couple of years of her own age.

"Ygraine. Chelinda. Enid. Caradoc. Pellinore. Clarion. Laudine. You'd like Laudine, I think. She paints things. Mark." Charlotte let the names roll over her. All rather mythic, really. Most of those, maybe all of them, were right out of myth and legend.

"Find a time, then. Supper, are they the sort of people

who can do a seven o'clock supper? Or I can get free next Saturday or Sunday, if I know by Wednesday, I think."

"Will you? Oh, you're grand. You are absolutely scrumptious. And I'll tell everyone you are." He bounced up, suddenly all cheer and joy and youthful vigour. "Come on, let's go see if you can soften Mother up a bit about me."

CHAPTER 2
MARCH 24TH IN TRELLECH

In the end, it had come down to a supper out at a quiet little place - emphasis on the little - on a side street in Trellech. Mama had let Charlotte come out for the evening, and she had plans to stay in the Trellech townhouse, so as not to wake anyone coming in. Papa was working some odd shifts for the Guard this spring, because of other people's training, apparently. Whatever the reason, they'd decided Charlotte was mature and responsible enough to be in the townhouse overnight by herself without anyone other than the ordinary staff there, Cook and the housemaid.

Which meant here was Charlotte. Figuring out what to wear had been a challenge. Victor had not given her much to go on at all. He'd just waved a hand and said, "Supper." He'd also mentioned a previous engagement, so she couldn't even get him to come round and meet her, with time to change if she picked the wrong thing.

It was easy for him. He'd turn up wearing the proper sort of suit, looking entirely dashing in it. Probably no over-robe, not for a supposedly informal meal with a small group of new friends.

Charlotte, though, had to make choices. If Mama had agreed to her getting something sleek in black crepe de chine, Charlotte could have gone for starkly elegant. Mama had pointed out - and Mama was annoyingly right, Charlotte knew it - that as an unmarried young woman, it was a little too on the nose as mature before her time. Also, that it was a tad harsh with Charlotte's colouring. Both she and Gabe had come out honey-blonde, some throwback given both Mama and Papa had darker brown hair. They all had the same paler eyes though. Whatever the reason, that kind of modish elegance was out.

Charlotte had spent a lot of time staring into the racks of clothes in her dressing room. There was a sea blue, rather simple, but it brought out those same eyes and was quite comfortable. That was what she'd wear if it were her friends she was dining with, without any need to impress anyone. The shimmering lavender and purple with little sparkles from charms was entirely too much for a purportedly simple supper. Besides, the net overlay tended to catch on things if she weren't quite careful. And if Victor weren't also careful. She'd worn it for a gala that winter at the Opera House, and got quite a few compliments, but that was too much for tonight.

After some consideration, she picked out one of her newest frocks, what they were calling the garconne silhouette, in a glowing forest green. She didn't quite have the figure for it - having more curves than straight lines to her body, on the whole - but it was cut to fit her perfectly. Seeing as it was March, it was a good excuse for another layer over it, and she had a deep purple wool coat, trimmed with fur. That was the right blend of all the signifiers of her sort of family and background, without being too obvious about it. Not for that restaurant, anyway. Plenty of others there would be dripping with jewels. She just wore the pearl and amethyst necklace Mama had given her for her eighteenth birthday. A few more amethyst-tipped hair pins made everything look deliberate and tied together.

Of course, Victor didn't say a word about it. He came downstairs, just as she came in the door. Apparently, his previous engagement had been with Morgen. That was certainly what it looked like. He offered his arm properly, at least, playing his part out, but he didn't say anything at all. It wasn't the done thing to elbow him hard in the ribs. She could take him to task about his assumptions sometime later. In private, once she had him in the wings. Never the dressing room, not for her, but definitely she could correct him in the wings.

Victor walked her upstairs, into one of the private dining rooms. It was immediately obvious the others in the party had been there for some time. The staff had certainly cleared some glasses and plates, but all of them had half-drunk glasses, and the wine bottle suggested it might not be the first round. There were four people there, besides the two empty chairs for her and Victor, at a round table.

Facing them, as they came in the door, was a woman in a vibrant ruby red, the sort of colour that was absolutely a deliberate statement. She could only be Morgen, given the way Victor had talked about her. It took Charlotte a moment more to take in the cut, eventually placing it as the sort of fantasy of a mediaeval gown. That wasn't at all like what they'd actually worn.

Mama and Papa didn't go in for illuminated manu-scripts the way some people did, but Charlotte had seen a few over the years. Someone then would have worn that sort of robe with a chemise under it, something that covered up much more of the woman's collarbones and the upper curves of her breasts. The woman's hair was loose down her back, too. That was an entirely romantic image, to have one's hair - and magic - loose and flowing, out touching the world in hundreds of tiny ways.

There was a man sitting beside her, to her right, and he was leaning on the arm of his chair, a conspiratorial tilt to his head. He was also wearing red, a shade brighter, a poet's shirt that was sure to give Victor ideas about his own wardrobe, and not necessarily practical ones. Also, she did not need two men who knew exactly how handsome they were in her life, let alone at the same supper table.

"Good evening." The woman's voice was as perfectly poised as her clothing, and Charlotte suspected just as deliberately chosen. It had a warmth to it, the sort that made her wonder not just about vocal training, but about whether she was applying an edge of a glamour to it. "We're delighted to meet you, Charlotte." Also, she had a gift for ambiguous grammar, applying the plural in a way that could almost have been regnal.

Charlotte smiled, the way she'd learned from childhood. It was a sincere enough smile, because Mama had taught her how to feed her curiosity into it. She did want to know about this woman, about the four people here, and what they wanted with Victor, after all. "Victor's been quite mysterious, but I'm so glad to get the chance." Charlotte wondered what he had actually said, that 'mysterious' was the word. They had long ago worked out how he could help her come across the way she wanted, as an appropriate society heiress with an interest in the arts, and that was a role he could play in his sleep. She supposed that it was evidence that the Albion Inheritance sorts would not ever cross Morgen's threshold, if he had been unable to come up with other topics.

Victor did manage to bow and then get her chair for her, pushing it in as Charlotte sat down, then taking his own seat to her left, next to the woman who had to be Morgen. It gave her a chance to look at the other two, and do some quick calculations. She didn't recognise any of them, either from her own schooling, or from the varying sorts of social circles she usually moved in. That meant two things, first that they were likely all a bit older, and that if they'd gone to Schola, over five years older. And second, that they didn't come from the sorts of families she and Victor did.

The woman in red went on, smoothly. "So considerate, Victor." It was like she was praising a hound, and Victor didn't seem to notice, just smiled back at her. "I am Morgen, of course. This is Gareth." She gestured at the man beside her. "Victor thought you'd get on well with Laudine." That was the woman, to her right, between Gareth and the other man.

"I'm an artist." Laudine had muted brown hair, flowing in an unlikely smoothness down her back, the kind of thing that almost certainly involved both charms and potions to keep it doing that. She had a touch of the uncanny about her, but Charlotte thought that was a glamour to change her eye colour. Maybe. She might have to ask Gabe more about spotting those in the moment. Her eyes were a startling green-blue, unusually vivid. Charlotte also hadn't forgotten that Victor had used nearly those exact same words with her. It caught the ear, the echo of it.

"And this is Mark." Mark was the dark, striking type, more typically Celtic in features and colouring, pale skin contrasting with dark wavy hair. It was the sort of appearance that a lot of women found dashing. Charlotte appreciated it on an aesthetic level, but honestly, it didn't do much for her personal interest. He didn't press the point, which was a nice change, just smiled and nodded.

There was a bit of quite ordinary conversation there. The waitress came in, looking for Charlotte's order - the others, including Victor, had obviously already placed theirs. She was offered the mead chicken, a bit of roast, or a mushroom tart, which was a fascinating and rather limited list. She chose the chicken, as likely to be interesting, and also the middle ground of the choices. There were people who considered eating a roast a statement about femininity or the lack of it, and she wanted more food than the mushroom tart, even if she could get a snack later tonight.

From there, the others at the table diverged a bit into chatting about people Charlotte didn't know. She kept track of the names, mostly the ones Victor had already mentioned, but she had so little to connect them to it wasn't much use yet. Once the food arrived, however, Morgen looked up. "Victor told us you've been quite busy with family matters, an upcoming wedding?"

"My older brother's, yes." Charlotte looked up, meeting Morgen's gaze for a moment, then looking back at her food. "I'm helping Mama with the planning, of course. All the family traditions. But it also gets a tad tiresome now and again."

"But you're not in a hurry to marry yourself?" Something in Morgen's voice made Charlotte look up again, quickly. Too quickly, honestly, she was off her game. Morgen laughed at that. "Victor's told us about your agreement. Really quite sensible, honestly, seeing as you're both from the sorts of families who think about the generations. We do that too, though rather differently. Not the family, or the land directly, but soul to soul, life to life, over the centuries."

"Oh?" Charlotte had to start with the too-simpler interrogative noise while the rest of her mind caught up. It also wasn't at all like Victor to expose that much to new people, especially when it touched on others. What was he playing at?

The whole thing was off-kilter. Sharing that kind of information was the sort of thing Victor did when all his masks were off and he was relaxing backstage. And yet, he was so obviously still playing up a role here. She didn't have a convenient name for this one yet, he wasn't exactly the Hero or the Young Nobleman. The Questor, perhaps, that might do for now.

"I suppose your family takes up a lot of your time. But perhaps you'd like to make your own way now?" Morgen flicked her fingers upward. An instant later - just long enough Charlotte was fairly sure she wasn't the one making it happen - there were little gold and red sparks of magic flinging themselves upwards and disappearing. "Your parents are, perhaps, very much of the current establishment? All those rules and restrictions, of a time before the War."

It was a remarkably general sort of statement, Charlotte realised, but it also was a sensible place to start.

"Papa prides himself on his honour and reputation, yes." That was the public sort of truth, because Papa was very obvious about it. As a Lord, as a magistrate, as a captain in the Guard, he'd shaped himself around keeping his oaths. It wasn't exactly the popular mode these days, it hadn't been for years, but Charlotte loved him for it. Papa knew what he valued, and he lived every day with that in mind.

Morgen was going on, her voice melodic and encouraging. "It's a new world, darling, but we bear the blood of the old. All four of us. And we think Victor has some potential, and you as well. Your family goes back to the Romans, doesn't it?" Her fingers twitched once. "Victor mentioned, dearest."

"So our family histories have it. The house does," Charlotte said.

"And Arthur?" Morgen leaned forward, the first active movement she'd taken, she'd spent the meal so far leaning back in her chair rather entirely like a throne.

"Kent is not a particular stronghold of Arthurian lore," Charlotte pointed out, deliberately leaning back a little herself now. Her chair did not have arms, though, which put her at a disadvantage with the posing, and she suspected that was deliberate. Victor's didn't have arms either. "More about Octo and Hengist and Horsa and Vortigern. Though there is that connection to Uther Pendragon, of course."

"There is." Morgen's voice had a cajoling softness to it, and it gave no hint whether Morgen actually knew the tale herself. "I'm glad you know your lore. So many people have forgotten it. I knew Victor was right to suggest including you. That's really quite promising. But Victor said your brother's marrying outside of anything like that."

He was. Charlotte wasn't sure if this was the usual sort of bigotry she'd learned to listen for from anyone who talked about Gabe and Rathna. Or it might be simply an utter disinterest in anything outside Morgen's pet topic. With what she knew at this point, it could honestly be either. The latter would be much easier to deal with. The former might lead Victor into the sort of choices that would make it a problem for Charlotte to continue to bring him home.

"Gabe will be himself. I'm told it's common for older brothers," Charlotte said, and if that wasn't an entire ship of truth by itself, she didn't know what was. "And I like Rathna very much, as I've had a chance to get to know her. They certainly make each other very happy. Unfashionable, perhaps, but it makes a lovely story."

Morgen raised an eyebrow, as if Charlotte had gone entirely off script, then she gathered herself. "Ah, loyalty to the family. That's a particularly Arthurian virtue, isn't it?"

Yes, it was. Not that it had gone well for them quite a lot of the time. Or perhaps it depended on defining loyalty and specifying which family, and which parts of the lore this particular story was currently wandering around in. Or whose interpretation. All the early things were rather a lot different than, say, anything after Chrétien de Troyes. Charlotte smiled and waited to see what Morgen did with that.

Victor leapt into the fray. Or rather, he leaned languidly into it, but at least he spoke up. "Charlotte is fond of her family." It baffled him, but his younger brother was at the bratty age. Gabe could be bratty, but mostly he was very busy, and anyway, he was older. Now, at least, Victor could be visibly baffled, making a show of it, but also how amiable he was about the whole thing. That her fondness was something he encouraged, then, or at least tolerated.

Charlotte knew this was another one of his parts, the gentle teasing. But again, why was he keeping that up if he'd already told these people their secrets? Also, this wasn't exactly kind of him, what was she supposed to answer to that? She wasn't going to deny she loved her family, because she did. It wasn't fashionable, perhaps, but truth mattered more than fashion.

On the other hand, she knew what this mode meant. It meant he liked these people, more than in passing. He wanted Charlotte to like them as well, he was using all the little signifiers of that, the indications of trust, of warmth, of making it clear he knew her well, nudging her closer. Or perhaps more like opening a door, even if Charlotte was still thinking she might want it to stay closed. He was acting with Morgen and these others like he did among their friends and yearmates where the intimacy had built over years.

"I can see." Morgen flicked her fingers, and again there was that tiny pause followed by sparkles. "I would like to get to know you better, Charlotte, darling. Could you get free for a fortnight, do you think? Could they spare you from all that wedding planning? Would you like an escape from it? The fortnight leading up to May Day, we have some delightful plans in mind. We're getting a few people together for a house party in Somerset, not far from Glastonbury. It's on a delicious ley. The magic is just bubbling up everywhere." There was a note under it Charlotte couldn't parse correctly, not with the twists this conversation was taking.

Charlotte glanced at Victor, who said promptly, "Morgen honoured me with an invitation, and of course I'm going. It's really quite remarkable, from the things I've heard."

Morgen tsked, just once, under her breath, and Victor shushed. Now, that was a trick Charlotte rather wanted to learn. Morgen wasn't obvious about it, not the way some people might be. She wasn't forceful or maternal. Just clear. And well, it wasn't like Charlotte was going to let Victor go off by himself for a fortnight without someone sensible around. Who knew what he'd come back thinking?

"I'd have to check with Mama. But the wedding's in June, and we're almost done with the parts that I can help with. I am doing a bit of an apprenticeship, but she'd mentioned wanting a break. I can see if that would suit."

"Darling, how delightful. Can you let us know in the next few days? We'll let you know what to bring, but we can put you up quite comfortably. Your own room, of course. And you might find someone there suits you, the ways Victor might find someone who suits him." That was right, she'd said Victor had explained their agreement. There wasn't any hint of the seductress visible, not aimed at Victor, as if she knew it was a waste of time. There was a little shift of her chest, a half-taken breath, that made it clear she applied those skills elsewhere, though. Gareth's hand shifted on Morgen's arm, and Charlotte couldn't see Mark, next to her. But he moved as well, leaning forward, she thought, just enough she could feel it from his chair.

Charlotte just nodded. "Through the portals, is there an address to send a note to? Or—" She hesitated, they were still quite expensive. "I do have one of the journals."

"Oh, leave that at home, darling. Not entirely compatible with the magic of the house, you know how it is. Gareth, a card?" Gareth produced one from somewhere on his person with a flourish of fingers, and it was ceremoniously handed around the table to Charlotte. Who, of course, then had to figure out how to tuck it into her little handbag without dumping everything in there on the floor. "There, just send a note through. Let's see, it's Saturday, by Tuesday? Monday would be even better."

"I'll see what I can arrange." Charlotte smiled, then glanced at Victor. "Tell me a bit more about what you think of Victor, then?"

That got her a lot of flattering nonsense, the sort she

wanted to dissect. It was exactly the sort of thing Mama would enjoy, not that Charlotte could actually take notes. A well-trained memory only went so far, especially when she was beginning to feel herself lulled into a certain sense of comfort by the flow of even, smooth voices. No mind, she could go home tomorrow and talk to Mama and Papa about taking a fortnight.

CHAPTER 3
MARCH 25TH AT VERITAS

"Just a fortnight, Mama." They were waiting for Gabe to come back for family supper, and Gabe was not here yet. It meant Charlotte had broached the topic she wanted an answer on without him.

It was a coin toss, honestly, on whether Gabe being here would have helped. On the one hand, Gabe was more of a general distraction to just about everything than usual. Given Gabe's normal, that was a great deal of distraction indeed. It was largely a very cheerful distraction, and mostly Charlotte enjoyed watching him, but he was even more likely to come out with something off the wall and unusual. It made framing her arguments that much harder.

They were in the library, waiting for him, with drinks before dinner. Mama sipped hers. "Middle of April through May Day. You'd miss the rituals here?"

Charlotte did not entirely want to, but she was, in fact, unable to be in two places at once. Even if there'd been a portal handy, being in both places at dawn at once was unfeasible, at least not when they were this close together. "I don't want to, exactly." She would be honest with her parents, whatever else. Victor didn't tell his parents much at all, and Charlotte had never been able to be like that.

For one thing, Mama and Papa both noticed things. It was a strategic error of the first order to think they wouldn't notice. Being honest sometimes got her somewhere. Hiding things rarely did.

Mama was looking at Papa now, with the half-raised eyebrow that was at least the start of a whole conversation. "And what do you know about these people?"

Charlotte was about to figure out how to answer that when the library door swung open and Gabe strolled in. He looked windblown. His cheeks were a healthy pink like he'd been exerting himself, but he wasn't wearing riding clothes. Or duelling clothes, either. He leaned the cane against his hip and took in the three of them. "Here we are, then."

"Here you are, yes, Gabe." Papa stood up and offered his arm. "Shall we go into supper? I gather it would be unkind to make Cook hold things longer than strictly necessary."

They made the usual little procession along to the small dining room, the one that was family and the occasional friend or four. Mama leaned a bit more on Papa's arm than she sometimes did, and Charlotte suspected the weather had been getting to her. Changeable weather often did, though to be unfair about it, so did damp, heat, and extended periods of rain. Sometimes, just to be extra difficult, it was entirely mild spring days. Gabe took up his place beside Charlotte, near enough bouncing and vibrating every step, though he didn't actually say anything. Some particular piece of news, then.

Gabe pulled out the chair for Charlotte, while Papa did the same for Mama. He did have manners. At least he did when Mama was around to remind him to use them. Mama nodded once they were all settled. "Yes, Gabe?"

"We got the flat." Now he really was bouncing, or near enough to it. "I wasn't sure we were going to, and it's exactly what we wanted. By Bedford Square, not Spital-fields, but we'd more or less resigned ourselves to that. Second floor, there's a sensibly designed lift. And we wanted to aim at the arty set, when it comes to the magical side, and see what that does for us."

Charlotte blinked. She knew, intellectually, that Gabe and Rathna had been looking for a flat. They wouldn't be living here, in some expansion of Gabe's existing rooms or whatever they settled on. It wasn't as if he'd be an entire stranger, but he'd have even more of a life she knew nothing about than was already the case. Now, she didn't know what she felt about it, and part of her wanted to burst into tears at the table. That was utterly the wrong reaction, and she wasn't going to do that.

Even if it meant pinching the skin between her thumb and index finger.

She missed whatever Papa had said, then heard Mama say, clearly, "And you'll be back for suppers."

"Of course. With reasonable warning, given the work." Then Charlotte felt Gabe's cane-tip nudge her under the table. It was nominally more civilised than kicking her, though it made her glad lower hemlines only went so far. The cane tangled in cloth more than a whole foot. "Hey, Char?"

She looked up, meeting his eyes. There was the nudge of the cane again. "Yes?"

"We'll figure out a new thing. Both of us. And besides, you've got your own life, too. You can come visit. There's a spare bedroom, even with a nursery and a nanny."

That was an interesting idea, especially if they were in Bedford Square, close enough to Bloomsbury and the British Museum, and the British Library and all. She nodded once, cautiously. "We'll see. You're not going to want to be bothered by bratty little sisters, I'm sure. It would cramp your style."

Gabe laughed freely. "Oh, sweet innocent, you think you can cramp my style? Even thou hath not that power." Then he grinned at his parents. "What were you talking about when I came in? Oh, thank you, Baker, this looks fabulous." It did, in fact; the starter was early spring vegetables and a quiche. Baker, the footman, went around serving things out.

"Charlotte has an invitation. Do you know anything about - what were the names?" Papa said.

"Morgen Priddy, she said." Charlotte offered, "I didn't get the other names, she was rather deft about not encouraging prying. She's maybe thirty, older than you, Gabe. Long dark hair, a fondness for ruby red, and a rather faux archaic style of dress."

"And you think we're going to let you go off and spend a fortnight with people who discourage prying?" Mama raised an eyebrow. "Honestly, Charlotte." It wasn't actually as scolding as it should have been. Mama was smiling. But Mama also had a point here, and Charlotte had to acknowledge it. Their family did notice prying, and more than that, knew it often indicated all sorts of other things, some of which were harsher than others.

Gabe leaned forward. "Why shouldn't she? Wait, back up. Who are these people, why are they inviting you, and everything else that I've missed since..." He counted back on his fingers. "Wednesday?"

"Tuesday." Mama filled that in. "You had that case in Skegness on Wednesday."

"Tuesday," Gabe agreed smoothly. "Go on, Char."

Charlotte sighed. Of course he'd ask. And it made sense he would. But she didn't much want to go through explaining it all just for her parents to come down like a ton of rocks. "Victor's fallen in with this new group of people. Morgen Priddy, and the others I met were Gareth, Laudine, and Mark. They all talked a little, Laudine's also an artist. There's a group, fifteen, maybe twenty, getting together at an estate in Somerset, somewhere not too far from Glastonbury, for a fortnight. Some sort of..." Charlotte frowned. "They weren't very specific, I was paying attention."

"What were some of the other names, anyone else mentioned? Last names?" Gabe was leaning forward now, something in that had caught his attention.

Charlotte had kept track, of all the things that were family expectations, that was perhaps the most basic of them. Now she grimaced. "I already thought of that. Victor mentioned, let's see." She ticked them off on her fingers. "Ygraine. Chelinda. Enid. Caradoc. Pellinore. Clarion. And Laudine and Mark."

"Arthuriana," Gabe said. "Mind, the Glastonbury's a bit of a giveaway. But not right in town, then, some sort of mystic connection to the tor or to Chalice Well, or whatever? The Glastonbury Thorn's actually quite interesting. There was a monograph about it, the uses for materia, but of course harvesting it's a trick and a half." He waved a hand. "What else? Schola, do you know?"

"I don't think so." Charlotte frowned. "She did the thing where she made coloured sparks off her fingers. I forget which one it is, but I'm pretty sure it was Gareth doing it.

She'd move her hand, and there'd be a half-second, then the sparks. Red and gold, both times."

"Like this?" Gabe flicked his fingers, a quick pass of his thumb over them. "Or this?" The first set of sparks went straight up, the second cascaded more like fireworks.

"The first. Straight up, dissipating after a second or so. Heavier on the red than the gold?" Charlotte watched as Gabe did it a third time. "Like that, yes."

"Paget's Second, with a - huh, that's an interesting angle on the thumb. Possibly a touch of arthritis in the joint, or some injury? Or perhaps it's deliberate, in which case I wish his thumbs well." Gabe stretched his hand. "Not very diagnostic about the level of magical skill. That's second year Incantation, though it's one of the supplemental readings at Schola, not one of the regular assignments."

"When did you learn it, then?" Charlotte asked, leaning to peer at Gabe across the table.

"From Aunt Mason when I was, what was I? Eleven. Useful for sending up a flare from a distance, across a field. It was when she had me out helping with surveying something." Gabe grinned briefly. "Do you want me to look into them a bit? Or rather, Mama, Papa, if Charlotte wants to go, I think she should."

Mama raised both eyebrows, and Papa sighed slightly. They had a short pause while the next course was brought in, which just let Gabe marshall his actual arguments better. As soon as they had their food, he went on. "Point the first, Charlotte's put up with a lot of things patiently about my wedding. I owe her. Point the second, she's got to take a break from the apprenticeship for a little, right?" Charlotte nodded. Her apprentice mistress had an incipient grandchild. "And point the third, there's something a little odd here, but people don't wander into the Guard Hall or the Penelopes and announce it. Maybe they'll tell Charlotte."

"We do not generally suggest people wander into iffy situations for pleasure, Gabe. Especially your sister." Papa said, though it was the sort of tone he used when he knew Gabe was going to argue his point. Successfully.

"Charlotte isn't just anyone. And besides, Victor's going, right?" Charlotte nodded again. This was clearly her part in making the argument. "You know what Victor's like. Easily swayed, and gods know what he'll get into if Charlotte's not handy. At least if she's there, she'll know if there's something to worry about. Where's the nearest portal?"

"It's by Ebbor Gorge, so not very," Charlotte said. "And they said I shouldn't bring my journal, too much chance of magical interference or something. Not that I believe them on that, of course."

Gabe looked rather distracted. "Ebbor Gorge, Ebbor Gorge. Some interesting caves - limestone, of course - at the south end of it. And there's something about the mineral content there. A lot of lead, maybe? I might be misremembering, I'll ask Rathna." He pulled a small notebook out of his inside jacket pocket and scribbled something down. "Credence, no. Credential. No. Crednerite, maybe? Anyway. They're wrong, but they might just have something that looks like a credible argument in dim light."

"Most likely either Morgen doesn't have one, or she doesn't want anyone else to have one, and communicate without her knowing," Charlotte said, obligingly. "None of you need give me that lecture. It's not that far from Wells, though, I could always walk and take a train."

Gabe nodded. "You could. We could look at the maps in advance, make sure you know your options."

Mama cut in. "You're assuming that we're going to say yes."

"You're not currently saying no," Gabe said, smiling. Impishly and charmingly, not that that actually worked reliably on Mama and Papa, who knew a great many things Gabe got up to. Perhaps especially when he looked like that. The thing with Gabe, however, was that he was always being himself, not putting on someone else's mode, like Victor so often did. "More seriously, Mama, we're grown up. Both of us. Charlotte has her reasons for wanting to go. We can talk about handling the more complex things. She can bring some books, lie around and read, if there's nothing to it."

Mama snorted. "Richard?"

Papa shook his head, then he turned his hands upward. "Give me strength. All right. Charlotte, you can go. If you do some research about these people. Gabe, you're to help. See what you can turn up. And figure out the reasonable ways home, if it's needed. You're to write, as you can, Charlotte."

"Of course, Papa." She stood, pushing back from her chair to come around and kiss him on the cheek. "Thank you."

"You know I have a terribly hard time saying no to you. Especially when Gabe's helping." Papa waved a hand. "Sit, sit. Tell us about your plans for the week, then. Besides your new research project. When do they want you there?"

"April sixteenth. Someone will meet us at the portal with a carriage or something of the kind. Carriage or cart, not an automobile."

"Not up on their later technology," Gabe said. "Well, if

there's a horse, you can always sneak away on horseback. Add that to the list."

Charlotte could, though on the whole she'd prefer a saddle and riding gear to sneaking a horse out of a field and hoping for the best. "Talk about it after supper, or do you need to be somewhere, Gabe?"

He beamed. "I'll have a bit of time. Did you finish that sketch you were working on?" Charlotte smiled back at him, and was glad to change the subject. Instead, she talked about something she'd been sketching, learning more about how to lay out the perspective lines in a way that anchored and reinforced the illusions that changed a scene, a scaffolding for them. Her goal was to be able to set out a scene that could then be charmed in different ways, such as a street moving through the seasons. Gabe had a dozen ideas for how to apply that, it turned out, and Mama added several more.

CHAPTER 4
MARCH 30TH AT VICTOR'S

"But they are letting you go?" Victor leaned forward. He'd been coiled up in the chair in the solarium again. They had been supposed to go out to supper, but Victor had changed his mind at the last minute. They'd had supper in the small dining room of the estate instead, before retreating to the solarium. Victor's mode tonight seemed to be oddly more fragile, some sort of Edwardian gentleman with a lurking secret. She did not have overmuch hope that the drama would progress far enough to reveal it.

"They are." To be fair to Mama and Papa, once they'd agreed, they hadn't changed their minds. Even when Gabe had turned up some curious information about the names she had, or rather a lack of information. A trifle more worrisome was that they hadn't been able to turn up much about the house either, beyond the fact it was on a long-term lease. The actual owners were apparently somewhat short on funds, and had been glad to let out the place for at least a year.

"Was it terribly hard to talk them into it? I mean, you

need to be there, you absolutely do." There was an edge to his voice now, the sort of passion she usually only heard out of him when he'd spotted someone he desired and was pining for. Not that was ever her, of course. Victor did appreciate her - he told her so regularly - but she never got proclamations of adoration aimed at her. She wasn't entirely sure she wanted them, actually, they seemed uncomfortable in some ways - but they weren't on offer.

"Gabe helped." Charlotte considered that note in his voice, and she wasn't going to address it directly, not just yet.

Victor turned out to be a help. "Your brother?"

"He's been on a tear about how Mama and Papa should treat us the same. Within reason, I mean, we do have different skills and training and all that," Charlotte said. "But he doesn't agree at all with me being tucked in a box until we get married, or needing chaperoning or whatever. And your parents have relaxed a lot about it."

Victor flushed. "Mother is actually quite clear that we're not going to do anything she'd actually have to disapprove of. She might have found one of my diaries, the one about Benedict. Maybe six months ago."

"Oh, Victor." Victor's infatuation with Benedict had involved alternating bouts of praise and despondency on an ever decreasing frequency wave. Damped oscillation, that was the term for it. And if Charlotte had to guess, she'd put good odds on the diary having rather a lot of explicit fantasy. "Did she say anything?"

"You know Mother." Victor rolled onto his back, staring up at the ceiling. "But she did ask a few questions. Enough that she was clear there wasn't any worry about my compromising you or any of that rot. The way people care about. Not that she does, but Aunt Mellicant does." He then lifted his head. "Your parents let you come over here."

That, there, was why she loved him, in the particular way she did. In a moment, he'd gone from masks and artifice to letting her see what he really was feeling. It wasn't just that he let her see that, though it was more than a trifle intoxicating. It was knowing that there weren't other people he could do that with. Even now, she couldn't imagine him having this sort of conversation with anyone who met the world like Morgen and Gareth did. Charlotte took a breath, leaning herself, so that he'd see her responding that way, as well as with words.

"Well, yes. But we don't have particular standards about my being an untouched maiden in the family. Mama was? But that was because people arranged things for her and Papa, and they didn't get much chance before the wedding anyway. And they weren't going to do that to me, no matter what else. And it's your aunt who's got a thing about it, but as long as we're not obvious about being alone in private, who cares."

"Certainly not like I'm an untouched virgin," Victor agreed. "Even if it's been a long drought. Though maybe..." His voice trailed off.

"Is that part of the reason you like Morgen and all of them? Someone you've got an eye on?" Charlotte had been considering this question. She had only a limited sample set to work from. Gabe had found photos of a couple of people whose names and ages matched well enough, and they were all about as handsomely attractive as Morgen and the others had been at supper. It wasn't just their features, either. They shared a mode, something that united the clothing choices and the way they did their hair, similar in style and priority. That was the right word, yes. They weighted things the same way, each of the images she'd seen.

"Mmmyes." Victor let out a cheerful purr. "Caradoc and Pellinore are both very to my taste, actually. And they've both been, I mean, there are ways to indicate that you might be interested. I've only met them for supper, though, or there was a lecture at the museum, so there was only so much we could do in public."

"And you've not seen them at one of the clubs for that sort of thing?" Albion's laws were not Britain's on this particular question. But the clubs for men and women who preferred their own gender did tend toward the private for all sorts of reasons. "When's the last time you went?"

"Oh, not for, what? Three months?" Victor counted back on his fingers. "I was going to go again, but then I met Morgen, and well."

Charlotte raised an eyebrow, then was rather glad Victor wasn't going to see her expression. He was still sprawled and looking up at the ceiling. "That long ago? You didn't say. Where'd you meet them?"

"Suppose I didn't." That had a note of something sulky about it, and Charlotte was not at all interested in dealing with that. Then he shrugged. "It took a while to meet everyone, but Morgen really wanted to make sure you were included, once she realised what we are to each other."

That was a tiny bit of a salve, though one Charlotte would need to think about more. She nodded. "So, when did you meet them. Where? Not your usual set, or I'd know them too, obviously, at least a little."

"A party. A quite small one. Liam Earhart, do you remember him from school? Also, one of the Muses. At his place. And Morgen was there, and Gareth, and I think Enid, and Caradoc and Pellinore, and they caught my eye, of course."

Victor had - unlike Charlotte - been part of one of Schola's secret societies. Not that the Nine Muses were actually all that secret, seeing as how it was tricky to throw lavish performances and hide who was part of them at the same time. She went to perhaps a third of the parties now. They tended to be a lot of avant-garde art, some of which Charlotte liked and some of which she had very little patience for. Writing an entire cycle of poems without using the word 'the' was an interesting personal challenge, but it should perhaps not be let out in public without warning.

"Of course," Charlotte said, more to say something while she was thinking than for any other reason. "And did you talk to them, or just admire them from across the room in a pointed manner?"

Victor giggled at that, entirely at ease again and all the sulkiness dispelled. "Well. I did that first. But then Morgen noticed me watching, and she came and, I don't know, reclined on the sofa and talked to me. I don't even remember about what now, but maybe half an hour later, there was a little crowd around us, her people and a few others. And then she invited two of us to go somewhere else for drinks, a little place down near Club Row."

"Who was the other one she picked up?" Charlotte asked, more idly curious than anything else.

"Oh, I knew her. She thought Gareth was gorgeous, obviously. I mean, he is, not that he's interested in men." Victor twisted and blinked, a little earnestly now. "It's all right if you think he is too." Victor wanted her to like them, that was the thing. He wanted to bring her along with this pleasure he was having, in the ways he could. If he was clumsy about it, well, it wasn't as if he'd done something like this before. Grand dramas, yes, certainly he'd designed and championed any number of ridiculous productions for the fun of it, or clever costume party themes.

Charlotte grimaced. "I do not need your permission to find anyone gorgeous or otherwise, remember? Second premise." When they were thirteen, the summer before going to Schola, they'd made out a list of agreements.

The first premise, of course, was the core of the agreement. If neither of them found anyone they'd rather marry by the time they were twenty-one or otherwise needing to marry after that, they'd arrange to marry each other. The second premise was that either of them could have an interest in other people, without limit. Not that they'd quite put it like that at thirteen, of course. Charlotte had nudged Victor through rewriting it several times. Puberty had brought certain kinds of new awareness, as had some of the more practically minded sessions with Matron at school.

Victor held up his hands. "Didn't mean that. Just. It'd be all right if you did. If that made you more agreeable about things."

This, now, was a gift of an opening. Charlotte stretched out, though she kept herself angled so she could see Victor's expression. "What makes you think I'd land on him, besides his features?" She considered. "Any particular reason to think he might be good in bed, or - I mean, surely he's wrapped up in Morgen. Aren't they together?"

"Well, yes, but not exclusively. Or not like you mean, anyway. I know he's been with several of the other women. Laudine, a while back, from something I heard."

"Did any of them go to Schola? They can't be much older than we are, I mean, not ages and ages. But Gabe didn't recognise any of the names, at least that matched the descriptions I could give him."

"Your brother's not that much older," Victor pointed out, annoyingly correctly. "We haven't talked about it? Honestly, it's sort of refreshing, not going on about Schola Houses and all that. I mean, not that we come out badly in that." Both of them had ended up in Fox House, like Charlotte's parents, like Victor's parents, the proper little ambitious scions of the best families. Not that ambition was a thing that Victor had any interest in, unless perhaps it had to do with ambitious numbers of notches on his bedpost. On the other hand, he had certainly got more than a bit of use out of Fox's training in social skills and charm.

"Still." Charlotte couldn't decide what she thought about them not having gone to Schola. She knew perfectly well that Schola was not the only way one learned magic, no matter how much some families thought it was. Her aunts - adopted, not blood - were proof of that, both Aunt Mason and Aunt Witt had gone to Alethorpe. There were others in the Penelopes who'd gone straight into apprenticeship. And if they didn't have Gabe's meteoric dash across the heavens, they had come out of their own training just as competent, if in different areas than him.

But it did mean she couldn't evaluate their magic. That thing Gabe had said about the sparks wouldn't get out of her head, especially since she was pretty sure it really had been Gareth casting them. She and Gabe had wrangled over it on and off for a week. As he said, doing that kind of displacement illusion without her seeing Gareth doing it was a particular level of skill. Gabe had tried to talk her into getting him invited along on this whole thing, and she had refused. For one thing, that would drive Charlotte up a wall. She could manage either Victor or Gabe's particular chaos at a time, not both of them together without additional limits. Preferably in the form of her parents or Aunts Mason and Witt, honestly, who did very well at suppressing Gabe when required.

"Very relaxing. Mother's been going on about it, the apprenticeship. Too, too tedious, Charlotte, darling." Victor sighed and draped himself artistically on the long couch again. Now he was back to the masks, and Charlotte let herself lean back. Dissipated gentleman, apparently, or one of the Bright Young Things, and neither was much to Charlotte's taste.

"You mean she'd like you to make progress on it." The thing of it was, Victor was magically gifted. Not just one way around, either. He had strong magic, abundant magic, whichever set of language about it she wanted to use. But he was also clever when he put his mind to it, and he had a good memory when he cared about whatever it was he was doing. He should have been just as good at his apprenticeship, which was in ongoing enchantments. He didn't need to work - his family had plenty of money without that. But in their class, doing something useful with it, for those who had that kind of magic available, was rather expected. And Victor did have significant swaths of personal magic to back him up, unlike a number of increasingly inbred families.

"I suppose." Victor let out a sigh. "It's just not interesting. Any of it. And Morgen is." He pushed up on his elbow. "Two weeks there, with nothing to distract me. Us. She said it will be tremendously inspiring, in ways I haven't ever dreamed of."

That just sounded entirely unbelievable, though admittedly growing up with Gabe gave one a larger scope of what people dreamed about than most. Probably. But it wasn't as if Charlotte didn't have some fairly abundant dreams herself. "Magic? You still haven't said what we're going to be doing. She hasn't told you, has she?"

"Well, no. Not details, like you want. But it'll be grand, and time to talk without having to go off somewhere and be ordinary. She promised there's very little ordinary about any of it. Not the food, not the house, not the magic, not anything."

Charlotte couldn't help feeling this raised some significant concerns on the whole. But on the other hand, it wasn't as if she were going to let Victor go by himself in that case. "If you think so. Me, I'm going to pack a couple of books I've been meaning to get to. But I hope you do find some inspiration. You could use a little more."

That got her a mock-grumpy. "Yes, mother." A moment later, a pillow came flying at her. She caught it, propped it behind her head. "Thank you, Victor. So, tell me what I ought to pack, then."

CHAPTER 5

APRIL 6TH IN A COTTAGE ON A SOMERSET ESTATE

Lewis wanted to be doing something. Anything. Or at least, anything in his usual range of things he did. Specifically, he wanted to be working on the new distillation. He'd read an article last night about a different way to concentrate the magical powers of the distillate. If he could do that, and refine the qualities of the wax, and solve that problem of the tincture strength, he might be able to help Theo more.

Instead, he was here, waiting for Morgen to arrive. She'd said 'afternoon'. Morgen was not a morning person, not unless that meant seeing the dawn after a long night. That wasn't the part that bothered Lewis, he didn't much care for mornings either. Certainly not being up and about and chipper about them. He liked to ease his way from sleep to waking, and then bury himself in his work as soon as he'd had some tea and breakfast.

The problem was that Morgen might turn up at one or at six. Lewis didn't want to start anything he'd have to stop in the middle, and that left out nearly all the alchemical work. He was caught up on his notes, he always was, that had only taken him half an hour, from one to half-one. Then he'd tidied all his ingredient stores, confirmed what he was running low on for the fifth time this week, and triple-checked the list. It was on his desk in the sitting room, in one of the little envelopes Morgen wanted him to use, with the sealing wax stamped carefully on the back.

That was an affectation of hers. It was an odd bit of work, too, a crown held up and thrust forward by a wave, as if offering it to the viewer. That was an interesting trick to do in sealing wax, and it kept catching Lewis's eye. Or something in the wax did, anyway, the glowing red of it, not a water sort of colour at all. But Morgen did favour that red, over and over. Lewis didn't know as much about cloth and dyes as he did about other alchemical aspects, but he kept wondering if her dress had cochineal in the dye. It had the flavour of those bits of materia that had come through death into magic, like ambergris.

Lewis took a turn through the other rooms of the cottage. It didn't take long, it wasn't as if there were many to choose from. The bedroom, upstairs, wasn't anywhere Morgen would go, but all his clothes were put away. The sitting room was tidy. The tiny kitchen was also tidy, it bothered him when it wasn't. The dining room at the far end was piled with books, he was using it as a study. Lewis really itched - yearned - to be in the lab, across the stone courtyard, but that wouldn't do. Not until Morgen had come and gone.

Finally, a bit after the clock had chimed five, there was a knock on the door before it was immediately opened. "Lewis? Where are - oh, there you are." He could hear how her voice changed, from something sharper to something smooth. "How are you, darling? I just stopped by for the usual, of course."

She said it as if she hadn't told him to be waiting for her. And as if it weren't Friday, and if she were going to show up, it would be on a Friday. Mind, he only remembered it was Friday and not Tuesday because he'd laid out his plans for tonight's work. It wasn't an ideal alignment, but he wanted to play the conjunction of Mercury and the Sun in Aries against Venus in her hour in Gemini. And after all, Morgen had been very clear she was interested in any combination of alchemical oils and incense that encouraged free expression of someone's inner desires, as well as the more obvious ones. He was fairly sure he could have an incense ready for her in a week, at any rate, though the oils would take longer.

"Come in, please. Do you want a seat? Can I offer you something to drink?" Lewis made the proper polite noises.

"Oh, no, darling. We're not staying long. Boys, do bring in the hamper and wait for me by the gate, would you?" Mark and - no, he didn't know the other's name - heaved the hamper into the sitting room, then into the centre of the kitchen floor. They always left it for him to unpack, which meant he knew where things were, but also meant he was left to wrangle the heavy, awkward thing somewhere less annoying. They took the empty one, last fortnight's, back with them.

"Now, that's got more than usual, we have things for your cupboards. Next week's hamper will need to last you through to May fourth. Cook will be quite busy with everyone at the house. And we won't have time to be running down here to bring you things. There are quite a few people coming."

"That's good, isn't it?" Lewis rather wanted to sit down, and he couldn't if she didn't. He had manners, Mother had made sure of that, and Theo since.

"Oh, it is divine." Her voice dropped into the rolling purr, the one that meant she was as contented as a cat in someone's lap. Mark and the other man went out, closing the door behind them. If Morgen hadn't been there, they'd have been noisy about it. They always were, when it was just them, as if Lewis wasn't important enough to avoid slamming doors. Because Morgen was standing right there, listening, Mark eased the door shut, only the little snick of the latch audible. "Now, then." Her voice dropped in pitch, though she was still being persuasive.

Lewis had heard her ordering other people, and she didn't do that with him. It worried him, actually, that she didn't. He didn't understand what it meant, that she didn't order him. "Yes?"

"I just wanted to check, darling, that everything will be absolutely ready for the fortnight. That I'll be able to come down and get everything next Friday."

"Of course, Morgen. I wouldn't want, I mean, I know what you need. I have all the lists. I'll be making it up this week, when we're close enough for it to last."

"There is that one. I'll have to send Gareth for it. On the seventeenth, yes?"

"Yes'm." The formality slipped out of him, almost automatically. "I'll need to finish it on the Monday. Let it rest in the bottle overnight." The moon for illusions, and a lot of what she wanted was illusions. Illusions, enticements, encouragements, the books laid it out in several different sets of terms. All of them made Lewis a tad uncomfortable, and that didn't matter to anyone at all except Lewis.

"Grand, grand. Do you have the letter for me? Oh, and I have one for you." Morgen shifted, drawing a letter out of a slit in her frock, at the hip. She held it out, and when Lewis turned back from the desk, two letters in hand, she took

46

them. "I'll see this goes out tomorrow. You've been a good boy, haven't you? Anything unexpected in the ingredients?"

"We're getting low on the ambergris, Morgen, if you want me to do more of the longer-term perfumes. It's the best fixative for what you want, that's why we go through so much of it." Lewis could hear his voice going faster, the pitch rising, and he couldn't stop himself. He never could, especially with Morgen.

"Oh, bother." Now, Morgen sounded just the ordinary sort of annoyed. "Oh, not you, darling." Her voice softened, almost immediately. "There are some of the things you asked for, in the hamper, for your other little projects. If you get everything to me on time, and it works as you've said it will, you'll get the rest after May Day. How's that?"

"As you wish, Morgen." Lewis tried to summon the sort of brightness and cheerfulness he knew she preferred. "And of course, I've plenty to be busy with until then."

"There you are, then." It was like being a dog, patted on the head and praised. The others - the ones he'd seen with her, anyway - seemed to lean into it as much as Lewis did. He wasn't like that with most people. But even if Morgen hadn't been making the potions for Theo possible, he'd have wanted to do what made her smile like that. "Is there anything on the list you need urgently? Before the ambergris?"

"Nothing terribly complex, but if you want that much of the protective oils, I'll need a lot of orris root. It's not terribly expensive. Either of the usual providers should be fine for it."

"Ah, so it's not one of those things that needs to be harvested once a year, under particular weather conditions. Those are so, so tiresome, darling." She then leaned forward, reaching out to touch him, trailing fingers along his cheek. "Right. I'll be off. Someone will check for any messages on Tuesday. And then Friday."

She swept out without waiting for him to say anything. Lewis waited until the door closed behind her - it didn't dare slam, either. Then he shook out his hands, before going to run them under cool water from the tap for a minute. Then he went to unpack the hamper. Whoever had packed it - not Morgen, he was fairly sure - had packed the oils and ingredients for his work on the top, not even in a separate box. They were just nestled in twists of paper. He took those out, settling them into one of the small high-sided tins. None of them had spilled or leaked, at least, but it was bad practice, and wasteful, besides.

Lewis put away the rest of the hamper quickly enough into the pantry cabinet that would hold the bread and cheese and milk until he needed it, without spoiling. There was quite a lot in there, actually, more than there probably should have been. He thought he'd used up more of it this week, but perhaps not. The eggs went in the pantry too, and then there were various tins of things, and jam and cream and a tin of tea. Tea, he went through. Someone had added a couple of bottles of beer, not that Lewis was likely to drink that. He added them to the others on the shelf.

Once it was properly put away, he could pull the hamper into a corner of the dining room, where he wouldn't trip over it. Finally, he could take the precious tin of ingredients across the stone-paved courtyard to the alchemical lab. He would put up with any number of uncomfortable conversations, any amount of carelessness with the materials from others, for this. The lab itself was some nine yards by five, plenty of space, with counters all around the walls, abundant natural light, shades he could draw if the light was a problem, and good ventilation.

It had not been adequate when he'd started. He'd had to spend the entire first month he was here adjusting the charms to keep the temperature and humidity in proper range. There had been endless rounds of clearing mildew both physically and with magic. Finally, though, he'd got it into proper homeostasis to be a suitable lab, and especially for perfumes. He'd cleaned everything up when he finished last night, and so it was all ready to go now.

Lewis did not do most of his own distillation, not for the perfume oils themselves. He didn't have the space or the equipment to do it in any quantity. Besides, many of the more delicate flowers had to be processed immediately upon harvest, and they didn't grow here. There were moments, though, where it was a key part of the process. He checked, automatically, that the glassware was clean and dry, but once he'd done that, he moved to the other corner of the room, where his stands of oils were. Vial by vial, he replaced the bottles that were empty, then set the others aside in the secondary rack. Finally, he could settle into his proper work, making the blends that Morgen required.

CHAPTER 6
APRIL 16TH AT A COUNTRY HOUSE IN SOMERSET

It was very odd to arrive to a house party on a Monday. Ordinarily, the things ran from Friday through Sunday or into Monday, depending on whether the people involved needed to be somewhere during business hours. The nearest portal was on the far side of Wells, a good four or five miles, so there had been someone to meet them with a horse and carriage.

The mare pulling it had more than a bit of draught horse in her, that was interesting. It suggested they'd arranged for a carter, rather than having a carriage on hand at the house, and, perhaps, that the group at the house didn't go out much at all, or they'd have their own horses. Victor sat with his back to Mark, who was driving it, and chatted on and off with him rather than talking to Charlotte. Today, he was all cheerful bonhomie, the best friend in some drawing room farce, ready to pick up any joke thrown at him and lob it back for an easy catch.

The landscape was rather lovely, though, rolling hills, and largely open farmland, other than the town itself.

Charlotte did notice that no one seemed to notice much when they drove through the town, which suggested look-away charms or something of the kind. Not the safest thing to have on a carriage, honestly, though she supposed there were probably not that many automobiles around these parts yet. At least they were easy enough to see coming.

Eventually, after some bumps and a tad more dust than Charlotte would have chosen, they came through a copse of dense woodland up a long drive to a house. The house was younger than Charlotte had expected, actually. She'd assumed the place would be from the Pact or earlier, but this was Palladian. If Uncle Gil's lessons had stuck, and they mostly had, this was more like the 1750s, give or take. No, nearer the late 1760s, perhaps, with that work on the entryway.

The carriage drew up outside, and two women, both in long and archaic dresses, came out, in a flurry of charms that scattered illusion flower petals. One of them was dark-haired, the same sort of striking colouration that Morgen had, only perhaps a tad less so. It suggested that Morgen might be picking for looks as well as whatever other criteria she had. The other had auburn hair, an unusual shade that Charlotte suspected owed at least a little to charm enhancements as well as some potion or dye. Mind, the illusion petals showed a nice eye for detail. The illusions, of course, did not get ground into the steps like real flower petals did or need cleaning up later. Nor did anyone have to hope the petals were at the perfect unwilted moment before tossing them into the air. Victor did turn to offer her his hand. "Enid, darling. And Ragnall." He seemed entirely at ease with them, falling into his personal role as charming flatterer immediately.

Charlotte thought their long skirts must be a tad difficult to manage, sweeping the ground as they were. She hung back, a little behind Victor, as he kissed both women on each cheek, asking them how they'd been since he'd seen them last week. He had seen them more recently than he'd implied to Charlotte, certainly.

It was Victor at his most generous. He plucked a little token out of his pocket, two of them, bits of ribbon with charms to make them sparkle, one for each of the women. He asked after a project Enid had apparently been working on, and how Ragnall's finger was doing, some tiny injury. In other men, it might have been a precursor to wanting to get them in bed or some other intimacy, but with Victor it was just letting his delight in people shine. It was one of the few places he could be genuine even when he was playing a part, and it made that persona sparkle.

It did give Charlotte a proper chance to look around. The average entry hall in this sort of place was usually meant to impress the visitor. Ordinarily, there would be portraits of notable ancestors or visible decorative pieces that hinted at the overall quality of the residence and its inhabitants. Here, the hall was hung as if it were out of some mediaeval tale, with woven banners down any exposed wall. They didn't have heraldry on them, like she'd half expected, or any symbol at all, just swaths of jewel-tone colours. There was a scent, too, something she couldn't quite place, more floral than herbal. She'd have thought incense, but it wasn't like any incense she'd smelled, not at the Temple of Healing, not in the family rituals, nor the occasional rites she'd been at with other families. It was a particular sort of scent, like it had some chosen meaning, but Charlotte couldn't figure out what.

Charlotte could see a double door, ahead, currently

closed, and several doors off the entry hall. The floor had a rather ornate rug on it, but Charlotte was fairly sure the pattern had been charm-dyed, or rather charm-printed, rather than properly woven in. The charms almost always looked less sharp when that had been done, if sharp were a thing that might be sensibly said about a wool rug. Something about it made her wonder if there would be something like a bearskin rug in whatever room Morgen preferred for the more showy parts of the gatherings. Perhaps torches, though the hall here had space for the more sensible charm lights, and a few candle holders on side tables.

"Here, this is Charlotte. Char, this is Enid, this is Ragnall, they'll see you set up all right, I'm sure." Charlotte looked up at that, catching the introduction. She ought to be a trifle annoyed at Victor, actually, he'd been going on for a bit, but somehow she couldn't bring herself to make a fuss. Scolding him in public always got him to put on the affronted and slightly pathetic dignity of a wet cat, anyway, and that was not the right mode to use here.

Ragnall - that was the dark haired one - giggled, the sort of giggle that likely did well with many men. Her fingers were threading the ribbon into her hair to tie it, a dangling reminder of being noticed. "Oh, we'll see you right up to your room. Mark will bring your case up in a minute. Here, come along this way. I'm sure you want to wash up a bit. The road is so dusty this time of year, until you get here, to our glen. None of that bother at all." She chattered along, saying nothing of any particular interest, though Charlotte was listening closely to it.

Ragnall led Charlotte through the house, up a staircase that was off the main hall, then came out into a hall with a number of doors. Ragnall took a left down the hall, then almost immediately right at a short flight of steps, opening the door on the left. "You've your own private bath, here, and your own room. Some of us share, of course, with people we're close to, but Dame Morgen gathered that you and Victor..." Her voice trailed off, as if hoping for a bit of gossip. "Anyway, he's up on the second floor. That's where Dame Morgen's favoured guests are. Just two doors down from me, he'll have a lovely view of the drive."

Charlotte had no idea how to explain to someone she'd just met that the man she'd arrived with would be decidedly more interested in her if she had at least another six inches and more relevant appendages? Also, less in the way of a bosom, Victor was notably uninterested in anything like that. Not that she'd let his secrets slip like that, though Ragnall not knowing did indicate there were layers in who knew what in the group.

Ragnall, mind, had her own bosom decidedly on display in a bodice that gave her frock a more baroque feel than a mediaeval one. The comment did give Charlotte something to ask about. "Is the proper form of address Dame, then?"

"Oh, yes. To be polite." Ragnall gestured Charlotte in. "Do have a look. See if you need anything right away. There are staff here, but they are very good about not being obtrusive. The best sort of staff are neither seen nor heard, don't you think?" Charlotte did not think that, though she did respect the skill it implied. Doing a fair bit of heavy labour was one thing, even with magic to help. Doing it while being invisible or the next thing to it was an entirely different challenge.

The title, though, that was interesting. Of course, Morgen wouldn't want the implications of using Lady. Charlotte had already known that there was no one of that name or that description who held a title in her own right, nor was heir. It was one of the things Charlotte had known since she was about twelve. For one thing, there weren't that many people who did - two hundred or so, through all of Albion. Charlotte could generally spot the symbology, too. But more to the point, Lord and Lady Hembry, who held the land magic for this part of Somerset, were both in their seventies. Charlotte did actually know their children and grandchildren on sight. None of them looked remotely like Morgen.

Charlotte was enough Papa's daughter - and Gabe's sister - to know the ways magic could alter a face. She'd considered it a time or two, to give herself a bit of the softness that seemed fashionable in a certain set, rather than what Mama referred to as opinionated cheekbones that she'd grow into in a few years. That kind of magic was time-consuming and painstaking to learn. If Gareth had been doing the spark illusions - a much simpler trick - it seemed likely Morgen wasn't shaping her own face. Or even - which was a hair more plausible - the perception of her face. Probably. Charlotte knew less about that sort of magic, actually, it hadn't come up when she'd been around and listening to the rest of her family.

So if she had ties to the land magic, Morgen wasn't related to the landed family near here. Nor to the Fouracres, who held the western half of Somerset. Nothing quite matched up usefully, and Morgen had remained a tediously unsolvable cypher. Now Charlotte looked around. The room faced out to the back of the house, a field, with a maze in it. "A hedge maze? I do love them."

"Oh, it's not for walking in. It's part of some of the gathering, but only when Dame Morgen permits." Ragnall clapped her hand to her mouth. "I shouldn't have said that much. Please forgive me. But you shouldn't go out on the grounds unless someone invites you. It's one of the rules here."

Charlotte automatically found herself demurring, saying of course she wouldn't mention it. She wouldn't. But Ragnall's reaction seemed too much for a minor slip of the tongue. She filed it away to think about later, but immediately got distracted by the room. There was a large mirror, facing into the room, that same scent as downstairs with something else, more flowers. She took a few steps into the bathing room, then came out. "That scent?"

"Oh, isn't it lovely? I miss it so much when I'm anywhere else. I even dream about it when I'm not here. Dame Morgen has it made specially, just for her. A signature scent, I suppose you'd say, though she has her own perfume, of course." Ragnall beamed. "Now - ah, here's Mark with your case. Shall I give you a few minutes to unpack and then come back in ten? Gareth - he's Dame Morgen's most devoted knight - wanted to meet you and explain our customs."

Ten minutes would not let her do very much unpacking at all, but most of what she'd brought was clothing. A few books, nothing that would raise questions, because Charlotte fully expected someone would be nosy about her things at some point. Even if this were just the ordinary sort of house party, that was not uncommon. In the current circumstances, she expected someone to pry.

Instead, she just nodded. "Of course. I understand. Ten minutes should give me enough time to make a start."

"Perfect!" It came out with a squeal of pleasure. "Be back in just a few." Ragnall nearly bounced out of her bodice as she went off. Charlotte listened to her feet down the few stairs, wondered who had the room next to hers, and set herself to unpacking. She finished the basics of it -

putting out her book, her toiletries, hanging her frocks - with two minutes to spare, giving her time to make use of the loo. It had been a long bit of travel, and she could really have used a chance to wash up properly, but a charm would have to do.

CHAPTER 7
LATER, IN THE DRAWING ROOM

T he tea with Gareth was quite odd. Oh, it certainly involved tea, though with an undertone to the flavour that Charlotte couldn't quite place. She drank a quarter of it. Then she surreptitiously applied the rest of it to a potted plant behind her in the corner when Gareth was momentarily distracted. That happened twice, when people came in, he nodded at them, and they bent to whisper something in his ear. He turned back to her, all smiles. "Arrangements for tonight, dearest."

The rest of the time, his attention was entirely on her. Most people would have found it flattering. Charlotte knew better. Or at least, she knew enough to be cautious. The topics of conversation wandered a bit, without ever getting in very deep. However, Charlotte was sure he was searching for something.

He was vastly less deft at the process that Mama was. If Mama had been conducting this interview, Charlotte would never have noticed. Also, the whole thing would have been vastly shorter. Or, well, she might have spotted the interview, but only because she'd had near two decades of

Mama explaining what she was doing afterwards. She likely wouldn't have spotted a stranger of the same level of skill.

Fortunately, Gareth was skilled, but not at all at Mama's level of expertise. It was one of those things where age mattered, and Mama had decades on him. He signalled, a few times, what he wanted to talk about, as if he were running down a list in his memory, covering for it with radiant smiles.

It made Charlotte curious, though. The man was attractive enough in a classic sense, though he still did nothing for her personally. The few times she'd had a glimmering of an actual pash for someone, it had been the brains she'd been interested in first, and the body somewhere well down the line. Perhaps the face a little sooner, the face showed a lot about a person, that and how they used their hands. Gareth would make an excellent actor, most likely, he was measuring his effect.

One thing she noticed was how he kept redirecting the conversation. It wasn't just the ordinary flow she might expect with someone he barely knew. There was a predictable sort of awkwardness to those. Here, though, he would mention something - the tea, say - and she would reply. He would mention that they always took their tea with local honey, and make it clear that asking for sugar or no sweetener at all was not the done thing. Then, on the next topic, it would be something else like that. No one walks in the garden by themselves, no one goes into the maze except on special occasions, meals are taken together except for breakfast.

The other thing that got to her was the sense of distance. Certainly, she'd been around for a number of such conversations, where distance was the point of the thing.

Mama had a gift for setting the right amount of distance, so she'd get the gossip she wanted without being pulled into volunteering for something that she wanted to avoid. Gareth was doing the same sort of distancing, while he asked some increasingly personal questions.

Many of them were - more or less politely - about how she felt about Victor. She was honest, so far as anything she actually said. For one thing, she knew Victor had explained their agreement, talked about her as a dear friend or nearly a sister, or whatever. Which was not true, she had a brother, and Victor was nothing like Gabe. She was fond of Victor, but it was a different flavour to the fondness entirely. Good friends, definitely. Conspirators, possibly, whenever Victor ever motivated himself to do anything that required a conspiracy. Though this gathering did actually qualify, really, only he was not actually conspiring with her.

That was what was getting to her. Victor had included her, of course, but it seemed a beat late. It had started at that supper where she'd met Morgen and Gareth and the others, and it had continued now they were here. While Gareth was focused on her, to an uncomfortable sort of degree, she had a feeling he was engaging with Gareth's idea of her, rather than anything about who she was. It wasn't Victor's idea of her, on loan, or even the respectable image he promulgated for her. It was reassuring that Victor seemed not to have let slip anything beyond the mode they had worked out, but Gareth didn't seem to be engaging with that, either.

The current unspecificity was intentional on her part, of course. She suspected her answers were not, on the whole, being informative in the way Gareth had hoped for. He asked for favourite romantic heroes from legend and literature. She mentioned Odysseus, who'd always intrigued with his cleverness, near as much as she'd admired Penelope's steadfast work to keep things together in Ithaca. There was the tale of Isabeau and Ammet, one of the tales laid out not long after the Pact, of clever solutions to complicated problems.

"Nothing Arthurian? You've lovely blonde hair, the wave to it. Quite like some of the paintings of Guinevere. You should wear it loose while you're here, certainly." Gareth leaned forward. "No handsome dark knights or blond heroes in your dreams, then?"

"I always preferred Tristan and Iseult's tale to Arthur and Guinevere and Lancelot, and of course he comes in rather later," Charlotte said, deciding to go blithely forward and ignore all the hints about the Arthuriana at the base of whatever was going on here. No one had actually spelled it out to her, and she was becoming curious what they'd do if she just didn't quite get it.

That answer absolutely wasn't what he expected. "May I ask why? Not the typical answer, you must know that. I'm told girls often have a favourite knight, when they're talking in the dorms or what have you."

"They didn't have much choice in it. Tristan and Iseult drink a love potion, and then they have to figure out what to do about it. It's not fair to anyone, and they make some awful decisions. But I think it's a much more interesting story than a lot of the more modern Arthuriana." There, she could give him that tidbit, that she liked older things. Which she did.

Something in that made him lean back. "Ah, I can see that. You've some fascinating depths yourself, darling. I think you're going to find this gathering most agreeable. But I also have someone you absolutely must meet." He touched a stone on the table beside him. About five seconds later, the door opened, revealing one of the women she hadn't met yet, in the same long flowing dress. "Can you ask Bedivere to come through, please?"

The speed of it all suggested that not only was someone waiting to be summoned to the door, but that there was at least one gentleman - so she would suppose for the moment, sight unseen - lurking to be selected. Perhaps a minute later, just long enough to plausibly deny that he'd been lurking outside, there was a knock.

"Come in. Oh, Bedivere, here, I've decided we simply must put Charlotte in your charge for her time here. It couldn't be anyone else. Now, Charlotte, you understand that we each take new names when we join the community. You'll be seeing a bit of that this evening. We're welcoming two new companions to our circle. Now, why don't you go for a circuit around the garden, until it's time to dress for supper? And Charlotte, there'll be a frock for you, if you'd like to dress more like the other women, feel more one of us."

Bedivere was a pleasant-looking man, sandy-haired, with green eyes she suspected had help from a charm illusion, well-built. He was young enough he'd likely not fought in the Great War. Or if he had served, it wasn't anywhere that had left him with ghosts and nightmares. Interestingly, his was also not a face Charlotte recognised, so he'd neither gone to Schola nor was from any of the substantial number of families who were at the same parties Charlotte was. Not a landed family, not Council, probably not any of the magistrates. That was, in itself, an interesting puzzle. And of course, if they took on new names - and just forenames at that - that wouldn't be any help.

The more of these people she met, the more she began to wonder where they came from, who their people were. Not the notable members of the Great Families, not magically talented in their own right, or she'd know more about them. Charlotte and Victor stood out that way. While she suspected Morgen had realised about Victor, she was suddenly not sure what these people had figured out about her.

Bedivere bowed in front of her, then extended his hand. All very noble. To be entirely fair to him, he pulled the whole thing off rather well. In many men of their generation, that would look ridiculous. He made it look more than a little appealing, especially all the little movements of draping sleeves and tunic over tight hose. They were not, rather obviously, playing with the historical clothing for accuracy, but rather for flattery.

She accepted the hand, he slid her fingers into the crook of his arm. Bedivere escorted her back out through the doors they'd entered through, back through the entry hall, and around to the right. "Ever sunwise, dear Charlotte." Bedivere's voice was also unexpectedly pleasant. Not a tenor, as she might have expected from the hero motif, but a baritone with a bit of depth to it. He certainly had the presence to be a performer of some kind, like others of the Nine Muses she'd met through Victor. "I'm so delighted to get the chance to spend more time with you, just us. When Gareth and Mark came back from supper with you, they couldn't stop talking about how lovely you were, and how well they thought you'd fit in here. Isn't this just splendid?"

Charlotte was, to be fair, trying to place his accent. He had the more plummy tones of her usual set, but something in it wasn't quite ringing true. Gabe didn't precisely shift accents, but he did shift registers, half a dozen in a minute or less, sometimes, and this was like that. Some note that something underneath had moved. She dimpled and smiled, before asking, "Can you tell me a little more about the house? My room's just lovely. I gather there are a lot of people here?"

"Eighteen of us, this fortnight, with you and Victor making twenty. We hope to become twenty-five, in not too long. That's a lovely number, isn't it?"

It was an exceedingly curious number, actually. Most of Albion ran on sevens, and when it didn't, on threes or fours. Fives were unusual. Charlotte set aside the mental digression of her brother's commentary on the topic. She could near hear him in her head, going on about five-petalled roses, elemental systems in some parts of Asia, the fact Venus appeared to trace a pentagram in the sky. Followed by the association with both Saraswati and Shiva, and an entirely unnecessary discourse on the natural history of the starfish. "Twenty-five? And you think—" She did the dimple and blush manoeuvre again, it tended to work well. "The two of us, possibly?"

"Oh, it's most promising. Dame Morgen was so delighted when Victor appeared. She'd foreseen it, of course. She's a mistress of divination and enchantment." With that chosen name, she should certainly be expected to be. That was the thing with taking names out of lore. They came with particular expectations. Then Bedivere hurriedly added, "And you too, but you were a bit more, what did she say, shrouded in mist."

It was a nice pat answer for her tagging along. Shrouding things in mist had a number of purposes, both reasonable and dubious. Sometimes both at the same time. Charlotte squeezed his arm. "Can I ask - my, I don't know what's polite here. May I ask how long you've been one of the..." Her voice trailed off, hoping he'd suggest the proper language.

"Our circle. Think of the Round Table, dearest." Charlotte was not his dear anything, but she'd noticed already the tendency to that term, and darling, and whatever other endearments wandered through that were remotely plausible. "That had, in some lore - and again, Dame Morgen has foreseen it - twenty-five. Women as well as men, of course, in our case. As it should have been then. All of the right sort, the proper choices." That was the mirror of how Charlotte usually heard it. In her usual circles, the right sort would be Victor and Charlotte. Here, it almost excluded them.

Now Charlotte rather wanted to give a lecture of her own, and part of her wits would very much like to sit down and outline it. One of the key questions with Arthuriana, of course, was what period one was talking about. It wasn't clear whether they were bringing in the French influences or relying solely on those of Albion and Britain. And that did not even touch the question of Merlin's role. She opened her mouth, then closed it, letting Bedivere see her uncertainty. He leaned in. "Go on, dearest, do ask? You ask such interesting questions."

Blast, she'd have to cut back on them. She didn't want them to be quite that notable, that it was the first thing he went to for a compliment. "This is probably very silly of me, but if you're forming the Round Table anew, shouldn't there, I mean, shouldn't there be an Arthur, or a Guinevere, or a Lancelot, or a Merlin?"

He laughed, cheerful and loud. "Oh, that's part of the mystery. It's a journey, darling, one we are all on together. Now, some of it isn't mine to talk about. It's for Dame Morgen to decide that. I, well." He bent, kissing her cheek decorously. "I simply get to join you in discovering the magic."

It sounded charming. That was the problem. Bedivere had an earnestness to him, like a setter or a working dog, so glad to be doing his task, tail all but wagging. He was certainly easy on the eyes. The estate was stunning, and everyone she'd met so far was likeable. And yet, she wasn't at all sure what the foundation was, and she was someone who'd been taught to look behind the curtains and at the cracks in the foundation. Most of all, she didn't really trust anything that hadn't survived a bit of tumult first.

Now she smiled again. "I won't press, darling. Show me the gardens, then, would you, until it's time to change for supper?"

CHAPTER 8
THAT EVENING AT SUPPER

"Of course, only a few may join us." Morgen was ruling from the head table, up on a dais with Gareth beside her, and two others flanking them. She was speaking, though, to the entire room, the other fourteen people at long tables, forming a decidedly mediaeval great hall. They were in what must have been designed as the dining room. It was entirely the wrong place in the house for a great hall, and besides, the building wasn't old enough to have had one. Charlotte had paid attention to Uncle Gil's comments more than enough for that.

There was a fireplace, but the three tables were set up in a broad U shape, decidedly more rectangular than round. She supposed in some people it might have done a lot to evoke pomp and circumstance. But it mostly made Charlotte feel like she was back at Schola, in the long rows of house tables in the vastly larger Great Hall there. That had been a proper keep, even if it only dated to about 1100, not all the way back to Arthur. But it had been designed to hold hundreds, not just over two dozen. She half expected Esme to kick her foot and remind her to pass the peas.

The room was meant to feel decadent, but it was the sort of decadence that relied on trailing silk and satin and velvet. Also, they'd deployed an excessive number of torches and braziers, and just enough reality to hang the illusion on. There was a scent in the air, a mix of roses and some sort of incense, and a note she couldn't quite place. The same one as earlier, maybe, but she did not have the best trained nose.

Morgen was extravagantly dressed, too. Her dress was the same sort of faux-mediaeval she'd worn to the supper. It had a decidedly ahistoric plunging neckline, fur trim around the collar. She'd had a velvet cloak when she came in, now draped around the back of her ornate carved chair. She was drinking - rather at ease, actually - from a goblet. Charlotte had started out doing the sort of sums she'd learned from Mama, about how real the silver was, when she saw how Gareth was concentrating, just a hair. Real enough objects, then, but enough illusion to make them shine and glimmer.

There were two others up on the dais, both wearing long white flowing robes. It was exactly the sort of fabric that might be reasonably described as white samite, because they were going to hit every single one of those notes, apparently. Though if she remembered correctly, the particular term in question was best known from Tennyson, decidedly later on. The woman on Gareth's side of the table looked nothing like Morgen. She had a pale complexion, blonde hair a shade lighter than Charlotte's, and very blue eyes. The man on Morgen's left kept watching her, raptly devoted, his dark hair making a mirror to her own.

It made Charlotte consider the room. Everyone in the room was young. Probably under thirty, by her best guess, most of them under twenty-five. All seemed to be visibly in good health, which was not the way the averages fell in the generation just a hair older than Charlotte and Victor. If any of the men had served in the War, she suspected it wasn't in battle conditions. If they had, they'd been exceptionally lucky. That suggested Morgen was choosing her companions carefully.

They'd been seated more or less in pairs. Bedivere was seated right next to her, on the short end, where he could lean over and murmur. Victor was at the other table, across the room, with a handsome young man she hadn't met whispering in his ear. Victor, bless him, wasn't paying as much attention to the pronouncements from the head table as he probably ought to be. She couldn't refuse the food - for one thing, she needed to eat and drink. But she was careful not to take anything that hadn't been shared by others at the table. At a feast like this, that was at least the ordinary way of things. The staff had passed plates brought out from wherever the kitchens were, processing up to the head table, then splitting up to bring things to the others.

Charlotte recognised a couple of other faces. Not the people, directly, but people where she knew cousins. Two others who'd gone to Schola, one of the women seemed to be quite senior among the current group. She was at Victor's right, leaning to speak with him now and again. Charlotte thought that maybe she'd also been in the Nine Muses. She had that sort of way of carrying herself they got, as if declamation might be required at any second, and a prop to gesture with. Victor was of course the same way.

The meal wound its way on through multiple removes. Bedivere tempted her to try this or that, all from the shared serving dishes. Charlotte was used to a reasonably varied table at home, for all Papa admittedly liked traditional foods, so she'd had most all of what was on offer before. Everything she tasted was well-prepared, the flavours balanced. At least whoever hired the staff had hired for skill. The spicing was a bit different here and there, though.

Charlotte had not, however, been prepared for some of the sauces. They were on the edge of being too sweet. When she'd tried to decline a second spoonful, Esme, next to her, had tsked softly. "We welcome all we're given. Some days, of course, we are more restrained, but tonight is for the pleasure of it. And you want to join us in that, of course." There was no sensible argument to make to that. Charlotte had dealt with the extra spoon of wine sauce, managing to get the excess to pool out of the way of the rest of her food.

When the last course had been cleared, they were left with goblets and carafes of wine, clearly meant for toasting. Two servants came and lifted up the high table entirely, moving it to one edge of the room and withdrawing. It made a showy bit of staging, leaving Morgen and Gareth near enough enthroned, with nothing between them and the rest of the hall. The two who had been sitting with them had stood, their chairs whisked away to the corners, hands folded behind their back.

Quiet conversation had continued through those shifts, but now Morgen spoke again. "Gentles, attend." She'd enhanced her voice, somehow, or perhaps Gareth had, because it rang out above the conversation. Not that it needed the help after the first two words, the entire room fell silent. "Sir, attend us."

The man who'd been seated on her left came forward, bowing and kneeling perhaps five feet in front of her. It looked like a rather hard floor, with no visible padding.

Watching his face from the side - she had quite a good view actually - Charlotte suspected a lack of a cushioning charm as well.

Morgen stood, posing to make her authority clear, the cloak falling behind her as if it knew it must obey properly or be banished for curtains. "You have kept vigil?"

"I have, Dame Morgen." Now the man bowed his head. "I would make my pledge to you."

The hairs on the back of Charlotte's neck stood up. She had made enough oaths in her time - not near so many as Papa or Gabe or even Mama did. But the way she'd been brought up, it was only proper to make oaths on the Silence, but also to some greater cause, whether that was justice or the Guard's work or to healing or whatever it was. Not to another person. Even in the Council rites, the Council was the human face of the exchange on behalf of the land, which had neither mouth nor hands to make its will known. She forced herself to take a breath and let it out. No one was asking her to make such an oath, not yet. Or Victor. And there were ways to unbind oaths, she knew that.

"Last night, you kept vigil. This morning, you told me your dreams. Make your oath, and then we will tell you your gifts." She spooled it out, like it was its own enchantments.

"I, with all the magic in my blood, do swear to give my body to your work, my heart at your will, and my magic at your calling, in all you see fit, from now until the end of days." Charlotte bit her tongue to keep from doing worse. It was an oath made for abuse in several forms, and poorly made, besides. He seemed glad to make it, though.

"Well said," Morgen smiled down at him. "Gareth." Gareth stepped forward, presenting her with an unsheathed sword. It seemed easier to wield than a blade of that length had any right to be, making it either a stage prop or charmed to be waved around. Morgen placed the flat on each of the man's shoulders, then the top of his head. "Rise, Urien. Your dreams today spoke of a lion, roaring. Here, then, is your shield, upon which you should gaze on rising and retiring, as you have been taught."

One of the others brought out a shield. Charlotte knew her heraldry well enough that the blazon came to mind first. Azure, a lion rampant or, armed and langued gules. In practice, a gold lion rearing on his hind legs, on a blue ground, with gleaming red claws, fit to match Morgen's gown. The shield was small to be used in many fighting styles, but certainly easier to move around, especially if multiple people had one.

Charlotte had a number of questions about this, about when they'd made the shield, for one thing, or if they'd decided on the blazon well in advance. Never mind what the rites Morgen had mentioned were supposed to do. Now, Morgen leaned to kiss Urien on his forehead, then take his hand and bid him to rise. "Yours is the lapis, and the calendula. These bring you power and shape your magic as we will."

Urien seemed a bit speechless at this point, nodding, until one of the men led him back off to the side, then handed him his shield. Morgen had already turned, gesturing to the woman who'd sat beside Gareth. She came and knelt like Urien had, her robes billowing out to cover her feet. Morgen nodded at her. "And you have also kept vigil, and whispered your dreams to me. Speak now, your oath."

"With all the magic in my blood, I swear my body to your work, my heart to your will, and my magic to your calling, in all you see fit from now until the end of days." Her voice wavered, just a hair on that 'body' and Charlotte had an awful realisation. They had been willing enough to bring in Victor, despite knowing his preferences, but an awful lot of the people here did seem to be paired up.

That included Victor, as well as Charlotte. She had been presented with Bedivere, without any particular choice in the matter, or even having met the other potential candidates. It made her wonder how they did that, and how Bedivere was lacking a partner of his own already. Victor looked much happier, if that was Caradoc, he was leaning into the man's shoulder now and again, or sneaking a bit off his plate, playful and boyish, deferring to the other man's maturity.

Bedivere was a reasonable dinner companion, in the circumstances, but not one she'd want more intimacy with, even just for an evening's mutual pleasure. He had not struck her as having enough brains to bring home to Mama. And whether she actually wanted to bring someone home, Charlotte had long felt that was a reasonable bar to set with who she bedded. Or mostly didn't. Also, she did rather prefer someone who had a personal interest in her, not a dictated one. At any rate, the oath did seem to suggest that the eventual provision of children might be covered, and that seemed a foolish sort of thing to swear away.

The woman, though, looked as if it were the happiest day of her life. There were tears at the corners of her eyes. Charlotte could see the glimmer of them. Morgen reached out behind her, to be handed some object by Gareth, and she touched it to the woman's head. Not a sword, in this case, nor a dagger, but a decorated hair comb. "Yours is the lioness, of course. Meditate upon your adornment on rising and before you retire, as you have been taught. I

name you Elaine, and yours are the carnelian and the iris."
As if she couldn't have symbols of her own, just those that
matched and reflected Urien. It rather underscored the
sense of mated pairs, and left her wondering, again, about
Victor.

Charlotte bit her tongue and kept her face carefully
neutral. Gareth came to escort the new-named Elaine to
Urien, then showed both of them out through the door
back to the drawing room. When he returned, he placed his
hand in Morgen's. "May the celebrations begin!"

All at once, the tables and chairs were pulled away,
making a space for dancing. The dances were more or less
ones that Charlotte knew, the sorts of country dances that
could be done in pairs of varying number. Three people had
pulled away to make the music: a drummer, a fiddler, and a
flautist. Before Charlotte could suggest she sit things out,
she was swung into a dance, then into another, then into a
third. The fourth, she was partnered by Victor, and then she
was swung into Gareth's hand for the fifth, which was at
least slower and longer, a walking pace.

"I could see you watching, Charlotte." He leaned in to
murmur in her ear, as if it were a secret from everyone else.

"It was impressive. M - Dame Morgen has a great deal
of presence." She remembered the proper title here and
now in the nick of time. "And you, I am honoured by your
attention."

He chuckled. "Of course we have an interest. We are still
learning about you, darling. We will need time before
knowing what your name of names is, what symbols and
ancient magics call to you. We've had more time to get to
know Victor." His mouth twitched up, as if there were
something amusing in that. "Morgen will wish to sit with
you for a proper divination in a few days. There are a

number of magical bloodlines, and we must name yours precisely, for the greatest blessings. For you, and for us."

Charlotte ducked her chin. "And the goals, sir?" She tried to make the question just hesitant enough.

"Oh, restoring Arthur's golden age to the world, what else? Morgen has the power for it, when all is in place. I am sure of it, convinced." There was an edge of something manic to Gareth now, the way his eyes glowed in the candle and charm light. Charlotte knew better than to argue with that, but she was desperately wishing she'd been able to bring her journal.

"May I ask, the process? How - I would not presume that to be welcomed as Urien and Elaine were would be quick."

"This fortnight will reveal much. Perhaps by the end of it, we might extend the offer - the magic of May Eve has a lot to answer for. If not, perhaps in June or shortly after." Gareth waved it off, as if the precise date did not matter. If they were not going to press her before May Eve, then she did not need to flee into the night. She was sure Victor would not come, for one thing. While there was a lot of abominable ritual language at play, there was nothing that would have permitted the Guard to interfere. Not that she knew of yet, at least.

Perhaps she could get free for long enough to make a long hike to the portal on the far side of Wells and send a message through. She'd only need three hours or so, she was used to a hearty ramble. Perhaps she could even go overnight, if they did not guard the windows too carefully. Most people might consider her bedroom not easy to climb down from, but most people did not have Gabe for a brother. She could consider her options.

The dance ended before she could ask other questions,

and Gareth handed her back into Bedivere's hands. They had another few dances, before his hands did become a bit more freely applied than previously, as if he and his restraint were slowly parting company. Before he could do more than have one linger lower on her back, the music came to a stop. "To bed, to bed. Tomorrow, we gather for dreams of old."

The phrase meant something to the others, there were delighted murmurs. Bedivere did not explain - he was not much for explaining anything, as she'd already noticed. Instead, he walked her up the stairs to her room, leaving her at the door with only a kiss on her cheek, despite the wandering hands. Odd. Most odd all round.

CHAPTER 9
APRIL 17TH AT THE COTTAGE

"Lewis. Get your scrawny...." Gareth's voice cut off as soon as he saw Lewis coming from the dining room, through the dingy kitchen. "There you are."

Lewis had waited in the sitting room all morning. He'd even got up early, though he knew by now it was almost impossible that either Morgen or Gareth would turn up before ten. But he'd sat there, a book in his lap from nine through to past noon. Then he'd moved to the little dining room with all his books, so he could at least take notes.

Gareth nearly dropped the hamper he was holding, before he visibly remembered that it did have breakables in it. "Your milk and those bits and bobs you insisted on. No food hamper on Friday, or the following one, but someone will drop off a small basket next week with milk and such. You have the new bottles for Morgen?"

"Thank you, Gareth. And I do." Lewis knew better than to argue. Most importantly, it wouldn't do any good at all. Gareth was not the sort of person who responded to logic, nor did he care about evidence, citations, best practices, or the practical limitations of alchemy. He wanted the flash and the show, the glamour of an illusion, and he thought everything ought to bend to his whim the same way illusions did.

Lewis was almost too distracted for a moment about what his brother Theo would say. Theo would have argued - back when he had the desire to make an argument - that getting what he wanted was bad for Gareth. That someone should tell him no, more often. Lewis felt just as caught up here as Theo did at home, like nothing he said would do anything good, so why bother? It made him understand his brother and the way Theo got tangled now, when there didn't seem to be any solution to anything.

Gareth strode around, four strides along each edge, pacing like a great cat in a zoo. He was wearing even more dramatic clothing than usual. He had on one of those Renaissance shirts with puffs of creamy fabric everywhere, a brown leather vest running smoothly down to tightly fitted red breeches that left nothing to the imagination, and tall leather boots. It made Lewis nervous, that he was dressed like that, honestly. It was the sort of outfit that made him wonder where the sword was, or the daggers he couldn't see. "You've been coddled too much."

"Gareth?" Lewis had no idea what Gareth meant by that. Yes, Morgen had given over this cottage - and more importantly, the studio for a laboratory - for his use. But she wanted so many things. It's not that he minded, exactly. She was also paying for supplies, not just for what she wanted, but for the potions and drops and salves that Theo needed. But it kept him busy, ten or twelve hours most days, or having to wake up in the middle of the night to tend something. The complexity of what she wanted really needed three or four people working on it, not just him.

"All this. We're feeding you, buying your supplies. You have all this space to work with. And there we are crammed into the house, everyone knowing exactly what you're up to all the time."

Lewis had only been in the main house briefly, when he'd first arrived, but it had seemed to have rather a lot of bedrooms. None of them had to share. He'd overheard that much, even if some of them wanted to. Which Lewis found a bit odd, because ever since school, he'd wanted his own space. Moving to his own room third year had been a tremendous relief in all sorts of ways.

"And I appreciate that, Gareth, no end." Lewis was grateful. "How are the new perfumes and incense working?"

Gareth wheeled around sharply. "Not well enough." He'd gone from irritation to a focused anger in a heartbeat. Lewis took several steps back, retreating toward the kitchen. Not that the half-wall there offered any protection. "Make something better."

"Better?" Lewis scrunched up the cloth of his trousers, then made himself open his fingers. "What's not working, please?" He could think of several reasons. There were components that didn't react reliably with certain kinds of magic. He'd told Morgen about those, he'd made her lists, and Gareth had been here for several of those times, but maybe Gareth didn't remember.

"That potion. The one that makes me more persuasive." Gareth took a step toward him, then went back to pacing. "Make it stronger. Today."

"I, um. I can't." For a whole range of reasons. Then, hesitantly, he asked, "What wasn't working, please? Maybe I can think of something."

"She kept asking questions. Most of them don't ask

questions like that." Gareth waved a hand, almost flinging something invisible away from him. "It might be fine, but what if it isn't?"

Lewis frowned. Morgen had told him that the potion - like the incense, like two of the perfume oils - was just meant to make it easier for people to learn what she was teaching. 'Not get in their own way' was how she'd put it. Lewis had thought, at the time, that it seemed reasonable enough. He didn't know all of what they did in the main house, of course not. He wasn't an initiate in their mysteries, or whatever they called it. But he knew the sort of thing they were doing, bring people together, doing rituals of some sort.

Learning that sort of thing could be very complicated. Lewis certainly wasn't good at it. Not that kind of complicated, anyway. Lots of people thought alchemy was awfully complicated, and that was mostly very simple for him? It had a lot of different aspects, but that was the fun of it, making something that worked, but that was also pleasant. Now he cleared his throat. "Someone new, Gareth?"

"Yes." Gareth growled it out, turning in another loop around the sitting room. "I dosed her tea yesterday. Not the wine, but Bedivere had some of the oils on. It should have - can you do something for her room? A spray, an oil, something that would make her more agreeable."

Given time and materials, Lewis could. That sort of encouragement was widely desirable. It was also - in anything more certain than he'd already made - the sort of thing that got alchemists in trouble with the Guard. That wouldn't do at all. But for another thing, even the current potion had taken a fortnight to make. They were in the wrong lunar cycle for it anyway, and he was none too sure he could coax extra potency of this batch of vervain. "Sometimes people have a resistance to something, one of the ingredients. There are studies about it. I'm sure you don't care much about the details."

"No." That was also growled. "Give me options, you." Gareth turned away, stalking around the room again.

Lewis thought furiously. "What sort of agreeable are you looking for?" He frowned, thinking through what he could put together quickly. "There's a spray that encourages dreams, fantasies of what might be. Nothing harmful, but combined with the other things, it might work well." It was legal, the kind of thing shops used to encourage customers to imagine yourself wearing whatever they sold. "Compatible with the incense, but a different strand of effect. It's based on..."

No, Gareth wouldn't care about that at all, even if it were an extremely clever application of Hereford's Tonality, and one Lewis had refined himself, as a journeyman project. "Pardon." Lewis cleared his throat. "That one, I think I can make up now, if you have a few minutes." He was running through his inventory, all the little vials and bottles and droppers. He'd have to wash everything out before doing more work this afternoon, but that was to be expected.

"Do it. I'll come watch." Gareth took a step or two back. "Get on with it."

Lewis scurried over, nearly out the door, before he remembered that he needed two things from the hamper. He opened it quickly, pulling out the container of supplies at the top, and then hurried off to the studio. Gareth was right on his heels, close enough Lewis could feel the other man's breath on the back of his neck when he paused to undo the warding on the laboratory. Everything was in place when he got the lighting up. "If you'd sit there, part of this needs proper ventilation."

It certainly didn't do to drug himself while he was working with volatile compounds. Morgen had handed the place over to him, and he'd had to do all the fitting himself. Most of it wasn't that hard. He'd learned the charms that drew the air above the vented workbench away from him, to disperse in the wide open fields beyond the tiny house and courtyard. Gareth half-flung himself on the battered sofa. "Go on, then."

Lewis began, as always, with checking the recipe. The memory was fallible - well, unless he'd used a memory enhancing potion at the proper time, which he had in this case. But he could check, and it was good habit. Then he went through it a second time, taking out each vial he needed. Frankincense, yes. Vervain, for the magical potency, he went through ridiculous amounts of that. He'd need two drops of the rose, and the newest bottle, that had a different jasmine. He laid out another five bottles, firmly setting aside the feeling of Gareth staring at him.

The work was a delight, as always, suffused with the faint whiffs of the scents as he worked with them. This wasn't the creative part, it wasn't exploring how to weave the magical effect into something pleasant to smell, memorable to smell. But it was satisfying, in a particular way. He poured his own magic into it, as he added and blended, drop by drop. Then, just as he was coming to the end, he considered, and added a single drop of chios mastic oil. That was the light of clarity, the fresh breeze from over the sea cliffs. He didn't know why, he just knew it was the proper thing.

It wasn't like Gareth would know it was different from the recipe. It should still work, just as Lewis had been asked, something to make the dreams and desires easier to reach for, easier to name. The mastic just added clarity to the mix. Perhaps that was what this particular person needed - a woman? Yes. Gareth had said 'she'.

He made sure to close up all the vials and bottles and put them back. It would be chaos if they went out of order, no matter how carefully he'd labelled them all. He tucked the rest of the newly arrived supplies into the corner of the table to be unpacked later. "I've the box for you, too. It's in the sitting room. Shall I fetch it?"

"I'll come. This is it? How is it used?" Gareth pushed himself up from the sofa. "Deadly boring, this whole thing. Why does it take so long?" He flicked his fingers, an illusion of shimmering rainbows spiralling out from his fingers like it was nothing. It was nothing for him, though Lewis knew that keeping the lines of colour in order in the rainbow did actually take some skill.

"It can be used as a linen spray, or added to a scent stone in the room. Perhaps the linen, for the greatest effect while she sleeps?" Lewis offered it uncertainly. Though it would encourage deeper sleep, likely.

Gareth grunted. "Give me the other box, then. Is that what Morgen expected? Any changes?"

"Just as she asked. Incense, oil, a salve that counters the effects for those who should have that." Coming up with the countering agent had actually been exceedingly interesting alchemy, a truly fascinating problem to solve. That incense was also right on the line of what was legal. Morgen had assured him that it would be used in ritual, with people who wanted to be there, a controlled setting. Not a regular party or anything like that. And it was the class of things where people who worried could use a charm to tell if they wanted to. Or any number of commercial products to test, actually.

Before Lewis could wool-gather further, Gareth nudged him. "The box. I've places to be and things to do."

Lewis hurried back to pick up the small wooden box, rather like a jewellery box, and bring it out. Gareth waited in the courtyard, and as soon as Lewis handed it over, he was gone, with no further comment. Lewis watched until he was past the hedge, into the maze, the little shimmer of magic where he'd disappeared. Then he swallowed. Tea, first. And then he had plenty to be doing. Morgen already had very specific plans for the solstice, and some of it required starting infusions now, so they'd be ready when needed.

CHAPTER 10
APRIL 17TH AT THE ESTATE

The morning had been slow to get going. Charlotte quite liked lounging around in bed. Honestly, that wasn't the problem. She had brought plenty of books, and there was apparently a library downstairs. However, the morning had an odd dreaminess to it that didn't quite make sense. It was as if everything - including Charlotte - were covered in a slight haze. Not a pea souper fog, like she'd sometimes been in when she was in London. This wasn't nearly that thick. But everything was slow. She wasn't imagining it.

There was a breakfast tray waiting outside her door when she peered out, but she had no idea how long it had been there. She brought it in to find a fairly ordinary sort of meal, eggs and toast and a bit of jam and tea. Nothing heavy, nothing that couldn't sit with the appropriate charms for quite a while, though that was always an interesting trick with eggs.

Charlotte considered the meal thoughtfully, because she kept wondering about the food. Or rather, she'd wondered about the food since that tea. She hadn't been able to keep a sample, and whatever had been in the meal last night, at least everyone was getting the same thing. But now? She had some options.

When she'd talked about this visit with Gabe, she'd thought he was being ridiculous. Yes, Morgen had been a bit overwhelming, and yes, Victor was having a reaction to the whole thing that wasn't entirely like him. But that didn't mean she'd need the kit. On the other hand, she had packed it, because when Gabe got that kind of stubborn, it was easier to give in. She chose her battles with her brother carefully, thank you.

They both had one, though Gabe's got far more active use. On the outside, it looked entirely like an ordinary sort of medicinal and cosmetic kit. A few pastilles for minor ailments in little containers charmed against breakage, a few vials and jars of what would be taken for perfume or cosmetics. She also had a bar of what looked like soap that she could scrape a bit off, actually a reagent to test for the presence of the most likely additives. She generally didn't visit homes where she was worried about that sort of thing, but she did have to from time to time. Everyone in their family did, or in their social circles. Just because she needed to make an obligatory visit didn't mean she trusted the people she was visiting.

Grandmama, for example, who had in fact been known to try to slip things into both Charlotte's food and Gabe's to get them to see her side of things. Not that it had fooled either of them for years. Nothing Grandmama had used had been terribly strong. As Gabe had said, a couple of years ago, she didn't tend to treat alchemists well. The ones who would take on that kind of work usually had other options. And she certainly wasn't competent enough in an alchemical lab to do it herself. Gabe was - mostly because he'd learned how to work up antidotes to the things people came up with. Charlotte could have followed instructions to do it, but the influencing potions tended to need a native talent for the thing, not just technical skill.

The question now was whether they were keeping some kind of watch on her room. On one level, she didn't want to know because she needed to dress and undress without being self-conscious about it. Knowing made it worse. On the other hand, if she were going to test the tray - and future trays, because she couldn't assume - then she'd need to do some obvious things. Though she did have the testing solution that looked like it might be a medicinal, that would do for tea. On the third hand, she certainly couldn't go a fortnight without eating and drinking. If they were drugging everything, she should just set out for the Wells portal at once and abandon her luggage.

She'd agreed with Gabe on that point. She hadn't brought anything she wasn't willing to leave. Perfectly pleasant frocks, but none of her favourites. Underthings on the older side, where she'd be thinking about replacing them in the next six months. Books that were easy to replace from secondhand shops, or where they already had multiple copies at home. Charlotte was an Edgarton, and that kind of strategy just was sensible, growing up with the sort of family stories she had.

Charlotte stood up, taking the cosmetics case into the bath with her, to brush her hair and cast the charm. One of the things in it was set up as a spray, a scent or an oil for hair, to keep hers from having flyaway wisps everywhere. Or at least, it also did that. It would briefly reflect green, however, if there were certain kinds of charms in play, including those used for observation. She could be fairly sure the mirror itself wasn't the problem here, it backed up on those two steps leading up to these rooms.

Several sprays made it clear that none of those charms were in play. Charlotte rummaged in her kit and murmured. "Oh, just a touch of headache. I'd best take that tincture, that will help. Perhaps it's something in the air, all the plants coming alive." Spring did make an awfully good excuse, even if she didn't suffer much from hay fever in actuality.

Once she was settled at the little table by the window, she pulled the lids off the tray. Next she put a couple of drops obviously into her tea, then one onto the bread, one on each egg, and one in the little pot of jam. The jam shimmered green for just a second, but the eggs and the tea and the toast itself looked fine. Curious, but at least that was easy to avoid and still make a reasonable breakfast.

It did mean she was both curious and a tad hungry by lunch. The luncheon was served in a different room than the feast the previous night, making her wonder how many rooms there were on the main floor here. There was an unmistakable green baize door, the boundary line with the servant spaces. Charlotte rather desperately wanted to go chat with them. But they'd likely have none of it, and they'd be at risk of their jobs if they told her anything of use, almost certainly.

Similarly, only about half the group were there, ten or so, plus Charlotte and Victor. It was the younger set, mostly. There was no sign of Morgen or Gareth. Or Bedivere, for that matter. Charlotte was swept into a seat and picked out food off the trays. No way to test it now. She'd have to take it as it came.

The luncheon itself was full of amiable chatter, mostly full of terms Charlotte couldn't quite place. It wasn't the specialist language problem, exactly. She was entirely familiar with that one. This was more about people using perfectly reasonable words in ways that didn't quite make sense if anyone stopped and thought about it.

There was a lot of natter about 'lines' and 'roots', and some - though less - about some magical theory that Charlotte suspected was just wrong. It was as if it had been passed through a chain of people who changed it just a little every time. The bits she heard about the incantation, for example, made her quite sure none of the ones here for luncheon had gone to Schola. Professor Ahamadi had his idiosyncrasies, but he really did quite a good job explaining the things that made an incantation or spoken or sung enchantment take hold, and those that had no real bearing except looking flashy.

After luncheon, she looked up to find Victor by her chair. "Walk in the garden? Bedivere's got something he needs to do for a few."

If she was always supposed to have someone handy, they'd been asleep on the job this morning, but she wasn't going to comment on that. "Your company's always grand. Which way shall we go? Bedivere took me through the gardens yesterday."

"I thought you'd get on with him." Victor said as soon as they were out on the path. "Thank you for making me look good. I'd suggested you might, to Dame Morgen and Gareth."

"Who was that you were with last night?" Charlotte thought about saying he looked nice, but she couldn't quite bring herself to it.

"Oh, that's Caradoc, he's grand, mmm. He came to my room last night, after. That's why I wasn't up this morning." Victor looked like a cat with cream and a canary feather sticking out of his mouth, honestly. He was, honestly, vastly easier to get on with when he had a direction for his quite reasonable lustiness, but it just put Charlotte more on edge right now.

"Are you - I mean. We don't really know any of these people. Not yet. Caradoc looks nice, but you know how you get sometimes." Victor had passions that could be scheduled to a clock. Well, not a clock. They weren't that fast, but certainly to a month or two. He'd fall madly for someone, it would be all about them. Then, if the other person took notice, there'd be three and a half weeks of bliss. It would be followed by a fortnight of on-again-off-again dramatics, and then some sort of climactic point with them breaking things off. He didn't do it all that often, fortunately for everyone's well-being, but when he did, it looked like this, and it didn't end well. Even before she got into the other aspects of the whole gathering, the undercurrent that Charlotte really wasn't liking.

"Don't you be like that." Victor stopped suddenly on the path, hands on his hips, furious. "I don't want to hear it. You and Mother and Father are always nagging me to make something of myself, to do something useful." The petulance and anger in his voice shocked Charlotte, it wasn't like Victor at all. He could be an idiot, but he wasn't angry. Not the Victor she knew, under all the roles and masks.

Also, the accusation was desperately unfair, Charlotte didn't nag. She didn't even bring up what Victor wasn't doing unless he did, or she was talking about what she was doing. She knew it was a sore point with him. She wasn't going to make it worse. She hadn't meant to. Now she took a step back, trying to understand.

He went on, before she could get a word in. "Dame Morgen has a plan. She can see what I'm good for. If I'm very lucky, she'll do the divination for me while we're here. You don't understand what it means, how finding out where I fit in, finally, will make all the difference. It's the thing I've been missing, the thing no one else has bothered to give me."

The thing of it was, it was a reasonable argument for him to make. He'd been forced into all sorts of expectations by his family. His parents weren't, well, as good at parenting as Mama and Papa were. Most people weren't, from what Charlotte had gathered in her school years. Victor kept trying to do what he was supposed to, and he kept failing. And at the same time, they kept forbidding him from the things he could do very well, and more than that, enjoy doing. No theatre, no passionate romance with a man, certainly no living a life of the mind and heart that didn't fit into respectable society.

He sounded so sure of himself right now, as if this held an answer he'd wanted at needed. How all the things that had been swirling around in him, pushed aside like stage curtains, were suddenly solved. And if that was what Morgen and Gareth and all were telling him, of course he'd chase after it.

Only that was a problem. Charlotte might be young, and she might be fairly inexperienced in the world, but she was fairly sure things didn't work like that. She opened her mouth, closed it, and then finally settled on something she could say with a straight face. "I don't want you to get hurt. I hope you know that."

Victor's expression softened, as if she'd said the right thing he hadn't been sure she'd say. "You're a darling, Charlotte. I know you don't. But this isn't like anything else. Trust in it, let yourself flow with the experience. Have fun with Bedivere. You didn't ask him to join you last night, did you?"

She shook her head, rather uncertain how to respond now he'd flipped that particular point around. "He was chivalrous." That seemed a suitable word in the circumstances. "He didn't suggest coming in. And a new place, and I'd only just met him. I mean, I wouldn't have had a good time."

"I gather he's scrumptious in bed. I mean, not from Caradoc's direct experience, but, shall we say, indirect?" Which suggested that whatever else might be on the menu for the favoured few, it might involve something properly described as an orgy. Or at least a bit of voyeurism. "And that hair, mmm. He is handsome."

Bedivere was handsome the way Gareth was handsome, and that was a sort of handsomeness that didn't actually do much for Charlotte. Now, she just said, "I'll think about it. And that is useful info. Knowing a bit more about people. Bedivere's not with anyone here, then?"

"No." Victor's voice trailed off, looking over Charlotte's shoulder at something back on the terrace. "He'd been paired up with someone who's not here. I didn't meet her, she didn't choose to continue. You're going to, though, aren't you? Even if you're not ready for it this visit." Now his voice had gone cajoling, the way he got when he wanted to talk her into the passion of the moment, but there was also something entirely earnest there, that he wanted this for her.

Charlotte would not make that promise. Every bit of her training - familial and otherwise - shouted about it. Mildly, she said, "I'm looking forward to learning more, you know that. What are you looking at?"

She turned to see one of the women - she thought this

was Elaine - running down, having picked up the skirts of her dress to run. "Victor? There you are. Dame Morgen has time to see you this afternoon. Will you come? Right away?"

Immediately, Victor stepped back, then bent to kiss Charlotte's cheek. "Must go. You come back and find Bedivere and have a good time with him, right? See you later." He was off, not quite running but striding briskly, without waiting for any kind of response. Elaine held out her hand. "Come back, we've some sewing in the solarium. Do you embroider? It's such a pleasant hobby really, so portable."

Charlotte did not enjoy embroidery, but she could be competent with it, so long as it wasn't anything complicated. She certainly knew when she was being manoeuvred.

CHAPTER 11
THAT AFTERNOON

It wasn't the embroidery that was the problem. In fact, Charlotte was handed something to hem, once they discovered she could do perfectly good neat sewing. It was one of those endless sweeps of a cape, the kind that had yards of fabric at the hem. A sensible person would have used a sewing machine, they were designed for this particular task, but apparently that affected the magic. How it affected the magic when Charlotte was not particularly applying charmwork with her needle was a question no one showed signs of answering.

There was a tremendous amount of other chatter, though. There were six of them there, all on the younger side. The conversation ebbed and flowed, but there were always at least two talking. It was as if they had walked into an opera. No, an operetta, this was definitely more the light soubrette sort of piece. All the men were somewhere else, and that made Charlotte wonder if they were off doing manly chivalric things in the distance. Or what that would look like. There were stables somewhere, she'd noticed that, but not terribly near the house.

"Oh, Charlotte, aren't you curious, though?" That was Elaine, who was working on some quite skilled embroidery, shading her stitches with the kind of delicacy that Charlotte managed only by luck.

"About..." Charlotte let the word trail off. "About all of this, what the - I'm sorry, I don't know how to put it properly, I don't want to be rude."

"That's why it's so good we've this time this afternoon. Dame Morgen asked us especially to make you welcome." There was a quintet of bobbing heads - Elaine, Laudine, Ragnall, along with Chelinda and Helsin, who Charlotte had just been introduced to. There wasn't, thus far, a lot to help differentiate them besides details of clothing and hair colour. None of them had ventured much in the way of personal information.

Elaine was embroidering flowers, and Laudine was doing something complex in entirely anachronistic black-work designs on cuffs of a shirt. Ragnall was doing some embroidery on what was likely a girdle. Chelinda and Helsin were working on crowns, Chelinda's out of silk flowers and Helsin's out of oak and holly, presumably for the men. That was entirely out of season, too, really. Unless they were being very prepared for summer solstice.

"Oh!" Charlotte did her best to put a bit of enthusiasm into that, the right note of surprised pleasure. From the quick smiles she got back, it must have been about right. "I mean, it's—" She lowered her voice, leaning into the slightly conspiratorial volume. "It's, to be honest, it's a trifle overwhelming. There was so much last night, and I'm sure I wasn't catching most of it."

"Your first time here, no. But Dame Morgen sees such potential in you. It's quite rare to be invited here, before you've known us, oh, rather longer." Ragnall leaned in. "It was nine full months before I was invited out here, of meeting Dame Morgen and listening to some of her talks. Gareth has rooms in Trellech, a really lovely flat, very well appointed. We'd meet there." She added cheerfully, "Up to the north of Trivium Way." Not too far from the family townhouse, then, in terms of both distance and degree of luxury.

Charlotte ducked her chin, ostensibly focusing on her sewing while she figured out how to play that. She adjusted the pools of velvet in her lap to work on the next bit. "Oh, I'm sure that's mostly because of Victor." Demurring was the ladylike thing. She could do that without thinking about it, and have it sound like she meant it.

"Victor is scrumptious. And kind, too." As if the kindness were particularly notable among this set, and that was an interesting admission. Not that Victor wasn't tremendously kind, when he wasn't being selfishly tangled up in his current passion of the moment. They all had a story about it. He'd helped Ragnall untangle her embroidery thread that morning, and she went on about how patient he'd been, not like most men. He'd remembered Enid's birthday, a fortnight ago, and had sent round a book he thought she'd like from a chance comment. She'd loved it, of course. And he'd told stories to keep Chelinda and Helsin laughing, during a previous gathering, when they'd been feeling out of sorts. It was all Victor at his best and most observant, and she was glad they'd seen it.

On the other hand, the line of conversation did make Charlotte absolutely certain Morgen and Gareth were courting Victor deliberately, ardently, and not for his kindness. Kindness was clearly not a common gift here, the way the women talked about him.

It must surely be because of his family. Not just the fact

they had money - they did - but that Victor was reasonably likely to inherit the title in due course. That meant the land magic, all sorts of resources, and access to a particular circle of the world. It would do as a working premise for now, but she needed more details. She had no hope of talking to Victor about it without them.

Then Chelinda giggled. "Though he's not looking at us, is he? Even, um. Is that something you don't want to talk about?"

"Oh, he's very enthused about Caradoc, and I wish them both good fortune." Charlotte shook her head. "I love Victor, but not romantically. A good friend, someone I'm glad enough to spend my life with, we're a good fit in other ways."

"And Bedivere? He'll come sweep you away sometime later, mind. He was going on at me earlier about how lovely you are. And you are, your hair is gorgeous." Charlotte felt her hair was well-managed most of the time, because she knew which potions and oils and such made it so, and it wasn't a particular virtue of hers. Women of her station were expected to be well-dressed and all the other bits that went with it, and she kept up the necessary standard. But it didn't say much about her as a person beyond that diligence and reliable access to all the dressing table necessities. Or having brilliant staff who knew how to manage things even better. Wallis, Mama's lady's maid, had a lovely family recipe for hair oil that did wonders, in addition to her skills with putting hair up elegantly.

"Bedivere was very charming last night." True enough. Then she dropped the pitch of her voice. "Chivalrous when he saw me to my door, too, but - I got the impression that..." She let her voice trail off.

"Oh, he won't ask to come in. Not until Dame Morgen

suggests it would be good for both of you. And she won't do that just yet, not until you've had a proper divination from her." Laudine took over explaining, the others looking to her for how to handle this a bit.

"A divination?" Charlotte asked it entirely open. There was no reason to hide her curiosity here.

Laudine's head bobbed up and down. "Dame Morgen has a gift." The way Laudine said it was properly 'Gift', with the capital rubricated and gilded to boot.

"What, I mean?" Charlotte let her uncertainty continue to show. "I've heard all sorts of rumours about that sort of divination. How it can be, well. Scary. Someone looking at you, your life, so close."

"Oh, she does!" Chelinda spoke up, delighted, her voice pitched to where it made one of the glass decorations shiver and chime for an instant. "But you needn't be scared, darling. It will be opening a door to the life you've been meant for, the one you were born for. All of us, each and every one of us, we're part of a tremendous lineage."

It was a bit like the more obsessed of the women in Albion's Inheritance and the other social and philanthropic groups of the Great Families, only there, of course, they already knew and proudly proclaimed their heritage. Discovering it would have missed the entire point. Charlotte wasn't precisely surprised by this turn in the conversation, but it had only been gestured at so far. "Lineage?" Again, she blessed Mama for teaching her how to do the earnest inquiry so smoothly.

"It's not for us to say too much yet." Laudine leaned forward, hushing the others with a gesture. "But we're sure you have something special to offer, particularly special. Dame Morgen has seen it." Seen it, and - Charlotte was sure - said it, in part to keep these women on their toes and a hair jealous. None of them were showing it overmuch right now, but it was the kind of thing that would cause dissension if not managed perfectly. Charlotte had learned that lesson extremely well at school. It wasn't excelling that was the problem, per se. It was how one person excelling made everyone else around them feel.

Now she ducked her chin. "I wouldn't dream of prying. So the divination, and then things unfold from there? Like last night's ritual?"

"Just so." Laudine beamed at her. "You have a gift. I can see it too, the way you know how to understand things. Intuitively."

It was not intuitive; it was a great deal of observation and training over time. It was just that people didn't talk about those skills much. Most people thought someone had them or they didn't. Mama thought most people could develop them, and certainly Charlotte and Gabe could. And Mama had been right. Though to be fair to everyone, it had come out very differently in Charlotte than it had in her brother. Now, though, it meant Charlotte could reasonably venture a comment. "That's so kind. It's—" Then it hit her, what might work here. "I'm sure you all had different experiences of the world, but I've often felt like I didn't quite fit in. I like Victor because I don't need to, I mean, we're comfortable with each other...." She let her voice trail off again. It was a start at a conversation, and it fit with what Victor had said - nearly shouted - earlier.

As she'd hoped, there was a chorus of agreement, how each and every single one of them - and the other women in the group, always except for Morgen, of course - had felt the same. "It's just so wonderful to have somewhere I feel like I belong." Elaine picked up the commentary. "Where I don't have to explain myself, where everyone's so chivalrous and encouraging. I mean, just look at this. And the men, too. That's a thing I like about the chivalry. They have a particular way they're expected to treat us, and we're expected to treat them, and it's all laid out properly."

Charlotte had to admit that had some advantages, having had more than a couple of young men trying odd ways to get her attention. Part of why Victor was comfortable was that he didn't go in for dangerous stunts to impress anyone, even the men he was interested in. Charlotte contemplated, wondering how to ask about the other part. After a moment, she figured it was a likely enough question. "Did, um. I don't want to hurt anyone accidentally. Upset them. But is there anything I should know about anyone's War service?"

The question apparently took all of them aback. There was an utter silence. After perhaps twenty seconds, Ragnall cleared her throat. "Oh, no, not here."

It made Charlotte desperately want to get a list of names - people's actual names - to Gabe to find out about their War service. Or lack of it, and why, which was sounding more and more likely. She did at least have something to say. "It's just, I've got a sort of older cousin, adopted into the family. He had an awful head injury in the War. He's generally very cheerful still, but there are some things he can't abide. Certain noises, all that. I hate to upset him, especially when it's something I could have avoided."

"There, you are so kind and thoughtful. Even to people you don't know yet." Chelinda lept on that. It made Charlotte wonder again what Victor had done that was so out of the ordinary. Though yes, Victor was kind and attentive, especially with people he was getting to know. "Nothing like that, not that any of us know of. The men, they have different mysteries, different magics that they explore with

Dame Morgen, of course. But connecting to their lineages, their inspiring lives, that's what Dame Morgen calls it, is a great help."

It would be, yes, in men who'd lacked courage in the still quite immediate and recent moment. Not Victor. Victor hadn't had a chance to go fight. He'd just grown into adulthood watching the years ahead of them go off to War. Which was a different kind of burden and wound, and Charlotte certainly didn't know what to call it. Gabe had something of the same kind of thing, if an entirely other flavour. Then she shook her head slightly. If she got off on that line of thought, she'd be no good for this conversation. "Can you tell me how to be ready for the divination? As prepared as I can be for it?"

That got the other four women chattering away. "Dame Morgen will ask that you fast beforehand. It's more potent when you do. It's such a demanding thing on Dame Morgen's soul and spirit. We must do everything we can to ease things for her, so she can continue her work. It's tremendously draining, you can see it in her eyes, afterwards." Chelinda was very insistent. "The room will be dark. There's incense, that sort of thing."

"I'd noticed how wonderful the house smells," Charlotte offered. "And it's not just cut flowers, of course. There was the incense last night."

"There's nothing at all like it. When we're not here, Dame Morgen makes sure we have oils and incense with us for our meditations and readings. Those depend on your divination, some of them, but they, mmm. They remind me just what it's like to be here, even when I'm up in my room at home." Laudine shook her head, a strand of loose curls coming free.

"Do you live at home, then?" Charlotte asked, before

adding, in the sort of consoling tone that went over well in this kind of thing. "I do. Mama and Papa think it's silly for me to have a flat on my own, or with friends. And besides, most of my school friends are married, or nearly." She did not all disagree that it was silly for her to have a whole different flat. She could stay in the Trellech townhouse easily when she wanted that, and she absolutely didn't want to run her own housekeeping just to make a point of it. When she married Victor, she'd be helping there, and that was quite soon enough for that kind of work.

The question got a little flurry of commentary. Three of them lived at home. Elaine lived in a flat in Trellech with one of the older women in the group, and apparently didn't have much in the way of surviving family. The others didn't seem very close to theirs. It was the sort of comments Charlotte heard at social gatherings. The younger women had their own interests, the older generation had theirs, and every so often two well-dressed ships passed in the foyer on the way in and out of the building. As it were. That was not how life was at home for Charlotte, where people might be coming and going at various times - well, Gabe and Papa, mostly. But there were also regular times they were all home. Or had been.

Gabe would come for meals. He had to. Sometimes. With Rathna, if he wanted, that was fine. Rathna had all sorts of fascinating stories to share that they hadn't heard yet. And Charlotte just honestly liked her company. Rathna had a new way of looking at things, really seeing what mattered about them. Charlotte missed the next sentence or two, before someone asked her something that was clearly a question. "Oh, pardon. Got lost in my own thoughts."

The question was repeated, something about Charlotte's general interests. She could talk about those, the public ones, readily enough. Nothing that could be used against her, or even particularly gossiped about. She'd learned that lesson very well her second year at school. She always kept a mental list of books that were fine to talk about, the most recent public concert or lecture she'd attended that she was willing to discuss, and so on.

She still didn't know much about these people, they didn't get her more private thoughts. Not now, and the way things were going, not ever.

CHAPTER 12
THAT EVENING

The day had bled into evening. Or perhaps oozed. There was an entirely curious sort of timelessness about the place, as far as Charlotte could tell. Victor had been absent all afternoon and into the evening. Once it had got dark, everyone went and changed, then there was the feast. Since that was in a room with only the two windows on one wall, it was hard to tell the progression of time.

When she saw Victor again, Charlotte was unsure what to make of him. The lighting was indirect, mostly from the fireplace and lanterns hung around the walls, but she thought he looked a trifle pale. Certainly, he wasn't energetic, leaning against Caradoc more than the night before, neither teasing nor gesturing much. It was worrisome, but no one gave her any chance to so much as speak to him, and Bedivere kept talking to her. At her, rather, it wasn't like he listened to her responses.

This feast had been less about the pomp and more about the hypnotic experience. Everyone had eaten more lightly this time. The menu actually made Charlotte think of one of her school assignments for Ritual class, about preparation for demanding rituals, and the historical Lenten fasts. This wasn't quite that - if she remembered right, they'd generally avoided dairy. But the first night had a roast, as well as copious spiced wine. Tonight's had fish, roasted vegetables, a fair bit of dill, and dates for pudding. And bread, with just a little butter.

She'd got more used to thinking about food because of all the wedding planning. Rathna's apprentice mistress was Jewish and kept kosher. Rathna more or less did the same but also avoided beef, given her own family traditions. It meant the wedding feast was poultry and fish, and of course no shellfish. Cook was actually rising to the challenge gloriously, Mama had said, but it took some planning, especially around the combinations of foods.

Anyway, the whole thing made Charlotte notice. More than just noticing, it made her remember that one of the arguments Professor Ottson had made about the whole thing. He'd had a twenty-minute digression as part of a discussion of ritual preparation. He'd gone on about how lighter foods made it easier for you to enter certain mindsets for ritual. Be less attached to the physical was how he'd put it. He had rather archaic turns of phrase, as if mentioning the body to students was just not the done thing. By the time she'd pinned that down properly in her memory, the meal was finishing and the tables were cleared.

Morgen had dimmed the lights, bringing them together by sheer force of will. Charlotte didn't entirely remember everything Morgen had said. There had been music playing, with a low drum beat that thrummed with her heartbeat. It wasn't just the sound, there was a particular smell in the air, something with resin and some warm spices. She couldn't have named it. It hadn't made her head hurt, exactly, but it had made it hard to think and easy to dream. She'd heard Morgen's voice, drifting in and out, telling a story. It was something like it must have been to hear Homer's epics told by a hearth fire or a bonfire, or the Norse sagas, or the Welsh tales. There was nothing in the room but the words and the flicker of the light and the images in her head.

The stories, or at least the images from them, hadn't had much of a plot. Charlotte had flashes of standing somewhere in a tower. Not Veritas, then. Veritas didn't have much in the way of towers. Certainly, it wasn't Charlotte's own rooms. They were tucked on one side of the family wing, on the first floor, with the nursery above. And while the nursery had a few lovely arched windows, it had neither towers nor the view she'd had from the tower. That had been something Morgen had suggested, Charlotte was fairly sure, because it didn't look like Kent, it looked like Wales. Northern Wales, she thought, but Gabe would have known better. He'd spent more time there.

She supposed that fit with the general Arthuriana, at least if they were looking to Merlin and Dinas Emrys as much as you were to Arthur. There had been a fad for it when she was in her first years at school, but Charlotte had always been more interested in some of the Roman lore. Or some of the Kentish lore, too, for that matter. She knew where she came from, and where her line of ancestors had touched, and where they probably hadn't.

Eventually, the whole thing ran down. It was around midnight when Bedivere deposited her on the handful of steps leading up to her room with a kiss. This one was on her other cheek, making her wonder if he would work his way around her anatomy over time. Would it be forehead next, or lips, or hand?

She'd smiled at him, thanking him prettily for his escort. She knew her part in the dance, modified for the local manners. He'd waited until she'd disappeared into her room and closed the door, then she heard his steps go back down the steps and down the hall.

Her room smelled different. It only took her a breath or two to realise it. Not only different, but something in it helped her shake off the muzziness of the great hall and the supper, all the out-of-focus moments of the last few hours. Uncle Gil would have described it as cleaning his glasses properly. It wasn't mint. She would have known mint instantly, but it had something of that sharp cutting herbal edge to it.

Charlotte shook her head, wanting to clear it out. After a moment's consideration, she went off to have a bath, wanting to wash off the evening, and see if it made her brain work any better. It certainly felt good to get into the hot water, to soap herself up thoroughly and get the smell of the incense out of her hair. By the time she'd soaked and washed and rinsed, it had been a good half hour. She let her hair dry a little in the air, then dried the rest with a towel and a charm. Then she could comb it out and braid it in a single plait down her back.

She ought to get dressed. On the other hand, if the others felt like she had, maybe it would be a good time to go explore the house more than she'd been able to. They'd only let her see a handful of rooms, the main rooms on the ground floor. She knew there were other bedrooms all round her.

And more to the point, she knew the charms about whether anyone was moving her way. Gabe had taught her, of course, though they'd only ever used it to sneak down and get a biscuit or two from the kitchen. Not that Cook and Mama and Papa didn't know when they had, but it was permitted if they didn't cause any bother. Startling someone in the middle of the night and making them jump had been firmly categorised as 'bother' after the first time they'd slipped up. Hence the charms.

She found her slippers, and the sort of evening clothing that could be a nightgown or could be 'I was checking to see if there was a snack in the kitchens'. Even if that would be stretching an excuse rather a lot. It wasn't too chilly out, just a little brisk. Her hair was fully dry now. It wouldn't drip on anything, or even catch. She hadn't used strong-smelling soap in the bath. She didn't actually know the invisibility charms. Gabe did, but wouldn't teach them to her, and she knew better than to rely on something that didn't work. But she could muffle the sounds she made, her breath and her steps, and she did that.

The halls had dim charmlights every ten feet or so. She eased her way along, staying close to the wall. Floorboards - as both Uncle Gil and Gabe had taught her, though for slightly different reasons - were more likely to creak in the centre, the places they had the most flex and movement. She also knew perfectly well how to navigate in a space she didn't know. Pick a side and work the way around, tracing that path with one hand. She picked her right, since she was starting there. A little jog-leg hallway was first, the door propped open. What looked like two bedrooms, each with one person in them, not moving much. The door at the end was probably a linen closet, with its narrow doors and what looked like drawers in the dim light.

From there, two small steps led left into another hall-way. Charlotte went carefully now. She was out of the spaces where she had an excuse to be. She could tell there were people nearby. Two in the bedroom at the end of the hall, and she could hear faint noises that suggested they were having a good time together. The left-hand door was another bedroom, with someone still in the middle of it. Charlotte circled around, intending to go up to the next floor.

The stairs nearer her room led up not to the second floor, as she'd expected, but to a mezzanine floor. She desperately wanted a look at the plans of the house, because sticking a mezzanine floor there made no sense at all. Slowly, she edged up, then down the hallway that turned sharply left at the top of the stairs.

She realised with a start that the noises she'd heard before had actually come from here. Someone hadn't cared much about the sound charms at all. Or perhaps they liked knowing people were overhearing them. Charlotte had gathered some people had a taste for that. It was a second later that she knew who it was. One of those was Victor. She'd have known his voice anywhere. Even if he wasn't actually so much with coherent language at the moment, mostly moaning with a touch of begging. The other voice was a bit quieter. She couldn't quite make out the words, but the baritone suggested it was Caradoc. Or at least, it plausibly was Caradoc. Pellinore was more of a tenor.

Something in it made her uncomfortable. Oh, Victor was quite willing, audibly and emphatically willing. But the other man's voice had a measured quality that suggested it was a quest rather than some mutual pleasure. As if he were keeping his head while driving Victor out of all sense and reason. That worried her, honestly, for all she knew telling Victor about it was impossible. She couldn't admit to overhearing this, and it's not like Victor could be swayed from his pleasures when he wanted them. But Victor deserved his pleasures with honesty, not calculation.

Charlotte backtracked just in time. She heard footsteps and the charm suggested someone moving through the hall just as she turned back into her room. She eased the door closed, glad that it was set into the wall. Someone just going past wouldn't see it closing. Of course, she'd left the light off. There was nothing to show under the door.

She sat on the bed for a good twenty minutes then, trying to decide whether to go out and try again. That, though, got her thinking more about the house. She'd seen a sort of terrace when they were out in the garden earlier, and she'd thought it might be right above her own room. Maybe there'd be a way to get a sense of what was above her. She wasn't in Gabe's league as far as climbing, but she was fairly good at an apple tree. When she peered out the window, there was rough stonework, there was a trellis, there were little ridges here and there from story to story. As long as people weren't actually on the terrace, she should do all right.

It needed different clothing, though. She'd packed breeches on the off-chance of a chance to go riding, and those would do very well. Her slippers, with a bit of broad ribbon to bind them into her feet, under the arches and around the ankles for a better grip. She tucked her braid down the back of her shirt, and then perched on the window.

Even going slowly, it was a challenge. Or perhaps because she was going slowly. Gabe had a theory, and it wasn't as if she was going to prove him wrong, that good climbing was all about momentum. Stopping was the worst. Charlotte, though, needed the pauses to think about where she was going next. First she got herself turned to face the wall, foot on a ledge, her right foot on the trellis, balanced by a hand. Then she could climb up, step by step, testing her weight each time. She had to shift three times, when the wood sagged as soon as she tried to trust it.

Ten feet, and she was up to the next floor. As she'd remembered, there was a narrow open ledge, with glassed in windows more like a greenhouse than anything. That room was dark, and as soon as she got over the balustrade, she ducked down, moving on hands and knees toward the terrace itself, moving her weight slowly.

There were voices there, talking. Morgen and Gareth, she could tell immediately by their voices. Both had shed the mystic softness they'd been using with the others around. Morgen sounded more relaxed, though, while Gareth's voice had a sharpness that didn't surprise Charlotte at all.

"What do we do tomorrow?"

"We see what the moment suggests. Lean into the dream of it, of course. I was thinking of a picnic in a bower. I told the girls to get up early and make it ready. It'll take them hours and keep them out of trouble. Bedivere's got his instructions, and so does Caradoc."

"And they're both quite capable of being distracting." Gareth snorted. "You're sure that's sufficient?"

"For tomorrow? Yes. And we'll see where we go from there. I need more information." Charlotte didn't have enough to make sense of Morgen's tone, she wished she could see the expressions that went with it.

"Victor seems distracted enough. Delighted in it, it's like leading a lamb." Gareth sounded perhaps a bit tentative.

"The pet." Morgen snorted. "Glad to know that our enticements work on him. It was a bother talking Caradoc into it, though apparently he's enjoying himself enough now."

"And you did offer quite a few incentives, darling." Gareth's voice had acquired a purr. "And well, it's a good thing we don't need to pair him up with a woman, for what we have in mind. A few solitary bachelor knights are a fine thing, willing to take up the quest in due course without ties at home."

"Just so." There was some small movement inside, Charlotte couldn't make sense of what.

Gareth's voice picked up. "And Charlotte? Did you have new thoughts on her?"

"Does she worry you, then? The girls said she was easy to talk to." Someone in the room moved, and then Charlotte could hear the clinking of glass, like a drink being poured.

"I do wish Victor hadn't insisted on inviting her. Oh, I understand why you said yes, dearest." Gareth was quick to reassure on that point, Charlotte noticed, as if he didn't want to annoy Morgen either. "But it would be so much easier if we were just focusing on one of them. And I haven't found quite the way in with her yet."

"She'll come round." Morgen sounded smugly sure of that. "Out from under the thumb of her family, we've seen that before. It always takes a little to try what we're offering. I mean, look at Laudine now, or Chelinda. Patience, darling. I'm sure we'll have her full attention within a few days." Then there was a sudden pause, the silence noticeable. "Go have a walk around downstairs, see that everything's all right, would you?"

There was a grunt and the creak of a chair. Charlotte could just see Gareth standing. He came nearer the terrace doors, and she leaned into the side of the wall, where she was best hidden. "It'll take me a bit. Want me to come back?"

"Come, give me a report, do. Half an hour or so, yes? And then you can go enjoy yourself." Morgen sounded languid. The sounds faded as he closed the doors. Charlotte didn't want to move, didn't want to risk causing a sound or catching the eye. She could stay out here for a bit. If Gareth would be back in half an hour, that would be fine.

She was not well enough up on her astronomy at the moment to tell time by the movements of the stars, but she could do the practical thing and did. Charlotte recited a bit of verse to herself, something she knew took ten minutes or so, then again and again. Not too long into the fourth pass, the lights shifted in the upstairs room again, and she waited until it had been quiet a good bit longer.

Finally, she eased her way back over the balustrade, down the trellis careful step by careful step, and back into her window, closing it behind her. She cleaned up everything, including charming the ribbons clean, before slipping into her nightgown and into bed. With any luck, they'd let her sleep in.

Sleep did not come quickly, though, because of course she was still thinking about what she'd heard. Some part of Charlotte was reassured that she was here because Victor had wanted it, had near enough insisted on it. He hadn't forgotten about her, even if he might currently be finding it a little awkward. More to the point, he'd been able to sway Morgen's decision, and that was intriguing all by itself.

Charlotte had been assuming the obvious - that was a basic investigational principle - that Morgen and Gareth had wanted Victor because he was a scion of a landed family. And, similarly, that they'd known that Charlotte was from the same sort of family, even if she weren't going to be the one to inherit the land magic. Gabe had that well in hand, though they both hoped it'd be ages and ages from now. But something nagged at her, as she rearranged her pillow for the fourth time, that while the answer often was the obvious solution, it wasn't always. She would have to think about it more, and see if there were any additional clues to be had as to their actual motivation.

CHAPTER 13
APRIL 18TH IN THE EARLY AFTERNOON

"Victor, don't you have a minute?"

Victor twisted away, back toward the central doors. "Caradoc was going to show me something."

"Five minutes? Please. Just out in the garden." Charlotte held up her hands, doing her best not to use the levers of influence she knew, the unfair ones. The thing about having known Victor so long and so well was that she knew what would move him. But that would also irritate him, especially in this mood, and that wouldn't be any good.

"All right." He said it grudgingly, but then he turned to Caradoc. "Give you five minutes to set up whatever you were thinking?"

The other man went off laughing, slapping Victor's shoulder a little too heartily as he went by. Victor then turned. "Five and counting."

They were out on the grass within thirty seconds, thankfully. Charlotte didn't hesitate. "Are you all right? There's something odd, last night." She didn't want to say what she'd heard of Victor, nor from Morgen and Gareth, and now she was standing here, she didn't know what else she could say. It wasn't that what she heard was terribly new, she knew they were being lured. She couldn't even say that Caradoc wasn't as interested as he seemed. Not after overhearing Victor in bed.

"Come on, Char. You were enjoying yourself, yesterday."

She'd been making a good show of it yesterday. She'd been deliberately avoiding being difficult. Charlotte had been going along with things. "I just..." She couldn't say any of that. Victor wasn't going to listen. That much was obvious. "Tell me what you liked last night? Besides ..." She gestured euphemistically at where Caradoc had gone.

Victor threw back his head and laughed. "They like me here. Caradoc, particularly, we had, mmm, the sort of time I've not had in ages last night. Even better than I thought it'd be. But everyone before that, too. They think I can do things, interesting things, powerful things. And the visions last night, all about charging off and..." He shrugged, flipping his hand in the little gesture he had. "Being a hero. No one's let me be a hero."

Victor was - despite the name - not much of a fighter. A bit better as a lover, she gathered, and actually not a bad poet when he settled down to it. But a fighter, no. And yet, here and now, his eyes were lit up. And, well, Mama had pointed out that not fighting, not having been old enough to go to war, would be a defining thing for Charlotte's generation. Whether they actually wanted to have gone or not.

"It. I. It." Blast, this was even worse than it had come out in her head, certainly a lot more stuttering and incoherent. "Can you be careful, please? Just. For me?"

Victor cupped her face in his hands, both cheeks, and she wanted to lean into that touch and warmth for a bit. All he did, though, was quickly kiss her on the forehead. "Let yourself enjoy it, Char. You deserve that. You absolutely should have men dropping at your feet and pining for your favour. You should have lovely frocks and perfumed oils, all the pleasures you want."

Then he was gone, taking strides with his long legs back across the terrace to the doors. "Caradoc, there you are. What did you have in mind?" It left Charlotte standing there, looking like some abandoned maiden out of legend. She wasn't a maiden, and she wasn't abandoned, but she was increasingly angry. Also frustrated, why wouldn't Victor listen to her? Why wasn't there anything plausible she could say to him?

She took a deep breath, then another. When she looked back at the door, Bedivere was coming out toward her, hand outstretched. "Come, do come. We have some amusements for you." She let herself be drawn along, out to a bower in the back garden. People came and went from the blankets and pillows that had been set out all afternoon, but Charlotte stayed there.

The conversation wandered back and forth, nothing serious or complicated. But while others came and went, she was encouraged to stay put. They were working on something. She should relax and enjoy the lovely weather. It was not in fact lovely. There was a chill to the air, though the bower had some quite decent charms against wind and cold on it. And there were plenty of thick rugs and blankets. Bedivere was there, offering her this treat or that, and she couldn't refuse, not when it was that direct.

Later in the afternoon, Gareth came out to join her. When he sent Bedivere off on some errand, something that would take a few minutes, Charlotte didn't think too much of it.

Then Gareth leaned forward. "Why are you here, Charlotte? You're holding back, we can see it." His voice had settled into a soothing murmur, the kind meant to lull to sleep. Or, she realised, like a mesmerist. Aunt Mason had taken her to see one, a few years ago, and pointed out how the various tricks worked, or at least the basic theory. The theory wasn't nearly enough to help her figure out what to do now, though.

"Victor." It was the truth, and it was also a sensible answer in the circumstance. It certainly didn't give anything new away.

Gareth tsked gently. "That's not all of it, is it?" His voice got softer. "You have dreams of your own, don't you? I've been watching you, you're as bright-eyed and curious as a raven." There was a bird of omen for you, and not all of them kind omens, either. Gareth leaned a little more on his hand. "We can't help you if you don't let us."

She didn't want to let them, honestly. All she had to work with were wisps and intuition and fragments of conversation with not enough context. Nothing that had made her walk away entirely - nothing that had made her willing to leave Victor here on his own. But somehow, last night, hearing him and Caradoc, she'd realised that losing him might no longer be the question. Winning him back, maybe, but even that seemed complicated.

If she left, he'd be on his own with these people who had specific plans for him. Plans that they weren't telling him about, absolutely not fully. If she walked away now, first, she'd hate herself. He was her friend, he'd been her friend for so long. They'd navigated the awkwardness of adolescence together, they'd studied together, they'd supported each other through projects and first failures and first successes, over and over. It hurt her, deep in her heart, to think about leaving him with people who didn't also want the best for him.

Honestly, Charlotte didn't know what to do. Part of her wanted to relax into whatever it was they had in mind for her. Which, to be honest, didn't seem that horrible. A fair bit of pleasure of various kinds, decent food, and a certain amount of mystical nonsense around it. She couldn't explain why she kept feeling there was something slightly sinister right under the surface. And Charlotte certainly couldn't explain it to Gareth, of all people, who was almost certainly neck deep in whatever the goal was.

"We've been watching you." Gareth reached over and poured a cup of tea, handing it to her. "Thinking about whose line of magic, whose lineage you match, as we rebuild Camelot. Victor's good-hearted, a hero's mettle, just waiting for a chance. But you're a little different." His voice turned into a purr. "Rather more interesting." The food had been saltier than she'd expected. Her mouth was dry, and she took a long drink from the cup before blinking at Gareth.

"Interesting?" Now she sounded utterly daffy.

"Oh, yes. Morgen is still deciding the best time to do your divination, but we expect it to be most illuminating." He was definitely purring now. "Perhaps you might rest out here and reflect on what your dreams might bring."

Charlotte nodded. She was tired, it was true. For one thing, she'd been up half the night, and for the other, the bower did rather incline one to sleeping, somehow. Gareth pushed himself upright. "Someone will come fetch you to change for supper. We've something spectacular planned tonight. There will be a costume in your bedroom when you get back." He bent, taking her hand to kiss the back one more time, then straightened up with a flourish of his hand.

Charlotte managed a little wriggle of her fingers before he strode back to the house.

She watched him go, then settled down on the pillows strewn around the bower, considering her options. She hadn't expected to be left alone, certainly not for very long, but she would enjoy the moment while she got it. Since she'd arrived, someone had been in and out, talking to her, expecting her to talk to them, all the time from when everyone woke until when she was deposited at her bedroom door. She'd take the time now, and see if she could sort out what to do next.

Or that was what she'd planned. Somewhere in the midst of her thinking, her eyes closed.

When she woke, she was not in anything near as comfortable as the bower. She was lying on something that felt like a wool cloak. It seemed like a sturdy one, a bit too much time in a cedar closet, and a far rougher weave than she'd have expected. It was that which brought her more awake, and she found herself in the centre of a hedge maze. Boxwood, her mind insisted, she'd been inside enough while at garden parties on other estates.

It was probably the centre. Two paths led out on either side, facing each other. The hedges were tall. She was fairly sure a bit more than her actual height, so someone outside wouldn't see her moving. And more to the point, she couldn't see over to find her way through. There were classic plans for hedge mazes, Charlotte knew that. But she also knew that there were magical mazes, where the very pattern itself could be altered by a series of gates and panels that changed the pathways.

Uncle Gil had done a monograph on them a few years ago. She'd helped him do the proofreading, so she'd heard the whole thing several times over. Or rather, it was about how to align such a maze with the period of the house in an aesthetically and functionally pleasing manner, both. Charlotte let her head fall back, listening before she did anything else. She had no idea how she'd got here, or why. It could be what Gareth had had in mind. Though it didn't seem to involve a costume. He had said something about a costume. It could be - she couldn't even sort through the options.

Listening didn't tell her very much. She could hear a few birds, none terribly close. Nothing roosting in the hedges nearby, anyway, or if they were, they weren't making any sound. There was an occasional small rustle here or there, that might be the wind or someone watching or some small mammal. Still lying there, she called her magic, using the same charm she'd used the night before to figure out if there were people nearby. It didn't work quite the same outside, but no, no one was terribly nearby. Not within the range of the charm, several hundred feet, at least.

That was curious. If Gareth had put her here, or someone from the house, she'd have assumed there'd be someone watching her. They'd want to see what she did, if she screamed or ran or explored. It would definitely be 'explore'. She knew better than to waste her energy with the first two. It wasn't like they'd help. First rule, Papa had taught her. Don't make the situation worse, whatever else you do. Take your time if it's safe and look at your options.

The ground underneath her was dry, at least, so she worked on slowly pushing herself upright. The ground was grass, that was fine, and at first she didn't see anything to tell the two pathways apart. Just two gaps in the hedge. She didn't even have a compass with her, and she didn't remember the charm for that.

Charlotte took stock, then. She was not starving, so chances were good it was the same afternoon. A bit later in the day, she thought. Sunset was around seven. If it were late afternoon, that way was west, that way was east. She had maybe two hours of light left. It was hard to tell in April. And while she was not terribly far north of Veritas, in the grand scheme of the planet, she wasn't used to adjusting for that. The last few days she'd been inside at this time of day.

She stood slowly, listening to figure out if anything moved or changed. When nothing did, she picked up the cloak and brushed it out. Just the cloak, nothing but what she'd been wearing. Blouse, skirt, a knit jumper, not at all fashionable, but she'd chosen it over one of her frocks to be a little contrary and firmly modern. Now, of course, it wasn't much help. Nor were her shoes, which were fine for an average walk, but not the ones she'd have chosen to go miles into Wells.

Charlotte could do that. It was four miles to the portal, probably, but that was an hour and a half once she got her bearings related to the estate. She didn't much want to go cross country. For one thing, while she thought they were on the east side of the rather large gorge, she wasn't certain, and she didn't want to fall down any outcroppings. For another, she had a countrywoman's strong respect for fields that might have bulls or goats in them. Either.

Circling through the central space, she looked to see if she could see any other mark. One side, on close inspection, looked like it had a few threads of bright red thread, more like Gareth's than Morgen's. It might just have caught from a scarf or cloak, she couldn't tell.

She'd go the other way. Charlotte set off that way, after scuffing a line in the dirt near the path she took, just one line across the path, another crossing it at an angle. Nothing terribly noticeable. She set off, remembering what Uncle Gil had told her about always tracing one direction. She chose left, this time, and she kept following it, turn by turn, for perhaps five minutes before it deposited her in the central space again. There was her line in the dirt, there was the red thread on the other entrance.

She hadn't seen too many turnoffs, either. The maze wasn't entirely unicursal, there had been one or two. But she didn't much want to explore the possible paths one by one. She didn't have food and April was no time to be sleeping out in the open, even with a decent cloak. Charlotte wanted to get out of the maze, and then she could consider her options. She could go back to the house, assuming she wasn't too far. There might be a barn or a farmhouse that would put her up for the night.

First, get out of the maze. She tried again, one more attempt at the east path, this time following her right hand, and taking the right-hand path when she had a choice. Five minutes later, she was back in the same spot. Annoyingly the same.

She could repeat it for the other paths, or she could, perhaps, try something different. She cast the charm one more time, and there was still no sign of anyone near, no one who'd come to find her. She couldn't hear anyone shouting for her, and it was getting on close enough to sunset that someone should have missed her by now. Unless, well. Unless Gareth or someone else had put her here.

Gabe would probably have wanted to work out the endless permutations. Gabe also usually had a much better personal kit with him than she had and knew how to use more of it. She was fairly sure he had something that would do for an overnight out in the open in anything bar an absolute downpour or blizzard. She knew he always carried something for food and drink.

Of the options, trying the other path was the sensible choice. She set off to the western path, feeling entirely mystical about it and also cranky about that. Going into the west was courting mystery and arguably also death. Charlotte was having none of that. She was in search of shelter and food and sensible people.

This path curved differently, which was odd in a maze. The other one had swept around. This one took tight turns, with no branching paths. She followed it and followed it, turning around and around, and she almost lost track of the sun's position a couple of times. Finally, though, there was a gap in the hedge, another opening, and she could see something beyond that didn't seem to be more of the maze.

Stepping out of the gap, she found herself in a small field. There was a wooden fence, running right up to the maze, with a gate. Beyond the gate was a path, worn down to dirt, and a small cottage, a farmer's cottage. She couldn't see a barn, or livestock, but she could see a little smoke coming out of the chimney. It suggested someone was there, at least. If nothing else, there'd be a bit of a windbreak.

They might not be safe, whoever they were. Her heart was racing as she realised that. It had been one thing to have a plan in the maze. Now she was realising it was an entirely different thing to go through with it. Whoever this was, it was entirely possible they weren't of Albion; they weren't magical, which would be an entirely different problem. But she could pass herself off as having been on a ramble, separated from friends, could she get a lift to the road? Figuring out what to say helped. On the other hand, Charlotte did want to figure out the next step.

And that involved this cottage. She took a deep breath, automatically brushing off her skirt, tidying her hair, then rebraiding it. She folded the cloak over her arm, out of the way, so she could cast a charm or two if she needed to, without it fouling her movement. One more breath, and she walked on, doing her best to feel confident.

The door of the cottage was slightly open. She knocked with no answer. After a minute, she pushed it open gently. There didn't seem to be anyone inside. She glanced around to find a small kitchen to the left, a room beyond, and a rather barren sitting room with stairs up in front of her. "Good afternoon? Hello?"

CHAPTER 14

APRIL 18TH AT THE COTTAGE, EARLY EVENING

Lewis wasn't looking at where he was going. He didn't need to. He'd never needed to, anyway. What he needed was a book from the dining room, while one of the perfumes he was working on sat for an hour. Then he could get a better sense of the balance and figure out how to adjust it from there.

Not more pepper. That would certainly spoil the effect of the blend. And it was too martial for what he wanted, on the magical side, too. Perhaps a drop or two of - no. He shook his head when he heard something move, and his head came up sharply.

And then he smelled it. The sillage, the scent floating around her, that was the bottle he'd made up for Gareth, along with the incense the house went through in pots, and a bit of fresh air and grass. It was a cacophony that didn't work at all as a scent.

There was a woman standing there. Not anyone he'd ever met before, or seen, and he'd at least seen most of Morgen's people at a distance now. He stopped dead, staring at her. She was standing in his sitting room, looking like she belonged there. And also like she didn't remotely belong there. It was exceedingly annoying of her already.

"Hello?" The woman leaned forward slightly, but she didn't move, just spread her hands out a little more. "I beg pardon, the door was open."

"Go away." There wasn't supposed to be anyone else here. Not for two reasons, both of them important. First, Lewis didn't want to be disturbed. He put up with Gareth, because Morgen insisted. And he supposed that Morgen needed to check in regularly, and someone had to bring food. That was fine. "You're not wanted here." Lewis put his hands up, the sort of childish gesture to avert the unwanted that Mother would have scolded him about. She wasn't here, it didn't matter.

"I can't go back the way I came. Is there a way out to the road from here? Down past here?"

"Can't." Lewis shook his head. "Just the maze."

"That can't be right." The woman took a step or two back again, then she considered, and held out her hand, as if to shake. "Let's try this differently. Pardon, I'm so sorry to have just walked in. My name's Charlotte. Sorry to be a bother. Can you help me get out to the road, toward Wells?"

Lewis didn't take the hand, though he did frown at her. She was younger than he was. Probably. Though she was a lot more confident, or at least comfortable in what - if she was telling the truth - seemed an odd situation on her end, too.

"How'd you get here?" It came out abruptly, and Lewis didn't care. He knew how to have manners, he practised having manners regularly. Well, he had before coming here, anyway. Here he hadn't exactly had many people to practise on.

The woman - Charlotte - held her hands up, and took another half-step back. "Through the maze and the gate."

"You can't have." Lewis knew it was impossible. His world was bounded by the fence. He'd been in the maze once, when Morgen had left the gate open, just out of curiosity, and it hadn't worked right. Even when he'd taken notes, it dropped him back in the centre again. "Were you up at the house? With her?"

Charlotte tilted her head, and now Lewis felt like some sort of insect being examined by a magnifying glass. He did not like the feeling one bit. "Do you know them up at the house?"

She wasn't actually answering anything. Lewis grunted and then turned away. She wasn't looking like she was too much of a threat, and she didn't know about the lab, or at least he didn't think so. If someone had wanted the things in the lab, they'd have gone right there. Probably. Then he turned back, because it wasn't like he knew what else to do. He just repeated. "Go away."

"You've just told me I can't. I tried going out through the maze the other way, and I couldn't. And you say I can't get out this way. What happens if I try?" She didn't sound like Morgen or Gareth. That was the odd thing about it. Oh, this woman was certainly posh, the sort who - if she'd gone to Schola, maybe she hadn't - wouldn't have given him the time of day. He wouldn't have cared unless she was between Lewis and the books he wanted. Or the lab door. Now, Lewis didn't know what to do.

Before he could figure it out - before he had to figure it out, to be honest - she went on. "Pardon, but - look, we seem to be at an impasse. I'd love to get out of your hair, that's apparently impossible." Then there was a sound of her stomach rumbling - decidedly not posh, and she grimaced. "Have you had supper? I suppose it's roughly supper time?"

It was getting on for dark. Lewis shrugged. "No." He hadn't.

"Tea?"

"Course not. I was working all afternoon." Some things should be self-evident. Or maybe she didn't know what she was seeing. He'd hung the protective smock up, of course. There was no point in hauling it around, but he was in shirtsleeves and trousers, the sleeves held in place by garters. Lewis had been busy.

"Lunch?" She was damnably persistent.

He had to think about that one. "No."

"Breakfast?" Charlotte said it with a note of something he couldn't make sense of.

He paused, longer this time. "I must have. I'd have noticed if I hadn't. By now."

"All right." Charlotte crossed her arms. "Can I put some food together? For me, and for you. We can't possibly have a sensible conversation until we've both eaten."

Lewis didn't know about that either. On the other hand, he was hungry, now he'd noticed. He was perfectly competent at cooking. It was easier than alchemy, obviously. Or at least the kind of cooking he did was. And it certainly shared a number of the same basic skills. If she wanted to make food happen, well, he wouldn't have to do it. "There are things in the pantry, there. Keep-cold box, tins, all that." He waved a hand in the direction of the pantry door. "They bring me food, in a hamper." Then, a little uncertainly, he added, "I'm Lewis."

Charlotte nodded once. "Right. May I put this down somewhere?" She gestured with her arm, then waved a hand at the cloak.

Lewis nodded. "Um. There. There's a hook." Then he looked at the cloak as she hung it up. It didn't match much of anything else she was wearing, and that seemed out of place. She didn't look back at it, just pushed up the sleeves of her jumper. She took a minute in the pantry, then she came out with something. "Where'd you get that bowl?" Lewis didn't remember it being there.

"It was on the shelf? Should I not use it?" She seemed all innocence. If she were someone who could produce a bowl out of thin air, that seemed fairly harmless. Though perhaps she was right, and he'd left it in there. She'd put eggs in it, she had a little jar of the cream in her other hand. "Do you have anything like a spice? Or a bit of cheese? I saw the bread. I'll get that in a second."

"Bread?" Lewis blinked at her. "Why bread?"

"I'm not a bad cook, but I don't have the most expansive repertoire? I was going to do scrambled eggs with a bit of cheese. And toast. Filling, easy, you can see me make it." She said the last part like she expected him to be suspicious, and he had no idea what to do with that. Both the idea that she was thinking like that and the fact she wasn't hiding it didn't make sense.

"Um. Cheese." He went and got the cheese. He had more in the pantry, but he'd had the last bit of this out on the counter, under one of the little stasis domes, for snacking on. "There's this?"

She peered at it, beamed, and then nodded. "Cheddar, that will do nicely. You have more? I can use all of this?"

Lewis froze for a moment. She kept asking him things, and that wasn't how people asked him things, as a rule. When he didn't answer, she didn't push. She just waited. There was a long silence, the sort other people considered increasingly awkward, but she didn't look impatient.

Finally, he just nodded. It was cheese. Why was she asking permission about cheese, when - as she guessed - he had more?

Once he nodded, she turned away, going to busy herself with all the small motions of a kitchen. She was efficient about them, the sort of efficiency that might actually have got a word or two of praise from Master Aylett. Likely even from Evans, who'd been the senior apprentice responsible for Lewis during most of his apprenticeship. Evans had been extremely precise about things, which was a virtue in a number of ways, but to a degree that had irritated even Lewis.

At any rate, Charlotte was deft and she was appropriately careful. Within a couple of minutes, she had a pan on the stove, adding a little of her own magic to heat it, and then got the toast going first, in the pan. When that was done, she had the eggs ready to go, and a little bowl of diced up cheese to go with them. A couple of minutes after that, she had everything in bowls and little plates. Well, only the two of each. He only had two of each. He'd never been sure why two. Either one, because it was only him, or two to allow one to wash, or in case of breakage? It seemed unlike Morgen to think about accidents.

"Where do you eat, please?"

"There's a table. A sort of dining room? It's mostly books, but, um. I can clear some off." Lewis went ahead of her, as she tidied up the pan and set it to cool, stacking books so they had half the table to use. When he turned back, she had found forks, that would do for eggs, and then she was bringing the food out, glancing around.

"The books are rather homey, aren't they?" Charlotte settled down, with a shift of her body that suddenly seemed very elegant, out of place. As if she were used to how she sat down, what it looked like, instead of ordinary people who just sat. Morgen was like that too, and Gareth. The show of the thing mattered to them. Lewis didn't much like the thought, even if it was a true one.

They ate in mutual silence for a little before the kettle sang out and Charlotte jumped. "Oh, I put that on. Can't have supper without something to drink. The tin was right there."

"No, that's fine." There was plenty of tea. He often brewed it three times anyway, liking the changes in the taste of each round. Charlotte went back and poured the water into the teapot, then brought it to the table before going back for teacups.

"Only two of everything?" It seemed for a moment like she'd been reading his mind earlier, but that was ridiculous. It was far more logical that she could simply count.

"That's how it's been. It's just me, here. Except when they visit, to check in." Lewis gestured.

He didn't miss the way she flinched once. That didn't make sense. For the one thing, it looked for a moment like she was upset, though she smoothed any sign he could read of it away almost instantly. For another, why would anyone feel like that about Morgen? Morgen wasn't always the kindest person, but she wasn't scary. Demanding, yes, precise, yes, of course. But Lewis didn't find that scary. No one who lived up to high standards should. He'd learned that lesson thoroughly in his apprenticeship, but honestly, he'd figured that out by the time he was ten. The interesting people had standards and lived up to them. Boring people didn't.

There was a quite long silence as she finished up her meal, and then poured the tea into cups. His first. "Do you take milk or sugar or anything? I didn't see any out."

"No, thank you." He thought about offering it to her. There was some in the cupboard, but she presumably had figured out he might have some if she wanted it. And she didn't get up. Also, he still didn't know why she was here, or what she was doing, or why she wanted to find the road.

CHAPTER 15
THAT EVENING IN THE COTTAGE

Charlotte wanted to figure out how to handle this elegantly, like Mama would, or Papa, or Gabe. Or maybe Uncle Gil, who was on the whole more restrained than all of the others. None of them, apparently, had bothered to fully explain what it felt like when you were in an absurd situation and had to make sense of it and keep your head. At the moment, it felt an exceedingly obvious gap in her education.

The thing of it was, she didn't exactly feel unsafe. She didn't feel safe, either. But she was fairly sure Lewis was not actually a threat. Nor, more accurately, did he seem likely to be capable of being a threat. He hadn't shown any signs of being a duellist; she knew those well enough. He hadn't reached for magic.

Mind, he also hadn't used even the most rudimentary warding charms on this cottage or his pantry. On the other hand, if it really was just him here and no one else could get in and out, or only in very limited ways, the cottage didn't really need its own protections. Still, his instincts hadn't demanded them, and Gabe's would have. Even Victor used

134

that sort of warding on his room, though admittedly that was more to keep his mother from his diary.

Now, she finished her food, and set down her fork properly, before folding her hands in her lap and looking at him. "Do you, I suppose. Do you have questions?"

"No." Lewis said it immediately, as if that were his automatic answer to things. Interesting. Also, for all there were things Lewis did that half-reminded her of Gabe, that was the complete polar opposite of her brother. Gabe was made of questions, and he had been as long as Charlotte could remember. Probably before that, too, just no one knew what they were until he learned to talk.

"I have questions." Charlotte tried to gather her thoughts more usefully. "May I ask them? If you don't want to answer any, it's not like I can make you, of course."

Something in that made him react. It wasn't a flinch. That wasn't the proper term for it at all. Questions were apparently a problem. That was a useful point to be aware of, but it made a conversation exceedingly difficult. Finally, she started with, "So, just to clarify, now we're fed. I can't leave. Ever? Someone brings you food. How do they do that?"

"They come from the main house, and they can get through the maze and the gate. Either Morgen or Gareth can do that." That answer was prompt enough. Then Lewis drew back. "Do you know them?" There was a cautious neutrality there, as if he wasn't sure what he thought about that.

Charlotte considered her options. Lying was an option, it was always an option. She wasn't sworn to truth-telling. And while she was not the most suave of liars she'd met, she could wander around the truth with the best of them. Sometimes she needed to do that. Besides, she was fairly sure even on this brief acquaintance that she was better at lying than Lewis was at figuring out she was lying. On the other hand, telling the truth, at least a little of it, might actually be informative. And it would certainly be a sign of good will, and she was a little more certain Lewis would recognise that when it was right in front of him.

"I was staying up at the house. I felt sleepy, earlier, and then I woke up, and I was in the maze. I don't know how I got there. There was a cloak around me to keep me warm, but that was it." Charlotte gestured with one hand toward the cloak. "And then I tried one direction, and it brought me back to the centre, and eventually I tried the other, and it brought me to the gate."

"It shouldn't have." Lewis sounded stubborn. Then he glanced off toward the door, and said, "You know Morgen and Gareth, then."

He had made it a statement, not a question. "I wouldn't say 'know' in any meaningful sense of the word, but I've had meals with them. I've been staying at the house. Will they be coming here anytime soon?"

"Not expecting them until..." Lewis stopped, counting on his fingers. "Gareth is picking something up next week. A few days before May Day."

"You've forgotten which day it is, haven't you?" It came out of Charlotte's mouth before she could consider whether it was a good idea. Gabe was a horrible influence sometimes. On the other hand, he had a gift for making that kind of thing work for him, and maybe it'd do something else here.

Lewis blinked, then ducked his chin. "There's a calendar. You've got me all turned around. I should be..." He stopped, suddenly. "I've got to get back to the lab."

"Alchemical lab?" It was the obvious question, really,

given that one word to work with. "Rather remote for one, isn't it? Materials and equipment and all that?"

Lewis blinked at her, owlishly. "I like not being interrupted. And I set it up, properly. I don't suppose you know much about it."

It made her giggle, but she repressed the sound. "Not my speciality, but I'm perfectly competent up through Hester's Fourth." She used the standard reference, which put her at mid-range apprentice skills. She'd never wanted to go further than that, but there were several things in Hester's Third and Fourth that were useful for illustration, adaptations of paints and washes and such. Charlotte had discovered she preferred making her own. "My brother's better."

Lewis was frowning now. "You aren't." Then he cocked his head. "How would you handle it if you discovered your vervain had a little less potency than you expected?"

"First, I'd want to find out why. There's that whole approach with a touch of enchantment, if it's just that it wasn't dried as well as it ought. But if it's old, I prefer Thompson's Sixth. My brother argues at length - he's better in a lab, so long as he's paying attention, but he's actually not wrong about this part - that it gives you more control. It's no good to overshoot, it's just as unstable in the final mix. Splotchy." It was one of the ones she knew fairly well. It enhanced the smoothness of the work, whether that was paints or ink or dye or whatever else.

"Huh." Lewis leaned forward a little. "Brother, you said?" Then he added, after a moment. "I thought I knew most of the alchemists."

This was a question, whether she was up front about the family. Because if Lewis knew much about the families at all, he might guess some other things. On the other hand,

Morgen and Gareth hadn't noticed. Charlotte considered her options, then asked, "Did you go to Schola?"

He hesitated, then nodded just once. "Owl House. Finished school in 1916."

That put him two years ahead of Gabe, then, and well ahead of Charlotte herself. They'd not have overlapped. "Gabe was two years behind you, in Salmon. And I started the year you finished, in Fox." Like Mama and Papa, and also the house that often produced alchemists in particular.

"Oh, then you'd have heard a lot from Professor Norton. I'm rather envious, though of course, he's very much a proponent of one line of thought." Lewis added, almost shyly. "I apprenticed with Master Aylett. It was all war work, at first. Preparation work, when I wasn't good enough for the rest of it, yet. And then he helped me get set up with other things, after."

Charlotte had heard about the Ayletts. Gabe - and Aunt Mason and Aunt Witt - had talked, where Charlotte could hear, about how he was steady enough with the precautions for his apprentices. But that was at least half because he left the apprentices to the journeymen to train, and the journeymen were still terrified of the Ministry coming down on them hard. But Wallington Aylett had a reputation for innovation, and the kind that Aunt Witt said only happened if people took risks.

Lewis did not seem the sort to take risks, but at the same time, she wasn't sure how to weigh any of that. And people picked up bad habits from all sorts of places that they wouldn't admit were a problem. She nodded once. "I'm a little familiar with his work. And his wife's, too." Then she ventured one more question. "You're doing something other than medical potions now, though?"

"You were at the house. I make incense and oils and such for Morgen. For her projects. I went into perfumery, mostly. It's a very delicate art, and Morgen's made it possible for me to work with oils and ingredients I'd not be able to manage otherwise." He hesitated, saying it, like he wasn't used to explaining it, and she wondered how much of the truth she was getting. No way to tell, at least not without a lot more understanding of his usual patterns. That was the thing she'd learned in Fox House, far more than the alchemy background. And from Mama and Papa, how to read between the lines, see what moved someone, what could be used as a lever to persuade them, without them actually telling.

It did make her stop, though. "I noticed the incense. The way the house smells. A lot of it was rather lovely, actually. Unusual, but in the right way? A scent that's completely different from what you expect, that would throw you out of it."

He rather lit up at that. "A lot of people have really rather odd ideas about perfumes and incense, and all that? Morgen isn't like that."

This was not getting her any closer to an answer about where to go from here, but the actual topic was also interesting. "Oh? What sort of odd ideas?"

"Do you remember seeing the news last year about an American buying those tapestries? In rather bad shape, compared to some of ours, of course, but causing quite a stir? The ones about the unicorn hunt?" Charlotte did remember that, yes. It had been rather a source of gossip for a few weeks of social events. She nodded, encouragingly. Lewis went on, "Well, there was quite a fashion for people wanting perfumes made out of things in it. Only, of course, a lot of the plants don't actually go together, or people want all the plants in one scent, and it's awfully muddy. Not good at all."

Charlotte considered what she'd heard. "And some of them have good scents, if you can make them in perfume, but aren't some of the flowers very difficult that way? Um. Sweet pea isn't one of them, but you know what I mean, obviously."

Lewis bobbed his head. "Just like that. And people never understand the delicacy of it. And they certainly don't want to pay for the materia to make an oil that holds the scent. And then they fuss that it's not just a perfect replica of the tapestry or painting or whatever it is." He looked up. "I like a challenge, but not an unreasonable one."

Talking about the perfumes had completely changed his face and voice. He was leaning forward now, not stiff and nervous, but somehow fluid, like something that had gone from wax to liquid seamlessly. The way he smiled amused her, that was very like Gabe in full flourish of an interest. It made her think better of Lewis, honestly. Not that this helped exactly with her current problem.

"I don't want to get in the way of your work." Not that he'd explained what he was doing for Morgen, though she had some suspicions about that. Asking him right out probably wouldn't work, though. "I—" She looked up, then at the window. "It's dark already. Is there, um, somewhere I could sleep tonight? And see if I can get out of your hair tomorrow?"

He grunted once. "Just the one bedroom. There's a couch. I can sleep in the lab. I'll be up for a bit, but I'm not doing anything that needs airing out the rest of tonight."

It was not the most generous offer, but it was a sofa which looked wide enough not to be entirely awful. It was about as good as she was going to get. And while politeness might impel her to say he wouldn't wake her, he would. And that might go badly. "I appreciate it a great deal. Is there, um, facilities handy? Or anything I should or shouldn't do?"

He gestured at a door behind them. "Bathroom and all that there. You've seen the kitchen, if you need something. Don't go upstairs or touch my books." Then he must have caught something in her face. She realised, all of a sudden, that along with all the other things she didn't have, she didn't have anything to read. "You could borrow one I don't really need? I've something on folklore, not very relevant?"

He was an Owl, he'd appreciate not having a book. Charlotte nodded enthusiastically. "Thank you. Soothing, a book is. And I'm sure I could stand to learn something."

Lewis leaned over to rummage in a pile, pulling out a slender volume in green bookcloth. "I sleep in. If you're gone when I get up, that's fine. If not, well." He grimaced. "I don't know. But I do have work to do tonight."

"Of course. I'll get out of your way." She stood, shifting the book in front of her place. "And I'll wash up. Do you need the ..." She gestured at the facilities, and he disappeared into them. Charlotte cleared the dishes, and was washing them when he came out, making a beeline for the door of the cottage without saying anything to her. She watched him go, before settling down on the couch when everything was dry, to make herself as comfortable as she could.

CHAPTER 16
APRIL 19TH AROUND NOON

In the end, Lewis flung himself on the sofa in the lab at about four in the morning. Around nine, he woke up and needed the loo, and went in through the side door. When he went to peer at the sitting room from halfway through the kitchen, he discovered that Charlotte wasn't there. She hadn't been a figment of his imagination, he was fairly sure of that. He thought about going back out to the studio, but it was cold and drizzling, and the sofa had a lump in it. In the end, he went back up to his bedroom, falling into bed for another few hours.

When he came downstairs again, there were noises. Cooking sorts of noises. Lewis rubbed his face and stopped on the stairs. "Hello?"

"Making soft-boiled eggs. Also some hard-boiled ones." Charlotte was at the stove again, peering at a pot of boiling water. "Do you have rice anywhere?"

"Rice? No." Not a thing Lewis ate. "Why?"

"I was thinking of making something. Well, two some-things. Do you want toast, or something for..." She then peered at the watch on her wrist. "Luncheon?"

"There's some ham. Sandwiches, maybe, and the eggs." He wasn't going to turn down someone else making the eggs happen.

"Right." Charlotte turned away. "I tried the maze again. I could get into the centre, and along one of the edges, but never anywhere near the exit. Wherever that is." She wouldn't look at him.

Lewis pulled a chair over to where he could sit at the edge of the kitchen and at least not stand there feeling terribly awkward. "Oh."

"And then I tried to get out along the fence, the other way. I didn't try the whole line of the fence, but the places I could see might have a gap near here."

"It's rather a long way round. I'm not sure why. I don't need a lot of space, and they're not using this field for anything, at least not this year. Maybe the apples in the autumn." Lewis wasn't sure what to say to that.

"I did hear people talking, though, by the hedge. When I was trying the maze." Charlotte kept not looking at him. Lewis noticed that, because usually people wanted you to look at them when talking. She wasn't. She had last night, and now she wouldn't, and he didn't think it was anything he'd done in particular.

Lewis nodded cautiously. But then she wasn't looking at him, so he cleared his throat. "Yes?"

"They were looking for me." She kept poking at the pot, and boiling eggs didn't need that much looking at them. "I'd leave if I could, you know that."

Lewis considered that. He barely knew her, and even if he did, he was lousy at figuring out people's motivations. He always had been. Lewis was fine with potions and alchemy, and especially with perfumes, but that was different. Perfumes had opinions about how they danced on someone's skin, but it wasn't about truth or lies. "But you can't. Like I told you."

"So what do we do about it? Do you have a way to get a note to anyone?" She stopped staring at the pot of boiling water and went to get the frying pan, presumably for toast. "Moment." With that, she disappeared into the pantry cupboard, coming out with some of the sliced ham, the bread, and another hunk of cheese. Then she went back, coming out with a jar of mustard. "What do you usually eat, anyway?"

The second question was easier than the first. "Sandwiches. Soup, sometimes, I'm all right making soup or stew." He shrugged. "I don't much care what I eat most of the time. It's a distraction."

That, of all things, made her look at him. "Well. I can do the cooking while I'm here. Anything you don't eat? Out of what's in the pantry, anyway?"

Lewis shrugged. "Not really. Nothing really spicy, but they don't give me any of that." He hesitated, then added, "They aren't bringing more food until after May Day. A few days after, probably. I think there's plenty, maybe? It's not like they checked what I use. Someone should drop off some eggs and milk, sometime, but they forget a lot. Or it's late." Or maybe he forgot when they would. That was also entirely possible. It was all under stasis charms, so it didn't go bad, though those only lasted so long on milk, not for weeks and weeks.

Then he remembered she'd asked about notes. "They'll take notes when they bring the food, but I don't think they go out very promptly."

"Right. I'll figure out some things to make, then. When do you usually eat?" She waved a hand toward the stairs. "Are you a real night person, then?" Most people made that sound like a bad thing, and maybe she wasn't. He couldn't tell.

"Usually. When I can. Do the prep in the afternoon, have supper, and then work straight through until I'm done. Last night it was four, maybe?" He hesitated. "If you're staying, we could make up something more comfortable for you. The couch wasn't very. I'd sort of like my bed. But we could figure out some cushions or something for you?" He offered it hesitantly.

"I'd like that. The couch wasn't very here, either. I might be able to do some charmwork to help, but that's not really my line of things." She added after a moment, "My brother keeps the oddest hours. I'm used to him wandering in for breakfast at two in the afternoon, if he was up late." It was one more bit of information about her. "Here, sandwich, egg will be a minute, and the toast. Or do you want your cheese melted?"

The idea of that was novel. Not entirely, of course. He'd had that before, but he never bothered with it on his own. "Please." Charlotte turned away, busying herself with that. After a pause, a not entirely awkward silence, Lewis cleared his throat. "You overheard them looking for you. Can I ask why?"

"I told you that." Charlotte glanced over at him. "I know it sounds like something out of a bad novel, but I really am telling you the truth. Went to sleep on the lawn by the house, woke up in the maze, and found my way here."

Lewis held up both hands. "I believe you? Or at least if you were making something up, I think maybe, I'm not sure, it would sound different from that?"

It made her snort, and he sort of liked that. He was beginning to think that her movements, the tightness of them, were something about her discomfort. But it wasn't the sort of thing he could ask about. "Anyway. I thought maybe someone from the house had put me there. I mean, someone must have, somehow? But it wasn't Gareth or Bedivere or the others he had out looking for me. I don't know all their voices, and they didn't use names. But three or four of them? Not Victor."

Victor was a name Lewis hadn't heard before. Also, it didn't match the set of names. Lewis knew his Arthuriana as well as anyone else in Albion. "Victor?"

"My friend." Charlotte turned away. "We're going to get married, eventually. We've known each other since tutoring school."

Lewis tilted his head. "And he wasn't out looking for you?" The way she'd put that didn't add up. It was one of those awful recipes where someone left ingredients entirely out of the list. She'd called him a friend, so maybe it wasn't the sort of arranged match people did. But while Lewis wasn't actually skilled at friendship in a general sense, he was fairly sure that worrying about where your friend - your betrothed, or whatever they were - had got to was supposed to be part of it. The show of it, at the very least.

Charlotte shook her head once. "Not that I heard. Mind, Victor's not much for mornings, though with less cause than you. He just likes a lie-in." Then she turned her head. "I'm making him sound awful, and he's not. He's funny and good-hearted and kind. Just also, I don't know. Thinks a lot about himself, and not always about the implications. He's still pretty young."

"He didn't - you're the same age. You don't seem young like that." He wasn't entirely sure what made him say that, but he knew it was true. It was like a well-aged vanilla note, or a beeswax accord, something that had some time behind it. Young women were supposed to be fleeting spring flower scents, and while that might suit her in some ways, it wasn't right either. Roses, definitely roses. They had history. Or a hint of something like dragon's blood, even amber, things that had age.

It got him a sudden smile. "That's a very fine compliment, thank you." Then she turned back, turning the sandwich out on a plate. "Let me get the eggs out." She busied herself with that for a minute or two, and Lewis didn't ask her anything else. Then she turned around with two plates and gestured. "The table? Do you want tea to drink, or is there something else?"

"Tea, please. Can I put the kettle on while you finish up?" He was entirely competent for tea, even in its nuanced forms, not that they were doing that at the moment.

"Thank you." There was a bit of a dance back and forth - the kitchen was not designed for two, really, though there was space for one of them to move behind. Finally, they were both at the dining room table, and honestly, the food smelled wonderful. She'd made another piece of toast, cut into strips, half for each of them, to dip into the eggs, and found egg cups somewhere.

Right. He could say so. That would be, actually, he wasn't sure what manners applied here, but Theo would look at him if he didn't have manners. Not that he was sure he'd tell Theo about this. There was quite a bit odd about it. Lewis put all that aside and murmured, "I do appreciate the cooking."

Charlotte opened her mouth, then closed it, as if he'd caught her off guard. "It's not something I do much. But thank you." She ate for a moment, taking the top off of her egg neatly, eating the white from that, then dipping toast into the yolk carefully.

"Um. Can I ask where you live normally?" As he asked it,

he wondered if it was a rude question. But it was a thing people asked.

"With my parents still, our family home. And my brother, for a month or so yet. He's getting married. They just got a flat in London." Charlotte looked up. "He says I can visit."

Lewis considered that. "London and not Trellech?"

"London. His wife to be's a Londoner, I think that's why? And she's got family there, getting on, she wants to be close at hand. Though it's a different one of the London portals, so I'm not actually sure how that helps. Gabe didn't really explain it to me."

That name seemed slightly familiar, but Lewis didn't ask about that. "Why didn't you call out when they were looking for you? The sound should have carried."

Charlotte paused, her spoon partway to her mouth, then she set it down, still loaded with egg. "That's a good question, isn't it? I don't know that I have a good answer yet." She shrugged. "They didn't think I'd come through the maze, though, from what I could hear. Which leads to the interesting question of where else they thought I might be."

Lewis nodded slowly. "I can - there are some books here. I moved them out of the lab. Some of them are about the local folklore, I don't know if there's anything there. There's no portal near here, though. I know that much."

"Just the one at Wells. And trust me, if I could get out onto the road, I'd walk to Wells." She looked down at her feet. "I'd rather not in these shoes, but needs must, or something."

Lewis considered that for an instant. "Um. Do you need clothes or things? I don't have much, but." Now he blushed. He certainly didn't have much in the way of things someone like her would want to wear.

"Oh, I can charm clean them today. Maybe when you go back to whatever you're doing, I'll wash up properly. If I'm here more than a day or two, though, I - I suppose I'll need something."

Lewis nodded, focusing on his food now. "I should get back to work in a little. If you don't find a way out of here, supper around six would be grand. Give or take a little, in case I'm in the middle of something?"

"That, I'm familiar with. I'll come up with something, and I know the food stasis charms well enough." She seemed happy enough at the idea. "Point me at the books, then, and I won't bother you."

CHAPTER 17
THAT AFTERNOON

Charlotte was not sure what to do next. Lewis had been true to his word. He'd eaten lunch, shown her which books she could rummage through and which she couldn't. And then he'd gone off to the lab. She'd watched him go from the doorway, then from the little dining room, a curving path that went across the courtyard. Of course, she hadn't asked to see it. For one thing, every alchemist she knew - and she suspected most of those she didn't - was territorial about their lab. It also seemed like a particular kind of intimacy.

On the other hand, at the moment, she had no compunction about a proper investigation of the cottage. She wasn't going to touch anything, she just wanted to see what spaces there were. It wasn't big from the outside, but that meant nothing in a magical building. Though it was also a good question whether this was a fundamentally magical building or not.

First, she took her time thoroughly exploring the downstairs. She had, in fact, seen all of it, because there was not much to see. The sitting room had a sofa with which she was a trifle too well-acquainted. Her neck was still stiff. There was the kitchen and the pantry closet, and she would do a proper inventory of the latter soon. Over here was the dining room with its stacks of books, and the bathroom and loo. There wasn't any room to hide anything, really, at all.

The stairs went up to a square room, just over the sitting room, with one window built into the slanting roof. It must be a little tight for Lewis to stand up straight, the way the angle of it went. She didn't actually step onto the upstairs floor, just came to the penultimate step, looking around. Lewis was tidy. She approved of that. All his clothing was put away, presumably in the cabinets around the room. There was a decent sized bed, a jacket hung up on a hook, and of course half a dozen books. She approved of the books, too. A bedroom without books, a variety of them, had always seemed a trifle wrong to her.

She was sure Gareth's bedroom didn't have books. Or Bedivere's. Or Morgen's. Or if they did, they were the sort of books meant to look impressive, all bound up in the same colour. Charlotte knew what that sort of library looked like, when it was properly lived in and used - the library at Veritas was like that, for starters, and the Trellech town-house. Even without Gabe wandering through and out again, leaving a trail of books on flat surfaces as he got distracted by something else. But it was a library made for use, and not for show. All the matching bindings in theirs were to make it easier to find what they wanted.

She wasn't going to look at the specific books in his room. That would be prying a little too much. Besides, they were probably mostly alchemy, given what was downstairs. Looking at things from the top of the stairs didn't tell her a lot, but she could see there wasn't a hidden room anywhere, except maybe some attic storage. And she should probably look at that, but she didn't much want to crawl under the eaves. There were likely spiders. Or bugs, anyway.

Charlotte went back downstairs and began a thorough inventory of the pantry. He'd said there wouldn't be a new hamper until after May Day, but they had plenty of food, especially if there was a replenishment of both milk and eggs. Charms helped with both of them, but the proper stasis charms always changed the flavour a touch. And Gabe insisted the milk charms changed the texture, which was a trifle ridiculous, except that Charlotte had to agree he had a point. It wasn't horrible, and it was certainly fine for cooking, but not as much for drinking or tea.

At any rate, there were plenty of eggs, several kinds of bread, and a host of other staples. There wasn't anything fancy, but Charlotte rather wondered if someone sensible had actually been packing up the hampers for delivery. Gareth and Morgen didn't seem the sort of people who would have thought about multiple kinds of jam, or including some flour along with the baked bread. There were pocket soups, gelatinous bits that would turn into broth when reconstituted with water.

And there were various tins and jars, including pickles of several kinds. Not a lot of fresh vegetables. On the other hand, it was April, and the new plants were still coming in, and Charlotte suspected that was more preparation than Lewis did routinely. There were various root vegetables, though, the ones that stored well over the winter. She found potatoes, carrots, turnips, a few parsnips, some onions, a braid of garlic.

She found various packages of meat in stasis, in servings for one. Ham in reasonable slices, and that shelf held a fair bit of bacon. There were bits of chicken, but no whole birds. In short, everything for a bachelor establishment with a bachelor who had some skills in the kitchen but didn't care much what he ate. And there were quite a few varieties of cheese. Whoever had stocked the pantry clearly felt - as Charlotte did - that cheese did a lot to make a meal better. Or to make an easy meal, especially with the eggs and bread.

That done - and with some ideas about what to do about supper - she took herself off for a deeper look at the books. By the time she'd found what she wanted to read, it was nearly time to do something about an evening meal. She went to work making a proper bit of stew with some of the chicken and some of the onions. It had been amiably simmering for half an hour, just waiting and filling the cottage with quite a nice scent, when Lewis reappeared.

He stopped dead in the doorway before he blinked. "That smells grand. Rosemary, and what's that? Tarragon? And I didn't know there was a lemon back there?"

It made her laugh. "You have a well-informed nose, yes. And you have quite a few lemons, I'll dig them out. I like them in my tea, actually, depending on the blend. If you want to wash up, there's bread to go with this." He went past her to the loo. By the time he came out, she had the stew in bowls, the rest set aside to cool and go into stasis. There'd be another three meals there, at least.

"Can I, um? You cook quite well." Lewis hesitated. "You don't mind?"

"I don't get a chance to do much of it, really." Charlotte hesitated. "We have a cook at home. Very protective about her kitchen, and she gets to be. But two of my aunts taught me. Different things. The stew's thanks to Aunt Rosemary."

"It explains the herb, then." Lewis inhaled. "You don't have to cook if you don't want to?"

"You might get bored with what I can cook, actually. Not the widest range." Charlotte settled herself for her own meal, and she managed three spoonfuls - and let him have a couple more - before the question bubbled out of her. "Why haven't you told them I'm here?"

Lewis looked up, baffled and owlish. "How would I? I don't have any way to get in touch with them unless someone comes here. Usually that's twice a week, but with people visiting..." His voice trailed off.

"So you don't have a journal. Or even a message pad." She did, everyone in her family did. Though they were still expensive, she knew that. Gabe had gone on about how the magic was quite complex, actually. But even Charlotte knew the charms to link two pads of paper. That was the first year of proper Incantation classes at Schola. Well, Incantation and Materia, both, if you had to prepare the paper, but that would be certainly in Lewis's skills. "Or linked notebooks or anything?"

Lewis shook his head. "Morgen won't have any of the journals around. Or anything else like that. She wants everything in letters, sealed and all."

"You know she's probably reading whatever you send out. It's easy to open a seal if you know how." Charlotte took another bite of her food, and when she looked up, Lewis was staring at her. "What?"

"How do you know that?" Then he shook his head and changed the subject or rather went back to the original one. "Um. Morgen gets rather odd about some kinds of magic? Most of what I'm doing isn't complicated magically. I don't even do my own distilling, most of it, just combining things, and a bit of purifying and preparing the base oils and perfumer's alcohol and all that." He brushed that amount of skill aside, because no one appreciated it anyway, even if it was foundational to the final perfume.

"I was reading one of the books, this afternoon. About - there's lore about a Fatae portal near here, I guess?" Charlotte frowned. "Not the caves in the village, somewhere..." She considered her orientation and the charms she'd done earlier. "That way? That's odd, I agree that's odd."

"Something like that. I wouldn't ever ask, Morgen doesn't like those sorts of questions." He said it like he was mentioning the existence of weather, not to be argued with, and Charlotte started to realise how much of the situation he hadn't questioned. Lewis finished up his bowl. "Can I wash up for you?"

"Oh. Just a minute. Make sure you leave things like you would normally. Just one out, or whatever."

Lewis had been clearing his bowl and plate and he stopped. He didn't drop them, at least, that would have been awkward. "Why?"

"If someone comes along and sees two bowls or plates or whatever, they'll know I'm here. Or be pretty sure." Charlotte wasn't sure whether spelling this out was a good idea, now she said it. Her friends at school - well, and since, including Victor - thought she was a trifle over-cautious. More than a trifle, to be fair to everyone in this conversation in her head. But she had the habits of her family. They included resetting a room to what was expected, as well as taking care of their own hair and nail clippings and all that. Charlotte said, "Can I borrow a comb tonight? I'd like to wash my hair properly."

"Oh." The change of topic made him blink. "I, um. Yes. Do you, I mean." He flushed. "Something to sleep in, or wear tomorrow?"

The blush was honestly rather fascinating. Victor

didn't, though he might comment on what she wore. "If it's not a bother. Please. And if we could sort out somewhere more comfortable than the sofa." Fifteen minutes later, they had figured out how to remove the cushions from the back of the sofa and tuck a spare sheet around them to keep them in place. Lewis had also given her a pile of extra blankets to sleep on and under. It was promising, at least once she'd applied a couple of charms to keep the sheet from slipping. Fortunately, she was handy with managing fabric. As a skill, it came in surprisingly useful.

As she was finishing that up, Lewis went upstairs. He came back with a comb, a spare shirt, and a pair of trousers, and a grey jumper that would hang down to her hips. Also he had something that looked like a very voluminous nightshirt. "Here? Um. If that's all right."

"It's better than what I've got," Charlotte said cheerfully. "I'm not taking anything you need?"

Lewis shook his head. "The trousers don't fit me very well. I charm clean. I can do yours sometime, if you want?"

It was awkward, but manageable. The whole situation was, that was the rub of it. Charlotte managed a smile. "I appreciate that. If you could clean them tomorrow? I'm all right with it, but I suspect you're better, if you've been managing all your laundry like that?"

"I have!" He sounded surprised she'd figured it out.

"You didn't mention them taking laundry away, or expecting more back? Anyway, I'm all right with spot treatments, but I'm not as good at doing all of a thing. The blouse and skirt aren't fussy, with a charm, or they shouldn't be." Mama refused to patronise dressmakers who used the fabrics that misbehaved with a charm. It wasn't just the cleaning, but also how that usually went along with poor wear in general, or a tendency to pick up splotchy stains when around certain reagents. And Gabe would get into things, before anyone got into what Mama sometimes found herself in.

"Oh." Lewis blinked up at her. "You're very clever. Look, I need to get back to work, if you want to leave whatever, um... At the top of the stairs? Do you mind if I come back in and sleep here? Would it wake you?"

"It's fine if you do, I'll go back to sleep. And I'll put together something for breakfast tomorrow." Saying that, though, had something nagging at her. Too late to do much about it now. It was well dark outside. She hadn't noticed that happening. But tomorrow morning, she wanted to go set a ward or two that would at least alert her if people came through the maze.

Why on earth weren't they looking for her here? That was the puzzle that she couldn't solve, and it was driving her up a tree.

CHAPTER 18
APRIL 20TH IN THE MORNING

As it turned out, Lewis finished up fairly early that night. It was one of those projects where the next part needed straining, and that took forever. Best to set it up to strain while he slept, and he could pick up with it whenever he woke up in the morning. He was in bed by two, with Charlotte curled up in a corner of the sitting room asleep.

Or he thought she was asleep, anyway. She hadn't moved when he came in the door, and he tried to avoid making too much noise going up the stairs. He was used to that, from being at home with Theo and Mother and his other siblings. Lewis slept like a log for once, the way he did when he took a sleeping potion, waking mid-morning, earlier than he usually did. He rolled over and peered at his watch, to find it was only half-nine.

When he came downstairs, the sofa was put back in order, and there was no sign of Charlotte. Or his clothes, which suggested, probably, she was somewhere. She'd left bread and butter on the counter. As he was trying to decide if he wanted to make other food, he heard shoes on the path outside, and Charlotte came in, a little out of breath.

She looked unreasonably good in his shirt and trousers. Lewis was not a man who paid a lot of attention to clothing as a general rule, his own or anyone else's. But she'd somehow gone and made it look like it was made to fit her. Her hair was down in a braid, with a bit of something like a ribbon, though coarser, tying it off. More of that same fabric was braided or twisted or something to make a belt, the shirt blousing out just the flattering amount over it. He hadn't given her the belt, but it had some sort of print on it, blues and golden yellows that contrasted against the white shirt and charcoal trousers. She'd rolled the sleeves up above the elbows, and left the top buttons open, just showing a v at the neckline.

He must have been staring with his mouth open, which was ridiculous, because she raised an eyebrow. "Did you eat? I can make something. Morning!" Even more annoyingly - or interestingly, it wasn't actually annoying him - she was remarkably chipper.

"Please?" Lewis gestured at the kitchen and got out of the way. "I could have a go at your clothes, too? Not that you're not welcome to those."

"I managed the belt out of one of the flour sacks. Quite clever, those." Charlotte looked - and sounded - rather smug. "There's about half of it left. I can make up a dish towel when I get a chance to hem it."

That sounded remarkably domestic. Lastingly domestic. Lewis cleared his throat. "Um. You're expecting to be here a bit longer?"

Charlotte looked over her shoulder from where she'd got started on something with eggs. "I can't get out." She waved a hand. "I tried again. No luck. Though I did set up something that should let us know if someone's coming this way, from about half way through the maze, and again at the gate." She paused and fished two stones out of her pocket. His pocket, seeing as they were his trousers. She put them on the counter, one lighter grey, the other darker. "If they start buzzing - I think it'll sound like buzzing there? There's someone coming. You can take those into your lab if you like. I did two sets."

Lewis stared at the rocks and then at Charlotte, then back at the rocks. Charlotte ignored all this, turning back to the cooking. Without turning around, she went on, as if there was no staring involved. "The thing I can't figure out is where they think I am. Or if they care. They might not care, but they were trying awfully hard to persuade me."

"I, um." Lewis had a sudden mental leap back to the last time Gareth had come here demanding things. "Your room, the second night, did it smell like - um. Do you know what chios mastic is? And there'd have been frankincense, rose, jasmine, a touch of chamomile, cinquefoil, a hint of vervain. Not that that has scent."

"The chios mastic is resinous, isn't it? A bit like cedar or pine, but of course not quite like them?" Charlotte still hadn't turned around. That wasn't helping Lewis figure things out at all. "I did. It cleared my head, actually."

"Oh." Lewis swallowed. "Gareth was trying to persuade you, then. It must be you? I think. He wanted something a lot more persuasive, the illegal sorts of persuasive. And I wouldn't do it for him. I told him what I gave him, for - well, it was your room, I guess - would lead you closer to your dreams." He hesitated, then admitted, "I probably would have if Morgen had asked."

"Morgen is extremely persuasive, yes," Charlotte said, still focused on the cooking. "So my dreams think I should be more clearheaded." She seemed pleased at that. Lewis went quiet at that. A moment later, Charlotte turned the knob on the stove down and twisted around. "More than just persuasive."

"How do you do that?" Lewis took a step back. "Hear things I'm not saying. Do you do that to everyone?"

Other people would have taken it as a question not worth answering. She didn't. Lewis had no idea what to do with that. Instead, she said, "Let me finish the eggs, and then we can sit down without burning breakfast. Can you set up a teapot? I think the kettle's about to sing." Before he could say anything else, she added, "Hearing things, the stones, what my plans are, all over breakfast. Promise."

He wasn't going to argue. For one thing, he had no idea how to argue with someone like her. She didn't work under any of the rules he'd learned, anything Mother or Theo had taught him, once upon a time, or most things he'd learned at school. She made her own rules, or she was using a set he'd never really seen.

Three minutes later, the tea was steeping in the pot, and they were sitting at the dining room table, such as it was. Charlotte had made toast, too, and Lewis spread jam on his, feeling like he needed it to buffer something or other. When he put the knife back, she was watching him, her head slightly tilted. "I confuse you, I think." It wasn't a question, and that meant he didn't know if he was supposed to answer it.

After a moment, he nodded. "You're not like other people I know. A little like people at school, but they mostly didn't talk to me? You talk to me."

Charlotte tilted her head. "Well, you are something of a type. And people like me - like the me I wear around in public, anyway - don't talk much to people like you. Silly, but there you go. I think a lot of them are silly, for a number of reasons." She brushed her hands together, the sort of gesture of averting bad luck some people made routinely. "Anyway, I like questions. My brother asks thousands of them. You can't possibly ask more. There aren't enough seconds in the day."

That made Lewis chuckle, despite feeling he probably shouldn't. But Charlotte smiled, so she didn't seem to be angry. It wasn't the angry sort of smile, like Morgen had when people did things she didn't like. "All right. Um. Is that about the hearing things?"

She tilted her head, then nodded. "It is. I come from a family that pays attention a lot. Honestly, I find it hard to stop, and I know it's rather rude. I'm perfectly civil about it. I don't tell people I've been putting all those pieces together about what they're saying. Usually." She peered at him, the way someone with glasses and a couple of decades more age might peer at him. "You seem to be a tad different there. I'm still figuring out why. For now, let's chalk it up to unusual circumstances until a better idea comes along."

Lewis had no idea where to begin arguing with that, though he felt someone - not him - possibly should. In the grand scheme of logic and reason, anyway. "And me?"

"Does it bother you when I say things? Like that, I mean. I can't tell if it bothers you or you find it a bit of a relief not to have to rummage around for the words your-self, but it is awfully rude."

"It'd be rude if you got it wrong, and insisted you were right." Lewis said, before he realised he was thinking out loud. "And it'd be rude if you didn't let me talk. But the way you do it, um. It is a relief, yeah." Suddenly, this topic felt a great deal less tenable, and he asked instead, "The stones?"

"Linked charm. They'll trigger if anyone comes near

them, and they'll have to unless somehow they can fly. Or there's another way in entirely. That part's the easy part."

"Why?" Lewis blurted it out, swallowed, then tried to pretend he'd meant to ask it like that. He was quite sure he wasn't fooling her, but he also felt he had to make the attempt at that particular dignity. "I mean, why are you worried about them finding you?"

"Ah, that leads into my plans, such as they are. I don't know how I ended up in the maze in the first place. It seems like it was a spur-of-the-moment thing. Because if someone had meant to abscond with me, why not do it at night, and bring at least some of my things? Instead, it was just me, what I was wearing, and one additional cloak. Not even any food." She brushed her hands together again. "Anyway. My actual plans are to see if anyone comes looking and what they say, and see if there's a way out. I did find a reference in one of your books, and I'm trying to figure out how to apply it to get out, to trick a break in the warding."

"Isn't that, um, not the sort of thing that's supposed to work?" The thing about protective magics, Lewis had always been told, was that if they were done well, if they worked in the first place, they were very solid. And besides, logically, they weren't any use if they could just be pulled aside by some random person without particular skills.

Her mouth quirked up, then she outright grinned. "Whoever designed them wasn't expecting me. And me on my own, I'm not much beyond what I've said. Scion of Fox House, capable of dressing up nicely and saying all the right things. But my family goes in for some odd skills, and I've picked up a few. Can't help not." Then she tapped her fingers. "Whoever put me in the maze must have assumed I'd come this way, and that's an interesting puzzle."

"No one's supposed to." Lewis agreed, because that was also a distracting consideration, now she said it. "That was part of the arrangement here, that I'd be alone to do my work. Without interruptions."

"And yet," Charlotte said, leaning back now, "from what you've said, they feel they can wander in and make new demands whenever they like. Especially if they bring you a little more food you don't really need. Well, all right, I'll grant the milk and eggs."

Lewis frowned at that. It was true, and yet he wanted to argue. "There are, um. Other reasons."

"I thought there must be." Her voice had suddenly got gentle, and Lewis had no idea what to do with that. "Something that matters to you a lot. To make it worth this. Though I suppose time to work on your own mostly must also be pleasant."

"It is. I can do large-scale production, but I really prefer perfumes, and I can't begin to afford ingredients for, oh, three-quarters of what I want to do."

"And Morgen can?" Charlotte's voice had picked up a sharpness again, though not at all aimed at him.

"The things she cares about." Lewis tried to figure out how to explain it. "Do you know art at all?"

"I'm apprenticing in illusion art, in a not terribly formal sort of way. Sketches, watercolours, things like that." Charlotte stretched out her hands, peering at them, as if expecting to see a wash of colour somewhere.

"Then you'll understand this." Lewis paused to gather his thoughts into a better explanation. "It's like working with a palette of watercolours. You can mix them together, if you start with the right set, to get all sorts of effects. What Morgen wants gives me an excellent starting palette. Not everything I want, but enough I can figure out what I'd need to make what's in my nose. My head. My head-nose?" Now he just sounded foolish.

Charlotte was smiling at it, though, then she nodded. "That makes a lot of sense. So you have time to think, when you're not making things for her. And enough of a palette to work with to test some of your ideas, even if it's not all of them."

"Yes!" Lewis swallowed. "And she gives me ingredients for other things. My brother needs a potion, you see."

CHAPTER 19
THAT MORNING

J ust as Lewis said it, he grimaced. He hadn't meant to bring up Theo at all. He never did, except with people who already knew. Before he could say anything else, however, the rocks began to vibrate, making a rumbling sound far outside their apparent size.

"Is that, um." Lewis gestured.

"That's the centre of the maze. Wash these up and dry one and put it away. So it doesn't look like there were two of us here. I'll scatter some books - gently, of course - and find somewhere." She didn't specify where, but Lewis got up to clear the table and wash up the dishes. By the time he'd washed and dried both plates, put them both up in the cupboard, there were books spread on the table again. Charlotte was nowhere to be seen.

Ten minutes later, the door banged open. "Where are - there you are." Gareth had been about to bellow, and he didn't so much deflate as hold it in reserve. He had Bedivere behind him, and Mark.

Lewis tried to look both put out and unsettled. It wasn't at all hard, he certainly felt both things rather strongly.

"What, I?" He thought about asking if something was wrong, but that might be too much, and besides, he didn't need to. Gareth was talking over him almost immediately.

"Bedivere, you look upstairs. Mark, look at the lab. Is there anything going on there?" That was a question to Lewis.

"No, erm. I hadn't - why do you need to go in there?"

"We're looking for someone. Is. There. Anything. Going. On." Gareth stepped up, taking Lewis by the shoulders.

"No. Sir." That seemed to mollify Gareth slightly. He had a temper like a couple of the journeymen, and like Mistress Aylett, and Lewis didn't want to be on the wrong side of it. Reflexive politeness - no, the word really ought to be abasement - was safer. Some part of him was scurrying around inside his head, wanting to find the right thing to do now, with no idea what that might be.

Gareth gave him a little shake, just enough to jar his teeth. "Mark. Go. Don't touch anything, but make note if anything is out of place, and tell me. We'll look at it together as need be." Bedivere had in fact gone upstairs. Lewis could hear footsteps over his head. He was pretty sure Charlotte hadn't gone up there. She'd have had to go past him, but he didn't know for sure.

"Why are you here, please?" Asking what they were looking for might give things away. He didn't know. It seemed like a logical jump. They were here out of season, not on schedule, and Gareth was upset. Not just peeved at making the trip, like usual. Lewis tried not to twitch at the change, the way the unexpected made him feel like he was itchy on the inside of his head.

"Have you seen anyone?" Gareth gave him one more shake of the shoulders, more lightly this time, then let him go. "Anything unusual at all?"

Lewis looked down, because he certainly couldn't look Gareth in the eyes. Not on a good day, and certainly not when Gareth was like this. The other man grunted, and stepped away, going to go peer in the pantry, then into the dining room. "Come on, man. Answer me." Then his voice turned wheedling, a false note. "You want to be a help."

"Of course I do, Gareth." The question was who he was helping. "How could I have seen anyone? You're the only ones who know how to get through the maze."

"There's that." Gareth grunted, circling through the dining room. "All these books? You sure you need all of them?"

"Yes, I do." It did put an entirely righteous note of fear and need in Lewis's voice. Another time, he'd have hated himself for that. He knew it sounded awful. Right now, it was at least something different to talk about. "I'm still trying to figure out the structure for what Morgen wants, how to tie it into the sensory memory of myth. It's really rather tricky."

Lewis was gifted at what he did. He knew that. Anyone who actually knew both their alchemy and their perfume figured that out too fast for him to be wrong about that. But what Morgen wanted, fundamentally - beyond the various persuasive incenses and the ones that let people drift and dream and be suggestible - was something that would anchor myth in the here and now. Not only anchor it, but expand on it, in a way that was personal to each body and mind it touched.

If he could pull it off, he could be set for the rest of his life. Only, no one had done anything quite like it before. Certainly not all the layers that Morgen wanted, scents that developed over hours of wear. Lewis wasn't sure he could do it, but he'd known when she put the challenge before him that he'd have to try. And then, of course, she'd sweetened the lure with the materia that would help Theo. That did help Theo, that was the thing. If it wasn't working, it would have been easier for him to leave. Not that he could leave, mind, now Charlotte had made it clear there was more wrong than he'd realised.

It wasn't just that the materia was rare and costly. Though a bit of it was, most of it was more on the finicky side, which was a different sort of supply problem. The problem was having time and freedom for every step, not needing to be bound by a particular schedule. If he'd had an outside position, he'd not have been able to do the distillations and the combinations and all that at the best points.

There was that sort of deadly silence that meant Gareth had asked something and Lewis hadn't answered. Lewis cleared his throat. "Pardon?"

"I said - you twit - that I wanted to know what you've been doing." Gareth was standing by the stove now, his arms crossed.

"My work, Gareth. And making meals, and all that. Mostly working and reading." And talking to Charlotte, but he wouldn't say that. He wondered, suddenly, where her clothing was. Right as Lewis finished saying it, Bedivere came back down.

"Nothing there. Just books and clothes and things. No one in the eaves, I did look." Lewis didn't know Bedivere well, but the man looked nervous.

"You lost her. Find her. Right. Go back to Victor, and see what you can get out of him. Keep him sweet."

Bedivere hesitated. "He wasn't, um. Was he right about what he said?"

"That would be why we're worried. Merlin's sake, he didn't think to tell us, and it didn't come up. I knew we should have—" Gareth cut off sharply. "If we don't find her by May Day, we'll be in deep trouble. Go on. Go be charming."

Bedivere grimaced, but made a slight bow at the waist and went off. That was both informative and deeply mystifying. They had some particular reason for worrying about Charlotte being gone, then. And it seemed like they hadn't been the ones to put her in the maze, whatever else was up. Before Lewis could chase down the other implications, Gareth turned back to him. "Lab. Now."

Lewis knew better than to argue. Mark was along the far wall. He didn't seem to be actually disrupting anything critical, but he'd pulled down the ladder to the attic space, and Lewis could just see his legs. He had no idea where Charlotte was, and that was starting to bother him a lot. Mark came down the ladder, then, leaving it down. "No one up there."

"Blast. Where the ..." Gareth cut off. "Lewis. You haven't seen anyone?"

"What, um. Does - you said she? - she look like?" Lewis asked. The stammer was at least entirely unfeigned.

"This tall." Gareth gestured and got the height at least a couple of inches wrong. "She was wearing, what, a blouse and skirt. Nothing unusual. Blonde hair, well-bred. Posh."

Lewis said, he thought rather reasonably, "What would someone like that want here? I've got my own work to do. And you know I don't work well with people around."

Gareth grunted. "Someone will be back with the milk and such on Friday. If there's anything unusual, you leave a note as far as you can go in the maze."

"Yes, Gareth. I know where." Lewis looked down. He didn't want to meet Gareth's eyes in the ordinary way of things, and especially not now.

Neither of the other men said anything else to him. Or to each other, at least where he could overhear. They went out the door, paused in the courtyard to look through the various cabinets along the edge. None of them had enough room for Charlotte. Lewis kept an eye out the window, and then watched them go back up, through the gate, and into the maze. Then he put the ladder back up, closing the trap-door. Finally, for good measure, he counted to one hundred before carefully coming out of the lab.

There was no one visible around as he came back into the sitting room. He went upstairs to see what kind of state Bedivere had made of the place. Two books on their edges, threatening the spines, and he immediately put those right, but not a lot more out of place. Just the drawers pulled open, things moved so someone could look in the storage cupboards.

He finished putting it right and came downstairs again to find Charlotte standing in the kitchen, balanced lightly on the balls of her feet. He thought of a deer, ready to dart at any angle away from the hunter. Or perhaps, in the circumstances, something more like a unicorn.

CHAPTER 20
A FEW MINUTES LATER

"Are you all right?" It was the first thing out of Lewis's mouth, which under the circumstances was a lot better than it could be. He looked nervy, a little white and twitchy. She'd come back in and heard him upstairs, and she'd stayed put. At least from the kitchen, she could take off for the dining-room door or the sitting room. And one set of stones was still in her pocket.

She didn't know what to say to that, exactly. She had a dozen questions, and she had no idea at all whether he'd answer any of them. "For the moment, anyway. Are you?"

He took a step toward her, hesitantly holding out a hand, then dropping it suddenly. "They were upset. I didn't like it. Who would? And they searched things. But nothing's too much out of order, and they didn't damage anything, and they didn't yell. How do you measure that?" His shoulder twitched. "They're gone."

"Not a convenient mark on a pipette, no." Charlotte ran her hands through her hair, tucking a wisp out of the way, then coming up with a small branch and frowning at it. That he'd commented on the yelling was curious. "Why didn't you tell them where I was? And do they sometimes yell?"

There was a long silence. She'd asked something reasonable, honestly. But to be fair to Lewis, no one had given him much time to think, including her, since he got up this morning. And she did rather want to be fair to him. It seemed the least she could do.

"I didn't want to. And Gareth yells. I'm too slow, too precise, things like that. He's not patient. This time he was sharp. And he was angry at Bedivere." He said it quietly, half to the floor, but then he held out a hand to her again. "Um. We should talk some more, probably. I don't expect I want to tell them you're here. I wasn't sure where you'd gone, anyway."

"I heard a little of it. You did quite well not answering that particular question, from what I caught." She gestured out the door from the little dining room. "I went up the apple tree. Took a chance I could get up before anyone saw me. I can't do the proper invisibility charms. Gabe won't teach me the precursors. But I can manage a look-away. So long as they didn't actually stand under the tree and look up, I figured I might get away with it."

"Good thing you were wearing trousers, I guess?" Lewis offered it tentatively, as if he weren't sure.

"It certainly helped. They didn't find my clothes, then?"

"No?" Lewis ducked his chin.

"Under the potatoes. Can't say I think much about the thoroughness of their search. Let me go grab them." It left Lewis standing there for a moment, before he turned to the stove and put the kettle on. Charlotte needed a chance to gather her own thoughts, not that she could take terribly long. She ducked out, bringing the clothes with her. "Glad I put the sofa back. Let me use the loo, and then tea sounds wonderful."

Five minutes later, they'd both washed up and were sitting at the table, staring mutually at their tea cups. When the silence had gone on too long, Charlotte looked up. "You mentioned a brother?"

"He needs a potion." Lewis wasn't quite looking at her, that was fine, she was getting used to it. It was rather restful, honestly. "And the ingredients are expensive. Specialised. You need connections to get some of them."

Charlotte set aside her immediate inclination, which was to ask about them in detail. "There are other ways than Morgen to do that, though, surely?"

"How much do you know about it?" He looked her up and down. "Or, I don't know, even bookkeeping?"

"I am actually trained to run a large estate. With competent help, not all on my own. But I go over the accounts with our steward and Mama every month. And we have rather an odd list of materia on our shopping lists, given Gabe. And spices, these days." She didn't mind the spices at all, though she wished she could get the various transliterations of the names of some of them to stick in her head better. Cheat sheets only went so far.

Lewis looked down sharply. "Oh. I guess I don't know much about you." He looked up, fleetingly. "Gareth said they'd be in trouble if they didn't find you by May Day. Why's that?"

"Oh, because Papa is a Captain of the Guard and a magistrate, as well as being Lord Edgarton, and Gabe is a very persistent Penelope. And Mama and our friends would, I suspect, dismantle this place from top to bottom for any hint of what happened. And they do know what evidence is needed for the truth magics. If I remember right, Lord and

Lady Hembry here in Somerset sort of owe Papa a favour. At least I think they do still. It's not the sort of thing Papa would ordinarily call in."

Lewis blinked at her, then weakly said, "Oh."

"Not what you expected? I am not purely ornamental, either." She looked down. "Well, less ornamental than usual, at the moment."

"I actually thought, um, you looked rather nice? Better than I do in them." It was ridiculous, but she could feel herself smiling. A proper sort of smile, not like when Victor complimented her. Victor was florid with his compliments. They were works of art, but they sometimes had theatrical momentum draped around, rather than sincerity. Charlotte was fairly sure Lewis couldn't make an insincere compliment to save his life, though he might just manage to dodge the question. She hadn't actually expected that out of him until she'd heard him with Gareth. "Your brother?"

"A Penelope. Investigating things, that's what they do. He's got a case right now, I swear Aunt Witt and Aunt Mason - they're also Penelopes - are trying to keep him busy right now particularly. But he knows I'm here, and so do Mama and Papa. Gabe thought I'd learn something interesting."

"I maybe remember him, at school." Lewis offered it cautiously.

"Bouncing between the library, the salle, and whatever classroom had his attention at the moment, driving half the professors up a tree? Not quite so literally as my morning, but you get the idea?" Charlotte gestured at her own head. "We look alike, in the colouring and the shape of the face and all that. But he can't sit still, and me, I do like a bit of lounging when the opportunity presents."

"But not purely ornamental." For a second, Charlotte

didn't know how to read that, then Lewis smiled, shy again. She beamed back at him.

"Exactly. Anyway. Tell me about your materia, I should at least be able to follow the outline." Charlotte leaned one elbow on the table and told Mama's voice in her head that it was perfectly appropriate in informal circumstances. Which Mama would have said herself.

Lewis cleared his throat. "I've an older brother. He was supposed to be - he was supposed to help us all. Set us up right. My father died when I was twelve and Theo was seventeen."

Charlotte could do that maths. That made him exactly old enough to have had a bad War. Still alive, apparently, given the verb tenses, but there were all sorts of things that changed the world in an instant that came from the War. "And the War came." She said it as gently as she could, so that Lewis wouldn't have to.

He looked down, but she thought he was a little relieved. "Exactly. No one's quite sure what's wrong with him. He has terrors, nightmares, but also waking ones? There's a potion that helps, but it's hard to make, and it takes some specific materia, and also, attunements. Here is wonderful, there's so little interference from other magic. Not the sort of thing you could make in Trellech, though, or even in someone else's alchemical lab. Not without a lot of warding and protections and the chance to set things up perfectly."

"And you've been making that for him." Charlotte said.

Lewis nodded. "It's a variant of something the Ayletts designed. They helped me, they knew about it. I think a lot of the research went into one of their later potions? But what Theo needs is..." His voice trailed off.

Charlotte considered. "Does it bother you if I talk about Gabe?" That first. She wasn't sure. Lewis was hard to read.

He looked at her, blinking, absolutely owlish. "Should it?"

"Some people might be bothered by it." Charlotte tried to figure out how to put this. "By someone else's brother being well and happy and doing all the things we're supposed to be doing, when yours can't."

"That's, that's foolish." There was more blinking. "Your brother - I don't know what I'm supposed to call him, actually," That was a bemused digression, not distracted, and it actually sounded very like Gabe in a particular mood. "He's not being like that at me, on purpose. Or at Theo. He's just having his life. You're having your life." Which brought him back to the moment. "Even if that's a bit constrained right now."

"It is. Call him Gabe, if you like. Besides, he's two years behind you at school. Or Edgarton, if it makes you feel better." Then she settled into that essential question. "I can't get out. You didn't turn me in. I'm suspecting that circumstances will change after May Day. For one thing, if I don't turn up as expected, Papa and probably Gabe will come looking. Along with whatever other friends of the family take an interest. I'm quite sure they can come and find us. And they'll have hair and all that. And blood ties to work with."

"Hair? Oh, for locational charms." Lewis blinked. "Don't they have your hairbrush and things at the house?"

Charlotte grinned. "I come from the sort of family that makes a point of incinerating the leavings from our hairbrushes and all that on a regular basis. Every morning, usually. Like brushing my teeth. Never entirely saw the point of the bother before, but Papa insisted. And anyway, even without that, my family can draw on the blood link. That's much more reliable." She cocked her head. "Probably reassuring, if they try that to check on me in the interim. I'm more or less where they expect me to be. They can tell if I'm injured."

Lewis said, slowly, after a long pause, "You have a very different sort of family than mine. I don't think I know how to make a perfume out of it. At least not right now."

"I'd be terribly curious if you did make the attempt. At some point. Mama is terribly difficult to buy presents for, and that's just the sort of thing she'd adore." Then Charlotte considered. "It's you and your brother and - other family?"

"Mother, she keeps everything together in the household. And there's some money from the Ministry, for Theo. But my younger brother's due to finish at Alethorpe next year, and apothecary apprenticeships are hard to come by." And expensive, though Lewis didn't say that part out loud.

Charlotte considered. "Assuming we get out of this still talking to each other, which currently seems plausible, I can introduce you to some people who might be able to help." Starting with Mama, of course, who had a good line on the relevant charitable funds. And then, of course, going on to Aunts Mason and Witt, who'd gone to Alethorpe themselves and knew a few skeletons in wardrobes that might incline people to be informatively useful.

"You can do that?" Lewis blinked again.

"Watch me." Charlotte beamed at him, muting it a little when she apparently hit 'worrisome' rather than 'reassuring'. "More seriously, point me in the right direction, and see what I come up with. If you don't like it, you don't have to say yes. That is, in fact, what I'm really trained in. The illusion artwork is a sideline."

Lewis nodded, then he looked away. "I, um. I ought to get to work, I suppose. Let me do something about your clothes and then do you mind terribly if I disappear into the lab?"

"Not at all. I have books. And I'll have something ready for supper. Six or so?"

It got her another one of those pleased little smiles, like he had no idea what to do with this story he'd wandered into. But at least he liked her cooking. Both what she was making, apparently, and that she was making it. Figuring out some options for the next eight or nine days would also give her some occupation for her afternoon.

CHAPTER 21
APRIL 21ST IN THE EVENING

Lewis wasn't very conversational the next morning. He wasn't, to be honest, very awake. He had been up until almost five, working through a series of combinations and waiting to see how they settled. At the same time he had been working on a reactant for the potion Morgen wanted. He was good at slotting things in, piece by piece, using his time well. The Ayletts had insisted on that, demanded excellence in it, and it served him well now. He'd only stopped because both parts of what he was working on had to steep for at least a few hours.

But it meant he had staggered downstairs, eaten and had tea, and then gone off to the lab without more than a brief good morning. Charlotte hadn't seemed angry, but now he thought about it, he wasn't sure what angry looked like on her.

When he came back into the cottage at nearly seven that night, there was a wonderful smell of food, and he was suddenly starving. Charlotte had curled up on the sofa, reading. "Evening."

"Um. Evening." He ran his hand through his hair. "I've got an hour before I can do anything else. The food smells wonderful. I hope it's not a problem?"

"Most of my cooking runs to either fast to make or it will hold. Given I mostly learned it from Aunt Mason, and she's as bad as Gabe for patience. So it's all things you can do in one go, or things where you can let them simmer on the stove for a long time." She waved a hand at it. "Beef stew. All nice solid root vegetables in there."

Lewis went to wash up, and then the next few minutes were about getting out bowls. He thought Charlotte had been reading more books. Some of them were in different places than he remembered. He thought the stack with the big blue book at the bottom had been on the other edge of the table. He more or less inhaled the stew, only realising he was doing so when he was halfway through the bowl.

"Roll? Whoever made the food has a good hand with bread. And there's butter, here." Charlotte pushed it over, with no hint of upset. Mother would have been upset, Lewis knew that. He'd had bad manners thoroughly squashed out of him by her silent disapproval. "I might try baking some, but that's harder without a recipe, and no one seems to have provided a cookbook of any kind."

That was curious, now he thought about it. "They didn't really ask how good I was at cooking. Now you say that." He focused on his food, but he caught her expression changing.

She held her tongue for long enough for him to have some of the bread and more of the stew. "What do you know about what they're doing, besides what you're making for them?"

Lewis shrugged. "Not a lot. That it's something where

they want, what was it Morgen called it, sensory persuasion."

"Manipulation. Near enough coercion. Not the scents themselves. I trust you when you say you're not doing that. But that, in combination with other things."

Lewis felt his head jerk up and his jaw drop. "What?"

Charlotte shifted, somehow. "If we're going to talk about that, we should be more comfortable. Do you want a beer?"

Something had gone sour in his mouth, but a beer would probably help, or rather the alcohol in it. And he wasn't doing anything early in the evening where it might be a problem. He nodded, weakly.

She stood up. "Finish your supper. I'll get that and wash mine, and be on the sofa."

Five minutes later, he joined her, having washed out his own bowl and spoon and the butter knife, before putting them all away. He found Charlotte on the sofa, her feet tucked up under her, her shoes off beside the sofa, a book in her hands. "You read a lot." Then, before she could take it as an insult, he hurried to add, "I like that."

She looked up and smiled. "I do. Books have all sorts of things in them, things I'm never going to get to do, because you can't actually do all the things in the world. And some of them I wouldn't want to experience. Anyway. More time for reading later. You have plenty to keep me entertained."

He realised then how artificial this must feel. Stuck in a cottage, not much she could do, certainly none of her own particular interests, or her own things. "You do art. I can rummage out a spare notebook and some pencils. I'm sure I have some in the lab?"

Something in her lit up, a glowing smile. "I'd like that very much, if you can run to a rubber, too. I understand all the best artists continue to need them, but I need one rather a lot."

How she put that made Lewis smile. "Fairly sure I've got one too. I'll look tonight." Then he swallowed, because if he didn't ask, he wasn't sure she'd press the point, and now he'd had it laid out for him, he needed to know more. "What's Morgen doing that is near enough coercion?"

"Her thing - it's her and Gareth, and a few other people who've been around for a while - is all pseudo-Arthurian. You'd probably figured that out by now?"

Lewis coughed. "I am known for being oblivious to things that aren't perfumes, but even I had figured that one out, yes. Though there's no actual Arthur or Gwenevere or Lancelot, is there?"

Charlotte shook her head. "Not that I've heard of. And that's an interesting question, isn't it? As is Morgen choosing that name. Anyway, it's not as if I'm at all in her confidence, but she was obviously much more interested in Victor than in me. I'm just a side effect."

"Victor's your friend, you said." Lewis had been chewing on that. "And you're engaged?"

"Near enough. We made a promise back when, in tutoring school, that if neither of us had someone we wanted to marry, we'd marry each other. He's funny, and when he's not stuck in careless mode, he's kind, and he's got rather a lot on his shoulders, family expectations." Charlotte shrugged.

"What's he like in, um?" He didn't know how to ask that. "Never mind that. Morgen's using the things I give her how?"

Thankfully, Charlotte didn't press him on the question. Lewis couldn't make sense of how she talked about him. Like a slightly foolish younger brother, maybe, and that didn't seem the right sort of intimacy for a marriage. Or a partnership. Lewis didn't understand romance, but he understood how working with someone, as a partner, worked. Not every version of it, but he'd seen enough apprentices come and go, or how they sorted out into working groups, plus his time at school.

Charlotte shifted a little. "There was this fancy dinner. Not fancy in the food, though that was fine. Actually, the food's been quite good. Whoever she got as a cook knows their work." She gestured at the pantry. "Like what you get, just well done. But there was a lot of pomp and fuss, and there was something in the air to make it easier to fall into it. That's not the iffy one."

"All right." Lewis wasn't sure where this was going.

"The next night, there was more of a meditation. They're a fad, in some circles, some sort of glorious, fantastic scene. And this one, we were supposed to find ourselves in some Arthurian space. Most of the people there, they've been through a divination session with her, and then they get granted an Arthurian name. I think when they actually formally make the oaths to join the group? But I'm not sure. It's just me and Victor who haven't, right now. There was a pair who did."

"A couple, together?" Lewis asked.

"That's the thing. They're encouraging people to pair off very deliberately, but it's all rather assigned. Bedivere was squiring me around. And Caradoc was dancing atten-dance on Victor." She looked up, and his face must have done something. "Victor's gay." She glanced at him briefly, then went on. "Homosexual. Only wants to be in bed with other men. I've known since we were eleven, it's fine with me."

"Oh." Lewis coughed. "All right. I can see how the

incense would, y'know, make people more suggestible. And she had me make things for people that would make it affect them less. It's hard with incense, of course, everyone is breathing it in. Easier to affect just one person with something on their skin."

Charlotte nodded. "Do you know if she's putting things in the food? If you're making things that would go in food or drink?"

"Nothing illegal. But the same sort of suggestible things, yes. And they do sort of stack on top of each other, but they're not entirely reliable. People have different reactions to them. Gareth was upset. You didn't seem to be affected."

"I haven't actually done proper testing, but the couple of times I know someone's given me something like that, it hasn't affected me as much. It's a little like some people get tipsy or drunk faster, and some people slower?" She shrugged. "Gareth gave me tea that tasted odd, but I don't know if it was the taste or some hint of the magic. I didn't drink much of it."

"Gareth was very annoyed. He asked me to make up something for your room. And then sat there glowering at me while I did." Lewis shook his head. "He's very good at glowering. I'm sure he practises."

"He was all smarmy at me. I'm quite sure he practises that too." Charlotte shrugged again. "Anyway, I was almost sure there was something in my tea, that last afternoon. Before I woke up in the maze."

"I didn't make anything like that." Lewis was now, however, distracted. "Morgen wanted something special. For May Eve. It's not exactly illegal? But she's been really taken with the love philtre from Tristan and Iseult."

"Because that story ends so happily for everyone

involved." Charlotte grimaced. "I mean, there are ways it's better than Arthur and Lancelot and Gwenevere? It's not like Tristan and Iseult were entirely acting from free will? But it's not the sort of thing I'd want to model my life choices on."

"It, um. It needs virgin blood." Lewis blurted it out.

"Of course it's the sort of thing that does. And obviously you're not getting that from Gareth or Morgen or any of them." Then her eyes narrowed. "What happens if it's not virgin blood? Does it not work? Can it be a virgin horse or something? Not that that helps, given we don't have any horses handy, never mind any idea about their experience. Nor sheep nor cats nor anything else that might pass."

"It works oddly? Not as well, more like a soporific? But they'd..." Lewis swallowed. "They know mine would work. That's part of why they picked me, instead of other people."

Charlotte leaned forward, covering one of his hand with hers, and that startled him so much he didn't pull away. "Lewis, I'm fairly sure that was a side benefit. They picked you because they could manipulate you, because of your brother. And they didn't care about hurting him, or hurting you. If they'd had more care for you, they'd have you somewhere you could write to him freely, or whatever, at the very least. Give you a key to the warding."

"I don't really want to go out." He then looked down at her hand. She still didn't move it.

"Talk to me more about what non-virgin blood does. I suspect there's a bunch of standing enchantments, at least in the rooms they use most often for gatherings. Is what you're making a potion, a scent, an incense?"

"A perfumed oil, something that can be touched to everyone. You could put it in an oil warmer, too, with a candle? It'd scent the air then. A lighter effect, but it'd multiply the effect of the oil on the skin, most likely." Lewis considered. "I think it might negate standing enchantments, but it might take a bit. An hour or three? Depending on how much was put out."

"Well, then. That's one solution."

Lewis did not know what she meant.

CHAPTER 22
APRIL 22ND IN THE COTTAGE

Charlotte had learned quite early how to read the signs of someone who had too much to think about to be any good at talking about any of it. Mostly, it was Gabe, who showed it differently, but this was definitely a transferable skill.

Last night, she'd seen Lewis hit that point, and she'd simply nudged him off toward his lab and said she'd see him tomorrow. He'd gone without complaint or comment. Not that he actually complained that much. She was beginning to think that he actually had a serious deficit in the complaint department, seeing as there were plenty of things reasonable people would dislike in his situation, even if he did find being left alone to work entirely appealing. They were not actually that good at leaving him alone.

She'd spent the early evening rearranging the pantry. It was obvious that however precise Lewis might be in the lab, he didn't care about the pantry. She might as well make it easier on herself. Not that she'd seen the lab, which was also fine. People were protective of their spaces, and anyone who dealt with dozens or maybe hundreds of small, nearly identical bottles would be even more so.

By the time she'd got done with that, she was actually tired, and she'd fallen asleep with a book in her hand and the charm light still going. When she woke up, around eight in the morning, the light had gone out. She hadn't heard Lewis come in, which was interesting. She had the last two nights, but maybe she didn't think he was anything to worry about now? Or maybe he was just very quiet. Or both. Both could be true.

She took herself out for a walk around the large field. Charlotte didn't expect anything had changed, and it hadn't. Then, she went up and into the maze, to see if she heard anything. No one was conveniently near the hedges, but she did take a few minutes to explore something one of the books in the dining room had suggested. It involved more or less using the nearby Fatae portal or whatever it was to brace against and pull the magic just slightly out of alignment to undo the annoying and unreasonable bits.

Not that the book had put it that way. But she could hear Gabe's voice in her head, dissecting it. He could probably have done it right away. It was the sort of magic he excelled at. She wished he was here, or at least that he knew there was something wrong. They'd talked about what to do if she had no means of communication - they'd expected that, honestly, given the prohibition on having her journal. But they hadn't guessed she'd end up somewhere she couldn't get out of at all.

By the time she came back to the cottage, Lewis had apparently come and gone again, disappeared back into the lab. He'd left his mug for his morning tea drying, and two of the rolls were gone, as well as some of the cheese. He'd left a single potato on the counter, which made her blink. It took her far too long to realise he'd meant it as a hint. Back into the pantry she went, and there were her blouse and skirt, folded into a towel, all cleaned and pressed.

It made her smile, and she went to put them on first thing. After a moment's thought, she left the clothes she'd borrowed at the top of the stairs, just to the side. They wouldn't look terribly out of place there if people came back. She kept his borrowed jumper, that was comfortable.

Once Charlotte had redistributed clothing, she realised Lewis must not have taken enough food to keep him going through a heavy day of alchemical whatever. She set to work making up more things he could grab quickly. Once she had a plate of sandwiches under stasis, she grabbed one for herself and settled in to do more reading. Maybe she could figure out a way to do something useful. If she didn't, at least she was keeping herself busy.

Keeping herself extremely busy, as it turned out. She kept reading through the afternoon, snagged another sandwich, ignored the sunset, and she was still reading when she heard steps behind her and a cough. "Pardon?"

She wheeled around, and there was Lewis. His hair was going about three directions, but he immediately reached up and smoothed it down. "Oh. Lewis. What time is it? And thank you for my clothes. Yours are at the top of the stairs."

Lewis blinked at her, as if that were entirely not what he'd been thinking about. "Um. All right." Then he cleared his throat. "You said there was a solution for the oil that Morgen wants. What did you mean by that, please?" He sounded incredibly cautious, as if he'd been working out one set of maths, but was certain he'd been working on the wrong problem set entirely.

"Oh." She dragged her own head back to this topic, rather than chasing down references in her head. "Use blood, not from a virgin." She thought that was fairly obvious, and she wasn't sure where Lewis had got caught up.

He flushed bright red, looking down. "I - they expect me to use mine." Oh, that put a different lampshade on it. Charlotte was trying to figure out what to say in response, something that would be kind and not shaming, when he looked up again. "And I thought you couldn't mean that. Fixing that. Changing that. I don't even know what the right word is."

"Right." Charlotte swallowed. "It wasn't exactly what I'd meant, but if you'd like to talk about that as a solution, we can do that. Um. Sofa? Definitely more comfortable than being here, staring at the floor. On the sofa, you can stare across the room and not look at me if you need to, and not get such a crick in your neck."

"Um." Lewis didn't argue. That was a kindness. She waited for him to start moving that direction, then followed him, letting him sit down before she joined him on the sofa, a reasonable sort of distance away. She neither wanted to shove herself against the arm, nor be too close for him to be comfortable. Fortunately, this was exactly one of the things she had been taught how to manage, and so she picked a reasonable six inches. All right, not for this exact reason, but it was right on the edge of the intimate space, without pressing that boundary.

Lewis was, in fact, staring off across the room, rather deliberately. Charlotte cleared her throat. "All right. Here we are, and I'm going to say right out, I'm glad to talk about this. Or glad's an odd word. But I'd much rather talk it out with you than have you worrying about something, or thinking you're going to offend me, or something like that. Talking's better."

He didn't look at her. "Why are you being like that? People don't talk to me, I don't know what to do with it."

"The usual way talking works is we take turns saying things, and we listen when we're not saying something, and we check in if something doesn't make sense. Like, well. Let's start right in the middle. You thought, do I have this right, that I was suggesting going to bed with you?"

He flushed again. "Yeah." He was usually precise in his pronunciation. She'd noticed that, the crispness of someone who was anxious about doing things right. "But then I realised you couldn't have meant that."

There were about eight things there that needed dealing with, but she had to start somewhere. "Can you promise to hear me out before you say whatever you say next? There are several parts here." He nodded, still not twisting to face her. "First, I was suggesting you use my blood. I'm not a maiden or a virgin. No unicorns for me, if they worked like legend, and I'm none too convinced about that, but that is an entirely different discussion. We can have it sometime later, if we actually want to." She pitched her tone to be amused and was rewarded with his mouth quirking into a little smile. "Ready for the next bit?"

He nodded once, looking more uncertain now.

"Second, while it wasn't what I was thinking of when we talked yesterday, I'd be glad to talk about going to bed with you, if that's something you're interested in. But I don't want to assume what you want." Honesty led her to add, "And while I think I'm willing, it's still a new idea to me, since walking across the room. So give me a minute to catch up with it and what I'd like to make sure we talk about that's relevant."

That got Lewis to actually almost laugh, the sort of snort that was impossible to entirely repress.

"And third, this probably goes without saying, but I like the idea of going to bed with you rather a lot more than I liked the idea of Bedivere." She wrinkled up her nose. "I'm fairly sure he has ideas about how it's supposed to go, and won't be budged from them." She let out a breath. "All right, now I'm going to stop talking and you can, and I'll listen?"

There was a dense sort of silence. Charlotte mustered all her skills to stay quiet and not fuss, not twitch her fingers. It mattered right now that she paid attention, and that she didn't get in his way. Finally, his voice creaked, "You'd actually, with me?"

"If you want to." She took a chance then, twisting a little to look at him more directly. "You're surprised?"

"No one's wanted. Or even suggested. People made fun. Just good for potions for other people's pleasure, all that." Lewis was still looking across the room, then he glanced at her for just a second before looking away again.

"Right. Well. Here are some more things to think about. Fourth, I've been to bed with other people, and I like..." She frowned. "This is odd to talk about, all right? I mostly don't. But I like figuring things out in bed, with someone. What it's like with them. It's never been a big romantic gesture, what we're going to be for the rest of our lives or anything like that, out of a story. So if that's what you want, I won't. Because that wouldn't be fair to you, and it wouldn't be fair to me, and we absolutely shouldn't do something like that while we're stuck living in the same cottage."

It got another of the little sounds from his throat, more or less in agreement. Charlotte went on. "Fifth, I don't know you terribly well. But I know that you pay attention, and you tidy up after yourself - which, trust me, puts you miles ahead of quite a lot of men. You make perfume and do your own distillation, so I'm quite confident you have a delicacy of touch. And from the perfume, I'm guessing there's something you love about the sensual, even if you don't know how to talk about it. Unless it's perfume."

Lewis managed another smile, then carefully shifted his hand without looking at her, closer to where she was sitting on the sofa. She took a breath and then rested her fingers on top of his. Some things didn't need words. They sat like that for a minute, maybe two or three. Finally, he cleared his throat. "How do I know you mean that?"

"That, sorry, there's no magic for. Even the truth-telling magics aren't great on emotional intentions. But if you want to ask me questions, if there are things where asking would help, please do." Charlotte tried to keep her tone even and relaxed, but she could feel his hand under hers. And some part of her was now very curious about what he'd be like in bed, with all that focused attention aimed at her. Also, what he'd be like if he actually relaxed, even just for a few seconds, in pleasure or in satiation. She was fairly sure she could show him a good time. Her past experiences hadn't been romantically passionate, but all four of the men she'd been with had their own particular gifts and interests.

"What would, how would—" Now he glanced up toward the stairs.

"I'd prefer a bed, yes. And some time and quiet. I don't know if you have things you need to keep doing tonight, or when would work for you. When you'd want to. You don't have to decide right now, if you'd rather not. I am, as we've determined, not going anywhere for another week."

Again, there was that half-laugh. "If we're, I mean, if I'm thinking about this seriously, I'm going to be distracted until I do. And actually, I was mostly done. I could start the next step, but it can wait for tomorrow. Better if it does, maybe. The longer steeping time would be a help." There, he was back on alchemy. That was reassuringly ordinary for him.

"There, that's a decision. How about we talk a little longer? You can wash up if you want. Then you can tidy your bedroom or put away anything you don't want me to see while I do the same. And we can see how things go? You can stop any time, you know. And I'll stop and ask if I'm not sure."

There was a long silence again. A waiting silence. Finally, he said, "What if you don't want something?"

"Lewis. I'm quite sure if I made a startled noise, you'd stop, never mind anything more energetic. I should, um. Tell you that if this goes well, I am going likely to make some startling noises, but I will do my best to make my enthusiasm clear in the moment." Charlotte twisted a little more now, settling her fingers to interlace with his. "I can protect myself, but I'm sure I won't need to."

"Because I'm not dangerous." There was something heavy and painful there.

"Because you're a decent human being, you've made it clear you don't want me to be hurt, and you didn't give me up to Gareth and all." Charlotte squeezed his hand. "Would you rather talk about what we might do here, or upstairs?"

"Upstairs." It was out of his mouth on the heels of her question. Then he ducked his chin. "I should go wash up?"

"You should go wash up. And I'll put together some snacks or whatever to bring up, just in case we want something."

He stood, slipping his hand out from under hers, taking a few steps toward the kitchen, like he was sure she'd disappear. Some moment of Orpheus and Eurydice, where looking back changed the world. Charlotte stayed where she was until she heard him close the door to the bathing room. When he came out again, she was almost done with a plate of cheese and two of the rolls and some dried fruit. He went past her, blushing furiously, and she thought she'd best give him a few more minutes. "Let me know when you're ready. I'll be a few washing up." There, he could work with that.

CHAPTER 23
THAT EVENING, UPSTAIRS

Lewis didn't know what to do with himself. He heard the water running downstairs, then it stopped and there was silence. He'd tidied up - not that there was much of that to do. Next, Lewis charm cleaned the clothes she'd left, and pulled out a clean set she could wear next time she wanted a change. The books were neatly in piles or even on the shelves, not all over the place or on the bed. It wasn't as if he could spruce the place up on no notice, or have flowers or something of the kind. Besides, she'd made it clear she didn't want the romance of it. He'd lit two of the charmlights, ones he could dim from the bed, leaving the room lit but not bright. He wasn't sure he could deal with bright, with being that visible.

He didn't understand that, either. Lewis figured he didn't need to understand how it worked for her. He just had to be clear about what she was willing to do and what she wasn't. But it didn't make sense to him how she could just blithely be with someone and then wander off. Mother would have talked about sex - if she'd mention the word, which she wouldn't - as a thing that created a bond. And

Charlotte didn't seem like the sort who'd be untidy about a magical bond.

But she'd been decisive about it. She'd done this before, and presumably she was fine with how it worked out. It wasn't like Lewis had any experience to argue from. That was part of the point. Thinking about that, though, got him distractingly aroused, without even getting any specifics.

He'd assumed that he'd go along in his life. Maybe Mother would find someone who was willing to marry him and keep house. For Lewis and Theo, maybe. If he could establish himself as an independent perfumer and build up a clientele, a reasonable flat in Trellech or a small house in some village would be within the realm of possibility. But he'd assumed, apparently, that it would be a sisterly sort of relationship. It would be someone who married him because it was reasonable for her, without a lot of mutual attraction or passion there. He certainly hadn't imagined anyone would want to go to bed with him without some assurance of ongoing security.

Charlotte didn't need any of that. She came from money and property. She didn't fuss about it, though, like a lot of the Schola women of her class had. Charlotte talked to him like a person with skills she was interested in. Not like someone who she'd use like a tool and discard. That phrasing made him shiver again, because parts of it, wasn't that what their agreement was? A mutual benefit, for different reasons. That was a thing for tools.

Now he was just tangling himself up entirely. Fortunately or unfortunately, he'd run out of time. He could hear her coming up the steps first, the way the second stair creaked. First her head appeared, then the rest of her. The bed was at an angle to the stairs, the foot near where they came out, and Lewis was right in the middle of the foot.

She'd just taken her hair down, and she was shoving something - the hair tie, maybe - in the pocket of her skirt and shaking the braid out. He hadn't seen her with her hair fully loose, and it was gorgeous.

People - Mother included - talked about long hair as a woman's magical glory. There was all sorts of lore about it. Right now, at this moment, Lewis was sure it was all fake. It was just there to give people a chance to talk about how stunning it was, in polite company. The lights caught on it, shimmering golden and with something more like new-minted copper without a hint of patina. It fell in loose waves down to her waist, like a cloak made of enchantment.

Charlotte smiled at him, then took a look around. Him first, then the room, then back to him. She didn't look him directly in the eye, she just came over. "May I join you?"

He nodded, feeling how jerky his movements were now. He didn't know where to look, or what to do with his hands, or even what to say. If he looked, he'd stare. He could reach for her, but he'd want to grab hold of her. If he tried to talk, he'd blurt out some part of what he was thinking, and that would be chaos.

"Before anything else. I use a contraceptive charm. And I had a proper check with the Healers, my yearly, last month. I don't know if you were worrying about any of that."

He should have been, but he hadn't been. It was good to know he didn't actually need to. Lewis was sure she was telling the truth, though if someone had asked him, he wouldn't have known how to explain it.

Then, even more gently, she asked, "May I touch you? Your hand, maybe your face?" He managed another nod, just as uneven. A moment later, he felt her fingers brush his, right hand to right hand, so it twisted her body toward him. Lewis tried to just be with it, to summon all the patience and attention he'd given to learning scents, letting them sink into him and change over time as they developed. He knew how to do that. He had so much practice with it.

She just let her fingers move, exploring. A hand was simple enough. People touched hands all the time, in handshakes, in the lab handing things over, in buying something from a shop. He hadn't had much touch of any kind in ages, though. Even Morgen had mostly avoided it. Morgen was overwhelming, though, when she did. Morgen's touches claimed things that weren't hers and stole them away.

Charlotte's were something else. Mother had never been terribly maternal about touch, not as long as Lewis could remember, though she probably had been when he was very small. It wasn't like Theo or one of the cousins clapping a hand on his shoulder. It wasn't the precise touches of one of the journeymen in the Ayletts' lab, guiding his hands. Her fingers weren't moving like she was petting an animal, not exactly, but it was maybe more like art. He thought of what it might be like to be her paintbrush, the changes in pressure and the damp of the watercolours, and he shivered. He couldn't help it, and then he flushed. Of course she'd see it and feel it and know it.

Her fingers hesitated for just a moment, then they went on. "You're nervous. That's normal. Very human. I don't want you to be scared, but I like that you're anticipating this. That you don't take it for granted, not one bit."

"How could anyone?" It burst out of him like a wave crashing over a pier in a storm. "You're right there, your hand is..." His voice caught in his throat. "I don't know what to do."

She just breathed for a moment, like she had all the

time in the world for this. "Am I right that you've got a lot of thoughts all tumbling over each other? And you're not sure which it's all right to say, or what to do?"

He nodded, a little less jerky this time.

"How do you begin to build a perfume? There are the base notes, the middle notes, the top notes. Things that make harmonies and accords, I know that much." The fact she was so deliberately looking for the language that made sense to him made his heart do flips. He could hear it pounding now. Not that it was hard to guess, but she was doing it, and no one else bothered.

It did give him something to anchor to. "A perfume for you? That is you?" That came out before he entirely meant it to. Her only answer was to reach with her other hand to cup his cheek. It wasn't erotic. Well, not more erotic than her hand on his fingers, not intentionally. It felt steady, and he hesitantly leaned into it a bit. That gave him the courage to say, "I was thinking about your hair. How beautiful it is, the way the light catches it, how to evoke that in scent."

"There you go then. Start with that." Then she smiled. He saw that, though he was mostly looking at the top of her right shoulder now. "Then work your way down, mm? Undressing me is fine. Asking me to do it is also fine." She hesitated for just a moment, then added, "I left off my underthings. They're rather tedious to undo, especially if you're not sure how they attach."

It meant her skin was bare under the silk of her blouse and her skirt. That brought him back to the full force of what he was apparently about to do, to a pulsing hardness that drove everything else out of his head for a dozen thumps of his heart. She didn't move either hand, just waited through it. Finally, he cleared his throat. "And me?"

"I thought I'd undo what you undo on me, unless you

want something else. Slower, faster." Her head tilted slightly, and that hand slipped from his cheek down to brush his shoulder. "I'm curious what you look like under your clothes. Lean, and - you're sort of like an engraving, the clarity of the lines."

No one had ever called him an engraving before. He ducked his chin. "Aren't there naughty engravings?"

"There are!" Now she sounded delighted. "Not that I've seen the widest range of them, of course, but I've seen a few. Perhaps if things go well, you'd let me try my hand at a few sketches along that line?"

She seemed to mean it. Lewis had no idea what to do with that, either. Everything was overwhelming, but she'd given him a clear instruction. He moved his right hand from under hers, then his left, reaching to the second button on her blouse. She'd left the top one open, with a narrow V of pale skin. It was still April, even if she seemed the sort of person to enjoy the outdoors. He went on to the third, before she spoke again.

"The other thing, of course, is kissing. Would you like that?" It seemed far more intimate, emotionally intimate, than touching, at least the touching so far.

"A middle note, maybe, kissing?" He might be coming up with a theory on how to build this moment into a perfume. If her hair, her face, her voice were the top notes, the things that showed first that glowed and glimmered and sparkled. The base note was what they were leading toward, the carnality of sex and musk and indoles that were all about bodies. Or so people said, and so he was coming to understand much better.

She smelled fresh. Like the soap in the bathroom, of course, that's what she'd been using, which had herbs in it. It blended with something still in her hair, a hint of almond and some sort of scented oil that hadn't quite faded or been washed out. And then, yes, there were the smells of what she'd been doing, cooking - more herbs - a hint of tea, a little milk.

When that train of thought released him, he looked up and met her eyes. "How - how does kissing work best?"

"You do ask good questions. There being a number of ways to kiss. I was thinking, wondering..." Her voice trailed off, suddenly breathy. "What would you think if I sat in your lap? It'd help the height, and I - I'd like to touch you more. And you could touch me. My back, my front..." She didn't explicitly say her breasts, but that rather strongly implied it. "Work on undoing a few more buttons."

He could only manage to nod, and to shift a bit to give her room. "Um. Show me what you're thinking." Doing was easier than words, though he liked how she was explaining the options in words first.

"You tell me if something doesn't feel good. Or if you're not sure. Please?" That had a more urgent note in it, something she was twining herself around. He nodded, and then she was straddling him. Suddenly he could feel her weight, settling to kneel with one leg on either side of his thighs. The warmth of her was right there. He was shockingly hard now. She had to realise that, though she wasn't doing anything that drew attention to it. Instead, as soon as she was balanced, most of her weight on her shins, she got a hand back on his shoulder. "Kissing now?"

It was a plea, like he might turn her down. Everything was overwhelming, everything was glowing, and he just managed another nod before she leaned in. Her mouth met his, at an angle, so their noses didn't collide. Then her other arm came up around his shoulders. He didn't know if she'd meant to be gentle, but it didn't stay gentle. Not on her part, and not on his. Instants later, his arms were around her back, like they knew what to do when his head had no idea. His mouth was opening, feeling her tongue, the way she moved.

The way her hips were moving, too. She was shifting back and forth, and now she was pressing against him. It made his breath catch before he was kissing her more and more urgently. There was nothing but her, nothing but responding, nothing but figuring out how they fit together right now, and making a blend that was something new and fascinating.

He didn't realise in time what was happening. It might have been seconds, it might have been minutes, but all of a sudden, he could feel heat and need bubbling up, with no way to hold it back. Lewis was clutching at her. His hips were bucking up against her, rude and primal and demanding something that wasn't going to happen. Then he could feel himself exploding into heat and damp and pulses of more into his trousers and against her clothes. He whimpered, pulling back and dropping onto the bed, unable to hold any part of himself up. He'd have run away with the shame of it, only he couldn't move.

She instantly settled to one side, an arm draped over his chest, then he felt her kiss his cheek, just once, gently. "There's a nice start." Her voice was a purr, a deeply contented cat, as if she were utterly satisfied with what had just happened. That made no sense at all, not in all the stories he'd heard about sex, about what a man's part was supposed to be.

"I, I, um."

"You threw all of yourself into it. Into feeling it. Didn't hold anything back. It turns out I like that very much." Her fingers traced down the side of his cheek. Absolutely an intimate gesture rather than a soothing one. "And I'm quite sure that in a little while, we'll work ourselves up again nicely, and you can show me a good time. Or if you're not ready for that, you can watch me make a good time for myself. If you want."

That, the straightforwardness of it, made him blink. "I, um?" Same words as before, but an entirely different intonation. She made sense of it, somehow.

"I expected it might take you like that. Or at least there was a good chance at it. There are a lot of new things all at once, and some of them are a bit awkward. That wasn't awkward at all, that was a lot of enthusiasm. Enthusiasm is excellent. Would you like some more?"

Lewis let his head fall back on the bed, weakly. Then, cautiously, he nodded.

"Grand. Maybe both of us more up on the bed, and working our way to less in the way of clothes? I suppose it's excellent you're so good with cleaning charms." Charlotte was utterly matter of fact about it, in a way that made Lewis blush and then feel himself growing hard again. Rather than try to say anything, he shifted, pushing himself up along the bed so his head was on the pillows. She moved with him, immediately settling to drape a hand over his chest again, very much as if she wanted that more than anything else.

"Do you, um? Yourself, often?" Now he was blushing again, but she didn't seem to mind.

"It's reliable. It's not as if I have someone handy I'm interested in going to bed with all that often. Do you?"

He nodded. "I was told it's more usual for men?"

"Some people don't think women should have any fun. And a lot of people think that just because our bodies are different in some ways, we don't like the same kinds of pleasures." Charlotte's shoulder twitched in a shrug. "It's like singing. I like singing with people. There's something about it. But I also like singing by myself. Or riding, or whatever other hobby there might be."

"Oh." He let himself lie there, her fingers just gently brushing his cheek, then slowly moving to undo a button of his shirt. She was only using one hand, so it went slowly, and he thought that might be on purpose.

Somehow, without either of them directly saying anything, they both slowly undid their clothes, taking their time with it. Charlotte had talked about his body with apparent interest, but hers was amazing, toned muscle in places, curves in others. She didn't have the sort of body that was currently fashionable, he thought. That didn't matter to him. Once she'd tossed her blouse aside, he couldn't stop running his hands over her skin, cupping her breasts, then sliding his hand down to the curve of her hip.

Finally, all the clothes were in a pile beside the bed, tumbled over each other to be dealt with later. Only when that was done did she take his hand and draw it down between her legs. There was dampness there, and a slickness that was a little like some of the perfume preparations, not a gel but not water. "There, that shows I want this. That I'd like very much to feel you touch. And that I'm ready when you want to slide into me." They'd been both on their sides, but now she shifted to end up on her back. "Unless you'd like some other position?"

There she was, laid out, her hair spread on the pillow, framing her face, her body entirely on display. He grunted, suddenly needy again, and her smile lit up the world. "Mmm, yes. This will do then. Later, if you like, we can try other things."

The idea there might be more, sometime later, that she

was just flinging that out there without any warning, made him whimper. Before he could panic again, she tugged one hand to the side. "Lean here. And your other hand here, and rock against me a little, get a feel for it. When we're ready, I'll help you find the right place."

"I.... will you, how do you, how do I do what you like?" That came out of him in a babble. While she obviously had found some pleasure with this, he didn't think she'd come close to her own climax.

"I'll show you. Bend down, kiss me. We know we like that." He could take that sort of instruction, lowering himself to one elbow. He fit between her legs the way civet did, something prowling and exalting everything it touched. And then there was the beauty, that was all rose and jasmine, lush florals that came from nowhere and couldn't be grabbed at, just enfolding him. Them.

Then he was kissing her, giving all his attention to that and the way it felt to have her move against him. What it was like to have weight in the mix, to know he was pressing against her. His hips began to move, without him making the choice, and her head came back for an instant, with a gasp of sudden pleasure. He did his best to do more of that, to lean into the movements without changing too much and making the angles all wrong. He could feel how he slid against her skin, how they were both increasingly damp, in a way that made everything slide easily.

Before he was aware of it, her hand shifted, then he could feel her guiding him, precisely as a pipette into a narrow vial. Whatever he'd expected, it wasn't this. He slipped in, filling her faster than he'd meant to. Her head went back. He heard her moan as her hips arched up, one leg coming around his thigh as if she wanted to pull him closer still.

"Oh, yes. You feel so good." It should have been inane, and it wasn't. Hesitantly, not wanting to pull too far out, he shifted a little before rocking into her again. "That, yes, just like that. Please." There was a pleading note in her voice, now, and he didn't know how he'd done that. Or if it had been him. He hoped it was him, that he'd found something that made her feel like he felt. Everything was buoyant, nothing mattered in all the world but the pleasure of the moment, and the way it was just the two of them.

It took him a little to figure out a rhythm. Then he was rocking in and out of her, steadily at first, until he risked bending to kiss her skin. Not her lips, that would be too complicated, but little brushes of lips against her cheek, her neck, her shoulder, the top of her breast. Her head was thrown back, her eyes half-lidded, and now she was moaning and gasping, reacting every time he filled her, whimpering here and there when he pulled back.

Somehow, it built up, until they were moving faster and faster. It was energetic, in a way he almost never was, using weight and speed and the lever of his arms to move his hips. He could feel it through his back and his thighs. Then she hitched her hips a little and all the angles changed again, so he was driving into her. Her fingers slipped from his hip to where they were joined. "I'm close." She got it out between a gasp and a sharp inhale. "So close. I want to feel you." Her hand twisted against him, touching herself. Her back arched off the bed an instant before he felt her clench tightly around him over and over again, too many times to count.

He shoved himself as deep as he could, holding there as long as he could bear, before he pulled out as her shudders were beginning to slow. Three more thrusts and he felt everything boiling up in him again, a desperate rush to release. Then he was deep in her, feeling himself pulse and explode like nothing he'd ever felt in a wave that washed away every insecurity and awkwardness in its path.

As it passed, he felt weak, barely able to manage to fall to one side, slipping out of her. He heard her make some sound he couldn't parse, then her arm was around him, and he was pillowing his head on her breast, overwhelmed.

CHAPTER 24

APRIL 23RD IN THE MORNING

There was sun in her eyes. Charlotte rubbed them, needing a moment to remember where she was. And why there was sun in her eyes, making her want to quote John Donne and pound a hand into the bed. Then she paused. Why was she like this? Unruly sun or not, first the poem was from a man to a woman, and the man in this picture was, where was he? She rolled over. The man in question was not only not in the picture, he was not in the room. And possibly hadn't been in the room for a while. His side of the bed had a dent in the pillow, but no residual warmth in the sheets.

She rubbed her face again, trying to get the sleep out of her eyes, and took stock. Lewis was not here. Her clothes were neatly folded beside the bed. Another stack had a set of his trousers and a shirt, as well as what might be a dressing gown when it was unfolded. She appreciated that.

Second, the poem was inaccurate because they had gone to bed for entirely different reasons than wanting to be the centre of each other's worlds. She had been clear about what was on offer. He had agreed to it, just as directly. She liked his directness. She knew where she stood with him. Perhaps the poem had just come to mind because of the alchemy reference. That made sense.

Charlotte stopped to see if she could hear anything from downstairs. Given that he'd apparently been gone for a bit, she expected he was in the lab, and would appear at some point more or less around a meal. Mostly because she would make sure there was a meal when he did appear. Even if that was circular logic or the ouroboros of time, or whatever label she wanted to put on it.

Besides, it gave her time to think about last night. She had been telling the truth, clearly, about the fact Lewis was going to be much better than Bedivere had seemed likely to be. She'd had a tremendously good time. Helped perhaps by the amount of time she spent on horseback, or she suspected her thighs and back would be complaining more. It had been, what, more than a year, since the last vigorous round of sex.

Had it really been that long? She counted back, using both her fingers and the various memorable moments. Just around when Gabe had gone up to Scotland, yes. A year. That was no good. She'd obviously missed that kind of romp a great deal, given how she felt right now. As if the world was, all right, she'd be fair, wreathed in sun. Not just that it was shining down on her from the single skylight window.

After a moment's consideration, she decided a bath was more important than a meal. She'd slept incredibly well, but now she could feel all the residual effects of having fallen deeply asleep without cleaning up. Bath, food, and then figuring out the meals for the rest of the day. Charlotte leaned over to rummage for the dressing gown, coming up with a rather lovely if well-worn robe of soft flannel. She took it and the clean trousers and shirt down to the bathing room and soaked for a bit.

Leaning her head back in the tub made her think about his reaction to her hair. The thing of it was, she had fairly ordinary hair, by her standards. It wasn't the shimmering pale blonde or black that drew the eye. It certainly wasn't the striking auburn of Aunt Kate's, or even the sort of rich woody brown. And yet, Lewis had been very taken with it.

And with the rest of her. Blast. She was going to have a hard time not thinking about that and wanting to stroke herself to another climax. It hadn't exactly been about what he did, though he'd turned out to have a lovely dexterity with his fingers once he got over his nerves. She'd told the truth - she kept telling him the truth - when she'd said it was his enthusiasm that got to her. He'd been entirely present with her, nothing in his world but her and her body and what they were doing together. Charlotte wanted to get drunk on that over and over again, and that was exceedingly unlike her.

Her growing hunger got her out of the tub, rather than lingering and thinking about last night. Once she dried off, she set about boiling some eggs. They'd make a good snack or part of a meal, whenever they were wanted later, and they still had plenty. It was tricky cooking without much of a recipe to work from, but she thought she might try toad in the hole. Aunt Rosemary had taught her.

More to the point, she'd made it recently enough - at supper with them, when they'd both been run off their feet - that she was fairly sure she knew how the batter should go. That would be nice and filling. For lunch, there could be sandwiches. She could do those whenever Lewis appeared. And she could make some scones. If she hadn't been able to do that by touch and sight, Aunt Rosemary would have had words with her.

It wasn't until sometime around one that Lewis reappeared, looking a bit uncertain about things. Her, maybe. Him, probably. He ducked his chin, then straightened his shoulders. "Charlotte. Hope you slept well?" It had the sound of something he'd been practising in his head, but it was satisfyingly pragmatic.

"Very, thank you. I hope you did too? Sleeping, sharing a bed. Some people find it odd the first time? It's a skill like anything else."

Something in that made him smile, the shy little smile he let her see now, every so often. "I did keep waking up. I hope I wasn't, um. Inappropriate."

With a sudden rush of memory, she flashed back to a moment of rolling in bed, barely aware of anything, and of the warmth of him. That was what she'd missed in the morning, as much as being woken by the sun. She shook her head. "Not at all. And besides, we'd just been intimate. Cuddling after is a thing a lot of people like."

He tilted his head, as if she'd just thrown something into the midst of his mental equations. "We didn't talk about that part before. So I didn't know what you wanted. And I fell asleep rather fast."

"You were delightfully energetic. I wasn't surprised. Or offended. Besides, it was all a new thing for you, and new things are so often tiring out of proportion, aren't they?"

He blinked at her several times, before he managed a hesitant nod. "I had an idea for something in the lab. I wasn't sure if it was all right to get up."

"I wouldn't dream of keeping you from your lab. I know better." She smiled as she said it. "Besides, it gave me a chance to have a nice soaking bath, and then figure out food. I appreciate the dressing gown. I hope you have something? And the clean clothes."

Lewis nodded. "I've an older one. But it must be hard not to have any of your own things at all." Then he fumbled in his pocket and brought out a small bottle. "And just the soap and all I use. I put this together. It's a fairly standard hair oil base, but I hope you like the smell? It's nothing complicated, just." He held it out, so she could see the more or less clear golden oil in it.

"For me?" It was a particular sort of gift, but it was a welcome one. At least generally speaking, she had felt her hair snagging on the comb. She opened the bottle delicately, not wanting to spill it, and sniffed at it.

Before she could say anything, there was another burst of words from him. "It isn't - I just wanted something I thought you'd like. It's not what I think would suit you best, that would take a lot more time to put together properly. Just. I wanted something nice."

She looked up to find him a little wide-eyed and worried. She sniffed the oil carefully, finding something that had a hint of the floral. There was nothing overwhelming, along with some definite vanilla or something akin to it, a little cedar, she thought, and half a dozen things she couldn't quite name. "I'd love to learn more about what you chose, when we've a little leisure. There's cedar, yes? And some spring flowers, but I can't tell which ones. And of course it's different in the bottle. May I?"

When he nodded, she untied the tail of her braid, shaking her hair loose before she went to pour a tiny bit, a dozen drops maybe, in her hands. Before she had to figure out where to put it, his hand was there, and she put the bottle there. Charlotte rubbed her hands together, then ran them both through her hair, focusing on the ends. She made sure to get all of it worked through, then shook her hair out. When she looked up, Lewis was smiling, but a different sort of smile. "I don't normally get to see people, you know." He gestured. "Enjoy it?"

She couldn't help beaming at him. "Oh, well, then." She then sniffed at her palms, thoughtfully. Normally you wanted the pulse points for perfume, but now she could smell the range of it. "A little like a meadow, isn't it? I remember reading something about the smell of hay, and that's not this, but it's sort of related?"

Lewis was nearly glowing with pleasure. The ensuing conversation took them through braiding her hair back up, tucking the bottle in the bathing room, and then putting together and eating lunch. Lewis nearly inhaled his, and she diagnosed that he hadn't actually remembered to eat breakfast.

CHAPTER 25
THAT AFTERNOON

L ewis considered, while they were eating. The conversation was delightful. Charlotte didn't have remotely his level of training or experience, of course. But she was far better at listening to what he knew, and asking sensible questions about it, than anyone who wasn't an alchemist he'd talked to. Certainly better than Mother or even Theo, though Theo was always patient with him about it.

Before he could think better of it, as she was clearing the dishes and washing up, he spoke up. "Would you like to come see the lab and talk there for a while? I need to do some more preparation for tonight."

"Tonight?" Charlotte dried her hands off. "And I'd love to. Tell me where I should be to stay out of the way. Or if you need things ground, I'm good with a mortar and pestle." She made a gesture with her hand, which suddenly made an entire set of jokes in his school years drop into place. Metaphor made real, right.

He flushed and ducked into the bathing room. "Minute,

I'll show you." He took his time, washing his hands a fair length under the cool water, not just for the ordinary sanitary reasons. When he came out again, she was leaning against the counter, just waiting agreeably. Still looking exceedingly fit in his clothing. "I, um. It's a good alignment tonight for part of what Morgen wants. A portion of it. And enough time for it to sit before it goes into the final version."

She raised an eyebrow at him. She didn't say anything; she didn't have to. "I don't know what I think about all of it, yet? But I can't make this later, and it has other uses, and ..."

"I wasn't going to stop you." Charlotte said, pushing away from the counter. "So I'll come sit, and make myself useful if I can, and then you'll be in the lab all evening?"

"Until at least dawn. Maybe longer." He hesitated. "You'd be welcome to sleep in the bed tonight. I can put something together downstairs. I had a nap this morning for a bit."

"Very early morning, very late night, I was going to say." Charlotte nodded. "Toad in the hole too stodgy for dinner, then? I was thinking of it, but I can do something lighter."

"Toad in the hole tomorrow?" Lewis said hopefully. It wasn't something he'd eaten terribly often outside of school. Nanny used to make it for them, when they were on holiday at some seaside cottage or another, and his parents were elsewhere.

Charlotte tilted her head, as if she were reading something in his expression. "Tomorrow. And thanks for the bed. You're, um. You're working. You're welcome to sleep there, or kick me out of it when you're ready to sleep, or whatever."

He waved a hand. Tonight, he'd be so tired it wouldn't

matter. He might just sleep on the couch again. Though maybe with a little more padding. It had worked all right for the nap. Or at least it had once he'd stuffed a blanket into the couch so he didn't slowly roll off the curve onto the floor. Instead of stammering again, he opened the door to the cottage and led her off to the lab, pausing to open the warding with his hand and a sigil.

Charlotte nodded approvingly. "Can they get in?"

"It needs three people, if it's not me. Morgen, Gareth, and Mark. Or a talisman Morgen has, but she doesn't bring it out often. Why?" He waved a hand to bring the charm-lights up, then gestured. "The sofa's a good place to sit. I might have something that needs grinding, let me check how things are."

"Oh, just thinking about the proper security, and who has access to materials in progress. Of course you ought, that's sensible. And it's not like Morgen traipses down here all the time."

He busied himself with checking that everything he'd left was doing what it was supposed to. Since what it was supposed to do was sit there and commune with the materia in the oil, and nothing had spilled, that was all set. Once he'd methodically gone through all of that, he turned around to find Charlotte sitting with her feet tucked up under her. She was leaning against the back of the sofa, just waiting.

"I don't know what sort of lab you're used to, other than school?" Lewis asked hesitantly.

"We have one at home. And a separate stillroom, actually. But not perfumes. Gabe's more likely to be doing identification work if he's not trying some off the wall experiment. You know, take something, put it into solution, and then test it against a lot of things to see what resonances you get. But the trick is getting the right solvent. Wax is different than oil is different than I don't know, copper dust."

Lewis snorted. "Right. Some of that's related to some of the modern distillation forms, but not anything I use. It needs a different kind of equipment, for one thing." He considered. "Let me start preparing things. Do you mind if we talk?"

"No?" Her voice went up at the end. She sounded suddenly uncertain. "About what?"

Lewis had been thinking about a lot of things today. Starting with the sex and what she meant by it and what he meant by it, and both were about equally baffling. He'd expected he'd at least have some idea about his own desires, and he didn't. Part of him very much wanted that again, but only if he knew what it meant for her in a lot more detail. So he wasn't going to ask about that. Not right now, anyway. More thinking was definitely required. Instead, he cleared his throat. "Do your parents expect you to marry Victor? I mean..."

He'd turned a little, timing the question to when he had to get something from the shelves along the back that brought her into his line of sight. He might not make sense of her expression, but at least he'd have it as information. It wasn't at all the question she'd expected. That much was obvious, even to him. She pulled one knee up to her chest. Charlotte didn't say anything until he was back at his main work bench with half a dozen small bottles to one side.

"I need to marry someone. And Victor and I get on well. He'll let me spend my time as I like, except for the necessary social obligations. There are a lot of people who wouldn't."

The words had the sort of pace behind them of an argument she'd made over and over again - maybe more in her head than out loud - over months or years.

He didn't turn around this time. "That wasn't what I asked, though."

There was another silence. "Victor's not a bad sort. He's trying to figure himself out. A lot of us are. You've got a thing you're passionate about, that you actually get to do. That's a huge help. And you're good at it. Or at least I'm assuming you are, since I haven't seen any reason to doubt that yet."

"I could be making it all up," Lewis offered.

"You trained with the Ayletts and you're neither dead nor disgraced. I'd know if you were disgraced. Mama and Papa keep up on that kind of thing, so does Gabe. People who get desperate are more likely to do something dangerous to other people. Not that they mean to, but - oh, Mama has a story about something she helped with, back when I was tiny. That was about people adulterating bread and sweets, because they were so worried about money."

"Skimping on ingredients," Lewis agreed. "But you didn't know who I was until you got here."

"I know the list of people to be aware of. And my memory's not like Mama and Papa's, but it's good. And trained." Now she sounded a little more relaxed and amused. "Goes with running a large estate. You can't constantly be going off and checking your notes when talking to someone at a party. I might not always remember the details of why to be cautious with someone. But I do remember the names, and I don't know, a general age and things like that."

Lewis puttered with the vials a little, then went to

work. He began by grinding some of the juniper berries in the mortar and pestle, a pleasantly small physical task. He needed more of the juniper, and the cardamon would likely be easier to grind. "And?"

He heard her cough. "You are insistent." There was another hesitation, but this time more like she was setting out ingredients or whatever one called it when it was words and not materia and oils and bottles. "No. I should marry. There's some complicated inheritances that would make it easier. One of them's settled on Gabe, one on me, and one between us, and if I don't marry, it gets horribly complicated in the next generation. And I don't know." She shrugged. He could hear it, and when he turned around to look over his shoulder, her hands were spread. "You've seen our generation. The one between me and you, mostly."

"Some. Tell me what you're getting at, though?" He turned back to his grinding. "Actually, if I get out another, do you have objections to cardamom?"

"Absolutely not. I love the smell of it. More than the other spices, except maybe nutmeg." Charlotte answered that one promptly.

Lewis set down his own for a moment to get the copper mortar and pestle. He hadn't intended to use it, actually. It wasn't what he needed tonight. But if Charlotte was here, and willing to help, no reason not to have a herb - well, spice - of Venus, and a metal of Venus together. It wouldn't hurt the work for Morgen's oil, and it would let him begin to put together the idea he'd got while they were talking. Well, and last night, too. It was all about last night, fundamentally. "Here you go." She took it, then asked, "Can I stand at one of the workbenches? I'm afraid I'll spill it in my lap."

"This one, here, the other end. And you can pull up that stool if you like." He usually didn't bother. He was back and forth so often, unless he was making the sort of blend that involved sitting there for an hour or so until his nose gave out. "You were saying about our generation?"

"Well, on one hand, we have people - a bit older than me, basically anyone Gabe's age and older - who fought. Or who were doing something else necessary, and a lot of that wasn't very pleasant. Most of whom have the, how do I put this sensibly, the weight of it on them? The scars from it, and a lot that don't show. And a lot that people won't talk about. Not that they should have to. But there are a lot of those folks who are a bit brittle."

"People you know?" Lewis asked it carefully. They'd swum into deep water and he wasn't sure what the right thing was.

"Not brittle, not close in. But Gabe and I have a sort of cousin - not actually related, but Mama and Papa have been helping him out since we were tiny. He had a head injury. It's not bad like some, he's still pleasant, not angry. You know how you count up all the ways it could be tremendously worse? But he's - he's different from how he was. He can't do most of the things he loved doing. And he's still happy, but it's hard to wonder what it could have been like for him."

Lewis almost talked about Theo then, more than the brief explanation he'd already given. Instead, he just nodded. "And others?" A lot implied some who weren't.

"How much have you seen of all of them up at the house?" Charlotte waited just a moment, then went on. "Now, I don't know about what's not visible. But there's not a one of the men with any sort of visible injury. And how often do you walk into a group of men where that's true these days? Who aren't over fifty?"

Lewis grimaced. "I don't."

"You were doing alchemy. There are plenty of individual reasons for it, many of them excellent. Health that wouldn't let them enlist. Skills that were desperately needed elsewhere, like you. Gabe didn't enlist. He broke his ankle six months before the end of the War, and he still uses a cane. Has to keep deciding whether to tell people the truth or let them make false assumptions. He says that's actually the most annoying part."

Lewis was momentarily distracted. "What does he do?"

"Tell the truth. But he doesn't always get a chance. People see him across a room or whatever. Anyway. The group of men in that house is statistically improbable at the moment. And the women aren't a lot better. I'm used to the chatter about what it was like for VADs, or the equivalents, or people doing their bit on the home front, keeping things running. I haven't heard much of that either."

Lewis didn't know what to say to that. After a moment, he settled into talking about something new, about the bits of the history he knew about cardamom. They went from that to other spices - Charlotte knew quite a few not common to British cuisine. By the time it got around to five or so, she paused. "Can I give this back to you, and go make supper? Something light, like I promised. Poached chicken and some veg, likely."

He nodded. "If I turn up in - um. An hour. Does that work for time? I'll even set the hourglass." He didn't usually bother unless he actually needed to time a process, but he had a set of them. He could time anything from five minutes to five hours.

"An hour is grand." She waited for him to take charge of the various items and the mortar and pestle again. Then she was at the door. Just before she slipped out, she stopped. "About Victor. I'm pretty sure I'll never have what Mama and Papa have. I'd rather have something where I know what to expect, given that."

Before he could say anything in reply, she was gone with the door closing smoothly behind her.

CHAPTER 26
APRIL 24TH IN THE MORNING

True to his word, Lewis had appeared for supper. He'd eaten quickly, without any comment on anything they'd talked about earlier, but he asked a couple of questions about what she was reading. A safe topic, and she suddenly wondered why he was so skilled in that. He knew how to talk about things that wouldn't offend, but he did it like he'd learned a skill. Or maybe a dance. He knew all the steps, but he wasn't dancing them terribly freely.

It wasn't like he did his alchemy. He had a degree of precision there that would make Aunt Witt beam in approval, and that was a rather hard thing to come by. She had the highest standards for a lab of anyone Charlotte knew of, even Professor Norton at Schola. But he had a fluidity in the lab - an entirely appropriate term - that wasn't just rote. The way he'd moved through preparing things that afternoon, the way he'd handed her the cardamom, for example. And that was a sensory experience of its own. She'd felt how the copper warmed against her hands as she held the mortar, and how the slip of the pestle ground the pods down to dust, and of course the amazing fragrance it released.

She herself had been a diligent Alchemy student, and she was certainly quite competent in the stillroom at Veritas. They made a fair amount of their own salves and potions and such, for all the household needs. Mama had one that helped her aches, and it was easier to make it on site. And then, of course, she and Mama took batches of useful things around the magical villages regularly, especially all those that needed a bit of a connection for the materia.

At any rate, she'd spent the evening reading. Then she had taken Lewis at his word and curled up in bed upstairs. She thought he'd come up at some point, but when she woke, she was entirely alone. Glancing at the clock, it was about half-eight. After a moment's thought, she got dressed. She went downstairs as quietly as she could, avoiding the stair she'd already learned squeaked.

There was no Lewis in the sitting room - the sofa there looked entirely untouched. And when she peeked into the dining room alcove, there was no sign he'd been there either. After a couple of minutes, she packed up a bit of food, some hard-boiled eggs and cheese and bread, tying it into a tidy little bundle. She thought twice about leaving a note, but where she was going, she'd beat back anyone who came looking from the house. It just said "Lunch at noon?" in block lettering.

Charlotte threaded her way through the gates, into the maze. She didn't have much hope of hearing anything this early in the day, but she thought she might if she spent some time near the lawn side of the maze. And in the meantime, she had a couple of ideas to try to see if she could navigate the maze better, and not get dumped back to the centre again and again. One of the books in the cottage had a small collection of Fatae lore. Charlotte had begun to wonder if the tips about distracting the Fatae tracking charms might work. There were dozens, about wearing a shirt inside out, spinning in place a certain number of times, all that. She had a list. She might as well be deliberate about her testing.

If any of it worked, Gabe - and Aunt Mason and Aunt Witt - would be delighted. If it didn't, at least she'd know she'd tried.

The first part of it took her a good two hours. Turning her shirt inside out didn't work. Looking for bits of stray sod, like one of the tales she'd heard, didn't turn anything up. There weren't any obvious charms or talismans hidden in the bushes near where she started having problems. She didn't have an embroidery kit full of different coloured threads, or rowan wood, or iron nails. Well, there might be some iron nails in the storage cabinets in the courtyard, but that seemed like an unpleasant rummage for several reasons.

But Lewis might have the herbs for what she wanted. And pulling them together into a salve wouldn't take long. There were recipes for clear sight, not to be glamoured. She knew the theory of them. There was an entire line of cosmetics built on the idea. They were fiddly and needed replacing every three months. And to be quite honest, the cosmetic effect wasn't at all as good as other lines. It was evidence of being suspicious, which made them next to worthless in Albion itself, though still potentially of use in other communities.

Right. She couldn't do anything more with that today. She checked the sun, and guessed she had another hour or so. As she'd feared, she didn't hear much of use from the lawn, though she could hear that they were planning something, for tomorrow, apparently. It required a grotto, with some sort of throne or - well. Fancy seating, throne would do for the moment.

By that time, she needed to get back and see whether Lewis had remembered that eating was good for a body. Especially since he'd been doing significant magical work last night, if she'd understood his plans correctly, not just the more physical parts of the process. When she got back to the cottage, he was on the sofa, as if he'd sat down and meant to start moving, and kept failing to do so.

"Sleep enough?" He rubbed his face and didn't say anything.

Charlotte came closer to get a good look at him. "You need lunch. And I'm guessing you don't feel hungry. Do I need to trot out the lecture on magical replenishment, or did you hear it enough at Schola?"

He grimaced, which was a good sign, at least. He tried pushing himself upright, but she waved him back. "Let me put together some soup and some eggs and some bread. And then we'll see what next."

Twenty minutes later, she had dragged a side table to eat from. They both had bowls of brothy chicken soup with ribbons of eggs in it, and a little in the way of green dried herbs, mostly parsley and, of course, some garlic. It went well with crusty bread, hunks of cheese, and mugs of tea. Once he'd eaten most of his bowl, she tilted her head. "More of that, or something else?"

"More of that, please. Not something I've had before?" He glanced at the bowl. "Not quite that flavouring, anyway?"

"A little honey in the broth, along with..." She glanced back at the kitchen. "Some scallions and some garlic."

"Oh." He then held out the bowl. "More of that, please? The broth is very good."

She'd made it two days ago, while he was busy, letting it bubble away and cook down on the stove. Aunt Mason and Aunt Rosemary would be proud of her for that. It was their recipe she'd started with, adjusting for the ingredients on hand, which were aimed at solid British cooking rather than Aunt Mason's Malaysian preferences. Charlotte went and refilled both bowls, bringing them back. "How'd it go last night?"'

"Well, I think. I won't know for a day for sure. You?" Lewis looked up, and she liked that he thought to ask, given that he'd obviously had a gruelling evening. Overnight. Whatever you called it.

"I was going to ask if you could make something, if you'd have time, but..." Her voice trailed off. "You're obviously exhausted."

Lewis looked down, more or less into his soup bowl. "What did you have in mind?"

"I tried a number of counter-enchantments on the maze, something in one of the books gave me an idea. But I don't have the materia for some of it, and what I could try didn't work, and I don't know any of the rituals well enough to attempt them." She looked up to get a look at him, blinking. "I'm better trained than to try rituals I don't fully remember, at least if it's not actually life or death."

"What are you supposed to do then?" Lewis sounded honestly curious.

"Think through which one is least likely to be dangerous if it doesn't work. And which one is most likely to be helpful - that's a combination of skill, my memory, and what it does. Decide from there." Charlotte shrugged.

"You have a very odd family, did you know that?" Lewis said. "All in a couple of seconds, if it's urgent?"

Charlotte grinned. "My family vastly improved my skills in a stillroom, so don't you complain."

"I was not complaining, just baffled." He sounded in much better humour, though, and the fact he was teasing like that was a good sign of his recovery. It was actually Gabe who had brought that bit of understanding home to her. He'd turned up unexpectedly nine months into his apprenticeship, having completely overdone it.

Which, as far as she could tell, meant he'd done about three times what the average Penelope considered reasonable. Even given they were not as a group prone to reasonable measurement on the topic of exertion. She'd got him up to bed, poured broth into him, and sat until she was sure he was on the road back to recovery. Then she'd dragged him down to the baths, more or less by one ear. Mama and Papa had been at the Trellech house. They'd had several days of obligations while Charlotte was home for the spring hols. From what she got out of Gabe - entirely unguarded, and that was also a rare thing in her experience - he hadn't wanted to worry them.

Fortunately, by the time they came home - with a little warning from Charlotte, she was sensible - Gabe was bouncing back. But he'd appreciated the effort, and he'd appreciated how she'd told Mama and Papa about it. Even how she'd let Aunt Mason and Aunt Witt know where he was. On that front, he'd apparently got a lecture of over an hour once he reported for training again. It had been followed a great many reminders about not pushing himself into backlash like that ever again. He had more or less expected that.

It was only that following summer she'd actually asked

what he'd been doing, and why Penelope Doyle, his apprentice mistress, hadn't been there. She'd got hurt - nothing bad, a sprained ankle - and had to seek care. Gabe had seen a way to defuse an increasingly dangerous situation, some sort of intersecting ritual magic that got less stable every time someone looked at it. By the time some additional help had turned up, he'd got it steady enough, and then he'd pretended he was fine for another hour until he was dismissed. At any rate, Lewis was now back to about where Gabe had been when she dragged him out of the baths. That didn't mean he should be encouraged to do anything complicatedly magical for a little.

"I was wondering if you have any of the herbs for seeing through glamours. I was going to ask if you could do a salve or something, but—" She gestured at him. "Not going to ask that today."

"Why?" It wasn't clear whether he was asking why she wasn't asking today, or why she wanted it. A moment later, he clarified. "Why do you want it?"

"They're up to something tomorrow. It involves a grotto and a throne or a fancy chair or whatever it is Morgen calls that thing. Probably a fair bit of impressive illusion. Whatever Gareth's up for that will hold in sunlight. I want to see what they're doing properly, but I also wonder if it'd let us get through the maze. Closer, at least, even if the way out's warded."

Lewis frowned, but it was a thinking sort of frown. "Why weren't you going to ask me today?"

"Look at you. You need rest."

"I've pushed myself like this for Morgen, plenty of times. Probably will again in a couple of days." He hesitated, then added, his voice suddenly softer. "I'd much rather do that for you."

The sheer honesty of it took her breath away, an instant before what it suggested about his feelings hit her. Before she could say anything, he said, a little more loudly. "I could walk you through it. In the lab. You'd do all the work."

Which was an entirely different kind of intimate admission, but she could deal with the complexities of it later. Charlotte really did want more options available to her. "That's fair. You have what you need?"

Lewis counted something out on his fingers. "I'd need a substitute for a couple of things. But I know I've got some St John's Wort, and red verbena. Plenty of clary sage oil and vervain oil." He considered. "Not sure about the clover, though if you wanted to go have a look for a four-leaf clover, that'd be a help."

"There's a charm for that!" That, Charlotte knew. Or at least, she was pretty sure she remembered it. If not, what she needed was the proper formal name of the plant, and she was pretty sure he'd have a book with it.

Lewis nodded, then looked up, cautious again. "If it works, and you can get out, will you?" He stopped and coughed. "I'm sure you'll go. Walk back to the road."

CHAPTER 27
THAT AFTERNOON IN THE LAB

L ewis said it, knowing she'd say yes immediately. She'd wanted to leave as soon as she'd got here. Why wouldn't she? She was trapped, and on top of that, it couldn't be entirely pleasant to be trapped with him. Or without any of her own things, in a curious sort of charitable obligation that she couldn't refuse. He didn't much like feeling on the other side of it either. He wanted to give her things and make her smile, but he wanted it to be for different reasons. Ones without obligations or necessity.

Anyway. Of course she'd leave when she could.

Much to his surprise, she didn't say anything for a moment. When she spoke, it was measured. "Let me go have a look for a four-leaf clover, and we can talk about what to do with the salve while I do the preparations. How's that?" It was practical, delivered in the sort of no-nonsense tone that half reminded him of Mistress Aylett, talking to the journeymen. He couldn't quite repress a flinch, and he saw her realise that he had.

Charlotte cleared her throat. "Sorry. I just did something I don't understand. Let me go look for the clover, and we'll regroup in - well. However long it takes me to find a four-leaf clover in a field in Somerset? I'm sure someone has actually done calculations about that sort of thing." She stood up, clearing her own dishes. "I'm sure there's clover somewhere in the field, so maybe twenty, thirty minutes at most? I need to check something in one of the books on the table. I'll go out that way. Meet you back in the lab?"

She didn't wait for him to do more than nod, leaving him alone with the remnants of his luncheon. He would want a nap in a bit, he could tell. But putting the salve together wouldn't take terribly long. He'd have to redo some of the calculations in the proportions, depending what he actually had for the materia, and how potent it was. He was assuming Charlotte knew the potency charms. If she did things in a stillroom, and given the other knowledge she'd shown, it seemed likely enough. Anyway, if things all went smoothly, he could be napping by two at the latest.

Not that they would. He did his utmost to make things go smoothly, but experience, near all of his life, suggested that relying on that was not the way to count. Even in the lab, where his odds were a lot better than average. After another minute or two, he heard Charlotte go out the far door. Lewis washed up his own dishes and gave her a good head start to the field before going off to the lab.

Lewis set one of the hourglasses going, more out of curiosity than anything else. He'd left anything that could wait when he finished early this morning. Now he took his time washing out the glassware, rinsing it in the potions that removed any trace of residue, and all that. Nothing that needed his own magic. He'd save that. Tomorrow, maybe.

Once he'd done that, he set out half a dozen dishes for

the materia, as well as putting together the double boiler for the salve and a block of beeswax. After a moment's consideration, he reached for the grapeseed oil rather than any of the others. He had a fair bit of it. He wouldn't need more for anything he was expecting to make. And it aligned with the Moon, so good for illusions. Only once he'd done that did he pull out the jars and bottles and pipettes for the rest of it. Finally, he went and pulled out his working notebook, thumbing through for the recipe he needed, and setting it in the book holder halfway down the long workbench.

Twenty-two minutes into the glass's sand, there was a rapping knock on the door, followed by "It's me." When he opened the door, Charlotte held up her palm with three four-leaved clovers. He nodded, holding the door for her. "Put those in the empty dish, if you would?" Nothing they'd be working with today was terribly reactive, so he'd used the glazed ceramic ones. They'd be easier to wash out after.

"Thank you." Once she'd done that, she folded her hands in front of her and waited for him. Lewis had to admit she had good manners in the lab, far better than most people who'd taken it at school. He gestured at the stool. "Sit while we talk? Or, um. The sofa?" He'd tidied it when he woke up this morning. Now, he settled on it, because it was more comfortable and he wanted something to lean back into. Being active, even for not very long, had got him tired again.

Charlotte took the sofa, surprising him by choosing to be closer. She twisted in her seat, as if measuring something. "Can you tell me what to do from there? When I start?"

Lewis opened his mouth, closed it, then nodded. "If you

could bring me things at a couple of steps." He then tried to decide what to say next.

Here, she saved him. Or plunged him into some new calamity, he wasn't at all sure. Looking straight at him, she spoke clearly. "Why do you assume I'd just leave if I could?"

Because the only people who'd stayed were his brothers. And then Theo had got hurt, and it had all changed. Paul had pulled away, burying himself in his own schoolwork, and Lewis couldn't blame him. He couldn't answer that, not with any words he had, so he just shrugged.

"All right. Look, I'd like the option to leave. I don't actually want to leave right now. I want to know what Morgen's doing, and exactly how worrying it is. And I'm not going to find that out if I leave. If I go home now, all I have to go on is feeling and supposition - and well, if you gave an oath, there's support for dealing with that. But even then, she could probably claim with a straight face that everyone chose to be here, and the rest of them knew what they were getting into. The truth-telling magics aren't great with nuance without a lot of detail to back up the specific questions."

Lewis opened his mouth, then closed it again. "And?"

"So I'd like to stay and figure out what they're doing. Listening closer to where they are, for example. Seeing what I can pick up from the gardens, if I can get a better look at them. Learning more about what you've made and are making, and whether we can pull together a tidy list for later." She hesitated. "Um. I'm making a lot of assumptions here."

That made him even more nervous. "Assumptions?"

"You haven't wanted to turn me in."

Lewis shook his head. "Still don't."

"And if I reappeared out of the maze, they'd keep

incredibly close watch on me, and use whatever they could to make me, mmm. Compliant with their goals, is that the polite way to put it?"

"It's a wrong way to put it." Lewis felt it burst out of him. "Use potions I made, incense and scent I made, to change your mind. To make it impossible to know your own mind clearly. I didn't..." He stopped and swallowed. "I didn't realise, until I looked at all the lists, how much I'd made? The layers of it."

Charlotte shifted a little closer on the sofa, then cautiously reached out a hand to him, leaving it in the middle space between them. He looked down at it, then took a breath and put his hand in hers. "I can copy out a list. Tonight, tomorrow. It's in shorthand, partly."

Then he swallowed, calling up the lists he'd looked at while things were simmering last night behind his eyes. "Salves, to help avoid being affected by whatever - either a block for the skin or something for under the nose, to mitigate scents in the air. Incense to increase openness, to encourage dreams, and one that's on the border of encouraging compliance. Oils for suggestibility. She swore she was just using them to suggest dreams, visions, how people could improve their lives. That sort of thing. But it's not as if the oil knows that. Or you can limit it like that. Things you put in drinks to encourage people to talk, to babble, say the things they wouldn't normally say out loud."

"Gareth kept wanting me to drink tea," Charlotte said, softly, and Lewis nodded emphatically. "And they test that all those things work, right?"

"Some of them they tested on me. Some on one of the others. Both giving it, and a charm. That was Gareth. He's a lot better at magic than Morgen, in general. She can't do most charmwork past Maxim Three."

Charlotte stopped, but she didn't move her hand. "All right. And obviously, we can't really switch out what they've already got. I assume there's both some amount of warding, or that sort of thing is stored, I don't know, in a trunk at the base of Morgen's bed. Not somewhere easy to get to."

"You have a suspicious sort of mind," Lewis said. "I wouldn't think of it like that. I'd be thinking of optimal storage - you know, constant temperature, no light filtering in, protections against external magical influences. All that."

Charlotte laughed, sounding more relaxed for the first time since she'd come back for lunch. "Family training. Anyway. Going and looking for it would be too risky. For me, anyway, I don't have those skills. So, what can we change that they're picking up?"

"Besides the one I'm still working on?" Lewis grimaced. "My blood will change that now. But she might want a new stock of a couple of others. I can have those ready?"

"The one that needs virgin blood. Is that something they can test on the spot?"

Lewis shook his head. "I've been thinking more about how it'd affect things. It's a complicated materia interaction, of course. When you change one thing, and not the rest, or anything about your process." He stopped. "Though, um. I could change the process. For anything, we'd have time to do. Three days, working time, realistically."

"You said that you thought it might be a soporific. Rather than encouraging compliance and lending their vitality or whatever that looks like for Morgen." Charlotte nodded. "Can you figure out what might work? Or point me at where to start with the research? Once we've done this salve?" Then she tilted her head. "And once you've had some sleep. In a proper bed."

"When anyone else says things like that, I feel like I'm nagged," Lewis said. "I don't with you."

"That's because you know I'm right." Charlotte said, almost cheerfully. "I might have more of a plan forming. I think that - we don't want to try going to the house before May Eve, but maybe we do that night. Or at least I do. I wouldn't make you go."

Lewis swallowed hard. If it were something out of legend, of course he'd go be a brave knight, charging right into danger. But this was something out of the old Fatae tales, and the women in those were fully capable of taking care of themselves. Often more than the poor mortal knights who stumbled across them, honestly. "With a little calculation, I can probably adjust the effect so it starts to wear off faster? Or we could bring something in a brazier to start burning that would counteract it. I'll have to think about the interactions." Then he coughed. "The salve, now? I probably do want a nap before I do anything complicated."

Charlotte squeezed his hand once, then stood up. "Is that the recipe here? Right. Oh, good, you have some St John's Wort in oil. That's a beautiful pure red, isn't it? And here's the clover, just one per batch, but I brought a couple just in case. Grapeseed - for the moon?" She craned her head around to catch his nod, then went back to talking through the ingredients.

"You'll need to do the charmwork to concentrate the dry materia in the oil. It's not as if we've time to let it sit for a lunar cycle, or anything like that." Heat and magic would do a great deal to draw out the necessary properties into the oil, but it took quite a lot of vitality to do that. He'd done a bit of that last night. It was still fresh in his mind. Or in his magic, it felt like he'd been far too active physically, only not at all in any actually physical way.

The actual work went smoothly enough. More slowly than he'd wanted, but of course it would. Charlotte made a point of checking each step. While she handled everything competently, she was careful and meticulous, and that never went fast. By the time she was done and the salve was cooling in jars for use the next day, Lewis was ready to fall over where he sat.

Charlotte apparently wasn't having any of that. She took his notes about which places to start research, chivied him upstairs, out of his shoes, and into bed. Though she didn't actually fuss about him undressing. Then she dimmed the lights, added a charm to shade the skylight from the sun, and went back downstairs. He remembered nothing after that.

CHAPTER 28
THE NEXT DAY

By the time Charlotte was ready to go to bed, Lewis had been up for a couple of hours. He had that sort of unfocused daze that Charlotte recognised from Gabe - and to be fair, Mama, Papa, and Charlotte herself - when there was a problem being worked on. She made a plate of sandwiches, waved it under his nose when he came in to grab tea, and didn't interrupt him while he was eating.

When he got up, he bent over - entirely without considering it - and kissed her on the forehead, before wandering to the lab again. Charlotte blinked after him, not sure what to do about that. Had he meant it as a sign of affection? He hadn't seemed prone to that sort of casual touch. Though, to be fair, it wasn't as if either of them had the largest range of evidence to base that sort of thing on.

He'd said he'd rather push himself for Charlotte than for Morgen. Blast, he was having feelings for her, of some kind. Currently undelineated and unspecified, but definitely feelings. She didn't want to hurt him. That was the thing. He didn't work by the rules of the First Families' social circles. He wasn't brittle and sharp-edged, like a lot of the generation a hair older than Gabe. They had reason to be, of course. And Lewis had reason to be as he was, shaped by the work he'd done, and the way he was driven to help his brother. Also his mother and his younger brother, for all he'd barely talked about either of them.

It wasn't as if she could talk about it with him. She read up until near midnight. After a lot of consideration, she went upstairs, and tucked herself into bed, wearing his shirt for a nightgown, or at least something like one. It came down to near enough her knees, if she didn't move much. Charlotte did her best to keep to her side of the bed. There was a sound sometime in the middle of the night, but when she rolled over, there was still space in the bed.

In the morning, she woke up, the room still dark. She hadn't changed the charm, had she? She rolled out of bed, putting a foot down before she brushed against something on the floor. A moment later, she realised it was Lewis, curled up in a little nest of blankets. Charlotte managed not to overbalance, then picked her way over him, step by step, until she could grab her clothes and go downstairs.

He came down perhaps twenty minutes later, rubbing his face and his hair sticking out at odd angles, though he'd put clothes on. She'd been making breakfast, rolls with eggs and a bit of bacon, that seemed fortifying. When he came back out of the bath, she offered him a plate. "Tea's almost steeped." Then, before she could lose her nerve about it, "I expected you to sleep in the bed, really. Was I being rude and taking it all over?"

"Oh." He rubbed his face again with his hand, almost hiding behind it. "The floor was fine."

"Lewis." Charlotte turned to face him. "Really?"

Suddenly, he blushed bright red. "I wasn't sure what I might do in my sleep. I mean. Yesterday." He gestured incoherently at the dining room, where he'd kissed her. "I didn't want to do something you didn't want."

That was absolutely no help at all, seeing as Charlotte wasn't actually sure what she wanted. She hadn't minded the kiss. And it had just been her forehead, affectionate kisses like that were an ordinary sort of thing. All right, she suspected it wasn't just ordinary friendly affection for Lewis, but he hadn't actually said that, or done anything else to make her certain of his feelings. Whatever they might be.

She could ask. Uncle Gil would say she should. But Uncle Gil was Bear House, not Fox, and asking showed vulnerabilities. Instead, she smiled. "The bed would have been fine. If you did do something, we'd figure it out." And she might well like it, but she couldn't say that. She went on resolutely. "I was worrying a little where you were." Then she changed the subject, a bit more abruptly than she wanted, but she was figuring this out on the fly. "I was thinking I'd go see what I could hear this morning. Did you have plans for the lab?"

Lewis hesitated, then took the plate she was still holding out. "I could come with you? I'm still thinking about some of the adjustments I could make. There's no reason I can't do it there."

Charlotte nodded. "I can probably do something to muffle our sound. And we can bring a blanket to sit on, I suppose. Less grass getting unfortunate places. Right. Breakfast, then. Can you take this in, and I'll bring the tea?" She handed over her own plate, and they made a little procession into the dining room. Bringing the tea meant she could fuss with pouring it for a minute and give herself a chance for some other topic of conversation.

What she landed on was perhaps not as useful as she

wanted. "If we do something about Morgen, you'll need to do something else, won't you? Do you have any idea about that?"

He shivered. "I - mostly, last night, I was thinking about having to trust it'd all work out." Lewis sounded entirely bleak about it, and Charlotte did not like that note in his voice at all. It was far too many echoes, an empty space ringing oddly at steps walking through it that shouldn't be there.

"I can't promise anything without talking to people. But Mama and Papa and Gabe and Aunt Mason and Aunt Witt all know people. What would you want to be doing if you could? If it wasn't just about keeping things together for your brother?"

"Perfumes. Proper perfume design. Room scents as well. Those are an interesting challenge, to do something that isn't in every corner apothecary. Something nuanced, individual, that suits the room it's in as well as the purpose. And the same thing with people. I'd love to do, maybe wardrobe is the best word for it. A range of scents that draw on the same anchoring notes, but that vary. By season, of course, but also time of day, or what someone's doing."

"Something different for an evening at home with a good book than a party, or a dinner with a couple of other people, that kind of thing? But all the same scent at the base?" Charlotte was intrigued by the idea. Mama had several scents, related, but that wasn't quite the same thing.

Lewis bobbed his head. "I could show you a simple version, if you like. When we get a little time. I can't spend all the time between now and May Eve on the other things. And the scent doesn't take a lot of direct magic, not at the blending stage."

That gave her an excuse to ask about the nuances of the magic. She'd done a competent job with the oils yesterday, she was quite sure. But that was obviously a different process than drawing out a delicate scent. Charlotte knew that the more delicate flowers were incredibly difficult that way, that there were some only magic could fix in a reliable form - sweetpea, for example. And that a large part of why neroli and jasmine and rose were so expensive as ingredients was how many delicate flowers were needed to make even a few drops of pure oil. The topic kept Lewis happily talking away until they were done eating, done drinking their tea, and ready to move into the maze.

"Now we get to see if the salve worked." Charlotte said once they were in the centre again. Lewis was carrying a rolled-up blanket. Charlotte had a satchel with a few things in it, including a notebook and pen.

Lewis nodded. "Need me to hold the salve?"

Charlotte hesitated, then reached for the jar in the satchel. "Would you?" It was another kind of intimacy, and she wasn't sure why she'd said it. Other than the fact she didn't have a mirror here, and it would work best if it covered her whole eyelid, and the area under her eyes. "You know where it needs to go?"

Lewis nodded, though he didn't meet her eyes. Instead, he reached for the salve, unscrewing the lid like it needed ferocious concentration. She closed her eyes - this would go better if she wasn't looking at him - and just waited. After maybe fifteen seconds, he coughed. "Ready?"

"Please." Almost immediately, she felt a gentle touch, fingers just under her eyebrow. He smoothed the salve down around the lower arch of her eyes, then finally the eyelid on the left. His fingers lifted, and she stayed still, waiting for the other. His movements there were a little more certain and comfortable. When she opened her eyes and blinked, she was sure it had worked. She could see the glimmers of the magic now, like a layer of illusion work over the hedges. More to the point, she could see the places where there was a mist or distraction, and the places there weren't. "Do you want some? It's working, I'm certain."

Lewis shook his head. "I'd like to see what it feels like if I don't. To start, anyway."

It was a fair point. She nodded, taking the salve jar back and tugging it in the satchel before holding out her hand. "Take mine and let's see how this goes." Following the maze back around, turn by turn, they came out to the opening on the other end. The last stretch twisted along the front edge of the maze, closest to the garden. There was a large trellis there, now draped with ridiculously out of season flowers. There were summer roses, sweet peas, campanula, delphiniums, hollyhocks, lupins, drowsy peonies, even some foxgloves.

Lewis opened his mouth, and she put her finger to his lips automatically, then held it up. She cast the charm she'd intended, the one that would muffle the sound more than a few feet away. "Whisper, all right?"

"Do you think they know how to handle the foxgloves?" Trust that Lewis would think about the toxicity before anything else.

Charlotte tilted her head, then looked more closely at the flowers. The light was not at a good angle for it, but after maybe ten seconds, she was able to see the same illusion shimmer on them. "Illusion. Gareth, I assume? They're out of season, too. Not that you can't do a lot with a hothouse."

"Illusion's cheaper." Lewis said, one of the first actually cynical things she'd heard him say. "What are they doing?"

There was a group of people maybe fifty feet further across the garden. The women were in long trailing dresses, with completely ahistorical hats trailing ribbons and fabric over loose hair, rather than veils or hennins. The men had tabards and hose, and some of them were obviously a lot more comfortable showing off their legs than others.

She caught a glimpse of what had to be Victor - she knew his legs anywhere - turned away, laughing, teasing someone. It looked like he didn't have a care in the world. Then she got a second look, as he turned back, and she was worried, the sort of worry that snatched at her heart. He didn't look well. On a Victorian lady, it would have been described as a pallour, perhaps a sign of an incipient swoon, before he caught himself and shifted one foot so he could lean a little. His eyes were too bright, too, the sort that suggested a fever or a potion or both.

Before she could say anything to that, there was a triumphal trumpet sound. Someone was playing. She saw the gleam of the brass, but not terribly well. It sounded fine, but it wasn't particularly compelling. At least, it was not terribly impressive to Charlotte, well on the other side of whatever illusion was enhancing it. Morgen took her seat in the centre of the bower, escorted by both Gareth and Bedivere. Charlotte couldn't decide - given she could only really see their backs - what that meant. Maybe Bedivere was in disgrace and Morgen was keeping a close eye on him. Or maybe he was just there because he no longer had a tidily assigned pairing.

Pair by pair, the others came up. Charlotte couldn't hear all of it, but the two-thirds she could hear clearly were enough to give her the gist of what was going on. Each pair was given some sort of quest that would require both cooperation and something they found uncomfortable. Or uncomfortable to do together. There were blushes, those were reasonable enough. But there were also more than a couple of flinches, or the places where someone went still, like any answer would be wrong and they knew it. It wasn't just the women, and it didn't seem to be something overtly sexual. More like it was something embarrassing, or something that could be used later to put pressure on one or the other or both.

Victor and Caradoc were assigned to something that at least sounded like less exertion, at least in the half Charlotte could hear clearly. It involved a foray to the dovecote on the far side of the house. Caradoc looked uncomfortable, though, as if it were making more public what he and Victor got up to, but Victor looked pleased, almost smug. However, he also looked a bit pale, like he was glad not to have to go too far. It might be Victor's natural inclinations to recline, but she wasn't sure.

Finally, all the pairs had been dismissed, leaving the trio under the bower. "Do go fetch the refreshments, Beddie, darling." Morgen's voice had shifted from the portentous elocution of a few moments before. Neither Morgen nor Gareth said anything until Bedivere was dwindling into the distance, across the lawn. Morgen's voice shifted again, the drawl she preferred in private. "So tedious, Gareth, darling. Do tell me there's something to look forward to."

"You could have any of them in your bed for the asking now. You know that." Gareth leaned over to pull a strand of hair over Morgen's shoulder. "So can I. I was thinking Laudine this evening. We haven't for a while."

"And it would do a wonder for her to have your attention, and leave the others panting. Oh, quite. Well played, dearest." Morgen considered. "And it might encourage her to make a bit more of an effort, she's been letting herself slip."

"I was thinking more that it might help Mark buck up," Gareth said, amiably. "He's lost some of his desire to excel."

As the others began to start filtering back, Charlotte nudged Lewis, mouthing "Back?" When he nodded, they carefully lifted the blanket, retreating into the centre of the maze before they folded it up or did anything else.

Lewis paused, then said as clearly as he could, "I don't want to help her at all. How do we stop her?"

"Good question." Charlotte let out a huff of breath. "Let's go find some paper and, I don't know. Salt shakers to stand in for her and Gareth, or whatever. I suspect we're going to need them."

Lewis let out a little chuckle. "Certainly, anything she says should be taken with a number of grains of salt?" He seemed very pleased with his humour, which, to be fair, was rather well-timed. Charlotte snorted and set off for the cottage again.

CHAPTER 29
IN THE AFTERNOON

That afternoon, Lewis spent a good chunk of time looking at books in the lab and checking ingredients. He had a couple of ideas, but he wasn't sure they'd actually work. If they had time to make it work. Around two, he came back out to the cottage, and said, "Could I - would you mind coming and helping? I need to check ingredients, and it'll take forever and..."

Charlotte was already standing up, all smiles. "Glad to. Show me what you need. And tell me if you need something else."

The thing about her, Lewis thought, was that he was having a hard time not falling for her. There had been that kiss last night, like he'd have kissed one of his brothers, or even Mother. Familial, not romantic, but the sort of kiss that was entirely comfortable with the nature of the current reality. She hadn't said anything about it, even though she'd had several chances.

He'd had several chances, too, mind. And what he'd done was sleep on the floor and not say anything, even when there was a reasonable opening. But the more he watched her, the more he let her closer, the more he wanted to. At the moment, she was perched on the sofa, three books set out beside her. She was cross-referencing lists for him, while he checked the location of all his oils and perfumes and dried herbs.

Lewis went back to setting out what he needed, concentrating hard on it. As hard as he could. But he couldn't help getting a glimpse of her when he turned around to grab something else from the other workbench, or to pull something out of the apothecary cabinet further along.

He could ask. Well, part of it. He knew the words. He had no idea what she'd say, but he wasn't asking her to do anything with him past May Eve. However that turned out, she'd surely go her own way, back to a life he didn't understand. She might come to him for perfume, if he was lucky and set up on his own, but it would be the curious intimacy of a client, not - well. Not whatever it was they did between now and then.

The thing of it was, he wanted whatever he could have. He wanted that the way he'd wanted alchemy, as soon as he knew he could, or perfume and scent. It was foolish and stupid and thoughtless. Nothing about what she'd offered would last. It was a Fatae tale, gold turning to dry brittle leaves in the dawn, without even any useful materia properties that lingered.

Charlotte cleared her throat, the sort of sound Theo used to use when he wanted a moment without interrupting. Lewis made himself keep putting out the bottles before he turned around, not rushing to respond. "Yes?"

"I think I've got the list. Let me know when you're ready."

"Just a minute." He turned back, his fingers shifting,

almost dancing, as he checked the ingredients he wanted. "Please read them out?"

That occupied them nicely for twenty minutes. Once he had everything in the proper place, she asked, "Can I help with something here, or should I go put something together for supper and get out of your hair?"

Having her there felt good. Unreasonably good. Lewis took a breath and let it out. "Maybe if you wouldn't mind making supper, but help me set up for tomorrow after?" And then all in a rush. "And perhaps we might enjoy ourselves in bed, after? I'd like to learn more about what you like."

It didn't quite come out in one breathless tumble. There were pauses in there. More or less. He flushed, but he refused to turn back to the bench, no matter how much he wanted to.

Charlotte didn't say anything for far too long, though it was really only five or six heartbeats. Then she nodded, once. "That sounds like an excellent evening." Then she smiled at him. "Supper in ninety minutes or so, if you want to set a timer." Before he could say anything in return, she went out, closing the door behind her.

Lewis stared at the door until he could feel the tension in his shoulders get to him. She'd said it sounded like an excellent idea. How was he supposed to interpret that? Other than a degree of willingness he could apparently anticipate. It took him a long time to go back to work and not worry about dropping anything. He kept getting distracted by later that evening, what it would be like to be in bed again. The intimacy of it, what that would feel like, when it wasn't all entirely new.

There was something about doing a thing the first time that he loved - working with a new oil or ingredient always had that rush. Discovery, Magistra Aylett had said, the spark of it. But he also liked getting better at things, a great deal. Knowing that he had learned the movement, the way to touch something, coax a resin out of a jar or bottle in just the right amount. And he wasn't going to turn down a chance to learn those things with Charlotte, even if he had no idea what they were leading to. If anything.

He had to keep telling himself this was just about the moment, about the experience of walking past a garden in a particular season. It was there, it would be gone in a fleeting moment, never again quite that combination. Perfume was simultaneously about the chance interactions of the moment and the body and the materia, and then about trying to capture the essence of it so someone could return to it over and over. It meant he had to know which was which, and not mistake one for the other.

Lewis didn't forget to set the hourglass properly, and so just before ninety minutes were up, he washed up, making sure everything he was done with was put away. They'd have an hour or two of work that evening, nothing complicated. But it would be easier with one person to keep stirring an oil on the warmer, while he did the other parts.

When he opened the door into the cottage, there was a wave of delicious scent, vegetables, and some sort of egg and pastry. It made his mouth water immediately, and then he came around into the kitchen to find a tart or quiche or something of the kind cooling in a pie plate. "That smells wonderful. I really appreciate you doing the cooking."

Charlotte turned back from where she had been mixing something. "Something you like then? I thought I'd try something a bit more elaborate. I wasn't sure how adventurous your food tastes are."

"I like everything you've made so far." Lewis considered. "I don't like some things. Nothing in the pantry here, though. Fish, sometimes. The texture, more than the smell of it, though I'm not fond of very fishy as a note in the meal in general."

The way he put that made her smile, which he'd sort of been hoping for. "Well, then. It's a little tricky not having much in the way of recipes, but I might try a few more things and see if I get them right. I think I can manage at least edible, even if they don't come out the way I hope."

Lewis nodded a bit vigorously. He certainly didn't want to discourage her. Once they had their plates, they took them into the dining room, to the table, chatting about what he had in mind for the evening's work in the lab. Charlotte seemed pleased - unusually pleased - that he wanted her to stir, and he walked through each step, partly to sort it out in his own head.

"That sounds like an interesting evening. I expect I'll learn things." That seemed to make her even happier. She was smiling broadly now. "And then we'll clean up, and explore learning some entirely different things, yes?"

Lewis wasn't sure, still, how to interpret that, but he could only assume it was positive. He was often not sure about people's expressions, if they meant them or not, but her words were pretty clear. He nodded. "Please." He wanted to say more than that, to explain what he was feeling, and that it didn't obligate her to anything, and he couldn't get the words out.

She didn't press, and he was hugely grateful for that. She just turned the conversation back to something she'd read that afternoon, a question about a bit of theory. That was the hell of it. It was easy to be with her. Most people, having them around was a distraction. He'd have thought that having someone around that he wanted like he wanted

Charlotte absolutely would be. And yet, when they were talking about his work, his creations, his ideas, it wasn't a distraction at all.

It was like she'd said the first night they'd been together, about liking singing with other people. A duet was different than a solo. An accord was different than a single note. He kept getting lost in the ways things melded together, different aspects coming as they shifted, the conversation changing focus. Before he realised, he had finished all his food, and they were clearing the plates.

The work in the lab went much more smoothly now. Charlotte was still cautious, checking with him before doing something new, making sure to match the pace of his movements. But she'd hand him this or that, when she could do so easily, her other hand stirring the pot. The water simmered, infusing itself with the herbs, and Lewis kept checking to make sure it was at the perfect place. Not too hot, not too fast, only the slightest shimmer of move-ment at the surface of the water to show it was in motion.

Then, of course, they had to cool it - that took a while - and strain it. Charlotte easily shifted to helping him measure out what he wanted tomorrow. Lewis was still working out the details in his head. He was hoping that something overnight would give him the final inspiration for how to make everything gel. Or whatever the proper adjective was, he was aiming at something that could be sprayed, and gel was awful for that.

That was not the point right now. Lewis dragged his thoughts back to measuring out the precise amounts they needed, and Charlotte had a light touch with the scale. And with making sure every last bit got brushed into the containers for storage overnight, even the fluffy bits of mullein that wanted to go everywhere.

"Why the mullein?" Charlotte asked once she was sure he wasn't handling anything.

"The solar associations, partly. They used it for torches. Still do some places, I think?" he said. "And it's a protective herb, warding against evil, but also for courage and protection." And in some traditions to attract love, though that wasn't why they were using it here, and he wasn't going to go near that topic.

"We use it at home for some of the rituals. Candlewick, I mean, dipped in wax and lit up like a torch." Charlotte said it easily. "Have you ever seen it? You could come this year, if you like. Midsummer and midwinter, usually, though now I say that it's not actually formally part of each ritual."

Lewis murmured something agreeable, turning back to the workbench to hide his confusion. Finally, though, there was nothing left to put away, and he had to talk to her again. He wanted to talk to her again. "I'm all set. Would you like a few to wash up and change?"

"Mmm, yes. Thank you. Five or ten minutes? I'll be upstairs." With that, she considered something for just an instant, then kissed him on the forehead before heading for the door. He watched her go, now entirely sure what the next hour or two was going to bring. He was fairly sure he wanted as much as that time could hold, even if he didn't know what the potion in process really was, or what it was going to do to him.

CHAPTER 30
THAT EVENING

Charlotte wasn't entirely sure what Lewis had in mind that night. On the other hand, it implied at least both of them would get a good night's sleep afterwards, and that he probably wouldn't insist on sleeping on the floor again. That was worth something.

The other thing was that, well. She rather wanted to. The anticipation was a thing, and not one that she'd really explored like this. Knowing, hours in advance, that they'd be in bed, that he wanted to be in bed with her. And not just for his own relief, though that certainly wasn't necessarily bad. But he'd wanted to be with her enough to ask, through his blushes and his nerves and the way it had come out all in one burst.

It wasn't like she'd be cruel, given that. So she'd gone off to wash up, and pulled on the dressing gown. The question was how to be when he came up the stairs. On the bed, she presumed, it wasn't like the furniture gave a great deal of viable options. Bed it was, the dressing gown starting out covering everything, but easy to move. And her hair was loose, because Lewis had been very clear he liked that. The oil he'd made her was doing it good, too, and she wondered if there was extra charmwork in it. She added a couple of charmlights, just enough for gentle illumination.

Lewis wasn't far behind her. He'd given her five minutes, but not much more than that. Just about when she expected, he was coming up the stairs; the sound caused shivers of anticipation. When she could see his head, he was blushing - he did blush, quite a lot. Charlotte held out her hand. "I'm glad you asked."

That was the thing of it. She was glad he had. She probably would have suggested it in another day or two, if he weren't wrapped up in his work. Or at least, she would have if she could be fairly sure how he'd take it. But Charlotte wasn't going to turn him down, either, and hurt him.

In another time, another place, with another person, she might have been worried about her safety, at least a little. Turning down someone while stuck in the same place had risks. Oddly, wonderfully, fascinatingly, she wasn't worried about that. She was absolutely sure Lewis wouldn't hurt her, that he wouldn't even be abrupt or dismissive with her, if she'd said no. But she would have hurt him, and she hadn't wanted to.

Besides, they'd had a grand time the first night, and she was decidedly looking forward to what they might get up to tonight. Probably nothing emphatically energetic. Charlotte wanted to see what it would be like if Lewis forgot all the things that held him back for just a little. She'd seen glimpses of it two nights ago, passion and desire all crashing like a wave at the moment, but she wasn't sure she could coax him to that tonight.

He'd stripped off the smock he'd been wearing for his work, just shirtsleeves with the cuffs already open, trousers, and his own hair loose. Then he stopped, taking in the scene. "May I?"

"Please. Get comfortable?" He hesitated once more, but then worked on unbuttoning and discarding the shirt, now alternating between glancing at her and down at his own hands. Interestingly enough, he didn't seem terribly shy about her looking at him, in the sense of undressing. Though Charlotte rather felt that her focused attention, even when he was wearing clothes and a working smock, still made him blush in an instant. She really would have to see if she could manage to sketch him sometime. Not right now.

A minute or so later, he was stretched out on the bed, a few inches from her, hand resting on the bed between them. He looked at her, meeting her eyes, then down at his hand, before moving it to touch hers, lightly. "I'm glad you said yes."

Charlotte wasn't sure how to answer that entirely. After considering and discarding half a dozen options, she chose what she actually wanted to know. "Did you think I'd say no?"

"I hoped you wouldn't." His fingers shifted on hers, just a hair, strength and pressure changing. "You made it clear that this is - a thing for right now. And I want to respect that, and you. But I also," He flushed again, and now he was looking at their hands, rather fixedly. "I wanted to know what it's like when it's not our first time. When we learn more about each other, what that's like? I think I might like it even more, and - last time was amazing. I was dreaming about it, and I keep thinking about it, and I don't want to pressure you, but I wanted more."

"More." Charlotte let it come out like a breath. Then she said, doing her best to speak lightly. Not dismissively, but not putting weight on the scaffolding that might not hold up to it. "I enjoyed it a great deal, and I like the idea of seeing what it's like this time. I've been looking forward to it since you asked. Enjoying the anticipation."

Lewis inhaled sharply, the sort of inhale that was making his own rapidly increasing arousal very plain. "And?"

He was entirely too tempting. Charlotte slipped her fingers from under his, moving to directly cup and touch him, making what she wanted just as obvious. "I was thinking, as you were getting ready, that I'd love to see what it's like when you forget to behave yourself, to be so controlled. I got glimpses of it last time. But, mmm. Can we see where we go with that, do you think? Or is that too much?"

There was a long pause. She could feel the way he was trembling, under her fingers. And also the way that something in that absolutely got him going. She was sure he didn't have words for it, and they didn't actually need words. Just they'd probably make Lewis feel better. She didn't add any provocation; she didn't move.

First he mumbled something. She couldn't make out enough of what he said, then he caught himself and tried again. "I don't want to hurt you."

"Can you trust me to tell you if you do? Accidentally. I'm very clear you don't want to." The imp of the perverse, sitting on her shoulder, provoked her to add, "Sometimes people do that deliberately in bed. Certain kinds of hurts that feel good in the moment. But that is, mmm. A play to work up to. You might figure out some interesting salves for it, too. I'd be curious if you did."

It was entirely too much, but in the best way possible. He went even more still and even more swollen against her fingers, and then he was reaching to undo his trousers and push his clothing away. He reached for her, pulling her closer into a kiss as he pressed his body against hers, already rocking with little pauses that were half breath and half moan.

That, now, was a wonderful thing on her end. The thing of it was, she was beginning to see what Morgen liked about having men panting after her. Not that she wanted what Morgen was encouraging. Ugh, no. But the intensity of his interest and his desire was utterly addictive. Or could be, with very little help. Then, thankfully, she was entirely too tangled up in the doing to be thinking. Lewis had got one hand down between her legs, had found how wet she already was between the anticipation of the evening and the words and the way he was already so eager. Now, finally, he looked up and met her eyes. "Less control, then? Show me how."

It was that last either of them said - that came out as words, anyway - for quite some time. They began with her on her back. He fitted himself between her legs, finding his way far more deftly than last time. Lewis didn't last - maybe ten strokes, before he was arching back, driving into her, and bellowing. It left her quivering and frustrated, before his hand reached to do what he could for her.

By the time she was beginning to come back to herself, he was beginning to recover, slowly rolling his hips in and out. It felt grand, but it was just a warmup for what she'd wanted. Once she felt she could keep her balance, she nudged his hands. "Rearrange?" Just the one word, but he backed up to give her the space to get onto her hands and knees, until she twisted her head to look at him.

Lewis was not a stupid man, not at all. Nor was he unobservant. The man took a hint beautifully, in fact, not that this was remotely subtle. She pulled one of his hands to her hip, and just after that, felt him press into her again. It had every bit of eagerness she might possibly have wanted. For all his thrusts were forceful, making her whimper each time, before she sucked in a breath as he moved to do it again. They felt wonderful. He had started eager, but he was rapidly gaining speed, filling her over and over with a delightful need that just kept building and building.

He managed to hold back this time until she'd burst into a second climax, but only barely. She could feel him thrusting three times before holding deep and filling her entirely, then following her down as her elbows finally gave up. They made a heap on the bed, but she wanted his weight and the knowledge of exactly where he was and what they'd done.

It couldn't last. He slipped out of her, and then to one side, one arm over her bare back, his thumb moving slightly against slick skin. Neither of them said anything for quite a long time. Charlotte didn't want anything to change. She could stay here, like this, in the glorious erotic satiation of the moment, and just enjoy it.

Finally, though, she wanted to breathe more easily, and she wriggled to shift to her side. When he tried to move his hand, she shook her head. "Like you touching." His fingers picked up, stroking again, now more on her hip than her back. That felt grand too, the way his thumb brushed the curve, like he was learning her by feel. "You?"

There was a silence, like he was picking through what words to say. She knew that sort of pause well enough. In the end, what he said sounded simple at first, but it had a lot of implications. "I could do this every night and find something new I loved." He didn't thank her - she thought for a moment he might. He had that sort of manners, even if this was an unusual application of the phrase.

The thing of it was, she wanted that too. She hadn't thought, two nights ago, that she'd get this. The freedom of it, and the care of it, both in the same bed, a bare few minutes apart. She wanted to try new things with him too, things she'd never wanted to risk with other people. Charlotte knew the theory of some of it, of restraint and a touch of pain in the right ways. Definitely sensation charms. She'd read the pillow books in the library just like Gabe had. And presumably their parents, though neither of them wanted to think about that in any sort of detail. The things in short, where trusting a partner really mattered, whoever they were, in ways that went far beyond the current pleasure.

Charlotte didn't know what else she felt about Lewis. She certainly wasn't fit to sort it out tonight, probably not this week. But she was more and more sure that she wanted to figure it out, and more to the point, do it in a way that let her do this again. Or something like this. Just repeating it wouldn't be nearly as much fun as exploring what else they could do together.

His comment needed some answer. She didn't have words for it, so instead she lifted her head, reaching a hand to curl into his hair, and kissed him. She'd have to trust that got something of the idea across.

CHAPTER 31
THE NEXT MORNING

Lewis woke the next morning slowly. He half-remembered Charlotte moving in the bed, the warmth and softness of her, and the way she kissed his shoulder. Then the bed had been empty, but he'd still been tired, so he'd rolled over into the warmth and gone back to sleep.

Now, however, there were interesting smells from downstairs. Something creamy and sweet, he could pick out those notes. Eggs, maybe. And definitely tea. He could smell the way that cut across the sweetness. He considered his clothes, then decided on trousers and his dressing gown over them, before padding downstairs in slippers.

And sometime in the night, his brain had sorted out some ideas, which was actually very helpful of it. Him. Both. Thinking of the inside of his head as distinct from the rest of him had benefits and complications, and he wasn't sure how he felt about it right now.

Charlotte was at the stove, stirring something, and with the oven on. It seemed like an awful lot for a morning, but she seemed happy, what he could see. Her hair was braided down her back, and the tip of it twitched now and again as she moved. She seemed to be focusing on something with the stove, because she only glanced at him. "Give me a minute. It's almost ready to come off the heat."

Lewis didn't interrupt. He had better manners than that, and besides, she was so careful about it in the lab; he wanted to return the favour. Instead, he went to the teapot, checking it had steeped, and pouring out two mugs of it, adding a splash of cream to his and then to hers. By the time he'd done that, she was taking the pot off the heat, some sort of improvised double boiler, with a metal mixing bowl in one of the cooking pots.

"There. It did come together." She sounded smug, more than anything, like she hadn't been sure it would.

He peered over her shoulder. "It smells fascinating? Um. What is it?" Though he'd told her he didn't have foods he avoided much, he hadn't expected this.

"If we had such a thing as coconut milk or cream, it'd be kaya jam. We don't, so it's a variation." He must have looked blank, because Charlotte explained immediately. "A Malaysian spread, usually it's coconut milk, sugar, eggs, a little salt. This time it's heavy cream. You spread it on bread. And the egg cakes in the oven should be out in a minute. They're, um. Sort of like madeleines? Only not quite. And I don't have the proper moulds, obviously." She waved a hand at the bowl. "It's not the same, but it's still tasty."

Lewis blinked several times. "Sure?" It needed a better answer than that. "Why?"

"Because I wanted to." She leaned forward and kissed his nose, which was very difficult to interpret with any sort of certainty. "Go wash up, I've got some sausage and scrambled eggs waiting too."

Lewis did as she said, because it was entirely sensible, and he was suddenly starving. Once he'd washed up, he helped her bring the waiting plates to the dining table, and then rummaged for cutlery. Once she was sitting down, he looked up. "Do I spread it on bread?"

"Mmhmm. And the egg cakes are just tasty." She pushed the plate over. They both ate in silence for a few minutes. Charlotte had been right. The spread was very tasty, temptingly so, though now he wondered what it was like with coconut. When they'd both begun to slow down on finishing their meal - he got the sense she had been near as hungry as he was - he cleared his throat.

"Last night, I hope it was as wonderful for you as it was for me." Mother had not really covered the proper manners for this sort of thing, nor had Theo. And yet, Lewis wanted to get it right, whatever that meant for her.

Charlotte broke into a reassuringly warm smile. "Oh, yes." Her voice had a note of a purr, something he hadn't expected. "Again, when you've the energy for it? I don't know what your plans for the lab are today."

Lewis waved a hand. "I've got a few ideas. And I do need to begin to pull things together for Gareth. He'll be here in two days. Everything's got to be bottled. Before that, though..." His voice trailed off.

"Yes?" Now she was leaning one elbow on the table, decidedly informal.

"I— sometimes you don't make sense?" To be fair, she often didn't make sense by any rules he understood. "Can I ask, um? Where you learned this kind of cooking?"

She laughed, her teeth showing, and her head thrown back. "I was wondering if you'd ask. I don't cook at home

- we have staff for that, and gods help anyone who gets in Cook's way. Besides, that's rude. I'd get to help sometimes when I was growing up. Things like shelling peas or picking out the good fruit from the fruit that really needed to be turned into jam promptly. But only with permission, as a special treat." She shrugged. "Aunt Mason's a really good cook. And so's Aunt Rosemary. They live together. And Aunt Mason, especially, thought it was important for both Gabe and I to be able to make our own food. Gabe, because he's a Penelope, and they end up in all sorts of places. And they knew he was going to do that, almost certainly, very early. By the time he was nine, maybe."

That was exceedingly early. Lewis hadn't figured out he wanted the alchemy until he was in tutoring school, and the perfume had come even later. He hadn't really even known what perfume could do when he was nine, except that Mother smelled nice when she wore it. That he could now give every note of it - the jasmine, the amber accord, the touch of vanilla and citrus - had come significantly later. Now, he just nodded. "And this?"

"Aunt Mason is Dutch-Malaysian. And she likes the things her mother and grandmother made. I like them too, even if they're not very authentic like this? She can do more, she stocks up on the spices and the proper moulds and things like coconut. But she also likes figuring out things that are close enough, that fill the same sort of food space."

It made sense to Lewis. Sometimes an ingredient or an oil or a particular kind of materia wasn't available, and the best alchemists knew how to adapt to that. It wouldn't get exactly the same results. But sometimes there were happy discoveries, and sometimes it ended up with something that was different, but - as Charlotte said - filled the same space. "I do like it. I was thinking I'd like to try the original, sometime, too."

"Oh, you'd get on wonderfully with Aunt Mason, I suspect. We'd have to tear you both away from talking materia. She doesn't do perfume, but she's an artist, makes a lot of her own paints and inks and things. I mean, besides being a Penelope." Charlotte beamed at him, and Lewis just wanted to bask in that feeling forever. It wasn't just her obvious happiness, though that was part of it. It was the way she wanted, apparently, through some miracle, to keep having him around.

That brought him back sharply to what he'd sorted out overnight. "I did have some ideas. So we can get to, um, the after better?"

"I like those, too." Charlotte now leaned both elbows on the table, and he was sure someone - a governess, if not her mother - had scolded her for that a number of times. It didn't seem to stop her.

Lewis didn't know how to interpret any of it. Charlotte was visibly more relaxed, even since last night. Languid might be a suitable word for it, something made of musk and indolence. And yet, there was also something delightfully sharp, with depths. Cedar, maybe, or a well-aged vanilla. Or roses. Complex roses, they always had depth far beyond the first impression. Now, Lewis swallowed hard, trying to remember how he'd wanted to say this. "I had an idea, sometime last night. After, erm, the inspirational part?"

"Inspiration, am I? I do like the sound of that. I can aspire to additional inspiration." That was entirely unfair. He had no defences against this at all. Not that he actually wanted them, so long as she wasn't teasing him to hurt. People had done that in school, and the memory of it left him cold. She must have caught some part of it in his expression. "To be clear, last night was delightful. I look forward to more, as circumstances allow. I - you also put me in a teasing mood, but if it bothers you, I'll stop."

"I did?" Lewis managed not to stammer. It was only two words, and no difficult consonants. Then he swallowed. "I'm not sure what you mean about the teasing. What we're doing. Besides the things in bed, which, yes, I also enjoy."

Charlotte was watching him carefully now. "I'm still figuring that out, I think. Can you cope with that, for the moment? That we do whatever we do in bed, and we work together on whatever we come up with Morgen. And that I'll be honest with you about whatever I sort out about other things? I know it's a bit unfair."

Lewis wanted to burst out with what he felt about her, but that would also be decidedly unfair. Also, it would come out in the sort of rush that would make her flee in the other direction, as far as she could, given their unusual circumstances. That wouldn't do either of them any good at all, and it certainly wouldn't stop Morgen from doing whatever she was doing to other people. After a long moment - longer than it should have been - he shook his head. "I'm - it's a challenge, to be clear? But I understand why, and sorting out Morgen is more important."

"Good. All right. You had an idea." Charlotte leaned back now, a sort of straight attentive posture that was what she must have done in school.

Time to gather his wits, which had been well and truly scattered. Part of him very much just wanted to watch her, the way her body moved when she took a breath, the flow of her hair, the tilt of her head. That wouldn't do right now. He swallowed. "How good are you at illusions in the moment? In a room, not on a page, I know they're different things."

Charlotte frowned. "I haven't practised them a great deal, but the way you learn is to do the room, before the page, usually. And what I learned in Incantation class, of course."

"There's a spray - I was working on something related, during my apprenticeship. It's an interesting problem? But it can enhance an illusion. You sort of use the spray and the illusion grabs onto it. It lasts longer, it's more solid? If I can come up with the spray, do you think you can craft an illusion that would work?"

"Possibly? What kind of thing were you thinking?" Charlotte leaned forward again, now entirely intent on the problem at hand.

"That's the question. I don't know what would intimidate Morgen. She's not exactly easy to intimidate." Lewis felt this was understating the situation, rather severely.

"Let's go at the other question. What would break the illusion she's trying to create with everyone there? She's in this Arthuriana mode, but had you noticed there's nothing like Arthur? And Morgen, of course, is an antagonist, in a lot of the stories. We wouldn't want to impersonate one of the Fatae ladies - frankly, I think Morgen's tempting fate there as she is. Though I have to say she's never come out with anything more than the implication. Oh, I do wish we had a larger library here."

Lewis had to smile a little at that. "We can talk it through, maybe? Can you help me do the preparation? And maybe stir the thing for Gareth, while I work on the rest of it, once I get it going."

"Absolutely." Charlotte stood. "Let me wash up, you figure out what you need to get out. I'll meet you there in ten minutes?" Then she started ticking off on her fingers. "Arthur himself. Guenevere. Merlin. Lancelot. Why is there no Lancelot in this? We have a Mark, after all." She went off with the dishes, still talking to herself about lore and myth. Lewis ducked upstairs to get dressed and figure out what he needed to make things work today.

CHAPTER 32
APRIL 28TH IN THE AFTERNOON

"When is Gareth supposed to collect things?" Charlotte had been finishing up washing the glassware.

"Tomorrow." Lewis said, not turning around. He was putting something away on his workbench. She couldn't see what. "We, um. Should we talk about that? And this morning?"

Charlotte did not want to talk about that morning. They'd gone up to see what Morgen and Gareth and the others were up to, right before lunch. Victor had apparently completely forgotten about her. He'd been sprawled on Caradoc's lap, as if he hadn't a care in the world. Someone had asked, even, if Charlotte would be joining them, and he'd waved a hand.

As if Charlotte were just lounging around her bedroom in the house, reading novels. Not that that was a bad way to spend an afternoon, but Victor hadn't seen her for days. More than a week, ten days. And he just waved it off. That had hurt, for all Charlotte knew, logically, that he must be under the influence of some potion or salve or incense or charm or enchantment. Besides whatever Morgen was doing with him or to him. Including, but not limited to, whatever Caradoc was doing with him in bed. And it wasn't as if Morgen and Gareth wouldn't have coached him or lied to him. Probably both. She was worried and she was upset, and the two didn't fit comfortably together at all.

She tsked slightly, but there was no ducking the conversation. Lewis would just continue dancing around it carefully, and that was also not something she could tolerate. "What did you want to say about it?" As she spoke, she finished up. "The glassware's all drying."

"Good. Can you bring this over there and stir it for me? Nice and steady, with the glass stirrer, for a couple of minutes."

"Of course." He handed it over, and she took it over to her bit of workbench, out of his way. It was a bottle, bigger than a perfume bottle, full of a liquid with an amber tinge to it, and it smelled wonderful. Cardamom, of course, she picked that out immediately, but also darker notes that gave it roots. She liked that a lot, and a touch of beeswax or honey, and several flowers she couldn't identify.

Lewis didn't say anything for another minute or two. She could hear the gentle clinking of glass on glass as she stirred, and whatever he was doing. It apparently involved a metal bowl of some kind, because she heard it ring once, when something hit it like a bell. Finally, he said, "I think you can do better than him."

"Are you jealous?" It came out of her mouth before she could think better of it, and she immediately winced. "Sorry. That's not fair."

Lewis didn't turn around, but she heard him clear as anything. "Doesn't matter how I feel about you. I think you can do better than that."

"Morgen's probably got him charmed. Or Caradoc. Someone. And I'm worried they're using him for something, I mean they are, but I don't know how." It sounded weak, as she said it. "Sorry. That's true, and it's also not helpful, is it?"

"Both of those, yes." Lewis didn't look at her, but she could see his shoulder shift. "I know I can't offer a lot of things he can. And I'm not going to try. But I'm going to be over here wanting better for you than that. Someone who makes you happy and gets you to laugh, and who you can do things with that you both enjoy. Besides someone you can enjoy in bed."

The thing of it was, Lewis had been giving her all of that. Last night in bed had, actually, been a romp that had been half discovering where the other was ticklish, and half something very sincere and earnest. There had been a lot of quiet, but a restful sort of quiet. He'd ended the evening spooned up behind her, rocking into her for a long time while his fingers explored. And he did have very deft fingers. No one sensible would argue with that. And Charlotte was trying to be sensible.

"I don't want to argue about it." It came out decidedly like a pouty toddler, and that was no good either. She took a breath and let it out in a puff. "You're right. I admit it. I just don't know what to do about it. And I probably won't know until - after. May Eve, however it goes."

"What exactly are we doing, then?" Lewis did turn at this.

"I was practising my illusions. I think we go with our plans. We sneak in, use illusions for a distraction, use your clever brazier to help disperse the effects of what Morgen's been using, and go from there. If my parents don't hear from me by May first or second, they'll come looking. If either of us gets a chance to make a break for it, we do that, and - you know how to find my parents?"

"Go to the Guard Hall in Trellech and ask for your father - Captain Edgarton, not his other titles - or try for Veritas." Lewis was good with that kind of detail, it was reassuring. "And if that doesn't work, wherever I can go that makes sense and get help from there."

"Exactly. And. Well." Charlotte swallowed. "Come find me, after, whatever else? I owe you some sketches, for one thing, and I'd - I meant it when I said I'd like to help in other ways, if I can. Mama and Aunt Mason and all know people who could probably help with the materia, or your brother's apprenticeship."

Lewis's shoulders went stiff again, and he turned back to the workbench. "And not on my own account?"

Bloody hells. Not language Mama would approve of, but suitable to the situation. Charlotte let out a grunt, decidedly unladylike. "I didn't say that. Don't put words in my mouth, please?" Lewis didn't turn around, and so Charlotte had to go on. "I don't know what I'm feeling. Except I do like you, and I'm enjoying being with you, all the ways. Here, the kitchen, the bed, all of it. But I can't make sense of it right now. I don't trust anything I feel this week, and I don't want to say something I turn out not to mean. I don't want to hurt you."

"Oh." It was a very soft sound, like something ancient crumbling into dust when someone excavated it from an ancient tomb. "Will you know later?" It had all the formality of some language that had tones and modes for that sort of thing, far more elaborate than English. Disinterested observer to one embedded in an emotional bog of her own making, if that was how one could describe a mode.

"I'd like to." Charlotte felt that was the truth, even if

everything was confusing. "Should I climb a tree again when Gareth is here?" It was not the smoothest change of subject she'd ever done. Honestly, it was the clumsiest since she was about eight, but it was what it was.

"You can probably go up the ladder into the attic here. That way you can hear. There's a trunk or two. We can rig up something so you can close it if you need to?" Lewis had, apparently, given a lot more thought to this than Charlotte had. She'd been planning to pack everything of hers up - well, wear her blouse and skirt - and go off to the far end of the field. The chance to overhear was too good to pass up, though.

"You don't think he'll search this time?" It was a reasonable sort of concern.

Lewis shook his head. "I don't think he wants to spend any more time here than he has to. He might ask me if I've seen anyone. I'll lie or duck the question or whatever, best as I can. Divert him." He shrugged one shoulder. "I have a couple of ideas."

There wasn't any help for that one. "Salve or spray or whatever to be more convincing? Use his own tools against him?"

Lewis did turn around at that. "Oh, that's clever. I do have some. Plus what we're making up for May Eve." Then he brushed his hands off on his smock and tilted his head. "Your illusions. You keep assuming there's a reason Morgen's avoiding Arthur directly. The major figures."

"It makes sense, though." Charlotte wanted to stick to this, stubbornly.

"But you're assuming Morgen is doing the sensible thing. Rather than the showy thing, or the thing that gets her praised, or the thing that gets her interesting presents. Putting herself forward as Morgen le Fay, without ever saying those last two bits, that's suggestive. Having Arthur or Guenevere or Lancelot around would spoil that. But it's more - I don't think she's thought about it that deeply. She wants to sweep people up in the moment and the romance of it, but she doesn't care if things have staying power. Lack of ambergris, is what she is. No age, no weight, no essential quality of whale."

Charlotte grimaced, stopped stirring, and then after about twenty seconds, started again. Before she could stir it more than a couple more times, Lewis came and took that. "Mood changed," he said, briskly. "More of that later. Can you wash out this bowl, please?" He handed her one of the copper bowls, and she set to work doing that while she thought about the question.

"So you're saying I should think about different illusions?" Charlotte had been experimenting with several. A great dragon - well, several variations. She'd mostly settled on either red or white, for the dragons famed to have been at the base of Dinas Emrys in lore. They were easy, she'd seen - and done - a number of illustrations of them.

"More dragon, fewer people?" Lewis offered. "Or, I don't know. Can you do a unicorn?"

Charlotte snorted. "Neither of us qualify for unicorns. Nor does anyone there."

"Certainly not Morgen," Lewis agreed. Then he turned around to face her. "Are you upset with me? For earlier?"

She took a long breath and let it out. "You're right. Or at least, probably right. About Victor, I mean. And about this too. It'd be shoddy of me to be angry with you for being right. That's no way to do anything useful." She glanced to the side, setting the bowl down. "I just don't know what to do about a lot of things now. It's not like I can get any traction with any of it until this - soon - is done." She didn't really want to think about it, as much as she wanted to get home and have her own things.

The thing of it was she liked this with Lewis. She liked making meals, and talking to him, and helping him in the lab. She very much enjoyed the evenings and nights. Especially now they were turning into a regular thing. He asked good questions, even if they weren't easy ones. He liked her cooking, and he liked her ideas about what he was doing when she had something to share. It was comfortable.

Victor was comfortable because they'd known each other for so long. But she was beginning to think he was comfortable because they avoided the places it might be prickly. She'd almost never pressed him about his parents, or his choice in friends, or the fact he wouldn't settle down to his apprenticeship. He was amused by her art and her illusion work, but he didn't much want to hear about it. Lewis had been curious about the process, how she was combining things, how the colours worked. Especially since she was improvising when it came to materia for a lot of it. Thank goodness he'd had a stash of cochineal for something, or it would be a very faded red dragon.

Lewis nodded. "I suppose that's what we've got right now." He half turned back. "Do you want to wash up and see about something for supper? I'll have another couple of hours here tonight, and then we ought to make sure we clean up properly, so there's nothing for the morning."

Charlotte considered the practicalities. "Let me go make supper, and then I'll clean up in the cottage, and you can do whatever you need to here? And we'll get up early enough to do one last pass, then I can figure out how to settle into the attic." It wouldn't be comfortable, but it was better than the alternatives.

Lewis nodded, then came over, offering her his hand.

When she squeezed it, he leaned in to kiss her, just once, quite tenderly. "I didn't mean to upset you."

"It's not you doing the upsetting." She swallowed hard. "I'm sorry. I don't have better answers for you. Don't let it stop you from asking questions? I hope whatever else we are, when this is all over, we're still friends."

That was all true, even if she didn't know about anything else she wanted. He must have read the sincerity of it well enough, because he nodded, kissing her forehead now. "Later, then." As if he had hundreds of questions, and he was letting them sit, like materia steeping in oil for its proper cycle. "Supper when?"

"About an hour." She hadn't planned anything fancy tonight. He nodded, and she took herself out the door before she said anything else that was too complicated for words or too revealing of how she felt.

CHAPTER 33
APRIL 29TH IN THE MORNING

L ewis wasn't sure what to say to Charlotte. She had been perfectly, properly, cordial with him, but it was exactly the sort of cordiality he didn't know how to read properly. It wasn't a neatly written recipe; it was something that used abbreviations and coded language that would have been simple for the creator, and had everyone else tearing their hair out.

Despite that, because of that, he didn't know. He'd woken up this morning with her curled up against him, one arm around him, her face buried in his shoulder. He hadn't wanted to move or disturb her, but they did need to be up and have everything sorted. In the end, he nudged her, gently. "Charlotte? Morning. We should make sure you get some food before the attic."

She made a sleepy, muzzy noise, then rolled away, stretching. "You're right. Did you sleep well?"

He had. They hadn't done anything in particular in bed. He hadn't wanted to press things. Instead, he'd talked to her a little about some of the stories of where perfume came from, the legends behind it. It had seemed a safe enough topic, really, intimate in all the ways perfume was and stories were, but not personal.

Now, she was getting up, dressing in her blouse and skirt, and he took the trousers and shirt she'd been wearing and shoved it into the hamper. "Let me put things away up here, like they'll expect. Breakfast in a few? I can make it if you'd rather not."

Charlotte shook her head and kissed his cheek. "I like to, when it's you." Right, he was clearly adding more unfathomable, impossible to interpret phrases to his list.

Once they'd had breakfast, they both did one final check around the cottage, before Charlotte cast a charm to draw anything that might be obviously hers to her hand. It involved hair - a little clump of golden strands shed over the course of a few days, and some other random dust. She grimaced at it, then said. "Pot? I can make them go up in flame, and then we can wash it out."

He gestured at the kitchen, staying well out of the way while she took the pot out to the terrace. She made a tiny, exceedingly local bonfire before she brought the pot back and rinsed the ash down the sink. It all seemed very thorough and also a trifle paranoid, and she didn't seem to think much of it. It made him wonder again about what her family was like to live with. And specifically, whether there was actually risk, or whether it was - as she said - just good habits for the occasional times it did actually matter.

Finally, it was time to pull down the ladder in the lab. Lewis had checked the night before. It was comfortable enough, and there should be plenty of warning if someone got the idea to go and check. They moved a large trunk to one side, half-buried under some old curtains or something of the kind, and Charlotte made a comfortable enough nest.

"I have a book. It'll be fine. And I have my set of stones, so I'll know when he's coming."

That made Lewis feel better. "True. And I'll knock when he's gone. Only, um. Only if I knock three, seven, three, all right? If it's anything else, it's not me, or at least not me doing it freely."

"I don't exactly have a lot of options if you're not, you realise," Charlotte pointed out. "But I might manage to go out the window or something, I suppose. We'll just hope it doesn't come to that."

Lewis felt it was rather inadequate as a plan, but it was what they had. And having her out in the field or tucked into the back of the maze didn't seem much better, honestly. Once he'd closed up the attic, he spent the next hour - it felt like days - working on things in the lab. The stones vibrated before lunchtime, which was at least promising. He'd been worrying Charlotte would be stuck up there all day. On the other hand, presumably Morgen had some sort of plan for the evening, and Gareth would be needed for that.

The door slammed open - or almost. Like in any sensible lab, Lewis renewed the cushioning charm on the door regularly, so that it wouldn't shake anything out on the benches. All right, where Charlotte's family ran to caution with hair and whatever else could be used for tracking, Lewis had his own things like that. That made him feel better. He turned, though, promptly, as he slid the vials of perfume further back on the table.

"Gareth."

"You couldn't even be waiting. Where is it?" Gareth was particularly abrupt today. It was the sort of abruptness that suggested too many potions for alertness and stamina. They weren't good for a body, and Lewis had seen a lot of people abuse them during the War. Not just in the fighting, where it made a certain amount of sense, but also in the various alchemical labs he'd been in. He felt a lot of those people didn't weigh risk sensibly.

"Right here, Gareth." He might have said more, but Gareth cut him off, taking the wooden box roughly, then grabbing Lewis's arm and pushing him back, so hard he staggered.

"Keep your distance. You swear this will work?"

Faced with a direct question, he could only nod. It would work, just not the way Gareth or Morgen expected. If Gareth made him take oath on it, though, that'd get tricky. On the other hand, it'd assume Gareth was good at pressing definitions under oath. It seemed quite plausible he was as bad at that as Morgen was at sturdy mythical foundations.

His luck held, because Gareth went right on. "Right. What day is it now?"

"The twenty-ninth of April, Gareth."

"And what do you do on the thirtieth?"

"Not leave this courtyard, not that I do anyway. Cottage, the lab, that's it. Not even out on the grass."

"And what do you do on the first?" Gareth had the box open, thumbing over the corked lids as he counted them up.

"Stay right where I am." Lewis took another step back, folding his hands in front of him. Though his arm hurt, Gareth had been far more forceful than he ever had been before.

"And what do you do on the second?" Gareth closed the box with a snap of wood. "All there."

"Wait for someone to come talk to me." Of course it was all there. Lewis knew what he was about, especially about delivery to touchy clients. Whatever else the Ayletts had taught him, they'd taught him that bit of it.

"Good boy." Gareth said it like a bit of praise he'd give a somewhat dim dog. "Small hamper by the cottage. Make it last. It might be the third before anyone has time to come see you."

It was, on the whole, a good thing that there had been plenty in the pantry when Charlotte arrived. They were getting a bit low on milk and cream, with both of them using it in their tea, as well as the cooking. On the other hand, they had no intention of being here on the first, or at least Charlotte didn't, so maybe it'd all work out. "Yes, Gareth. Is there anything I should be working on right now?"

"There's a note. I don't know what's in it." He sounded irritated by that, too, and Lewis wished it hadn't come out like that. "Morgen has plans. You know what's good for you, if you want the materia, and for it to get to your brother safely."

Lewis shivered at that, and he didn't try to hide it. He wouldn't have managed, anyway. It wasn't as if Gareth and Morgen didn't know what they had on him, to make him dance to their particular tune. "Yes, Gareth. I understand." Now, he could only hope Gareth would get bored and go away.

"And you haven't seen anyone around. A woman, more or less your age."

"No one new like that, Gareth." Charlotte wasn't new. Not anymore. Not new in his life, not new in this place, not even new in his bed. Not that he could let any of that show.

"Let me have a look round the cottage." Gareth strode out, the door hitting the charms and not banging again. Lewis trailed along after him. He was absolutely sure they'd cleared everything, but Gareth went to peer at the table, the kitchen, the sofa. Though he only went upstairs and came right back down, with barely enough time to turn around at the top. "Not like you'd have a woman up there. You wouldn't know what to do with one."

Lewis couldn't decide if he was glad Charlotte wouldn't have heard that, or if he wished she had. She'd likely laugh her head off, but he could tell her in a little. Once they were sure the coast was clear. Gareth swept around the sitting room one last time. "Right. Stay put. You know what's good for you."

"I do, Gareth." Lewis hesitated. "I hope everything goes well." He offered it nervously, the way he would have before. It would be rude not to say something.

Gareth grunted. "Of course it will." And then he was gone, long strides taking him up the path to the gate.

Lewis stayed in the sitting room, just standing there, for a minute or two. Then he went back to the lab, closing the door behind him, and puttered about, as if talking to himself. "I'm glad that's over with. I'll just work on something simple, in case he has a reason to come back. Half an hour or so should do it." What he wanted to do was work on what he was making for Charlotte, but he was in no state to do the more delicate work of it. His dexterity was just not there, and his magic wasn't settled either.

Instead, he flipped the half-hour hourglass, and set to work making a simple salve for scrapes. It might come in handy tomorrow, who knew, and if not, it'd be useful for someone sometime. It kept well. And it was easy to make, that was part of the point of it. Though he rather preferred his adjustments to the recipe to the ones he'd learned in school or from the Ayletts. He leaned harder on the rosemary, for one thing, and he felt it helped a lot with healing the cut. Plantain too, of course, but that was a given, and it didn't have much in the way of smell.

When the sand ran out, he grabbed the hook for the trapdoor, and rapped the ceiling, right where the trapdoor was, three, seven, three. Then he reached for the hook and pulled down the door and the ladder. Charlotte was waiting, right at the top, a bit wide-eyed. "Are you all right?"

It was the first thing out of her mouth, and Lewis had been about to ask the same thing. Instead, he nodded once before getting out, "You?"

"I heard you tell me you were giving it half an hour. He's gone, I'm sure." She clambered down before Lewis could offer a hand to help her. Though honestly, it wasn't as if another person's hand were much help on a ladder. Instead, he could put it back up while she brushed off her hands. "Lunch?"

"I'm not sure I can eat. But there's another hamper. We should probably see what's in it." Lewis did get the door, peering out into the courtyard just to make sure. "Actually, let me check one thing in the cottage first."

Gareth had gone upstairs, he'd been up there almost no time, but there was a chance he might have dropped something. Charlotte hung back, leaning against the lab, as Lewis went ahead. He went upstairs, then looked around, frowning. Something smelled wrong. Magically smelled wrong, he thought, not an actual scent. He then turned around, looking carefully, and after a minute, found a little terracotta disc, the sort of thing that took a listening charm well enough.

He left it where it was, and then went back out downstairs and to the lab. "There's a disc, this big." He held his fingers up an inch or two. "I don't know what made me spot it. It was tucked by one of the cabinets. Listening charm?"

"Probably. Good grief, why do they have to try to be clever? How long was he up there?"

"Just a few seconds. Enough time to shove it out of the way. It smelled wrong. What do we do about it?"

"If he doesn't get sound from it, he'll wonder. On the other hand, if it was out of the way, you could have piled sheets or blankets or something on it." Charlotte rubbed her face. "We can't put it outside. He'd hear birds. We can't leave it where it is. He'll hear us. Possibly even downstairs. Do we think he'll come back if he doesn't hear anything?"

Lewis considered. "He seemed awfully busy. And likely on some potion to help make there be thirty-six hours in the day."

Charlotte nodded. "I vote for a bottle, some water, a few stones to rest it on, and a silencing charm. If he comes looking, we'll have to deal with it then. But then we can stick it out the back door or something. You'd know enough to do that, yes?"

"Water and glass to distort the sound, the stones to make sure there's water under it, to buffer vibrations. Yes. I did take third year Incantation."

"Oh, that's right. I forgot about that exercise. And it's all things you have on hand. Right. If he does cause trouble, say you saw it, and you weren't comfortable with it or whatever."

Lewis hesitated, then took her hand. "I - I'm not. I'm not comfortable with any of it." Then he winced. "Gareth was - careful of my arm, here."

"You must have bruise salve, somewhere? Right. Listening charm first, then the hamper - I'll unpack that, save your arm. Then we'll see about salve and lunch, all right."

Lewis was glad someone had a plan. He could, in fact, find a jar and water, and a few pebbles, and take care of the listening charm. He brought it ceremonially outside, setting it on the far side of the courtyard, where it would mostly be exposed to a few rather vocal rooks. Once he'd done that, Charlotte went ahead of him, picking up the hamper with some visible effort and setting it in the kitchen to unpack it.

There was, in fact, plenty of milk and cream and eggs, as well as some fresh-baked scones, still warm from a charm, and clotted cream and jam. Charlotte unpacked things, taking various items into the pantry and coming out. Then she felt on the bottom of the hamper, then pulled out something tucked in the fabric at the bottom. It was a bit of ribbon, as for hair, a comb, and then a set of underthings.

Charlotte blinked. "These are mine. And they're... someone must have known I'm here? Someone still at the house. You'd never have looked though, perhaps?"

Lewis shook his head. "I'd just have unpacked it and left it for the next time someone came, with the empty milk bottles." He frowned. "Do you think someone knows? Someone in the house?"

"Someone on the staff, maybe?" Charlotte grimaced. "All right, that's entirely too much mystery before lunch. Let me go comb out my hair and all, and then what do you want with the scones?"

CHAPTER 34
THAT NIGHT

The rest of the afternoon had been taken up with various practical things. Charlotte had left the pantry and the kitchen in as good order as she could. She'd made several things that would keep in stasis charms for a few days, if - well.

There were a whole set of potential outcomes from tomorrow, and some of them were not at all pleasant. She was reasonably sure she wouldn't come to lasting harm. Even if she did end up in the clutches of Morgen and Gareth - it sounded melodramatic, but clutches was the best description she had - she was confident her family would notice. There was always a chance of some fluke horrible thing going wrong, but she couldn't refuse to act based on that tiny chance. There was also the fluke chance of falling off a horse or off a cliff or an ancient ladder collapsing or who knew what else. And she did most of those things often enough. Not the cliffs. She left cliffs to Gabe for a reason.

But there was a decent chance of some ongoing unpleasantness, and that was the part she really needed to talk out with Lewis. Not a conversation she wanted to have. It would touch on a number of uncomfortable points.

Fortunately, there was plenty of work to do in the alchemy lab for the rest of the evening. Lewis was working on something he obviously didn't want to talk about, and he handed a whole set of things to Charlotte to bottle to specifications. She honestly found messing with the little metal funnels and the caps rather satisfying. And the incense pellets for the brazier smelled like they'd cut through any mental fog imaginable.

It wasn't until nearly midnight that they retreated upstairs to bed. Charlotte meant to bring up what she needed to say, but before she could, Lewis encouraged her to stretch out on the bed. "I haven't had a chance to try my own arts on you." Before she could ask what he meant, he went on. "This is only a first go. I'm not satisfied with it yet. This deserves perfection. But I believe it's a very interesting working model, and I do hope you'll consider it when deciding if you'd like further engagements. Robe off, if you don't mind?"

He said it lightly enough, but Charlotte was painfully aware in that moment exactly how easily she could break him, even by gently backing away. He had gone and fallen for her; she was almost certain. She would be certain, as soon as she saw him when this was all over, without tomorrow night's confrontation looming over them like a badly managed dragon. Then she'd have to figure out what to do, what was fair to him and fair to her, and with any luck, good for them both.

"What should I do?" She wasn't going to argue. There were plenty of ways she was making things far more difficult for Lewis than he deserved. She could at least be reasonable about this.

"Lie down on your stomach here. Head to either side, but can you pull your hair out of the way? Close your eyes if you like."

It was an easy enough instruction, and though he was speaking lightly, Charlotte knew, deep in her heart, that this was a fragile thing for him. She settled herself, head turned so she could see him enough to be going on with. "Yes?"

Lewis considered, then reached to brush a strand of hair off her cheek, then adjusted the rest of her hair well up away from her neck. Then he pulled out a small case with four different small bottles in it. He pulled one out, checking the label - it was just a colour to her, she couldn't read the label, something orange-red. Then he dropped a few drops on her back, and she felt a burst of heat. It wasn't wrong, it wasn't painful, but it was quite blatant. Like the beat of the sun on the unprotected skin at the height of a summer day.

A moment later, there were Lewis's fingers, pushing the oil against her skin, drawing a pattern like a branching tree. Charlotte let out a small sigh, and his fingers stopped. "Not too hot?"

"Just right." It was something out of a fairy tale. Oh, she knew there were charms for this sort of thing, and for pleasure. But there was a sensuality to the oil, the way it slipped against her skin, the way it was his fingers rubbing it in, that added layers to it. And it felt wonderful, his thumb pausing to press into the knot she'd been feeling in her shoulder, before his fingers continued on in spiralling, draping patterns. Charlotte let herself drift with it, though it seemed a little selfish. When she tried to move, though, there were fingers pressing down on her back.

"Just like that. I've others to try. We can come back to the warm at the end, if you like."

"Others?" This was wonderful. It wasn't arousing, exactly, but the intimacy of it definitely was. The idea that he'd made this for her, for them to use together, now, that was a spark that fluttered and danced through her.

"Mmm. Yes. Moment." He set the bottle aside after tightening the cap, then cleaned off his hands, deliberately, before rubbing her back with a clean cloth. He pulled out another, this one with a purple label, and then let a few drops fall on her back. They were like drops of ice water, a delightful contrast to the warmth. It made her body tighten, something in the contrast making her whimper louder. "There you are. Tell me if it's too much."

It was a lot, but Lewis's fingers moved lightly, this time, leaving dots and dashes of cold against the heat, cutting through it and making her gasp her or there. When he finally lifted his hand again, she was quivering with it. His fingers brushed once against her hip. "Oh, you do like that, don't you? I'll remember that. Warmth to relax you, cold to make you arch and sigh and quiver."

It made her snort, because he was being entirely practical about it. "You are brilliant." She added after a moment. "I don't know of anything like this out there, not in oils. Charms, yes."

"I'd not want to sell them without a lot more testing. Not safe on sensitive parts, either of these, and I'm none too sure about the others. And people will do foolish things with alchemical potions and salves." Oh, quite. Lewis went on. "Want to try the other two, or is this enough for tonight?"

Charlotte let out a huff of breath. "One now, and - one as a promise for later, sometime?" She suddenly wanted that, an explicit invitation to come to bed again. Whenever and wherever that was.

His hand went flat on her lower back, then he bent to kiss the back of her neck. "As you like. I like that idea. The one I'm not choosing is pleasure. Tonight, then...." He repeated what he'd done before, cleaning off his hand and her back thoroughly before he reached for another vial, this one a green. "This is more like the cold, to let you brace."

It was and it wasn't. When his fingers brushed along skin, again in smooth lines, it was like the feeling when her foot had been tucked under her for ages. The prickling sensation that was just a hair too much. Feeling it on her back, that was like hearing some amazing piece of music, being somewhere that moved her, only it was a physical sensation bringing that sense of awe.

She did whimper now, even whine in her throat, over and over, her hands grabbing for a bit of the sheets so she had something to hold on to. She'd teased him, just a few nights ago, about pain being a thing people did, and if this was what he'd made of it, it was perfect. Something about it made her toes curl tight, her back arch, all of it too much and just the right amount. Inside a minute, she was panting with it, making the most undignified noises, and she didn't care at all.

It couldn't last. She couldn't have lived, if it had, the way it took up all the space in her head, every last corner. But she didn't know how long it had lasted, either. All she knew was that eventually, she was able to breathe again, without a cascade of new sensations dancing along her spine and her back. Charlotte could look up at him, and Lewis had cleaned his hands, looking down at her, so smugly. He should be smug. He'd been brilliant, and he knew it.

She inhaled more slowly, then let it out. "That could make you a fortune. Once it's safe. I'm sure of it."

"I like this." He moved to clean her back, the cloth soft and steady. "Bringing you like that. I didn't - you didn't, I mean."

"Oh, almost." It came out breathy. "Let's do something about that. Well. Let's do something about your pleasure, your particular pleasures." Talking could wait. Talking needed to wait. She wanted to seize the moment and coil around him, and let him have whatever delights he wanted. "And yes. After all of this, I want to try the other. And all of them again."

"Especially this one." Lewis held up the vial one last time, before putting it in the wooden box, and twisting to set it down on the floor, out of the way. "I have other ideas, too. But I'd need specific materia for them."

"More reason to sort out your supplies, then." She twisted onto her side, mostly so she could get a hand free and start touching and stroking him. "What would you like right now?"

She'd thought about offering her mouth, but she wanted to do that when they could take their time, and this was not a moment for that. Almost immediately, Lewis nudged her onto her back. They became a tangle of arms and legs and sounds, rubbing against each other and feeling skin on skin until she was begging him to fill her. When he finally did, he found a rhythm that had them both moaning, her legs and hips hitching to let him move as freely as she could manage. In their mutual aftermath, he collapsed on top of her, his weight steady and reassuring, before settling against her, head on her shoulder and an arm across her stomach. Then he lifted the hand, waving it at the lights, and they dimmed entirely, leaving them in darkness.

The darkness made it easier to speak, and yet she didn't want to break the moment. She let herself just be there, feeling him, the breath against her cheek, the weight of his arm, until she took a breath and he shifted slightly. "Lewis. About tomorrow."

"Yes?"

"I'd understand if you decided not to come with me." It came out badly, her voice cracking at the end. His hand moved against her stomach, stopped, then started again.

"I'm going to." There was a long pause, so long she almost thought he wasn't going to say anything else. Then came the words, as carefully measured and precise as Lewis was when he was measuring perfume. "Morgen's using the tales of knights and ladies for her own advantage. And I would not presume to be your knight, not without you wanting that. But I want to do the, the chivalrous thing. The courtly thing. Because you shouldn't go in there alone. Because we don't know what will happen." Then, his voice very soft, he added "Because maybe I can help, and if I can, I will."

Charlotte shivered, the sort of shiver like a hatching egg about to crack, a moment before life burst out in an entirely new way. His hand slipped down to her hip, steadier, his head a little more on her shoulder. She couldn't say anything, and after another few seconds, he asked, "Is that a problem?"

"No. I just - I don't want you getting hurt." It was the truth, and it was a very simple one. She wanted good things for him, all the good things he ought to have in his life. Security for himself, and steady support for his brother, and happiness, and people who appreciated his art and his skills. He ought to have all the materia he wanted to work with, and a pleasant space to do it in.

"If you hadn't come here, I'd have got hurt." His voice was right in her ear. "At least this time, I'm choosing. Besides. Helping you is right. Not helping you is wrong."

"It's that simple for you?" She let out a long breath. "You're certain."

"I am. Nervous. I'm not going to lie to you." His hand cupped her hip again. "I don't know what's going to happen, what Morgen or Gareth might do. But that's not going to stop me from being right there. And I think the incense will help."

"The way it smells, I should hope so." Charlotte tried to keep her voice lighter. Then she couldn't. "Just. Thank you." Before she could figure out other things to say, she twisted against him, burying her face against his neck. A moment later, he was hugging her tightly, both of them wordless. Neither of them figured out something new to say for quite a long time. She almost thought he was asleep when he spoke again.

"Stories don't talk about after. Other than the pomp and formal celebration. It's not going to be like that, I know. I'd feel better if I knew what the after would be like."

"So would I." She hugged him again, just holding on this time, rather than clinging. "We'll." She stopped, took a breath. "We'll figure out the after together."

He must know she was committing to something, here and now and also then, in the future. She felt him kiss her cheek, just once, before he nestled closer. No more words, apparently. She slept, tangled up with him, all night, half-waking a couple of times to find him curled around her, attentive and just the right amount of possessive, even in his sleep.

CHAPTER 35
APRIL 30TH IN THE AFTERNOON

Lewis woke up the next morning - well, nearly noon - determined to do the right thing. Even if he still wasn't sure entirely what the right thing was. Supporting Charlotte, that was right. He knew it, unalterably, the same way he knew perfume notes he'd spent time with, or the steps of distillation.

Charlotte was up and about. He could hear the small comfortable noises down in the kitchen. They'd laid out their plans, and most of hers involved coiling and then letting her magic fly. He didn't think she was inclined to archery as a sport - though honestly, he wouldn't be surprised by it at this point. But that was the image he kept getting, of an arrow loosed with precise aim, arcing over the sky.

Lewis had fallen for her, and hard. He hadn't meant to, but here he was, in love. He couldn't change his heart, but he could make sure it wasn't her problem to deal with. Pressing her would not do any good, as well as being unkind. She'd made what she was up for clear. And if she changed her mind after - after whatever happened tonight

- well, then it would be after. A lot of things would change, one way or another.

He came downstairs, dressing gown around him, belted tight. "Can I help with anything?"

"If you like, set the table and bring things over?" Charlotte hesitated, then added. "I made up some pasties, or something more or less like them. The crust isn't quite right? But if you're back here on your own tomorrow. Or. Well."

She was looking at all the ways things might go, as much as he was. Probably rather a lot more, given that he was sure she wasn't telling him all of her possible plans. His part of it was simple, really. Light the brazier, make sure it stayed lit, and keep out of the way. Charlotte had the far harder part, or at least the far more obvious part.

Of course Lewis hadn't tried to talk her out of it. A proper knight would have, would have gone charging off at the dangerous thing on his own. Lewis, though, couldn't get the half-faded memories of the story of Geraint and Enid out of his head. It had been some years since he'd read it, but it had all the tangles of a Fatae tale - hunt for the white hart and all. But what had stuck with him was how badly Geraint had treated Enid, a maiden of excellent birth, and with a number of skills and wisdoms of her own.

Back in school, he'd sworn not to be that sort. He didn't know better. He wasn't any braver or wiser or more skilled than Charlotte was. Not that he didn't have his own skills, but they were the quiet kind, not the questing kind, and they both knew it.

So now, presented with a chance to show what he could do, he wanted to do the other thing. Charlotte had skills he did not. She had experience of the world he did not. She knew what an investigation would need, far better than he did. Charlotte could call illusions to her fingers. Lewis suspected she could do it nearly as well as Gareth, if given a chance and incentive, for all she had less practice. Gareth was fundamentally lazy, and that came out in his magic, even if his hands were strong.

No matter. He would set the table, they would have lunch, Charlotte would likely want to rest for a bit. And the evening would come. What would happen would happen, and all he could do was be as steady as he could manage and be there. They ate in near enough silence, but at the end of it, Charlotte looked up. "You will write. Come see me when we're done. Tell me you're all right?"

Lewis nodded just once. "Of course." He cleared his throat. "Did you want to rest for a bit? I've something, before we set out, it won't take very long."

"Something else?" Charlotte looked away, out the window and across to the lab, through the courtyard. "You've done so much. Far more than I expected." Then she stopped, holding up her hand. "That came out badly. Let me try that again. You've been so kind. You didn't turn me in. This has been - you made me welcome, in all the ways you could. I don't think you understand how much."

He was fairly sure he didn't. Even if he understood his part in it, which was not a sure thing, he was certain he did not understand what it had meant to her. "It was the right combination. The proper accord. I don't have better words than that."

She nodded now, just once. Then she stood and kissed him on the forehead. "I will lie down for a bit, if you don't mind. Can you make sure I'm awake by six?" Sunset wasn't until half-eight. Whatever they were doing in the house would only be getting started then. It would give plenty of time for their last preparations, and to get through the maze in good time.

He spent the afternoon finishing up the last few things in the lab, and then packing up those things he absolutely didn't want to have out of his control. That was the time-consuming part, packing the vials into a padded case, adding the protective charms, and making sure they'd fit in a satchel. There was the vial for Theo, enough to make doses for a month or two. There were several other things that Theo might find useful, or Mother. The only two he left out, for the moment, were what he had in mind for the evening. The vial for Charlotte, and the salve for their eyes, so they could get through the maze.

At six, he went up and gently shook Charlotte's shoulder. She rolled over, blinking, before she smiled up at him. "Evening. I'll be down in a few, all right?"

"That's fine. I'll - you had the cheese and such for supper in mind, right?" She nodded. Lewis had his duties, then. "I'll put that out. No sense doing this on an entirely empty stomach."

It made her almost giggle, which was his goal. Some rituals wanted to be approached fasting, but this wasn't a ritual sort of evening. This was something else, the kind of magic that wanted fuel and connection to the real bounty of the earth, and the land under their feet. Lewis suspected Charlotte had more of the theory about that, since her father was a Lord.

Charlotte was thoughtful while she ate, making a couple of comments, but the conversation didn't want to flow. When they were both done, she washed up, then said, "It'll take me twenty or thirty minutes to put myself together. Will that leave enough time for what you wanted? And can you do your own salve, or do you want me to?"

Lewis nodded. "Yes to both." She swept off to the bathing room. He could hear the water running twice, then silence. While she was in there, he did apply the salve to his own eyelids and around his eyes, carefully.

When Charlotte came out, her hair was in an intricate sequence of braids, looping and curling. It seemed like a cross between the most Victorian concoctions and something that grew like nature. A mediaeval maiden's fantasy, or something of the kind. With it she wore her blouse and skirt, and the overall effect was striking.

And she looked fully put together, cosmetics and all. Charms, that must be, almost certainly. It made him suck in a breath, and then bow, the sort of courtly bow he was sure he was going to mess up in the middle, and actually didn't.

When he straightened up, she was smiling, then laughing. "The right effect, then. Mama always swears the right clothing is armour. Though in the days of the corset, a tad more literally, depending on the construction." She bobbed, bending her knees. "Good sir knight."

"You look—" Lewis stopped, rummaging for words. "You look like someone who knows what she wants, and what she will have. And what she won't do."

"That is the effect I wanted. Being somewhat limited in costuming. I suppose I could have rummaged in the lab's attic for something, but none of it looked promising yesterday. And I really am not terribly good with a needle, comparatively." She paused, and said, "I'd been practising illusions as costuming on and off for ages, so I suppose it's good to try it out and see how it goes," with a very peculiar tone to her voice, like she was thinking of something specific and not at all sure how she felt about it. Then her voice softened. "You had something specific in mind?"

Lewis nodded. "I need my case. Come into the sitting room, where the light is good?"

Charlotte went ahead of him, and he watched her walk, steady strides, the skirt shifting back and forth, the sway of her hips. She had all the proper underthings on, and they might not be a corset, but he thought they were a sort of harness, a shape to do work in. She was using the container of her clothes the way he used the container of a mortar.

Once she reached the sitting room, she stopped in the middle, turning to face him. "Here?"

"There." He set the two bottles he'd brought down, then picked up the vial. "I made this for you. For tonight." Now, he was nervous, his hands were shaking.

"What—" She stopped, then reached out a hand to brush her fingers against his. "Will you tell me about it?"

To make it, he'd built the foundation of a scent, the kind of thing she might wear in a score of different ways. For her, it had two kinds of rose, ambergris, a single drop of civet. A few drops of vervain oil, but that was for the magic, not for the scent, it didn't have a scent. And of course the cardamom she'd ground up for him, a brush of honey and beeswax. With it, he'd added a layer of citrus, the blend he'd been working on for days, to add brightness and clarity, all the solar protection against the fogs and mists of night.

Some other night, perhaps he'd get to know her in a blend of all the night-blooming flowers, rich with scent. That was not tonight. "An oil, a perfume. Clearheadedness. Protection from magic. Good luck. All the blessings I could make in the time we had." He had so many others he wanted to try, but he'd been limited by what he had on hand, and the time. No chance to soak things for a month, to line up the perfect timing, or even to collect much in the way of summer dew.

Charlotte looked at the bottle in his hand, then back up at him, meeting his eyes. "You made it. This week?"

"This week. May I?" He didn't know what else to say about it. He could list the notes, and he would if he asked. But perfume was something for the other senses, not for the mint-sharp clarity of words. It had soft edges, not precision.

"Please." She dropped her hands to her side, then asked, "What should I do?"

"May I unbutton your blouse for a moment?" Gareth, he was sure, would have just reached for the clothing, would have taken past permission for present. Lewis would do the other thing. Still. Again. For as long as he could. She nodded once, and he reached to undo a couple of buttons, enough to expose that v of pale skin. Then he opened the vial, getting a few drops on his fingers. He smoothed it along the collarbone like paint, first on the right, then on the left. Then he let his fingers slip down, to touch over her heart, before lifting to the pulse points under her jaw, behind her ears, a dot under her nose. He touched the vial again and again, to make sure there was plenty, adding a brush of his fingers against the back of her neck, then finally each wrist. "There."

She'd moved a little, standing so her weight was evenly balanced, her eyes half closed and her chin up. For a long moment, he wasn't sure what she thought, whether she hated it. When she spoke, her voice was the sort of whisper that grabbed attention. "A perfect accord."

It shook him; it felt like it shook the room, and she reached to take his hand before he quite dropped the vial. He'd capped it. He had more of the base oil, of course, but that would have been a shame, and now his mind was running away with him. From him. He sucked in a breath, and in that moment, she squeezed his hand. "It's wonderful. I feel like I could do anything. My way. How I choose."

Lewis met her eyes and he just nodded. He had no words for this, and maybe, just maybe, he didn't need them. Lewis didn't need to justify anything or explain. He could just let it be. When he could find any language again, he cleared his throat. "There's a spray, too, for all of you. To help the protective part."

"When you're ready, then." He almost fumbled again, but he brought out the little perfume atomiser. It was the bottle he'd had, though this was mostly water with enough of the perfume oil for the effect. He sprayed it, the mist settling around her like a cloak, something grand and majestic, and he could smell how it settled into her hair, how it encompassed her. Charlotte asked, only when he was done. "Will it work for you, too?"

"Not as well. But it would help."

She held out her hand. "Let me share, then." Lewis wasn't going to argue. He held out his hands, letting her walk around him. She made a ritual out of it, step by stately step, the scent settling on him like a blessing. It was something like walking out into a summer rain, the kind that drenched to the skin and made everything new and clean. And it was something like armour, something like a wall between him and the world. It wasn't made to suit him, and somehow that didn't matter. She was lending her cloak and her protection, and she was choosing to include him there.

When Charlotte had come round to face him again, she stepped closer, kissing him tenderly on the lips. Lightly, and just for a moment, before she stepped back. "Shall we?"

He nodded. First, he turned to put the vial and atomiser in his bag, then he picked it up, taking up the brazier in his other hand. He'd light it when they got much closer, and the pellets for the incense were already waiting there. She led the way out of the cottage, pausing just long enough for him to close and latch the door, before they walked side by side up into the maze.

CHAPTER 36
APPROACHING THE HOUSE

The closer they got to the entrance to the maze, the more Charlotte could feel something running through her. The poorly tutored would go on about magic, or ethereal energy, or some such thing. Charlotte knew better.

It wasn't the land magic. It wasn't reaching tendrils of Fatae magic, swooping up from some chthonic realm. Well, probably not, given that the nearest site was in fact an underground cave and thus the very definition of chthonic. It wasn't enchantments and wards from the house. She knew how to feel those, even if she could neither make nor remove them.

She had painstakingly worked through what might be there, based on her own experience of a few days in the house and her moderately educated guesses based on what she had seen and heard. She was neither a trained Guard, nor a Penelope. But she was Papa's daughter, and more especially Mama's. And that did count for something. With luck, a significant number of somethings sufficient unto the tasks of the evening.

Those were, she thought, threefold. Or at least she hoped for three, because seven began to get unwieldy, and five had resonances had to be accounted for in other ways. Three was manageable by two people with certain resources but not nearly enough of them for comfort.

First, to stop Morgen doing whatever it was she intended. This was the climax, the point on which everything would turn. On a practical level, Morgen would have invested a lot in whatever she had in mind, and so would Gareth and the others. If Charlotte and Lewis were lucky, whoever was actually competent there wouldn't have the energy or the time to bring in their best skills.

Second, she wanted to neutralise anyone who wished to be difficult, long enough for the Guard to get there. There would be extra people on duty tonight, though probably not Papa. Everyone knew he had a specific set of duties starting before dawn tomorrow for the land magic.

Probably Aunt Kate, who would do very well at the resolution of something like this. Captain Donovan would be good - terribly stern, but entirely competent - but with her other hat on as Lady Donovan, she also had obligations tomorrow. That might mean Captain Willoughby, who was competent. Papa had made sure to say so. But he did like to presume on professional connections for social reasons, and that seemed like it might become messy here.

Anyway, that part of it wasn't up to Charlotte and Lewis. If Charlotte could manage to get them where they couldn't cause problems, that would do. A sedative potion, thoroughly deployed, locking them in the feasting room, even a charm or two. Any of those would work. She wouldn't know which made sense until they had a better sense of where Morgen had set things up. From there, well. One of them could make the long hike to the portal, or maybe one of the staff could be persuaded. Maybe there was a horse in the stables. Three miles on horseback would be fast for Charlotte, though she didn't much like the idea of leaving Lewis behind.

Third, and last, to make sure that everyone who wasn't being actively difficult was all right. Including, Charlotte very much hoped, Victor. There was really no way to plan for this one. She had no idea how many people would be difficult, who would seem to be easy-tempered and then become difficult, or what. Locking everyone in a single room seemed like an increasingly good plan.

Instead of worrying about later, she focused on what she knew about illusions. She did know a fair bit. She'd started practising the appearance illusions with Victor as soon as she'd got the skill to try, to be able to give him what he wanted most when they were married. Now, she was going to use the same skills to save him a wholly different way. It was the part of why she hadn't considered leaving she had not explained to Lewis; she had refused to leave Victor behind. And of course she wouldn't leave Lewis, not to have his work twisted further. At any rate, she had put her time in learning and practising, and she would have to hope it was enough.

Now they were at the entrance to the maze, and Charlotte waited for Lewis to come up beside her. "I am thinking they're in the hall, where we had the evening things. But maybe also the public rooms along the north. They might have used the breakfast room for staging or costuming or whatever. But the gaming room, the sitting room, the morning room, and then the dining room, along the east wall." She frowned, considering the space. "There's a bit that sticks out on the end. We'll want to make sure whatever is there is locked, too."

"I do remember the map." Lewis spoke quietly, but when she looked up at him, he was watching her intently. "But I've only been inside a couple of times. You've got a better sense of all of it."

Charlotte considered. "Let's circle around to that side of the house, see what's lit up and all that." She peered across the lawn. The timing on this had the feeling of the uncanny, with the full of the moon smack at the same time - well, allowing for a few hours - as sunset, on May Eve. She could not have picked a better general timing for this sort of illusion work if she'd tried. That was probably at least part of the point here. The sun had set at two past eight. The full moon would be at half-ten. In the two and a half hours between, well, anything might happen.

Charlotte wasn't enough of a ritual astronomer to be sure of it, but she'd known Lewis must know this. He had, and he'd pointed at how the moon was rapidly moving into conjunction with Jupiter tonight, and it would be by the middle of the night. He'd shrugged, and said, "I don't think we'd like what happens if she uses that."

It was what had made sure that they needed to stop her, and to do it in a way that meant Morgen couldn't try something like this again. Whatever that looked like. Now it came to the moment, Charlotte was all nerves. She tried to focus on what was next. Lights on the north wall.

First things first. She cast the charms she knew to muffle sound and distract the eye. With any luck, anyone seeing a shift of a shadow would think it a deer or something of the kind. Did they have deer here? She hadn't seen any. Then she brought her mind back. No distractions. There wasn't time for them.

She touched Lewis's hand once, then slipped through the opening of the maze, sticking close to the hedge and circling down along the edge of the garden. If there were people in the kitchen or the related rooms, she didn't want them to glance out a window and see shadowy shapes coming toward the house. She had no idea if any of them could be trusted, if they'd tell Morgen or Gareth immediately, or what.

As it turned out, the breakfast room lights were out, but there were dim lights in the other two. The question was going to be getting into the house. Charlotte remembered that the ground floor windows on this side were raised up a bit, which meant both a chance of staff below stairs seeing them, and the problem of getting in at a window. After a moment, she nudged Lewis, leading the way around to the east corner of the house.

There was a door to the garden here. Charlotte paused on the stone of the terrace, then as silently as she could, eased the door open, to see if there was anyone inside. She knew the charm for that, too. Gabe had taught it to her, because it really was very practical in quite a few situations, like checking if someone was in the library or not.

No one was there. She put one foot in the room, then another, and she could feel Lewis following right behind her. The room was dimly lit, enough to see what they were doing, but not so much it would be jarring to enter it from out of a dark room. She looked around, finding a few boxes and containers, but no sign people were actively using them at the moment.

There were sounds through the door, though. Nothing that Charlotte could make sense of. They were far too muffled for that. However, there was something that sounded like a flute and maybe a drum, people reciting things in unison, or rather a call and response. There were louder bits, with both men's and women's voices, and ones with just a woman. After a moment's more thought, Charlotte pointed across to the next room. If they could get to the drawing room, they could get to the hall. From there, they could get to the little enclosed foyer that had two doors to the dining room and a bit of protection from being seen by any of the staff. Not that the staff had seemed to be very prominent all along.

Their luck held. The drawing room felt even more empty. Charlotte desperately wished for the range of charms Gabe had at his disposal. She'd have given a lot to know when the last people in the room had come through. The lights were a hair brighter, and Charlotte moved well away from the windows. Not that there were likely people out there.

Charlotte took a deep breath, then considered whether now was time for the incense. It would, in all likelihood, be obvious once it went on the brazier, both from the effect and from the smell. Light it too late, and they might get pulled into whatever enchantments Morgen and the others were weaving. Light it too soon, and they'd give their presence away.

Lewis gestured at it inquisitively. Charlotte gestured, little finger movements of walking through the hall, to the alcove with the stairs up, then lighting it there. It all depended on if someone was lurking in that alcove or foyer or whatever she wanted to call it. It was the sort of architectural feature which Uncle Gil would have frowned at, for several reasons. No defensive purpose, a chance of opening a door into someone in the hall and awkward for anyone who actually wanted to go upstairs. Charlotte had certainly found the last one true enough.

The only thing was to do it. Charlotte eased the door to the hall open, then wider - there was no one there. The door to the alcove was closed, but she had enough of an angle to cast the charm again. There was no one there, through the next door, though she had an impression of rather a lot of people not far beyond. And not on the far side of a solid door.

It suggested curtains, maybe, or just having the door open. Charlotte didn't know the variations on the charm results near well enough for this. She nodded at Lewis, indicating with her fingers that she'd walk across. He should count to ten, and follow.

The alcove was, in fact, lacking in people. There were a few items that suggested some pageantry might have been arranged here, but the items were tucked out of the way. Heavy velvet curtains hung against the doors, both of them. Lewis joined her, right on time, and she gestured at the other curtained doorway, then at the brazier. He nodded and set about lighting it, silently. Charlotte took a deep breath and began to set up the framework that would allow the illusion she had planned.

CHAPTER 37
IN THE GREAT HALL

Lewis couldn't be the one to start this. For one thing, Charlotte was the one in charge of the illusions. For another, nothing he had available was active, except the incense, and he had that going.

It wouldn't affect the illusions, that was the thing. Just the muzzy-headed agreeableness that Morgen had been encouraging. People could see what they saw and make the sense of it they made. The illusions - Charlotte's were meant to be distracting. Charlotte had talked a little about what she thought they might manage. At the worst, they might manage to lock the doors and summon help somehow. Or at least get away.

She'd admitted, up front, that it wasn't an ideal plan. It wasn't even within a good afternoon's ramble of an ideal plan, was how she'd put it. But it was what they had, she thought neither of them would actually get hurt directly. They were both too valuable for that. And she was confident that if she were actually hurt or restrained in the more obvious ways, her family would figure it out right quick.

He was trusting a lot to that analysis. Now, he swallowed hard, shifting the brazier a little to let the smoke begin to curl and fill the space. Charlotte had her ear to the hanging fold of the curtain, concentrating so hard her eyebrows were furrowed. He could hear bits of it too, as he carefully walked to the other curtained doorway. It came a bit clearer as he got his own ear facing the larger room, through folds of velvet.

They were mirroring each other now, he and Charlotte, both facing each other. There was a steady drumbeat, the entrancing sort he'd heard in some of the Ritual class workings. Morgen was talking, her voice rolling and rich, a purring control that felt like it was sending vines up around his ankles to hold him in place. He took a deep breath, smelling the salve under his nose, the way it broke the enchantment.

She was building up a picture of something Lewis wanted to believe in. It wasn't the things she was saying about lineage, about the great families of Avalon. Not Albion, but a place and time none of them could touch, not anymore. Those would be compelling to some people - Mother, maybe - but they weren't to Lewis. He liked his modern tools, honestly. The last century had brought a great many practical improvements to both alchemy and perfumery, even if Lewis had no interest in the synthetic scents beyond the purely inquisitive.

Despite that, her comments felt compelling. He had another moment where he wanted to fling himself forward, prostrate himself at her feet, and offer up whatever she'd take, and that was no good at all. He swung the brazier in another circle, getting a huge whiff of the smoke, and the unnatural inclination passed. It did, however, make him add several more of the incense pellets to the brazier itself; they could use all the clarifying smoke they could get.

Charlotte did not seem to be as affected. She'd drawn out the small bottle of the spray that would stabilise the illusion, and she was spraying it. He supposed that what Morgen was offering wasn't nearly as attractive to someone like Charlotte. The Edgartons had their history, their personal mythology, and all that already. Charlotte certainly had seemed to have a solid sense of what she wanted out of life, even if - if anyone asked Lewis - some of those choices weren't all they should be. Victor.

It got Lewis peering through the tiny slit between the curtain and the door, to see if he could figure out which one Victor was. He knew Caradoc on sight, though not terribly well. There was a younger man, nearly draped in his lap, in the sort of pose that suggested that rather direct sorts of intimacy might happen the next breath if either of them could be bothered to move. That was more or less the posture of the other people he could see, half the room. Men and women, in various combinations, draped against each other. There was nothing inappropriate, but the whole thing was terribly suggestive.

A fortnight ago, he'd have been blushing so much he could barely see. Now, it made him think of Charlotte, how she was when she was stretched against him. It was nothing like that, for all the poses were often similar. Lewis was quite sure 'passive' was not actually in Charlotte's vocabulary in any meaningful way. Even when she was lying still, it was with purpose.

Now she was beginning to move. Her hand was shifting. He knew that was preparing to cast an illusion. She'd practised a few times in front of him, though he suspected she'd done a lot more in private. Now, there was a shimmering form taking shape, glistening like moonlight and diamond, all sharp edges to go with the myth and the beauty.

Thirty seconds later, there was a unicorn standing there, pawing the ground with one foot, head up and the tip of the horn just brushing the curtain, not quite indenting it. Well, as an illusion, it couldn't move the velvet. It certainly looked persuasive, though. Charlotte took a breath, and then she pulled the curtain back silently, and there was a sudden sound of hoofbeats.

Lewis thought he heard four sharper sounds, like a lock turning, but he could only see Charlotte's fingers twisting, and that could have been the illusion. The unicorn charged into the room, heading straight for Morgen down the centre aisle between the seats, hooves coming a few inches from a couple of people on the cushions. There were people crying out, and Morgen held up her hands, as if she could make it stop.

In some storybook tale, it might have been a magician's duel, then. Not the Twa Magicians - Charlotte would not have spurned a blacksmith's magic, Lewis was quite sure. Nor was she - as he well knew - shy about sharing her bed. But it could have been that sort of challenging dance, duck and drake, hare and greyhound, sheep and ram, mare and saddle. Eventually it'd have run down to bed and coverlet, or perhaps, if one changed mythology a tad abruptly, chicken and seed.

Lewis's mind had, he realised, swung into that curiously analytical place he sometimes found when he was working on the most complex potions, the ones he could not do by feel and intuition. He found himself taking in all the details, the way Morgen had taken a step back, the movements of Gareth's hands. Lewis almost called out a warning, but Charlotte did something with her own that pushed Gareth back, four or five feet, until he nearly had the wall at his back. That was Lewis's cue to come and spread the smoke as far as he could. He could do a charm to move air, and set it going widdershins, banishing all that was lingering here.

The unicorn took another step forward, and Morgen stepped back, visibly this time. From the side, nearest Lewis, where the brazier had had the chance to work the longest, there was a muffled sound, then a "I say, what?"

It was very much a young aristocratic sort of man, whose world had suddenly become less ordered than he expected. Lewis had heard that sort often enough at school. Charlotte took it as her cue, and now she was glorious. The light from the charms around the room was catching on all those twists and braids. He saw all of a sudden that there was some charm that made it seem like her hair itself was golden. A shimmering gold, the same sort of - ah, illusion - shimmer of the unicorn's horn and hooves.

She walked forward, the soles of her shoes clicking, beat by beat, to match a dance of hooves on the parquet floor, each piece of the different woods echoing slightly differently. Charlotte didn't rush, she didn't twitch. She didn't so much as make a breath she didn't seem to intend for a purpose. She looked straight ahead, entirely focused on Morgen. When she spoke, Lewis thought her voice was amplified a touch, but that was a charm near any Schola student could do. "What did you think you were doing?"

It had a sharp edge of humour to it, as if whatever Morgen had been doing was like a child trying on an older sister's dress. As if the whole thing were slightly ridiculous, but of course you wouldn't actually laugh at someone, not for that. Lewis had heard that sort of tone of voice from Theo often enough, though in those cases, Theo had actually been near laughing.

Morgen's mouth opened and closed and opened again.

"You..." She didn't say anything else before her mouth moved and no sound came out. Charlotte raised her hand, and something pushed Gareth further back against the wall. Charlotte didn't look behind her, Lewis didn't see her fingers move again, but there was a new shape forming up, a great golden lion - glittering like her own mane of hair - that stalked up the centre. It prowled up to her left, the unicorn on the right, before it leapt in one great leap, landing neatly in front of Gareth, head cocked inquisitively.

It looked to all the world - from the back - like a great dog, hoping for a bit of play. And yet, from the front, much nearer the teeth, it must have been terrifying. "Do lower your hands, Gareth, and keep your palms pressed against the wall to either side of you. That way we won't have any trouble." Charlotte said it almost conversationally, though Lewis could suddenly hear a little shiver in her voice.

Morgen made a little abortive twitch of her own hands, and Charlotte shook her head once. "You too, Morgen. Stand against the wall, hands flat against it." When Morgen didn't move, Charlotte's pinky twitched, and the unicorn advanced, horn now lowered to heart level.

Lewis never wanted Charlotte angry with him. Certainly not in any way that involved a chance to plot. It wasn't that she was even being directly threatening - they had to know it was illusions, certainly? It wasn't as if anyone had seen a unicorn in the flesh in centuries, not since the Pact. All the tales said they'd disappeared through the portals to the Fatae lands. And one absolutely couldn't go down to the corner shop and acquire a lion.

When Charlotte spoke again, it was entirely conversational. "Everyone else, please seat yourselves comfortably. I would like you to make oath that you will stay seated, not attempt any act of magic or threat against anyone in this room. And that you will ask if you need to move or need attention for your health. Repeat after me."

She led them through the oath, using some framework that she knew well enough. There was no stumbling, no hunt for memory. Lewis wasn't deft enough with ritual magic to feel or see or sense the Silence oath taking effect, but he did get a faint whiff of the ozone note he often got in such oaths. Of course, then it was blotted out again by the sharp scents of the brazier. Once everyone completed the oath, Charlotte spoke to him without turning her head. "The brazier, all around the room, if you please, and then put it down in front of me." It was a question, and it was a regnal command, and Lewis was already moving when she finished speaking.

CHAPTER 38
IN THE GREAT HALL

Charlotte had a vast and new respect for both Papa and Gabe at the moment. A number of other people she knew, too. Papa and Gabe had resources she didn't have, but she was using all the ones she had. She had her looks; she had her illusions. And she'd had deportment lessons from the age of six, including walking around with a book balanced on her head for most of a summer. The last one was, currently, doing just as much work as the first two.

She was particularly keeping an eye on Morgen and Gareth for any twitch of movement. Both of them seemed stunned. Gareth must know it was an illusion, and Morgen surely could guess. All that was keeping them back against the wall was a shielding charm, a wall made of air. It was possible to push back against it.

If someone managed to distract Charlotte, it might drop or at least fall back - holding it in place was awfully hard going. Charlotte could feel sweat beginning to gather at the hollow of her back. Though that was at least partly because the room was ridiculously warm. If Morgen's plans had involved frolicking outside in the nude, in the dew - May morning had traditions - the contrast seemed even more absurd. Or likely to lead to all sorts of unpleasant lung complaints.

She took a breath, like Mama had taught her. Always breathe before saying anything. Make them wait, make them wonder what you're going to say, and gather your thoughts even if they're fleeing like confused baby chicks. Morgen almost made a movement, and Charlotte curled her finger, the unicorn taking a threatening step a hair closer, pawing the ground.

Charlotte had never held an illusion that big and that detailed in front of this many people before. Or even more than one or two people. As Lewis circled the space, she took another breath. "Did you think I'd conveniently disappeared?" She kept her voice pitched for calm amusement, though it was a struggle. "There I go. You'll just order your people around a bit more, fill in the gaps. A bit rough on Bedivere, I suppose, paired off with a ghost, now." She caught Bedivere's twitch. She suspected he was staring at her, nothing quite making sense.

She needed to wait longer, for whatever good the incense would do. First things first. "Morgen, Gareth. Make the oath after me." She didn't tell them in advance, just said each half phrase, waiting to hear them both repeat it. When they didn't leap to it, her hands shifted a little more, ring fingers curling in, so the lion and unicorn menaced, rather than just guarded. Gareth broke first, repeating, but Morgen was only a syllable behind.

To stay standing where they were, palms against the wall. That would keep either of them from casting most charms. An oath to keep silent unless asked a question was next. She couldn't call the truth-telling magic, of course, but oh, she really wanted to. It must be such a temptation to Papa, in so many circumstances, small and large. When they had finished up, when Charlotte could see the snap of the Silence magics against them, the way their faces changed for just a second. Charlotte raised her hands, palms up, and the lion and unicorn parted, as beautiful as any equine parade team. They circled around behind the assembled witnesses and victims and collaborators on the floor, before disappearing out through the open curtained space behind her.

There, at least she didn't have to hold the illusion anymore. She could stand and breathe, and move onto the next stage of this. "Thank you," she said to Lewis. "Wherever you are comfortable, please." A bit to her surprise, he took up a place just behind her, to the right, where a chosen knight might be to escort his lady. She nodded just once, as if that were just what they'd discussed in advance. Now she turned her attention elsewhere. "Victor, are you sensible?"

There was a cough, and she knew that cough, and then a tentative, "Rarely, you say."

It was a more truthful answer than she'd actually expected. And it was absolutely Victor, the Victor she normally saw, unmasked, playing no part. "Tell me about the days since you last saw me. Briefly, what have you done, what have you not done?"

It wouldn't have worked on anyone else, but she and Victor had habits. Charlotte had listened to Mama and Papa talking about how to do an interview - especially when pretending it was just a conversation - so that the person was lulled into talking along. The process began with easy questions, the ones they'd answer without worry, before trying anything harder. And Victor had more than a decade of answering things she asked him. He paused, but then there was his voice, to her left and just enough behind her she couldn't see him.

"You'd been out in the garden, and then I guess you weren't. I was with Caradoc. We were distracted." He coughed, as if he were now a little shy, that was unlike him. "Having an excellent time. I didn't know you'd gone missing until - I don't know. A day later? Two days? I don't remember a lot of that time. It was all very pleasant, golden like honey. Morgen talked to me, several times."

"That was a potion, darling. Several potions, all meant to make you feel like that and not think about things you should worry about." There, that would do nicely to get the rest of them to possibly start thinking. She didn't want to push too far right now, but she suddenly was sure Morgen had also been using his magic, taking it for her own. "What happened when you found out?"

"Gareth had a lot of questions. He was very angry. At me, when I told him things, at Bedivere." Victor's voice shifted a little, suddenly distressed. "I bet Bedivere still has a bruise. All around his arm, it was all blue and purple." He sounded a little shocked at himself, even, now that he was sober enough to actually think it through and realise he had not marked it properly at the time.

Charlotte nodded briskly. "And then?"

"It's all a dream. A very pleasant one, all the pleasures I wanted, all the pleasures I don't get to have. The food, the wine, the bed..." Victor's voice drifted off. She wasn't going to get much more sense out of him for a little, she suspected. It wasn't as if Charlotte had experience with someone having their magic drawn from them like this, but that and the potions combined must make it hard to think. Like being anaemic, that was about the right model to be going on with.

"Morgen." Now Charlotte made her voice a wedge. "You were just interested in Victor. And a number of these other people here. What you could get from them. What gifts they could bring you. Some were about information, but I'm quite sure some are about money. That fine velvet dress and cloak you're wearing are very impressive, and silk velvet doesn't come cheap, especially with the charms to prevent marks."

Entirely conversational now, but Charlotte was guarding her own information. "You didn't think to look for me properly for at least a day. And then, someone - Victor, I have to assume - told you who I was. Who my people are." Charlotte let her voice arch, making space, hoping she could make this work. "You're lazy, you know. You rely on charms and potions and perfumes to make people compliant. You don't think you could persuade them, and you certainly don't bother to try. There you are, dangling pleasures in front of people who have their reasons for wanting something to fill them up." That innuendo got a snicker. That was bad planning, but Charlotte forged on. It was at least a sign people were coming back to their own minds.

Morgen made a strangled noise, but of course Charlotte hadn't asked her to reply. She'd been careful to avoid that. "And I'm quite sure that you threw a fit. You demanded Gareth do all your work for you. He searched the garden, he searched the maze, he searched the cottage. He wasn't actually very good at searching, all storm and fury and not much actual observation. Same thing with Mark and Bedivere." That brought a grunt from behind her, on the right, but no attempt to interrupt.

"You have attempted to claim the throne of one of the great magicians of an epic age. I don't know what your magic is, not right now. Nor what your name is, though I'm increasingly sure it's something like Ethel or Gladys or Bertha. All fine names for the right people, but nothing enchanting. They do not fall off the tongue in a wave of power."

Charlotte didn't hesitate now. She forged ahead. "You have drugged people. You have lied to them. You have taken their magic for your own. You have set them up with others, without caring for their well-being, or anything about the match except your amusement and personal benefit. Given all this..." Charlotte waved a hand at the trappings and Gareth actually flinched, as if he expected that sweeping hand to bring trailing vines and thorns in its way. Well, she could oblige. She'd been practising roses last month, just in case the gardens were a bit bare for Gabe's wedding. Now, she called up trailing branches, green and sharp-thorned and indubitably white, putting a stamp of King Richard's Pact on the veneer of Arthuriana.

Gareth rather obligingly shrank back, as Charlotte let the roses trail off toward the edge of the room and the door in the north. "Given all this, Morgen, Gareth, I'm quite sure that a proper investigation of your books will make it clear you've been taking in money. Using it for your own pleasure, and not in the ways you said you would. Either that or you've been using coercion magics so people will agree." She shrugged once, sharply. "The Guard and the Courts will sort it out promptly, I'm sure of that."

Now it was Morgen's expression that changed. Charlotte smiled, and she knew it was a smile that belonged nowhere near the sort of lady she was bred and trained to be. Except, of course, that she had been born into the kind of family where knowing how to defend her walls and protect her own was the key to everything she was and did and might become. She didn't hide it. "As for you, Morgen, you didn't do your research. You didn't know I'd be cautious, or why. You didn't know my family was quite aware of where I was, and that they do worry that I might be a target for something unduly unpleasant."

Charlotte swallowed, because it hit her again in that moment just how badly wrong so many things could have gone. Then Morgen tried to speak, and Charlotte lifted her fingers. "No. Stay quiet. Both of you. We will be summoning assistance, and all of you will stay where you are until they arrive. Pity it's so far from the portal, but I suppose that's what you get for picking a secluded country house for your poorly planned plotting."

There, that was a suitable concluding line. Charlotte got the satisfaction of letting it linger in the silent room for a good five seconds before there was a sharp rapping on the door, followed by a voice pitched to carry. "Pardon, Mistress Edgarton?"

Now that she had not expected. The way Gareth and Morgen's eyes opened, they had no idea what to do with it. Charlotte half-glanced at Lewis. "The door, if you would, if you feel it appropriate."

His fingers brushed her elbow for just a moment, a gesture she found entirely soothing. She hadn't been able to check on him. She was juggling too many things, far too delicate, to break her focus. But she heard him move, the slight slip of the fabric of his trousers made easier to follow because she'd worn his clothes and knew exactly how they sounded.

There was a sound behind her, conversational, before there were steps - three sets of steps behind her. "Noble lady," Lewis's voice didn't crack, but there was a note in it she couldn't make sense of. It wasn't humour, exactly, it wasn't formality. If she had to put a name on it, it would be ease, but that didn't make sense. "The household cook would like a word, if it pleases you."

Charlotte inclined her head. "If you'd come up here, please, Cook?"

A moment later, there was a comfortably plump woman, perhaps in her late forties, who looked remarkably familiar. Not someone Charlotte knew, or at least well, but a familial sort of resemblance. "Mistress Edgarton." She made a little bob of a curtsey, careful not to put her back to Morgen and Gareth. A sensible sort, then. Charlotte inclined her head. "My sister was second cook at Veritas for some years, and I visited, a few times, when you were a child."

"Oh!" Charlotte did remember her. "Alice Barrows. She wrote a few weeks ago. And you would be." She frowned, names were complicated for guests when one was little.

"Olive, ma'am. I was the one saw you got out of the place, if you don't mind me saying so. And I've sent the scullery boy to the portal. He's got the pony, should be getting a message through within five minutes or so."

Oh, well. That did simplify things. Charlotte swallowed, trying to keep up the impression this was all part of a plan. Her plan, ideally. "That is very well done, Cook, thank you. Might we put a few sturdy stableboys or some such to keeping an eye out here?"

"Yes'm. And I have refreshments for yourself and for Master Wright. I hope the provisions have been satisfactory, sir. Mistress." That, now, was in the tone of someone who thought Lewis needed feeding up. "You're welcome to check they're not having anything to do with any potions or whatever she did." There was a growl on the pronoun. Of course any respectable Cook would not approve of that sort of nonsense. And of course she'd know the charms - as Charlotte did - to check, given a moment's privacy.

Charlotte inclined her head. "Please. And if someone could bring a chair, I will sit and make sure no one causes further trouble."

Within five minutes, Charlotte had food and drink she trusted - and had not made herself. She'd been provided with a sturdy chair. They'd moved everyone else where she could keep an eye on them. And now there were two brawny stable boys, two footmen, and three maids properly provided with cast iron frying pans in case anyone got unnecessary ideas.

It left Charlotte to glance at Lewis - not that they could talk now - and to do the mental calculations of how long it'd take someone to let Papa know and how fast they'd arrive from the portal. It was like the most ridiculous maths problems from her governess. Posit one Guard contingent, pausing for horses at the stable. If a horse can canter at ten miles an hour for at least thirty minutes, when will they arrive compared to the denouement of an unsavoury event?

They'd arrive when they arrived. That was the only answer she had. All she had to do until then was keep calm and hold everything together a little while longer.

CHAPTER 39
IN THE GREAT HALL

L ewis found the waiting to be nearly intolerable. Charlotte looked almost relaxed now, though he could tell that at least some of that was show. He was close enough to know she was breathing more shallowly, that her knuckles were a little white, where they were holding the arm of the chair. He didn't try to talk to her, because what would he say? The people around them would hear everything, anyway. Whatever conversation they had, that would matter, it needed at least a bit of privacy.

There wasn't any clock, and Lewis didn't want to fumble for his pocket watch, so he had no idea how long it was before the Guard showed up. Long enough that he'd had something to drink, refused something to eat, and still wasn't terribly hungry. Long enough that his back and thighs were starting to complain about the chair. An hour, perhaps two. Somewhere in that range, that seemed plausible. He was far more used to telling the passage of time by distillation and evaporation and so on, and this had none of that to work with.

There was a sharp knock on the door, the sound of someone letting the Guard in. Quite a few of them, it turned out - there were five in the Guard uniform, and another two, both women in black jackets and skirts with a green vest. It must be a uniform, but it wasn't one he knew on sight. Then one more joined them in the same outfit, looking so much like Charlotte that it had to be her brother. Which made the others Penelopes too, Lewis assumed. He had the same hair - well, minus the shimmer of the illusion - in a braid down his back, a satchel over his shoulder, and trousers instead of the skirt. He immediately went to speak to one of the other Penelopes, murmuring in her ear.

Right, Lewis wasn't getting any chance to talk to Charlotte tonight. He was fairly sure of that. There was a brief bit of conversation behind them. Then an older man strolled to the centre, where he could see both Lewis and Charlotte and Morgen and Gareth. He had salt and pepper hair, the sort that looked distinguished, and he moved like an alchemist, all controlled motion, no energy wasted. "I am Captain Nonus Powell, and I will be overseeing this investigation. Graves, Belford, see to those two and make them secure. We'll work through questioning everyone in turn. I gather from the housekeeper that there is a breakfast room and an office we can use, suitable to purpose."

The man glanced around, considering the scene, before focusing on Charlotte. "Are they bound, Mistress Edgarton?"

Charlotte shook her head once. "Not by charms, but by oath. So is everyone else, with provisions for health and well-being. It seemed the safest thing at the time. I didn't know how quickly the Guard might be available." Her voice was clear, but the resonance of earlier had dropped away. "I can release that, if you like? Or transfer them, as you wish."

There was a little negotiation on that point - Lewis didn't understand the nuances of it, but Charlotte seemed to, and her brother was nodding slightly at each piece of it. It involved everyone taking oath under the specifications laid by the Guard Captain, one by one, then releasing them from the prior oaths made in that room. That made something that felt like a snap, and Charlotte's eyes went wide. The Penelopes were immediately whispering, before one of them - the woman who seemed to be senior, said, "Quite a few oaths here, Captain. Two of us will start here, and one in the lab, if you please."

It had the tone of something that didn't seem to be a question. Captain Powell waved a hand. "Loft in the lab, then, if you don't mind. I believe you've the best alchemical skills." Lewis tried not to flinch. He'd known when they started this that whether they were successful or not, it wasn't really his lab anymore. Captain Powell seemed to catch it. "You, Master Wright, if you'll make oath to keep quiet unless asked a question and not to interfere with the search in any way, I'd like you to go with Penelope Loft and..." He made a decision more or less on the fly. "Guard Cottering. I'll speak to people here, but I'll likely want to have a word in an hour or two."

That was that, then. The Penelope - the younger of the women, who seemed to be in her thirties or perhaps forties - stepped to one side. Lewis stood carefully, hoping his feet hadn't actually fallen asleep or anything awkward. He cleared his throat at Charlotte, but before he could say anything, she met his eyes, just briefly. "I'll be in touch, one way or another. Message to your club, if nothing else."

It would have to do. He nodded, and then he was being led off, out of the house and down through the maze. He had to show them where to go, and it seemed almost unfathomable that he knew something they didn't. Both were brisk, but they did exchange a few bits of conversation on the way down that made him think they'd worked on something together before. Lewis was abominably bad about that kind of thing, but it sounded agreeable, not friendly. But also not hostile.

Once they were in the lab - he was required to open it, after making a formal statement sworn on the Silence that he had been the one to lock it - he let them into the lab.

"Before we begin, do you need anything? Drink, food, the loo? I assume that's in the cottage?"

Lewis considered. "If you don't mind. And maybe something to drink. There, I mean, not here."

"Never in a lab, of course not." The woman nodded. "You are being questioned, so I need to escort you." She was pleasant about it, keeping him in sight unless he was actually in the loo - though she had a look in there first. And she asked a couple of questions purely about the layout of the cottage. Not, he noted, about when Charlotte had turned up, or where she'd slept, or where he'd slept. Just the layout.

Once they were back in the lab, she nodded at the sofa. "Have a seat there. We need to do an inventory, and obviously that will take a bit. Do you have a current one somewhere? Tell me where it is. Please stay put."

It was terribly difficult to manage, but Lewis nodded, explained where the inventory list was, that he'd updated it yesterday. And then he answered their questions as it came up. Why he had six different variations on jasmine, twelve kinds of rose oil, and that was before they got into the ambergris and the civet and so on. They clearly both knew their way around an alchemy lab - a few questions about specific bowls, but they used all the proper terminology, even for more esoteric devices. However, they didn't seem to know much about perfume. Neither of them asked him any questions about Morgen, or what he'd made for her, or anything like that.

He wasn't sure how long that went on, though he'd guess an hour or two. Cottering and Loft had made it halfway down the storage on the long workbench. It usually took him about an hour to get that far, and he knew where everything ought to be and what it did. Maybe closer to two, Lewis was feeling aches again, though in different places. He couldn't decide if that was good or bad.

At some point, there was a noise from something the Guard was carrying, and he pulled a journal out of his bag. Lewis knew what it was, of course, but he didn't have his own. Far too expensive. The man flipped a few pages. "Himself wants to come down. Would you rather show him the way, Loft, or shall I?"

The Penelope considered. "You go. I've got one more test I want to do about that residue." The Guard nodded, and took off at a fast walk - perhaps he'd break into a jog, once in the maze. Penelope Loft waited until he was well gone before saying, without looking at Lewis, "It will go best if you tell the truth. We'll find it out, anyway. You know that."

"I want to cooperate, ma'am." He wanted to say he was nervous. Lewis wanted to ask if Charlotte was all right. He wanted to defend her, whatever she needed defending from, and he couldn't. Lewis knew perfectly well that this was the challenge he had, and he could only face up to it and carry on.

Maybe ten minutes later, the lab seemed far more crowded. Captain Powell seemed to take up a tremendous amount of room, all by himself, and he'd brought one of the other Guards with him. "Is there space in the cottage for a conversation?" The question was to one of the others, not to Lewis.

"A sitting room, sir, with a comfortable enough sofa. Tea, if you need the refreshment, no alterations to it or any of the pots, nor anything recent, other than the usual cooking and cleaning charms I'd expect."

Which raised an interesting question of what she'd actually expected. Now Lewis thought about it, but it wasn't as if he could ask. "The cottage, then. Come along, Master Wright. You've found yourself in quite a mess, haven't you?"

It was the truth, so Lewis couldn't disagree at all. He nodded cautiously, not venturing to say anything. A couple of minutes later, they were in the sitting room. The Guard who'd come down with the Captain was perched on a chair ready to take notes, and Lewis was even more nervous. Neither of them was giving anything away.

"Right. I'm going to have you make a series of oaths about your testimony. That will include you speaking only when I ask you questions, for the duration of this session. We will see what we do when we've worked through my increasingly long list of questions."

"Yes, sir. Captain. I want to help, please." There, that seemed neutral enough, but the Captain looked very dubious. In short order, he led Lewis through the oath. That made it clear the Guard was taking detailed notes, and that this information could be used in the Courts, including under the truth-telling charms, with any discrepancies between this and that would be noted. He made that into a threat, even though Lewis was sure people forgot things all the time. And that he would, for that matter.

"If I'm not sure about something, sir, what's the appropriate way to indicate that? If I don't remember a date, without my notes, say."

"Then you should say so, provide what you do remember, and mention if there might be any confirmation." The Captain considered. "I gather you have notes, then?"

Lewis nodded. "In my bag, sir. There." He gestured at it on the floor. "And a few other things. I was hoping they could go where intended. Not to Morgen and Gareth."

"Ah. That seems an interesting place to start. Tell me if you need to consult your notes as we go, and we will see about that." Captain Powell leaned back a little, listening intently.

Lewis began at the beginning, then. He felt small and hollow, trying to explain Theo and what Theo needed, to this imposing man. The Captain gave no hint of anything away, listening to all of it with an impassive expression. He asked detailed questions, though, coming back to things Lewis had said five or ten minutes ago, without consulting notes of his own, as they went on. The questioning continued until Lewis's voice was going hoarse, and they'd got through the events of the evening.

"If I asked Mistress Edgarton about you, what would she say?"

That was a trick question, and Lewis knew it. He didn't know how to answer it, though, and he felt stuck. The oaths made him feel stuck. He couldn't say that he loved her. It wasn't like Lewis had said that to Charlotte herself. He couldn't begin to think what she thought of him, outside of their time in bed and the way he'd helped, wanted to help. How he'd liked her cooking.

That might do. "That I appreciated her cooking a great deal, found her tremendously helpful in the lab, coming up with what we used tonight. I expect she'd say that I'm single-minded, always on about perfume. And I hope that she'd say that once I understood how Morgen was using the potions she'd asked for, the perfumes and the ointments, that I didn't want to let that continue. I still don't. Even though..." His throat choked up at that point.

"Right." Captain Powell stood. "We'll have more questions in the morning, I expect. Will you swear oath to go upstairs, stay up there? If you need the loo, there will be a Guard here, working on notes. Call out before you come downstairs. I need to confirm a number of details with others before I can release you. I'll want to know where you are until the case is resolved, where you spend the night and can be found."

That was a whole mess Lewis hadn't begun to figure out yet, but he supposed at least he could put off that problem for tomorrow morning. Or later tomorrow, anyway. It must be past midnight now. "What time in the morning, sir?"

The Captain glanced at his wrist and grimaced. "It's near three. Eleven, call it. Someone will fetch you. We may talk up at the house."

"Thank you, sir." Lewis stretched, a little, testing how he felt, before there was one last flurry of releasing him from the existing oaths, and then he was sent upstairs. Rather like a schoolboy sent to bed without his supper. And no Charlotte, no way to hear anything from Charlotte, or even to ask about her. He was sure asking about her wasn't approved of.

CHAPTER 40
LATE THAT EVENING, UP AT THE HOUSE

Charlotte had found herself told to take a chair in the hallway outside the morning room. She was there perhaps twenty minutes, with absolutely no sign of anyone else besides the Guard coming in and out. Charlotte knew several of them by sight, besides Captain Powell, but none of them well, and she was fairly sure that was intentional on someone's part. She was rather surprised Gabe was here, actually. But the Guard couldn't actually forbid one of the Penelopes to turn out, and he was obviously making sure to be observed by Lucy Doyle, his former apprentice mistress. Who Charlotte did know quite well, better than she did Loft.

Gabe presumably had his journal, and could at least let their parents know she was visibly in one piece and not horribly injured or something of the kind. It wasn't as if Charlotte could do anything about writing to them, so she sat with her hands folded and waited.

Finally, the door of the morning room opened, and one of the Guards stepped out. "Mistress Edgarton?" Technically, it ought to be Miss, she was neither married nor had she completed her apprenticeship. But being Papa's daughter did bring a certain formality to everything. And it wasn't like she'd get referred to as The Honourable Charlotte Edgarton, like they might among the non-magical.

She stood, let the man show her into the room, and sat in the chair indicated. They'd moved the table to one side, and had brought in a smaller table to serve as a desk, with Charlotte's chair facing it. The Guard sat at the end of the long table, with papers out, clearly about to take notes.

"Oaths first, if you don't mind." Captain Powell was brisk. "I'd prefer everything on record, for everyone's sake." Charlotte was together enough to read that properly. She'd have to be half-dead to miss it. Powell didn't want accusations of mistreatment in the aftermath, but neither did he want any hint of favouritism.

"Of course, Captain Powell. I am very glad you and the Guard and Penelopes are here."

He led her through the oaths, in the form she'd expected, meaning that they couldn't compel truth-telling, but that any attempt to lie would show up in later examinations in the Courts and thus have consequences. There were the usual phrases about how to indicate she didn't want to answer something in this context. She knew all the theory of it, nearly as well as any Guard apprentice did. Once he'd done that, Powell considered. "I will want you to go back to the beginning, when you first met Morgen, through when you had concerns, your disappearance, and so on. But before we do that, tell me what you think the risks are here, what might fall under our remit."

Charlotte had given a great deal of thought to this likely request, and to the wording. "Based on the information available to me, I am certain - sufficient to swear to it in court - that Morgen was using coercive potions and other alchemical substances that fall counter to the law. I believe they were to sway people to her cause. I do not know her complete list of goals. From what I observed and heard, I have reason to believe they involved manipulation for financial gain, social benefit, and I strongly suspect syphoning of magical potential for her own use. Victor, in specific. He has a strong magical wellspring, and he does not look in good form at the moment. I do not have absolute evidence of that last, but it fits with other information, and I hope you have the resources to investigate that aspect fully. A Healer with the relevant expertise, perhaps. He was not in urgent need earlier, or of course I'd have mentioned it immediately."

Powell raised an eyebrow, sighed, and the Guard with the papers stood, going out the door. Powell didn't say anything more, not without a witness, and Charlotte folded her hands in her lap and waited. Perhaps five minutes later, the Guard came back, and nodded. Powell lifted a hand, and the Guard waited by the door.

"I should have inquired sooner. I presume you are in good health, and do not need attention from a Healer, or immediate refreshment. I know you would request it if you did." In other words, he knew she knew her particular rights in this circumstance, and also the Guard's customs.

"Thank you, sir. I am well enough for now." Charlotte inclined her head and waited. She could wait him out. Probably.

There was a long silence, another slight sigh, then he cleared his throat. "Crofts, if you'd take notes." Once the Guard was seated, pen in hand, Powell nodded. "Begin at the beginning, please, Mistress Edgarton."

She laid it out as precisely as she could, beginning with Victor's first mention of the group. When she finally concluded, with the arrival of the Guard, she added, "There is a statement in the cottage, tucked into one of the books on the shelf in the dining room. It's in an 1860 children's encyclopaedia, with the appropriate identifying charms. Lewis does not know it is there, and I doubt very much he'll look in that volume. It includes all the dates and times I could recall, as well as various other notes."

That definitely did get a sigh from Captain Powell. "Very well. Let me think about the next step for you. I am sorry to say that your bedroom here is off-limits, and your things."

"I would expect so. I assume Morgen and the others searched my things, and would be the last ones to handle anything." Charlotte would very much like her own bed and a change of clothing, but she could scarcely ask for that.

Powell considered. "Let me see what the options are. Do you have any questions?"

"Not at the moment, sir." She wanted very much to ask about Lewis, but she didn't dare put more weight on that relationship. Instead, Powell stood, escorting her out to the hallway and having a brief conversation with one of the Guards, what seemed like an update on the status of half a dozen pieces of the investigation. Gabe was there, looking entirely professional and controlled, and she was terribly glad to see him.

"Captain Powell, sir." Gabe nodded once.

"Don't lay it on with a trowel. We all know better." Powell waved a hand. "Yes?"

"Penelope Doyle wanted me to let you know that we have concluded the immediate investigation in the hall. But we need some additional reagents and a different specialist - Murgatroyd - to come out and check the layers of the alchemical effects. There's a cart going back to the portal for anyone who needs to go to Trellech, and to pick him up." It must be quite a complex thing to roust Helios Murgatroyd out of his bed at this time of night. They must be worried about the effects degrading quickly.

Powell grimaced - just briefly, but Charlotte was watching him carefully. "Right." He considered. "I'll send two of the Guards back with you, and likely have two coming back. Are you going for the night?"

"May Day celebrations at dawn, sir, and if at all possible, I'd like to be there for them. Penelope Doyle can confirm my skills can be spared for the moment." Gabe did not exactly look like an eager bird dog, but he was, in fact, laying it on thick.

Powell considered. "Mistress Edgarton, if you promise not to stray from the estates or - the local village, yes?" Charlotte nodded. "If you stay put for the next few days, I can release you to your home. Is there anything else you wish to say now? I expect we'll have additional questioning to come once we've spoken with everyone else."

Charlotte hesitated. It was tipping her hand several ways. "Is Lewis all right, please?" Then, after what was entirely too long a pause, "And Victor?"

"They are both being treated with appropriate care, and yes, we're getting a Healer in to look at everyone. We expect the questioning to take a bit, we're waiting for the various potions to diminish." Ah, that meant Victor likely wouldn't be interrogated for a while.

"Thank you, Captain. I appreciate knowing that. I would very much like to go home, if at all possible."

Captain Powell waved a hand. "Give me a minute or two to figure out who's coming with you, Penelope Edgarton, but you can go out to the cart now."

Gabe and Charlotte walked out to the front door, Gabe's cane making the only noise as it tapped on the floor. Neither of them said anything until they were well away from the house, on the grass of the turnaround. Then Gabe cleared his throat. "I have your journal. Write to Mama and Papa so they can go to sleep."

She took the journal, silently thumbing through to the page for her parents. She began to write - nothing long, just that she was coming home with Gabe. They'd be maybe an hour at most. As she was partway through the message, Gabe cleared his throat. "You can talk to them or you can talk to me. But you're going to have to talk to one of us. Soon."

"Don't you mean I can talk to them and I can talk to you?" Charlotte glanced up, then stopped writing. "It's just a choice of who first. How worried were you all?"

"Rather a lot, though we knew from the charms you were mostly fine? But, I don't know. Something felt very wrong. Papa was remarkably restrained in doing anything about it." Gabe let out his breath. "What's it going to be?"

"You. When we get back. And then you and Papa and Mama, once we're through the festivities. And maybe a nap." She yawned suddenly. "What time is it?"

"Only about midnight, but that's not much sleep, no." Before they could say anything else, the other Guards came out. There was all the fuss of being helped up into the back of the cart, and the jolting ride back down various roads to the portal. She'd managed to slip her journal back to Gabe, but that meant she could neither check to see if their parents had written anything, nor have something to clutch and keep her hands busy. He had his open, as well as a notebook, so she could only assume he was updating both their parents and both Aunts Mason and Witt, plus likely some number of other people.

They came through the portal at Veritas, and she could see that Mama and Papa's bedroom was in fact dark. It didn't mean they weren't lying there wondering, but at least they weren't sitting up. "Do you want to stay up?" Charlotte asked hesitantly.

"Potions and coffee? Sure. Let me round that up. You go wash up a bit. Your room in fifteen? I'll write a note, too. And Rathna." He leaned in, kissing her cheek, and disappeared down the hall, while Charlotte went up to her rooms on the first floor. It felt wonderful to wash up with her own soap and brush out her own hair. She wondered if Rathna were sleeping here, to be around for tomorrow morning - well, later this morning. It would make sense, given the imminent wedding.

By the time Gabe knocked, she was in a nightgown and dressing gown, in her own bed - if she did get a bit of a nap, no harm to it. Gabe came in with a tray, coffee, and two potion bottles. "We need to be up and moving by five. It's one, now."

Charlotte grimaced, then nudged the end of the bed. "Sit. Or whatever pillows you want."

Gabe did, in fact, take a big gulp of the coffee before setting it on the side table and sprawling on his side. "So, how have you been? What on earth have you been doing?" Then more gently. "Is there anything I need to be careful of? What's Victor's role in all this, and do I need to go defend your honour?"

Charlotte had been about to answer that. Only then Gabe had to go and mention Victor, and she froze. Gabe would see it, of course. He near enough always did. She'd have to be a lot faster off the mark to hide something from him, and she certainly wasn't going to manage it tonight.

"I've been wondering if Victor was up to your standards for a bit." Gabe had got quieter now, and when she glanced at him, he wasn't actually looking at her, but more or less out the window. "You seemed happy with him, and I certainly wasn't going to say anything. But if you want someone to be sympathetic about him not doing the right thing - whatever that was here, which is still unclear to me - then I'm your man." Gabe tilted his head then. "Also, your older brother, and I believe I am expected to be demanding of your suitors. Or Papa is, and I'll stand in for him here."

Despite the seriousness of the thing, Charlotte couldn't repress a giggle. She'd never explained all of it to Gabe, actually, the reason for the agreement with Victor. When she'd been younger, it had been awkward. When she was older, it had been settled already for so long bringing up the reason felt odd. It built all of a sudden to the sort of full-blown fit of laughter that ended up with her burying her face in the pillow so she didn't wake the house. Not that the soundproofing charms wouldn't help, but still.

When she'd finally caught her breath the third time, after two more rounds of looking up and seeing Gabe's expression setting her off, she swallowed. "I expect I'll be calling off the assumed engagement with Victor, yes. Whatever else I do."

As she'd pretty much expected, Gabe pounced on that. "Tell me about Lewis, then. Mind, I've only heard the barest outline of the evening's events. Other than that it was very much you and him against the world. Also, some rather impressive illusions, you have got better, haven't you? Necessity is the mother of improvement, as Aunt Witt says."

Charlotte snorted and let herself fall onto the pillows and onto her back with a little thump. "I don't know what he wants. I told him I wasn't interested in a romance."

"But?" Gabe was like a kitten with a loose strand of yarn.

"But now I am. And I don't know what to tell him. Do we know anyone with an alchemy lab needing someone to take it over? Perfumes, ideally, but he could likely do other things for income until that's fully self-supporting." Charlotte couldn't bring herself to look at Gabe for this.

There was a certain long silence, the sort that made Charlotte worry quite a lot. "I'd need specs," Gabe said finally. "And I expect Mama and Papa will have opinions. You want to keep him, then?"

It wasn't like that. And it was. That was the thing of it, and trust Gabe to hit on it. "If he'd like to be kept like that. He's not from a bad family, but not like us at all. And he's got an older brother, had a bad time in the War. No money, lots of uses for the money they do have, and the materia for what Theo - that's the brother - needs, it's quite dear. And the younger brother's at Alethorpe, wants to go into apothecary work, and there's no money for that either."

"You have a list? Or can gesture at one?" Gabe shifted on the bed, propping himself up on his elbow and reaching for his journal. Not to write it in directly, but on the slips of paper he kept tucked in the cover, for some later point. "Remind me later. Or Wednesday, when people are back at work."

"I can do that." Reminding Gabe would be the easy part, honestly.

"All right. Start at the beginning. When you arrived at the place, where they put you, all of it." Gabe hesitated for just an instant. "Anything you tell me, I might have to share in court. If that makes a difference."

Which meant she'd have to figure out how to handle explaining she'd slept with Lewis, and several times. She hadn't lied, in the questioning Captain Powell had done. She'd just made it clear that she'd quickly come to trust Lewis, to understand how much had been kept from him, and that they'd comfortably figured out ways to share the living space. Presumably, any competent Captain of the Guard could read between those lines, but it wouldn't be in the formal record.

"Demarcate the personal things with something you can share? If that works, fine. If you have to share it all..." She thought. "I'd need to check with Mama, but I think it's the kind of thing that can be covered in the judge's chambers. And I'd rather that. I don't know what his family thinks about things."

"Fair. Yes, reputational effect on innocent parties. I'm sure Mama can lay hands on the relevant citations. It's not that uncommon, it's just not the sort of case I'm usually handling." Gabe considered, then he added, "You know, you're continuing a grand family tradition. Mama and Papa improved things immensely working on a case together. Rathna and I. She's in the green guest room, for the record, so you're not surprised at dawn. And now you and Lewis. If that works out."

"If." Charlotte swallowed hard. "All right. Let me start from when we got to the estate." In the end, the telling took them right up to half-four, until it was time for both of them to get dressed. One of the maids must have been warned in advance. There was a knock on her door, precisely on time, with the frock for May Day, pulled out of the attic storage and pressed. Ten minutes later, her hair was braided up in coils around her crown, fresh flowers woven in. When she met Gabe, Rathna, and her parents down at the front door, Mama and Papa just hugged her, not saying anything, as they all piled into the pony cart for the ride down to the village.

CHAPTER 41

MAY 1ST IN A SMALL MAGICAL VILLAGE
NEAR HOLME LACY

Lewis found himself deposited in front of the Wells portal at three in the afternoon with very little ceremony. Captain Powell was releasing him, though he was likely to be needed for further questioning in Trellech in the near future. He had been permitted to pack up his personal effects under the supervision of one of the Guards.

They were all in his hold-all, he'd left the trunk because he didn't want to carry it. It could be sent on at some future point, or he could figure out how to go and reclaim it. Whether he'd get to keep any of the materia was entirely another question. Some of it had been payment for his services, and he had had the sense to get receipts for that. On the other hand, his services were legally a problem.

In the end, they'd let him take the extant vials for Theo. And - after taking a sample - the perfume oil he'd made for Charlotte, not that he'd entirely explained who it was for. The Penelope who'd examined his kit - the one who had seemed to be in charge the previous night - had just nodded over it and said there was nothing of any risk.

348

The questioning had been exhausting, though everyone had been civil. They'd fed him lunch in the middle - which had been excellent. He'd made very appreciative noises at Cook both for her food then and throughout. He'd managed not to enthuse about Charlotte, because half a dozen people had been listening. Then he'd had to wait for the cart down to the Wells portal, and he hadn't known what he was allowed to say or not.

Captain Powell had made it clear he could tell his family only the barest details. And, of course, no one had specified what he might talk to Charlotte about. If he talked to Charlotte. She'd promised to write, but he had no idea when he might be in Trellech next. Though any letters at the Owlery would at least get forwarded along to him, but it might take a bit. The Holme Lacy portal was not the sort of place that got mail four times a day. Just the once, usually, unless something was marked urgent and the extra fees paid.

Five minutes later, he was through the portal, standing in the grove of trees, with the village to his right and the magical village to his left. It wasn't exactly a village, more like two dozen houses, with their own shop, which had a few shelves for a lending library. Mother and Father had preferred Trellech, once upon a time, but Mother had insisted the country was better for Theo. She was probably right, but Lewis could feel the uncomfortable stillness settling over him.

Down the road he went, shouldering the bag. By the time he got to the house - half a dozen houses standing near their neighbours but with hedges and fences to defend their territory - his back was aching. He didn't knock, knocks might disturb someone. Instead, he checked the door, pressed his palm against the panel on it, and then opened it, coming into the hallway.

He waited perhaps two minutes before he heard footsteps above, then his mother coming down the stairs. She was looking unusually severe, and by that he suspected she had not been out of the house. Just a plain blouse and a charcoal grey skirt, with the locket she always wore at her throat. Mother gestured him into the sitting room, with the sound charms, leaving a crack open to hear upstairs. "We didn't expect you."

Lewis had thought about what to say to that all the way to the portal and all the walk from this end. He still didn't have a good answer. In the end, he said what he could. "There's a Guard investigation, and I've been sent away. I've doses for Theo, enough for six weeks, but I need to figure out beyond that."

"And you'll be doing that first thing." It wasn't a question, it certainly wasn't encouragement. It was an expectation and an order.

"May I see him?" Lewis swallowed hard. "I can go to Trellech, if you'd rather. After."

She sniffed, once. Lewis noticed she hadn't asked how he was, or what part he'd had in anything. He suddenly wondered exactly how much she might have wondered about his employment already. Mother had encouraged him in it, at least once it became clear that it would be a steady supply for Theo. But of course, Lewis hadn't explained most of it. Mother didn't care for the technical details of his work, by which she meant anything beyond an occasional anecdote of a bit of materia. About one every five days, on average. "He's not having one of his best days."

In some other family, maybe that would have come with an explanation. It wasn't that Lewis couldn't read between the lines. There had been shouting, certainly. Nightmares, probably, and the way they left Theo unsure what was real and what wasn't. Any sensible person would be wary in the wake of something like that. At least what little Theo had been able to articulate. It might also have involved food thrown across the room, or something of the kind, and Mother never did like that.

"May I go up?" He'd left his bigger bag in the hall. He had the smaller one over his shoulder. She just nodded once, and he extracted himself, taking his time walking up the stairs. Part of it was to let Theo hear someone was coming. Some of it was to brace himself.

Lewis got to Theo's room. His room looked out on the back garden, and Mother made a point of saying she'd given him that room, given it up. It was the larger room, but Mother made use of the entire rest of the house. The door was slightly ajar, and from inside, Lewis heard, "Go away."

"Theo, it's me. Back for a quick visit. May I come in?"

There was a long pause, the sort of pause that made Lewis fairly sure Theo wasn't sure about his senses at the moment. "Why are you back?"

"There's a story in that. Guard and all. I wanted to see how you were doing before I go off to Trellech."

Another long silence followed, and Lewis just waited. Unlike the questioning, he at least knew how the pacing of this went. More importantly, he knew what the pacing meant. This morning, he'd been thrown off-kilter by which things took time, and which seemed to happen almost instantly. About when he'd expected it, he heard, "Come in, then."

The room was still as sparse as it had been. There was the single reinforced rocking chair in front of the window, the desk with the plain chair to one side, and just one book and some paper. The bed had two pillows, a cotton blanket - a bit light in this weather - and the wardrobe to one side.

Nothing fancy, nothing that could be picked up and thrown easily except the pencils and book. And the pillows, but those were not generally the problem.

Lewis didn't sit. Theo didn't like anyone sitting on his bed, though Mother did quite regularly. And he didn't want to move the other chair, for the same reasons. Sometimes Theo was fine with it, sometimes having it put back just a hair out of place set everything off again, like a burning nerve of injury.

"Well?" There was the note there that was still his big brother, torn between wanting to comfort and thinking he needed to scold. And better Theo than Mother, before. Still, probably.

There were so many places he could start. "The job I had, they had me doing things that got the Guard's interest. I didn't realise it at first. It wasn't like they told me how they were actually using them. The perfumes and incense and a few potions that make people suggestible." Lewis swallowed. "I have your doses for the next month or so. I'll figure out something before then, I promise."

Theo made a little abortive gesture with his fingers, the kind where his hand stopped moving part way through, then clenched. "And?"

"And I met a girl, and I fell in love, and I don't think she wants that, and I don't know what to do now." It all came out in a rush before Lewis bit his lip to stop more of it. How he'd been terrified when she'd confronted Morgen, and how he'd been proud, and it wasn't as if he'd done anything to be proud of. Except maybe make a perfume that approached suitable for whatever sort of glory Charlotte was.

There was a long silence, so long that Lewis wanted to

come and settle on the floor in front of Theo, so he could see the reactions properly. Finally, softly, Theo said, "Who?"

"Charlotte Edgarton. Her father's a lord, and a captain in the Guard and a magistrate. Why would she want me?"

"Did she?" Trust Theo to get right to the heart of it. It had been why Lewis had needed to come back here, however briefly he stayed. Even if Theo had limits now. Though Lewis seemed to have picked a better day for his mind than some.

Lewis blushed. He could feel the heat of it, up his cheeks, down his chest, all the other reactions in his memory. It wasn't just the sex or the time in bed, either. It was eating meals with her, or having her curled up on the sofa in the lab. "She spent a good bit of time in the lab. And." He swallowed. Mother hadn't come up. He'd have heard the stairs. "And in bed. But she made it clear it didn't mean anything. Emotions or after or anything."

"Ah." Theo grimaced, staring off out the window. "What did she say? Last?"

"She said. She said she'd write. To my club, the Owlery." It was the one everyone meant, talking to someone who'd gone to Schola and they didn't know to have some other context or club in mind. "She was in Fox, of course."

Theo sniffed once, and Lewis didn't know how to make sense of that. There was another long silence, during which Lewis did lean back on the wall. "See what she writes. You could write to her. Was she..." Theo went quiet, as if all the words and the context had got tangled.

"She was a guest. Only she didn't want to be, and someone got her away from the house. We had ten days together, near enough? And she." He wouldn't babble. Babble wouldn't do any good, and if he got started, he wouldn't hear if Mother came upstairs, and that wasn't anything he was at all competent to deal with. "Just."

"Did they tell you not to talk to her?" Theo's fingers twitched again, and Lewis thought he had best cut the visit on the shorter side.

"No. Just what to expect from questioning. I've got to let the Guard know where I'm sleeping." He wanted to stay and talk more, to have something that felt like he had a place to come home to, and he couldn't. This house wasn't that, not anymore, and if he was honest, it hadn't really been for years. "I should get to Trellech, probably. So I can get a room. I'll leave the doses with Mother, and I hope come see you in a week or two, when I know what I'm doing next."

Theo swallowed hard, like he wanted to argue, then he shook his head, more or less agreeing. "Come see. And." There was a longer silence. "Lewis. I hope she writes."

"Me too." He smiled back at his brother. "Soon, I hope." That was ambiguous. He meant it about the visit back here, but it was as much about Charlotte writing, and he wouldn't take it back now.

Theo just nodded, and Lewis took that as his cue to disappear out the door, leaving it ajar. Mother was still in the sitting room, and he knocked once, waiting for her permission before entering. "I'll be going. I don't want to be in the way. Here are the doses." He rummaged in the bag for them, bringing them out, still carefully wrapped. "Six weeks. I'll let you know when I've got more options."

She just nodded once. Lewis wished things were different - as he had many times. Mother had done what she needed to, keeping things together. And Lewis respected that. He wanted the same for Paul, their younger brother, too. For all Paul was stubbornly insisting on doing it himself, without much obvious help. But things weren't different, and all he could do was not make matters worse for anyone.

In the end, all he said was, "I'll let you know how I'm getting on. And maybe come visit, when I know where I'm working next." His mother didn't say anything else, so after leaving enough time in case she did, Lewis nodded and went back to the hall. He set the bag on his other shoulder. It didn't hurt any less, but at least it was different.

Frugality meant he hauled his bag all the way down to the Owlery, a good mile across Trellech, without waiting for a tram or hiring a cart. There was a room available, one of the cheap rooms up at the top of the club, with just the bare minimum of furniture. A bed, a washstand, but of course both a desk and a bookshelf, they were the Owlery, after all. He didn't mind the bath down the hall, and it had sounded like the club was not terribly busy that night. Once he'd set the bag down, he went back downstairs to pay a messenger to run a note to the Guard, addressed as he'd been told. Then he went to the library to find a book, and to the dining room for something filling and cheap, whatever that was today.

CHAPTER 42
MAY 1ST AT VERITAS

Charlotte knew there was no avoiding this conversation. And to be entirely fair to them, Mama and Papa had not rushed it. They'd arrived in the village just before dawn, and the festivities and rites and traditions had pulled them all in immediately. It was Rathna's first time at their May Day, though she'd mentioned she was familiar with Schola's version. But Rathna apparently hadn't expected - neither had Gabe - the procession of young girls bringing Rathna her own flower crown. Nor had she expected the costumed dancers drawing her in to open the dancing.

It wasn't a thing the family could have asked about in advance. But it was a decided gesture, a deliberate one. Gabe's wife-to-be, who in some distant year would be Lady of the land, was welcome here. Still learning her place, as she was learning the dances, but of this place and this people, no matter where she'd started. It had an open-heartedness that couldn't have been forced. Though, of course, everyone here respected the portals and the people who helped them keep working. Plenty relied on travel through the portal for the hops and other harvests, as well as for all the other reasons. That had been a help in accepting Gabe's choice of a wife in general and Rathna herself in specific.

The dance wasn't complicated, deliberately. It was supposed to be something near everyone could join in, from children of five or six to the older grannies. Mama had even managed a few rounds before settling onto the seating to one side to clap and laugh and sing and keep the beat going. Charlotte had swung from hand to hand as the younger folks kept going, faces she'd seen year after year.

In the midst of it, it hit her. She didn't want to leave this. If she'd married Victor - not that she was seriously considering that any longer - she'd have had to. She'd have been obligated to his family's rites, their traditions. They weren't so different, but they weren't the same. They weren't Kentish. If she found something with Lewis, they could come here, wherever they lived. At least some of the time. That particular thought, the implications of it, kept coming to the surface, like fish seeing food after a rainstorm had washed new treats into the water.

They stayed a little longer than anyone had meant to, perhaps, up until nearly luncheon. Then they'd retreated to the house, and the cold collation, since of course the staff had the rest of the day to their own celebrations. No one had wanted to talk much, other than Mama's "We'll talk over tea, shall we? I rather need a nap." Charlotte heard the implied commentary there. She certainly needed a bit more sleep if she were going to manage the challenges of her parents at teatime.

Half-four found them all in the library, with a tray of

sandwiches, biscuits, three pots of tea to satisfy the various preferences, and Gabe's coffee. He and Rathna looked slightly mussed, but more as if they'd been talking than doing anything more vigorous. That would, she expected, come tonight. It was one of the oldest of the celebrations. Her parents would too, almost certainly, and she refused to think about it in any more detail than that.

Now, she took her cup of tea, her plate, and her seat, in that order. Mama cleared her throat. "Your choice, Charlotte, dear, on whether you'd prefer Rathna to stay for this. We'd understand if you'd rather not."

There were a great many implications in there, and Charlotte was fortunately not too tired to spot them. First, Mama had been worried, that had been obvious, but she was not upset. That meant Charlotte probably wasn't in trouble, per se. The part she actually had to figure out was how to handle Rathna.

Rathna was marrying in quite soon now. That had implications. Charlotte could say she'd rather it was just the four of them, but it meant things later, not very long from now. And besides, Rathna might in fact have useful thoughts somewhere in here. Charlotte liked her, though they'd had very little time to talk without Gabe somewhere in the mix. She shook her head. "Please do stay, Rathna. Gabe, do you have to be anywhere any particular time that's relevant?"

"I have begged off going on duty tonight, but I need to be in by seven in the morning, spell some other people. Going through Trellech to pick up a few things. So I'd be obliged if this conversation didn't last all night." Gabe considered his options and draped himself over half the arm of the sofa, leaving the rest for Rathna. It was one of the uncomfortable positions he favoured, like a cat who was proving a point.

Charlotte took a breath, squared her shoulders, and looked at her parents. Mama had taken the chaise - it had been a very long day. And Papa had pulled up a chair beside her, close enough to touch easily, or hand her something. Charlotte had no idea how to describe that expression, except that she'd more commonly seen it pointed at Gabe rather than at her. She did not care for the new experience one bit. "Where would you like me to begin, Mama, Papa?" Then, before they could actually answer, she went on. "I am sorry for worrying you. But can you also clarify what I can tell you?"

Papa picked that up. "If Rathna weren't here, it would be simple. We're all bound by Guard oaths, one way or another, in terms of evidence. As it is, be suitably unspecific about anything you've been cautioned about sharing, and if we need to, we will ask you privately later." Normally Charlotte was the one on the outside of that, and it struck her that now at least she'd have company. Portal Keepers had their own confidences, of course, but they weren't the sort of investigative issues Papa and Gabe had as their daily bread and butter. And Mama helped as a consulting analyst often enough that she was used to it.

Charlotte nodded. "To begin, I had the chance to leave at one point, but I was not at all certain I'd be successful. I was safe enough where I was - well, until last night's choices. And." She swallowed. "I didn't want to leave."

Saying it out loud made it real. Or more real, somehow, than being in Lewis's bed and Lewis's lab and Lewis's company had been. She went on, not lingering on that, though she was sure Mama and Papa had caught enough of it for her own embarrassment. One more time, she went through the basics of what happened.

They knew what she'd known, before she left. That meant she could pick up with arriving at the house, the odd things she'd noticed, the fact they'd thrown Bedivere at her and the matchmaking generally. She didn't explain about Victor, not right now, not that part of it. She didn't specify the adulterated drinks, but she gestured at them, and she was sure both Papa and Gabe would have questions later. She did make it clear she'd followed all her training about hair and such, and it must have worked, or they'd have found her far more easily.

When it came to talking about Lewis, she had to stop and consider how to put things. Part of her wanted to dance around it, Mama and Papa would read what she didn't say, Gabe already knew it, and Rathna could ask him for an explanation. But something in her last ten days, something in Lewis's rather relaxing straightforwardness, made her speak plainly. "I won't be marrying Victor. He doesn't know that yet. But I would like to see what Lewis and I might sort out for ourselves. If you're going to forbid me, I'd like to know that now, please."

No one spoke for far too long. It left Charlotte counting heartbeats.

"Well. That's settled then." Gabe's voice cut through it, easily. "You said the man needs an alchemy lab. We can sort that out. What I saw of him seemed quiet but promising."

Before anyone could say anything else, Mama cleared her throat. "Gabriel." Mama's voice was very mild, but the full name was warning enough. "Let your sister speak for herself. Besides, I think you've made at least one significant error of scope."

It was as stinging a rebuke as Mama had ever delivered,

actually, to either of them. It was not the disappointed expression - that was even worse, and Charlotte had only ever been on the receiving end a handful of times. But Gabe went entirely still, before swallowing hard. "I beg pardon, Charlotte, for overstepping. And Mama and Papa, for getting in your way."

Mama's mouth twitched, more amused than annoyed. They could both read that easily enough. She spoke to Rathna, though, first. "Domestic negotiations are a touch delicate. And we were quite worried, Charlotte. Having no idea what you were up to, other than your general safety."

"I'm also very sorry for that." Charlotte considered her options, then said, "I'd like to talk about the maze with Uncle Gil when I can. Actually, it was rather clever. We might think about one here, perhaps? Not so restrictive, of course. And it was very handy to have a lab and skilled alchemist to make up the salve. And that he had a recipe for it." There, she could toss everyone a bone of academic interest, as a peace offering.

Mama, of course, was not distracted. "About the alchemist, dear. Tell me what you know about him."

That, of course, meant the sort of Fox-trained precis of his background, training, family, and anything else she'd picked up along the way. This part, she'd given quite a bit of thought to, because she'd been sure someone would ask. And over ten days, she'd learned enough. That he cared about his brothers, but there was some distance. That his older brother was dependent on a potion, and what she knew about that. Charlotte had pieced together some details of his training with the Ayletts, though that wasn't a connection the family had much experience with directly. All the Penelopes they knew had trained elsewhere, and Lord Carillon's pet alchemist as well.

Of course, both Mama and Papa had more questions. They were dancing around how intimate she'd been, which was on the whole a good sign. They went through things what felt like five times, only of course it wasn't. Neither Mama nor Papa would be that inefficient. Gabe managed to contain himself until Papa had nodded and gone silent again. "Victor, what are you going to do about Victor? And what are we doing about this Lewis? I would like to know if I'm supposed to challenge him or show him around the place or what."

Charlotte straightened her shoulders. "I'm not allowed to leave until they finish the investigation. Not that that's much bother, Captain Powell thought it wouldn't be more than a week at the outside. And more awkward to have me run into someone elsewhere, related." She didn't want to do that, and it wasn't like she'd be bored on the estate. "But might we invite him out for the afternoon? Lewis, not Victor. In a few days time, when we've all had some more sleep." And when Mama was a touch less achy. Hopefully.

Mama considered. "Saturday? Richard, you're not on duty, are you? Or Gabe?"

Both men shook their heads, in nearly an identical gesture, before Gabe grinned and shifted to lean against Rathna instead of draping over the furniture. "I can take a note, if you like, first thing in the morning. Do you know where he is?"

"I said I'd write him at the Owlery." Which Gabe knew. She'd said that, but of course he'd have her lay it out for their parents. Figured. "Saturday, Mama? And a nice tea? He needs feeding up. Cook, at the manor, was making a good effort."

Her mother nodded once, but then, of course, picked up the thread. "Victor, Charlotte. You'll need to invite him out here before that, if he can visit. Otherwise, we can see about arranging a suitably supervised meeting. What will you say to him?"

There were quite a lot of things Charlotte wanted to say to him. Very few of which she actually wanted to say to her parents. They would likely be understanding - eventually, if not perhaps right in the moment. She took a breath. "Besides how he handled things this week - potions or no, I don't trust him to have a care for me. That seems a poor sort of marriage, even if we'd more or less been planning on our own lives." Saying it didn't exactly surprise her parents, but something in there had done something unexpected. It gave Charlotte a reason to go on.

"I didn't particularly want to marry someone who'd be awful. And there are so many chances for that. I was fairly sure Victor would be tolerable, better than tolerable. Up until this fortnight. And I don't hate him. I'd be glad to still be friends, probably." Though now she said the words, she wasn't entirely sure how much they had in common. "We have history, anyway, and I'm not going to throw that away. But I was, I was choosing something because I didn't think I could have what you have, Mama, Papa. Or what Gabe and Rathna are building. Growing..." She used the term for the portals rather deliberately, and was rewarded with a smile from Rathna, as she slipped an arm a bit more comfortably around Gabe's shoulder. "And maybe I could."

There was a cautious sort of silence now, before Mama nodded. "And what else?"

"I don't want to leave the land. If I married Victor, and he becomes the heir, it'd be his land. And someone ought to take good care of it, but I think maybe I don't want to. I don't want to marry out like that. I was thinking, this morning, that - wherever we lived, obviously, we'd do things there." She was decidedly getting ahead of herself a dozen ways. "I mean, I don't even know if Lewis is interested. I told him I wasn't, all sorts of things. But building a hypothetical palace here..."

It made Papa actually chuckle, and he waved a hand to encourage her to go on. Charlotte sucked in a breath. "If Lewis and I worked things out. Or someone else, I suppose." Which seemed a very poor second indeed. "We could be here for at least some of it. Or sometimes. I wouldn't - I wouldn't have to give it all up."

Mama nodded. "I didn't come from a landed family. It must make a difference. I was thinking, this morning, what it was like watching Rathna have her first time here, and thinking it might be one of your last. I liked the one much better than the other." She bestowed a smile on Rathna, and then the same one on Charlotte. Charlotte knew she was largely forgiven for the fortnight of worries, more acute in the last day. "And Lewis?"

Charlotte could feel herself flushing. "I just - being with him is wonderful. Ridiculously. And I want him to be happy, and not worried about his brother, and not needing to work for horrid people to keep things together. And can we find a way to help with that? Maybe both his brother and with the lab, whatever else? I don't know a lot about what sort of Healers they've talked to. There have to be other people. It could help, too, the potion, or something based on it."

Mama lifted her fingers. "We can work through that. Tomorrow, I think, for the details. After lunch, here. Richard, would you please check in the morning about whether Victor may visit, or whether Charlotte may go there? The first, by choice. I would prefer to be available." Which meant Papa would do his utmost to do that. And it did mean that it would be a more controlled sort of visit than if Charlotte went there. It might well save her storming out of the solarium at Victor's in a snit. Not the proper way to end things, on anyone's account.

Papa nodded. "I'll check in first thing. No, Gabe, not you. Powell trusts that Lucy Doyle has the Penelopes in hand for this case. Don't let him think otherwise, it will just muddy things."

Gabe snorted, this time good-naturedly. "Sir." That was him being decidedly agreeable. "How much can I ask him, Char? On Saturday, I mean?"

"Anything you like about alchemy or perfumes or anything like that. Not so much about his brother unless he volunteers it. Fair?"

"Fair." Gabe stretched. "I'd love a walk, actually, before other pleasures. I should be home for supper tomorrow."

Rathna cleared her throat. "I need to be in London tomorrow. I'd normally spend Friday night and Saturday with Morah Avigail, but I'd be glad to come out here if I wouldn't be in the way?"

Charlotte didn't have a strong opinion at first, but then she considered. "It might make Lewis feel better. Slightly less intimidated, maybe? Both because you're - I mean, you didn't grow up here either." And also because Rathna was not at all intimidating. "Besides. You have better odds of good results if you elbow Gabe than if I do."

Rathna laughed at that. "We seem to be working it out." She then eyed Gabe, who was already standing. "Yes, I'm coming. Thank you for including me, and it's not a bother if I make arrangements for Friday?"

"Not at all. We're delighted to see more of you." Mama smiled generally. "Right. I would like to lie down upstairs.

Charlotte, you may have tomorrow morning to your own amusements. I'll want your time after lunch."

"Of course, Mama. Thank you, Mama. And whatever else you want to ask, of course." Charlotte did know that dance, very well indeed.

Papa just nodded once, and that was going to be all right. There would be questions. There might well be prying. But it would sort itself out, given a little time, and that was the important part.

CHAPTER 43
MAY 5TH AT VERITAS

L ewis stepped out of the portal with no idea what to expect. Charlotte's three notes had been warm, confusing, promising, and baffling. There had been one waiting for him when he made it downstairs for breakfast on Wednesday morning. It had clarified that Captain Powell did not object to correspondence, or to Lewis visiting the Edgartons on Saturday. There'd even been a brief note from Captain Powell confirming it. That first note from Charlotte had been all about practicalities. She had included an idea of clothing, the card with the portal address for the attendant in Portal Square, and a token for the fee.

Lewis had stared at the note for a long time, before finally beginning his own with "How are you, please?" He hadn't gone into anything about the questioning, or about his family, just that he was staying at the Owlery and trying to figure out what to do next. He'd managed three paragraphs about the reading he'd done the night before. Also, he'd expanded on an idea for getting more benefit out of floral materials that might reduce costs and also create a depth of scent, thanks to a passing reference. It would need more research, but at least he had a good library to work with.

He had been relieved - if not entirely surprised once he caught his breath - by the remarkably thick bundle of papers from Charlotte that arrived on Thursday morning. It was like she was sitting on the sofa in the lab, chatting away, only in writing. One of the Owlery staff had brought the note to the library around ten. She'd waited a few steps from the desk and old chair in the corner that Lewis had claimed. He was young, and it was rarely used. Better spaces were for more esteemed and established members. Charlotte had, apparently, chased down three related references in her library at home. She'd copied them out in a clear and readable hand, and added several annotations of things she apparently intended to hunt up as soon as she had a chance.

He didn't know how to ask how she was spending her time, or at least the parts that weren't about research on his behalf. She didn't say, just that her mother was also keeping her busy. She didn't seem to be in trouble, exactly, but he also wasn't sure how he'd tell. Thursday evening, he'd written back, this time more about how he was thinking about the research. Or rather, what he wanted to do with it. They'd touched on that sort of conversation a few times, while they'd been thrown together, but he'd never talked about it much with other people. At school, it was all about the method, and the theory was separate. Now, he was more and more sure that he had to combine the two to do what he wanted.

Her letter on Friday had been reassuring on some points, and baffling on others. She had made it clear - in small precise words - that she was looking forward to seeing him. "I miss you, I have so much I want to talk about with you," was in fact remarkably unambiguous. She was of Fox House. Surely she meant six other things there? And yet, he kept reading them, and they kept being clear and plain. He must be missing something important.

She'd been just as clear about what to wear, though she did have a good sense of his likely wardrobe. He didn't need to be formal, but it would help if he were the sort of presentable that went well with her family. Which, in this case, apparently meant her parents, her brother, and her imminent sister-in-law. It had also included one of the references she'd found, and apologies she hadn't had time for the other two.

He had stared at the clothing notes, but it wasn't as if he could arrange anything other than what he already had, so he'd have to assume her instructions were right. Lewis had arranged to have things cleaned and pressed, and he'd had a bow tie that he thought suited him. Grey, with little gold potion vials, which more or less suited an afternoon visit. Besides, he didn't have a better one. The other three had stains or were for funerals.

There was nothing for it but to make it to Saturday at one, then to come through the portal. It came out in a small grove of trees. Charlotte was there, and she looked absolutely gorgeous, like she'd just stepped out of a pastoral painting. Her hair was pulled away from her face, but loose down her back. He'd expected she'd choose something more fashionable, all pins and curls, and she hadn't.

Her dress was modern - not that he had the words for much of that - a summer green that reminded him of one of his favourite potions. Haley's Sympathy was not only an interesting challenge to make, but it relied on both scent and colour to bring it to proper fruition. It was a little like a flower blooming in the perfect moment, and that link suited her very well indeed.

As far as Lewis could tell, they were entirely alone, though there was an exceedingly large house looming to the left. Charlotte sucked in a breath, and then she was flinging herself at him for a hug. His arms went around her, automatically, then deliberately, hugging back, burying his face against her neck for a moment and inhaling. He didn't try to kiss her. That seemed too much.

When she pulled back, she was beaming at him. "You're here. I didn't, I mean, it seemed like a dream?" Then she gathered herself. "Papa will welcome you properly when we get inside, but welcome to Veritas. Be welcome, please. And I promise Mama and Papa want to meet you, not scare you."

Lewis was not at all sure how to weigh that against, well, anything. He didn't know what to do with this sort of place, not at all. It was the sort of estate he might come to consult with the lady of the land, or one of her daughters, or something of the kind. If he could build up the perfumery. It wasn't the sort of place he'd be a social guest. Yet, here he was. Finally, he managed to stammer something out. "Thank you for inviting me, and your parents, and I don't know what we're supposed to be doing, and how are you, really? You're not in trouble, are you?"

She squeezed his hand and kissed his cheek. "My family was very worried, especially at the end of it. They are now reassured. What we're going to do is have a few minutes to ourselves, partly so I can tell you something that I hope you'll like?" Her own voice suddenly quavered, and Lewis wondered what could make it do that. "And then we'll go in and talk to my family. And you can stay for tea, I hope, and supper? If we don't scare you off?"

That made Lewis half-smile. "I'm very nervous. This is all intimidating. And they can't - do they really want to talk to me?"

Charlotte nodded, emphatically. "Gabe has even promised to behave himself. We'll see how long that actually lasts, but both Mama and Rathna have promised to rein him in if required, and Rathna's really quite good at it already. I mean, Mama can usually do it with a raised eyebrow and a faint cough, but she's had decades of practise."

It made Lewis laugh, then. "Both like my mother and not, maybe." Then he swallowed. "You had something to tell me?"

"Come sit? It's the sort of thing where you might want to sit. Or at least I might want to sit." Now she really was babbling, and that was very unlike Charlotte on the whole. Lewis let her tug him over to the bench near the portal, a sturdy, broad bench made of stone, comfortable for them both to sit on together.

He didn't know what he felt, except that now he was here, talking to her - touching her, even if in the acceptable public ways - he didn't want to stop. Lewis had had rather too much time to think, really. That was at least half the problem. Though if he added in the worries about more questioning, or possible charges, or what he was going to do to support himself as soon as possible, the maths definitely did not add up properly. Finally, he managed a faint, "Yes?"

"I wrote this part down. I missed you. Quite a lot. I've told Victor I won't be marrying him. Mama and Papa want to meet you. And, I mean, they don't think we should do anything obvious and public, not yet, but that doesn't mean we can't see each other, or that you couldn't visit.

And Mama and Aunt Mason and Gabe have some ideas about some lab spaces for you, if you don't mind some quirks? Gabe can tell you more. He's seen them all."

It was so overwhelming that Lewis had to squeeze her hand. "One thing at a time?" It came out entirely plaintively, but he didn't know how to say it otherwise.

"I missed you. I - whatever I said about not wanting anything romantic or lasting, I was wrong. If you're willing, I want that with you, please. Whatever it looks like for us. It wasn't just the time in bed, though actually, I'd like more of that, as soon as we can reasonably arrange it? I mean, when you can come stay overnight, which isn't yet." Her voice trailed off, then she said, hopefully. "Will you kiss me? Easier to show you that way."

He managed a nod. A moment later her arms were around his shoulders, she was half in his lap, and kissing him so thoroughly there was no space for doubt. Not until she pulled back, anyway. As he caught his breath, everything rushed back in on him again, and he leaned his head on her shoulder. "Victor?" It came out a bit muffled, but she got his meaning, anyway.

"He came out on Thursday, and it was all rather awful. He wanted to abase himself, and gods, that is not attractive. It always seems to be in a certain kind of novel, but it was not what I wanted or needed or anything like that. And besides. I'd already decided. I'm glad to be his friend, but I don't want to be his wife. Even with agreements about other people in our terms of marriage. He's getting sent off to a family cousin in America for at least six months, once the trial's over. He needs to figure out what he wants and who he is. I wish him well with that, but I don't want to be the one making him do the work. Wondering if any of it will last."

"But you don't, um. Are you upset at him?" What Charlotte described was not a kind of relationship Lewis had any model for. Colleagues, yes, or school friends, where you might not be close. He wasn't sure about friendship with that kind of limit.

"No. And - assuming the Guard doesn't say no - I've made arrangements to go riding with him on Monday. Though I can cancel it, if you'd rather?"

"I do not ever want you cancelling something because you think I might disapprove or - um. Whatever that was? I don't want to..." Lewis swallowed. "I want to be a catalysing agent with you, not a limiting one."

There was a silence, a bit weighted, then Charlotte was nudging his chin up with her fingers and kissing him again, this time short and much more tender. "That may be the nicest thing anyone's ever wanted for me." Then she kissed his nose, apparently for good measure. "All right. I will go riding with Victor now he's realised more about what happened, what nearly happened to him. He was awfully confused, when we talked, his head's all tangled up still, and he's figuring out how much they betrayed him. We'll sort things out when it's a little less awkward with everyone hearing. And then I will tell you about it, and you and I will find time for all sorts of other things."

Lewis blushed, but it wasn't as if he wanted to argue with any of the parts of that plan that involved him. Then he swallowed. "Lab space? I don't have, I mean, I'd need materials."

"We should probably talk about that with Mama and Papa and Gabe, and then you can hear all the details. Are you ready to do that, or do you need a few minutes?"

"I'd like a lot of time with you, in private. But that's not today, like you said." Lewis took a deep breath and let it out. "Do I get time to talk to you after I talk to them? With them? Meet them?" He wasn't sure what verb applied here. Possibly several he hadn't figured out yet.

"You do. Conversation with everyone, a nice walk - I can show you the pond? Or if you like, our stillroom and lab. You'd probably like that more?"

"The pond would also be lovely," Lewis assured her. Though he did rather want to see what the household standard for alchemy was, honestly. And at least he knew all the etiquette for being in someone else's lab. He had no idea what to do with someone else's pond.

"Come along, then." Charlotte wriggled out of his lap, dropping his hand long enough to smooth her hair back and straighten her dress. Once he was standing, she held her hand out. "I'll be right there. Of course. You're not dealing with them alone. And I promise, they want to give you much better terms than Morgen did."

"That isn't exactly hard," Lewis pointed out. But arguing wasn't going to do much good, and neither was standing here. "Please. Let's do this. Like walking into the great hall, Monday night." It felt like it had been years ago, decades, but he could remember what it felt like to be brave. He could be brave again.

CHAPTER 44
A FEW MINUTES LATER, IN THE LIBRARY

Charlotte took a breath just before they knocked on the library. There was Mama's "Come in." She squeezed Lewis's hand, and they went in, with her nudging the door closed behind her. Everyone was arrayed in their suitable places for conversation and a touch of intimidation. She hoped it would only be a touch.

Mama was on the chaise, and Papa beside her, rather than the sofa. They'd left that for Charlotte and Lewis, actually, with Gabe and Rathna having pulled up chairs to make an open square. It framed Mama and Papa with the lawn and garden and pond behind them through the great glass double doors and windows. A deliberate nod to the land, to the estate, and to the implications of those things, Charlotte was sure. What she wasn't sure of right now was whether Lewis would read any of that. Or, actually - and this was a novel thought - whether it would matter if he did. He made his own judgements on different things than she did. That might, in fact, be a very good thing.

She nodded. "Mama, Papa, Gabe, Rathna. Thank you for giving us a moment. I hope we didn't keep you waiting too long. May I introduce Lewis Wright? Lewis, these are my parents, Lord and Lady Edgarton, my brother, Gabe, and his fiancée, Rathna Stone."

Something in that made Rathna smile. Charlotte just caught it. She was watching her parents much more intently. Lewis dropped her hand, taking a step forward to offer his. He made a proper little formal bow over Mama's and shook Papa's and Gabe's firmly, before offering a milder form of the bow to Rathna. There were the little murmurs that went with the introduction, but she couldn't quite hear them, since she'd already found her seat. As Lewis straightened up, Mama spoke again.

"A pleasure. Please, Lady Alysoun and Lord Richard, if you'd rather, given the circumstances." That was a sign of approval, and another one where she wasn't sure if Lewis would read Mama's etiquette correctly. "Do have a seat on the sofa. Rathna, would you mind pouring?"

Rathna shook her head and stood to see to the pot waiting on the tea cart. Normally, it would likely be Charlotte, if Mama didn't herself, as daughter of the house. Mama usually didn't. The chance of spills was high enough Mama avoided it if possible. But Charlotte was assigned to the sofa, and her role here was clearly to steady Lewis. It did not really leave hands free for pouring tea.

Once Rathna was busy with the tea, Mama turned back to Charlotte and Lewis. "May I ask what you've already mentioned, Charlotte?"

There was no way through this but smiling and going forward. "Near the first thing I told Lewis was that I'd missed him a great deal. That I'd like very much to see what we might figure out ourselves. Of course, I mentioned the conversation with Victor. Briefly, only. We can come back to that."

Lewis squeezed her hand then, and didn't quite inter-rupt, but inserted himself in her pause for breath, rather smoothly. Maybe the metaphor she wanted was reaching to stir something that had just come to the proper simmer. He had seen the moment that wouldn't disrupt anything. "Charlotte did check if I had any objection to her friendship with Victor, specifically around sorting things out a little more thoroughly there, and of course I don't."

Something in that honestly surprised Papa, for one, and it wasn't like Papa to let that show. He leaned forward a moment, suddenly intent. "May I ask about that, then, your reasoning?"

Far stronger men - in whatever sense of strength you might name - had folded before Papa in that mode. Lewis kept holding her hand, and he didn't rush into the answer. "Lord Richard, Charlotte has shown a tremendous ability to manage herself in all sorts of complex situations. And I—" He hesitated, as if making a decision. "I don't have friends like that. Acquaintances, colleagues, of course. Perhaps that will change. But I don't have anyone who goes back to when I was eleven, not except my brothers. I would not take that away from anyone, without excellent reason. And I suspect, on the whole, I wouldn't be successful, in this case, no matter how hard I tried. There's no sense in setting up a fight I would lose. It would spoil everything else around it by contagion."

Papa nodded once, letting his satisfaction show, before he underlined it. "Well said. And that is a more rounded view of the problem, the scope of the problem, than I expected to hear. A mature one, and one that I think tends to lead to a good relationship."

Mama laughed. "You mean that it reminds you of Magni."

"I was thinking of Mason, but Magni, too." Papa smiled, more at ease. "Has Charlotte spoken of her adoptive aunts and uncles, Lewis? We should not drop names at random into the conversation. It is entirely rude."

"Yes, sir." Lewis straightened up a little. "And, pardon, Penelope Mason's partner, Rosemary. Charlotte cooked a few things she'd learned from Penelope Mason."

"Which things?" There was Gabe. He was irrepressible.

Charlotte said, mildly. "We were working with a reasonably well-stocked pantry by English food standards, and not so much in the way of spicing or coconuts. But Aunt Mason's variant on kaya jam and the egg cakes. And a fair bit of the other cooking. I do have some skills, you know."

"Quite a few skills." Gabe held up his hands, laughing. "I do not deny your skills. I just don't usually get the joy of the culinary ones."

Papa nodded. "Magni Torham was my apprentice master, and he is Duelling Master for the Guard, still, though getting on toward retirement now. Not that he's slowed down much." And in a more delicate position when it came to his choice of a partner in all other ways. Charlotte hadn't wanted to get into that in the cottage.

She cleared her throat. "I asked Uncle Gil last night, Papa, if I might. When we were looking at some of the research."

"Ah." Papa considered, then nodded once, giving Charlotte permission to go on.

"Aunt Mason and Aunt Rosemary live together as partners. And this is - this is private, to the family." Charlotte said, waiting for Lewis to nod his agreement. "And Uncle Magni and Uncle Gil are. Uncle Gil does architectural magics. We were talking about stones in building labs, and woods, and things like that. Not that that's his speciality, but he knows a fair bit about a lot of things."

"Oh." Beside her, Lewis went still for a moment, then he cleared his throat. "Of course, I honour your confidences, as a family. And theirs, by - by relationship?" He fumbled a little on the last word, and Charlotte patted his hand.

"Just so," Mama cut in there, smoothing things over. "The two pairs of them have given us quite a lot of good advice over the years, when it comes to a lasting relationship." Charlotte hadn't expected that from Mama, the nod at it. And again, she wasn't sure if Lewis would read that correctly. "Speaking of Mason, she and Gabe have been consulting about several lab spaces that might be doable. Let me be clear, Lewis. May I?" That was an inquiry on the name, and Lewis promptly nodded. "We'll have some plans for you to look at, and the details, but we should probably lay out what we've been talking about."

"Please, Lady Alysoun. Charlotte said she thought that you would have ideas as a family, but I admit I don't know..." Lewis frowned, then he went on. "I am a perfumer, please, by preference. I am used to taking different things, notes that at full strength and matched amounts, would clash. But in the proper proportions, they come into a relationship with each other. I know how to do that. I know how to follow a recipe. I do not know how to make something like this, the practicalities, outside of that."

Mama smiled rather more warmly. Charlotte suspected it was the admission of his limits, the honesty of it. Mama always did have a soft spot for people who didn't brag or make assumptions about what their gifts meant anywhere else. "That's a fine way to begin. Now, we are glad to support getting yourself set up to make perfumes. Charlotte has spoken emphatically and enthusiastically over the last few days about the range of your skill. You might need to see about some apothecary work as you get started, and we would need a proper business proposal. But she has argued you could make a going concern within a reasonable span of time for the investment."

"By which Mama means, Charlotte has drafted out several versions, allowing for changes in ingredient costs, glassware, along with several approaches to bring in custom. Two of which are quite inventive, and you should consider them."

"Only two, Gabe?" Charlotte wanted to get a word in edgewise.

"I'm still not at all sure about the scent cards, how you'd prevent them getting the scent all over everything. She had an idea about little cards that would let people sample the scents," Gabe said.

Lewis considered it. "I consider part of the art to be the relationship of the perfume and the individual." He then stopped. "I - pardon, Charlotte, I had thought to do this more privately. But I have a vial of what I made. Perhaps your family would care to smell the difference between it on you, and - Lady Alysoun, either you or Rathna, perhaps? It's not suited for a man, quite a lot of florals."

Rathna said, agreeably. "I'm curious to try it. Though if you can manage the spices I love, I would very much want to talk about something on my own account." Gabe almost said something, and Rathna elbowed him. "It is also good for Gabe to know what he can get me that I will use. I am a practical sort, when it comes to gifts, it keeps foiling him."

"I buy you books!" Gabe said, a bit plaintively. "And interesting mineral specimens. And you won't let me actually do anything about your working stones until we're properly married."

Lewis laughed. That was a relief. He was relaxing now, that helped a great deal. "I would be glad to consult, Rathna. And I do intend to work out a proper line of hair oils and lotions, and so on. Did Charlotte explain my larger plan, then?" He leaned a little toward Charlotte to reach into his shoulder bag and pull out a small case with the vial in it.

Mama nodded. "About a wardrobe of scent, adapting the same base, suited to the individual, to the different ways they are in their life. I admit, the idea intrigues, and I do think if you can pull it off for a range of different people, it would be quite successful. Artistically and financially." Rathna stood, coming over to their sofa. Lewis carefully took her hand after making sure it was all right, before touching the wand from the vial to the inside of her wrist. Charlotte smelled it there, first, but Lewis was right - of course Lewis was right - that it didn't come across the same. It wasn't bad, but it wasn't settling into her the way it had on Charlotte.

She stood, once Rathna stepped back, and held out her wrists. Lewis dabbed a swipe on each of her wrists, inside, by the pulse, and then crooked the fingers on his left hand. Charlotte leaned in, and he added a dot right at the hollow of her throat. Again, it felt absurdly intimate, for something that was, in fact, entirely in front of her parents.

She turned around, and together, she and Rathna went off first to Charlotte's parents, letting them both smell and compare, then to Gabe. Rathna settled back in her chair, Gabe still holding her hand where he could get a better sense of the smell, while Charlotte returned to her own seat.

"What's in it?" Gabe asked after a moment. "Rose, of course, cardamom. Honey?"

"Honey and a little beeswax accord. Both a *Rosa centifolia* and a *Rosa damascena,* both as attars. Cardamom, ambergris, a drop of civet, a few drops of vervain, as a magical fixative. The version I made for May Eve had a citrus accord in it. This one leans a little more on a simple amber accord. I didn't have the varieties of musk I'd like, or the quality of frankincense I preferred."

Gabe snorted. "People do prefer to save money there, don't they? The frankincense."

"Yes." Lewis ducked his chin. "Actually, it was something of a help. It left gaps in the potion and incense work Charlotte could suggest something for. Oh, and I didn't have the jasmine I wanted, either. I'd like to try a variation for - well." He nodded at the garden. "A summer's day."

Mama and Papa let the conversation go on, amiably. Charlotte let Gabe bubble from the discussion of the perfume into the discussion of what was needed to make it and store it. Along with, of course, what ingredients would provide a good start, which could be added as the business grew. Lewis didn't have a complete list, not yet, but he had notes of his own ideas. It became clear that they could put something workable together once he had a firm idea of the budget.

Finally, Papa broke in. "It seems that the next task is for you to look at the available spaces and see what you prefer. I gather you need housing, as well. Two of the spaces have rooms attached. If you prefer the other two, I believe..." He glanced at Mama, who nodded once, "We could see our way to providing rooms in our Trellech townhome. Convenient enough to the labs, and it would also strongly suggest our blessing. Once the immediate fuss blows over, and Victor is travelling, perhaps." It would also give them quite comfortable and private space, and Charlotte liked that idea a great deal. Though the townhouse would mean less cooking for Lewis, and that would actually be a shame.

"Of course, sir. Lord Richard." Lewis stopped before he babbled, she suspected. Then Lewis took a breath. "I didn't expect any of this, and I'm very grateful. Not just for the opportunity to do what I'd been hoping, but for your willingness to permit me to court your daughter. Since she is, in fact, willing." There was something in how he said that, a bit of awe, a bit of delight, a bit of everything that had been there during their first night together.

"Very willing." Charlotte said firmly. "May I take Lewis off for a bit, please? I wanted to show him our lab. And the stillroom. And possibly the pond."

Mama smiled. "Do. Back for tea at half-four, please, and then we'll be dining at seven, Lewis, with a chance to wash up first. We aren't changing for the meal, but I am hoping Mason and Rosemary can join us, their work allowing. They both have a few ideas for apprenticeships for your younger brother, I believe, as well."

That set of practicalities sorted, Charlotte slipped her fingers into Lewis's again, guiding him along the hall on the ground floor past the workroom to the stillroom and alchemy lab. He didn't say much while he was looking through things, bar a few questions about specific items. It wasn't until they were outside in the sun, walking down to the pond, arm in arm, that he said anything more personal.

"I can't decide if your mother is more imposing or if your father is." He leaned in, as if saying it out loud in the open air was too much of a risk.

"Equally imposing in different ways," Charlotte said, more or less amused. "But they do approve. Oh, and Mama said to tell you, when you did the proposal, that you should include a journal in the necessary equipment. She will be overseeing the expenses, and it's the easiest way for her to keep track of everything."

"Oh." Lewis let out his breath in a huff. "You mean, as well as seeing you, I could write to you, whenever?"

"That is the idea. Or at least, as much of whenever as time permits between your brilliance and your perfume and getting things running." Lewis fell silent again. She let him go on walking, till they were down at the edge of the pond. "Talk to me, would you?"

"I'd like to see if I can help Theo more. Do you think, is there a chance? Would that be a problem?"

"I am fairly sure that's why Aunt Mason and Aunt Rosemary are coming for supper, actually. I mean, not that they don't sometimes? But they're making a special effort, both of them together. Aunt Rosemary's a midwife, not a Healer, but she knows a lot about medical potions and who to talk to. And Aunt Mason just likes solving problems and puzzles. You wait, you'll see how she and Gabe are, tossing ideas back and forth. It - um. They can be a lot. But I'll be right there?"

"That's the part that matters," Lewis said, venturing to move his hand around her waist, letting her lean against him. "And you'll get them to slow down and explain." He swallowed again. "I like how you and Gabe are. It's how Theo and I were, once. Teasing. Caring but teasing. I told him about you. When I wasn't sure if you'd even write, after they let me leave the cottage."

"Which I did." Charlotte shifted to kiss his cheek. "We'll figure it out. How to help Theo, and maybe other people like Theo. How to make sure you can make amazing perfumes. And we'll see how we get on. I don't want to rush into things."

"Me either. And all that will take a bit," Lewis agreed.

Charlotte hesitated, before she decided best to be truthful. "I did mean it, earlier. I mean, working on the idea that Mama should be prepared to plan another wedding. In a year or so. Probably."

Lewis pulled back, just enough he could look at her. "You're sure."

"Absolutely. Sure as a maiden on a unicorn hunt."

EPILOGUE
JUNE 7TH AT VERITAS

L ewis had not known what to expect from today, despite Charlotte explaining it to him. She was careful about that, putting it in terms he understood. Not that the previous iterations had been that complex, just various combinations of her immediate family, chosen and born. He was intimidated, of course, and not just by her parents, but it was the sort of intimidation he was familiar with. Competent people, all with their own ideas of how to get things done, and with the skills, influence, or willpower to make it happen.

It did make him think, a great deal, about how faded and shallow Morgen had been, in comparison to them. Each of the people he'd been introduced to individually - Aunts Mason, Rosemary, and Witt, Uncles Gil and Magni - had their own expertise, but they also had their own shine. Or, in the terms Lewis preferred, their own collection of scent notes, complex and changing.

Lewis had begun to construct useful patterns, not just about the people, but about the social events. Mind, they'd all been tea or supper, or the time between the two. It was a relatively narrow range of activities, after all, and it was good manners as well as good sense to let the older generation guide the conversation. Charlotte admitted she'd been on good behaviour since returning from Somerset, not pushing the edge of what was indulged as much as she might. That had been for her mother's sake, and for Rathna's, mostly.

Rathna had a particularly challenging bit of this dance, Lewis supposed. If, as he very much hoped, he and Charlotte married sometime in the next year or three, he'd have his own experience of it. Preferably sooner than later, he would very much prefer to spend every night with her, and the daytimes too, as opposed to the once a week they'd managed thus far.

At any rate, when they married, it would be a big public fuss, but it wouldn't be the kind of big public fuss that had happened at Veritas yesterday. Gabe was the heir. Rathna was skilled and in a respected profession, but from nothing like the same sort of background. And so the whole thing had been a dance of making Lord Richard and Lady Alysoun's approval visible in every possible way, in front of several hundred guests. Along with all the necessary and relevant rites.

Charlotte had written to him in his new, much treasured journal, when the festivities finally let up around ten that night. It had all gone well, people had been fed, the happy couple had been feted, all the rituals and all the omens had been splendid.

In time, he'd have a better model for the formal events. December, that seemed likely. The trial would be well over with - it was currently anticipated for September. He could escort Charlotte to the Council celebrations and whatever number of formal social affairs made sense. He'd have to learn a lot of names and details, but as Lady Alysoun had pointed out, he'd want to do that as he looked at building a customer base. Lewis was good at learning things, and Charlotte - who seemed to know all of them on sight - had promised to help.

That left today. If yesterday had been the public celebration, this was the one for the family. Not just the people he'd met so far. There were more people coming. His role was to turn up at two, plan to stay through supper, and at the end of the meal, Gabe and Rathna would depart for their actual honeymoon. It apparently involved a remote bit of the Orkneys where Rathna could commune with ancient geology and Gabe could enjoy the wildlife. It was not what Lewis would find restful, but he was glad they were getting time to do what they enjoyed.

And so, Lewis turned up at two on the dot, stepping through the portal from Trellech to find Charlotte waiting for him. She was wearing blue today, with touches of vibrant embroidered ribbon, and she immediately held out both hands to him. "You ready?" she asked.

Lewis took a breath, leaning to kiss her. "Now I am. How are you? What should I know about yesterday?"

"Mama's tired. We're not making her get up. Everything went smoothly. We're mostly eating wedding leftovers, but they're delicious. And people want to meet you."

Lewis had felt that the food, the three times he'd been out to Veritas, had been excellent, so he had no objections. He said, mildly, "I was not here for the food." Then Charlotte was tugging him off by one hand, into the house, along the hall and into the library.

There were, in fact, a lot of people there, with more chairs brought in than usual. Half of them he'd met. More than half. That was reassuring. Lady Alysoun, with Lord

Richard hovering behind her for the moment. Gabe and Rathna, enthroned on a small sofa, with people pulling up chairs. Penelope Mason and Midwife Ditson, and Penelope Witt, of course, and Captain Torham and Master Oxley. There were others, too. A woman in a tailored jacket, rather like the Guard uniform, was chatting with Alysoun and Richard. The man beside her had smoked glasses on his nose, his head tilted as he listened to the conversation. As they came in, another man - perhaps the same age, a decade or maybe two older than Gabe and Charlotte - pulled a chair over. He was presenting a monocle apparently for Lady Alysoun's approval.

About at that point, everyone realised they'd come in. Gabe lifted a hand, and Lewis murmured to Charlotte. "I do have a present for them."

"Of course you do." Charlotte said it fondly. "Oh. Wait. Did you really?" She lit up with delight. "Oh, that's clever. Of course you did. Mama and Papa first, but then Gabe, yes."

Lewis grinned, suddenly sure he'd done the right thing. He hadn't been certain until he'd seen her face. She tugged his hand over to her parents, and Lewis made his proper bow. "Lady Alysoun, Lord Richard, thank you for inviting me to the family celebration. I have something for Gabe and Rathna, if it's convenient."

Lady Alysoun snorted. "Please, do give him some further occupation." Then she considered, "First, though, let me make some introductions. Carillon, Giles, Kate, this is Master Lewis Wright. Lewis, you've not yet met Lord Geoffrey Carillon, Major Giles Lefton, and Captain Kate Lefton, who is one of Richard's particular favourites." Lord Richard made a noise, mostly muffled, and Lady Alysoun continued, blithely. "None of you are on duty. You are allowed to have personal opinions." That got a guffaw out of Captain Torham, who had been over by some of the bookshelves, a large hearty laugh that didn't apologise for anything.

Lewis made the proper polite gestures, but no one seemed inclined to ask him anything that needed a further reply. These people weren't like anyone Lewis had known in so many ways. It was an entirely new set of ingredients to learn about. But possibly, it might be within his grasp. Enough to be a match to Charlotte. Who was now, he realised, tugging his hand to bring him over to Gabe and Rathna with a bright and cheerful, "Lewis has a present for you."

"For me? For Rathna?" Gabe leaned forward to kiss her cheek, as if it were entirely impossible to keep still.

"For both of you," Lewis said, doing his best to keep a straight face. "I did also include the working theory behind it, though not all my secrets." With that, he handed over the gift. He'd wrapped it up in a long shallow box, a tin for each of the sensation salves. That way the salve stayed put better. And he'd thought to put in a tester, with more of the warming salve, to demonstrate the degree of effect.

Gabe took it, and ceremonially handed it to Rathna, who went at opening it in small precise gestures. Then she was undoing the latch of the box, and peering at the row of tins, each with a matching colour on the lid. Paint wasn't his best skill, it wouldn't do for any kind of artistic work, but he'd worked out one that did well for a label on slick surfaces.

Rathna blinked up at him, and Lewis nodded. "They create particular sensations when applied to skin. Heat, cold, a prickling sensation that's actually quite pleasant.

They are safe for the skin, but I'd avoid, erm, sensitive areas. You can try the little one there, if you want an example?"

Gabe immediately picked up the smallest of the tins, sniffing it, then dabbing his finger into it, then peering at it. "Oh, yes, do try this, Rathna. And the smell's quite pleasant. That isn't cinnamon, if it's meant for the skin, but something that evokes it." Then Rathna reacted to the strip he'd just laid on the back of her hand, her eyes wide.

"First, can you make up more of this? How long does it last? Alysoun, you might enjoy it for that, among other things." She spoke clearly enough to cut across the other chatter. Within a minute, Lewis found himself sitting in a chair someone had pulled over for him. He found himself promptly engaged in a rather detailed discussion about the theory and practicality of the work, with - well, near every couple there interested in a set of their own, of course they'd be glad to pay market rate.

Charlotte had settled beside him, perching on a footstool, so she could hand things around, or a couple of times tap someone's hand to get them to share. She bumped her shoulder against his, just grinning at him, as if this had come out just as she hoped.

It was certainly an excellent way to go forward, with whatever accord they were making together.

THANK you so much for reading *Perfect Accord*. I love to share extra scenes and moments from my books, and this book is no exception. Get your copy of the two conversations Charlotte and Victor have at the end of the book.

It'll give you a chance to sign up for my mailing list, the

best place to hear about everything I'm up to and get more extras as they come out.

Your reviews (on whatever review site you use) are much appreciated, too!

Read on for more historical details about this book and where to find more about the various Edgartons.

AUTHOR'S NOTES

Thank you so much for joining me and Charlotte and Lewis for *Perfect Accord*. I'm delighted to get to share Charlotte's romance with you, in particular - I've known pieces of it for a long while. As always, tremendous thanks to Kiya Nicoll, my friend and editor, and to my early readers, whose comments made this a much better book. (They always do. Especially, in this case, improving how Victor comes across).

Charlotte, of course, has appeared in a number of other books at various stages in her life. Her parents have their arranged marriage to love match romance in *Pastiche* when Charlotte is 4, and *The Fossil Door* covers Gabe and Rathna's romance in 1922. Charlotte also appears in *Upon A Summer's Day* in 1940, as Gabe prepares for a new challenge. Fortunately, being Gabe's sister turns out to be good preparation for understanding Lewis!

You can find all the details about where the Edgartons appear on my authorial wiki at bit.ly/celia-lake-wiki (or look under the "More information" menu on my website at celialake.com). Under "Series and Arcs" on the wiki, you'll find a page for the Edgarton family.

We have fairly short author notes this time, which could honestly mostly be summed up as many gestures at the long history of natural perfumes, the materials used for them, and the way that plays out. I'm going to start with three general sets of comments, and then get into the chapter details.

The text itself explains enough of how **perfume** works to get started: a given perfume is made up of a variety of notes, some of which linger in the scent for longer, meaning that a given scent can change over time as it's worn. Similarly, different perfumes - particularly natural ones - work differently on different people's biochemistry. Accords are a combination of notes that evoke another, such as amber accord, and can be used as the basis for other scents.

One of the interesting things about setting this book in 1923 is the way that plays with the state of perfume. Up until the 1880s or so, perfumes were made from various natural materials using a variety of techniques. These include distillation, enfleurage, infusion, and many other approaches. Some plants are so delicate that you need tons of material to get a small bottle of oil (roses, for example). Others are so enthusiastic about scent that a little of the plant goes a long way. And of course, sometimes we're not talking about plants at all: ambergris comes from whales, civet from the glands of civet cats, castoreum from beavers, and musk from musk deer.

However, beginning in the 1880s, there was a surge of interest and development of artificial perfume notes. These had some advantages: in some cases they're vastly more humane (the ingredients of animal origin), in some cases they're much less expensive. They're also more likely to be stable: a given perfume on two different people is likely to smell much the same if it's using artificial notes. Obviously, that has a lot of commercial benefit, though there are (and have been all along) perfumers who do amazing things with natural perfumes.

In Albion, obviously, there's a preference for natural perfumes because those natural sources can also carry magical properties that have relevance to the wearer or the purpose. Lewis is thinking about these when he constructs the scent for Charlotte just before they make their way to the manor house at the climax of the book. But he's also thinking about what represents her, in specific, and what she will find appealing. It's a fascinating multi-dimensional puzzle.

I've been interested in natural perfumes in a low-key way since discovering Black Phoenix Alchemy Lab (often known as BPAL) back around 2004 or 2005. There's definitely something absolutely magical about a combination of notes and then how they smell when they're on you, in specific. I did a lot of reading then that's come in handy for this book, and I went back and reread several as I was getting ready to write.

If you're interested, I highly recommend any of Mandy Aftel's work, especially her *Essence and Alchemy*, which both talks about the history of many perfume ingredients and walks the reader through putting together a scent, including making an amber accord. I got the oils she mentions and have had a great deal of fun experimenting. Her *Fragrant* is also a great discussion, and focuses more on the role scent plays in our lives.

There are hundreds of other books out there, about specific ingredients, but I liked Celia Lyttleton's *The Scent Trail: How One Woman's Quest for the Perfect Perfume Took Her Around the World* for its rather epic journey to explore the origins of some of the ingredients.

Not all scent has to be complicated, either. I loved thinking about the various scents of the food Charlotte makes, and thinking through what she knew how to cook and what she doesn't. (Given that she's always lived in a home with household staff.) But of course her chosen aunts wouldn't let her get away without being able to cook a few things. The dishes she makes that she learned from Aunt Mason (who is of Dutch, English, and Malaysian background) are modifications as she describes, for ingredients more readily available in Albion. Sometimes you have a coconut available and sometimes you don't.

The second thread in this book is obviously about **cults**. The term is hard to define - academics and people with experience in coercive groups have done a lot of conversation about this in recent years (and earlier ones). In this case, though, we have a relatively small group with a charismatic leader (Morgen), an equally charismatic sidekick (Gareth), and some specific desires about shaping the world around them. That includes coercing people for their own benefit, using other people's magic, and the money and luxury that often comes with that.

There are a profusion of sources about cults (especially in the more modern experiences of them) out these days. There are documentaries (with various motivations and level of quality), there are books, and there are podcasts. I've read and watched enough that trying to do a list is impossible. But while writing this book, I have thought a lot about episodes from the podcasts *A Little Bit Culty* and *IndoctriNation*. They both focus more on 'what made this attractive in the first place', what kinds of behaviours to watch out for, and what happens when you begin to want to get free of them.

We don't always hear as much about cults in the 1920s - though there are some notable ones out there. But many of the things that make people vulnerable to coercive groups and manipulation were present in abundance in the period. People were struggling with the aftermath of the Great War, whether that had to do with their own losses, changes in options for the rest of their lives, or figuring out what they valued now. Having a place that courted you, that said you were meant for something special, and that gave you a focus could be tremendously compelling then - as it can be now.

There are also a lot of resources out there now if you or someone you know is concerned about a particular group or community. Both the podcasts I mentioned above have more information about these resources and tools on their websites, if that's helpful.

Arthuriana is such a huge topic I'm not going to attempt any sort of cohesive explanation. That makes sense, given these stories have flourished for well over a millennium, in multiple languages and cultures. As Charlotte and Lewis figure out, Morgen is leaning harder on some of the older and more obscure tales, rather than the central Arthur,

Lancelot, and Guinevere (in her many spellings) focus that has become most familiar.

And of course, Morgen is picking and choosing those elements that work for her other goals, rather than being consistent about any particular set of tales. Naturally, that's easier when the tales themselves have hordes of contradictions in names, in places, in the role of magic, and basically everything else.

All the names I've chosen do appear in the Arthurian legends in some form. Over the centuries, people have come up with all sorts of layers of additional information. I drew the **heraldry** in the scene where two devoted followers get their names and associated items from a list of Arthurian heraldry originally drawn up by a French nobleman in the 1500s. in a treatise called *La forme quon tenoit des tournoys et assemblees au temps du roy uterpendragon et du roy artus.* This is of course nowhere near a contemporary source for Arthur, whatever historical Arthur there was, but it made a great starting point for some interesting designs and associations.

Onward to information about specific chapters.

Chapter 1: Charlotte briefly mentions both her own family's **wedding** customs (such as the yellow veil), which largely draw from Roman custom in varying forms. (These can also be seen in the first chapter of *Pastiche*, for Alysoun and Richard's wedding.) She also mentions Rathna's background in passing. Rathna was born to Hindu parents, but spent her adolescence and young adulthood in a Jewish household. While she isn't Jewish, she prefers to keep their food customs (as well as not eating beef, in her own right), and of course the wedding feast needs to accommodate that.

As Charlotte notes, both June and Wednesday were considered particularly fortunate days for a wedding. In the period, the kind of event that is described in the book is not that uncommon. They're hosting a large gathering, but most of the people invited to the more public parts of the wedding can easily take a random Wednesday for a wedding, rather than pushing it to a weekend.

Chapter 3: Priddy is derived from the Welsh "prydydd" meaning "bard". It's definitely not Morgen's legal name. The stones Gabe mentions are all local to the area, but the formal mineralogical names were not entirely established in this period.

Ebbor Gorge is a fascinating geological location, with both the gorge and nearby caves that have been used for a variety of purposes. There are also some interesting legends of the surrounding area, including what Albion would consider some strongly linked to the Fatae or fairies and other magical beings.

Chapter 15: The Unicorn Tapestries are widely known - they've been on display at the Cloisters in New York City (part of the Metropolitan Museum of Art), since 1938. John D. Rockefeller Jr. bought them in 1922, and had them hung in his home until the Cloisters were built, something widely discussed at the time (and chronologically well-placed for my use here!)

Made right around 1500, the seven tapestries depict a vivid and detailed world, including the hunt for a unicorn. They may well come from multiple sets, but a monogram indicates they were likely from the same maker. That detail includes over a hundred different plants, with over eighty-five identified by botanists. That's a rich source for magical associations!

Chapter 24: Charlotte is referencing John Donne's **poem**, "The Sun Rising" which begins: "Busy old fool, unruly sun, / Why dost thou thus, / Through windows, and through curtains call on us? / Must to thy motions lovers' seasons run?"

Chapter 25: Magical and botanical lore often links specific plants with particular planets, elements, or other associations. **Juniper** here is a herb of the Moon, and **cardamom** (a particular favourite of mine) with Venus. The latter's particularly on point for a romance, obviously.

Thank you again for reading. Again, you can get your copy of the two conversations Charlotte and Victor have at the end of the book. While you're there, you can sign up for my mailing list, the best place to hear about everything I'm up to and get more extras as they come out.

Thank you again for joining me for this journey and a glimpse into the theatrics of Albion. The next book in the *Mysterious Arts* series is *Facets of the Bench*, focusing on the courts and legal systems of Albion along with jet carving. It will be out in August of 2024.

ALSO BY CELIA LAKE

Pastiche

Sailor's Jewel

Four Walls and a Heart

Land Mysteries

Best Foot Forward

Nocturnal Quarry

Old As The Hills

Upon A Summer's Day

Illusion of a Boar

Three Graces

Other stories

Complementary

Winter's Charms

Forged in Combat

Learn more about the world of Albion and future books at my website, celialake.com. Additional information linking characters, places, and timelines is available at my authorial wiki at bit.ly/celia-lake-wiki (or get there from my website under the menu that says "more information").

Sign up for my newsletter to be the first to hear about future books and learn about fascinating bits of research. Happy reading!